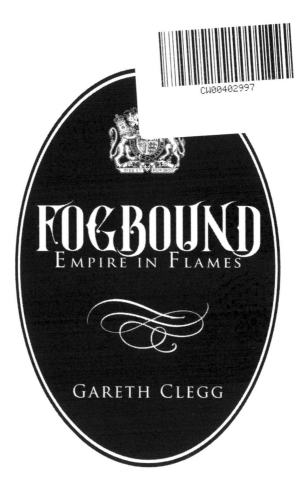

FOGBOUND
EMPIRE IN FLAMES

GARETH CLEGG

DEDICATION

For my Family (immediate & extended)

The Wednesday Night Crew
Antz Howley, Kevin Allmond,
Nick Simpson, Skye Alterskye

But especially for Jayne, my beautiful wife who has supported
me through it all and kept me on track when I was struggling
to focus on getting another two thousand words out that day.

I love you all.

CONTENTS

1

Fingers of toxic red fog clawed at his clothing as he stepped over yet another dead body. Sir Pelham Simmons stalked the Fogside wastes with his rifle slung over his right shoulder. His greatcoat hugged him tightly, holding the fog at bay.

An acrid smell hung thick in his nostrils: too thick. He coughed and tapped his respirator. He thumped it again, harder this time, and gasped as cold air hit his throat with a taste of charcoal. *Damn, I need to change these filters.* He blew a long breath between his lips and bent to inspect the night's latest victim. A tangled mass of hair splayed around the young woman's head where she lay face-down in the filth.

He rolled the body over with the tip of his boot. Crimson tears streaked her pallid face, dark veins prominent beneath the skin.

He'd seen plenty of tainted before, but this was just a child, fifteen at most.

Rubble shifted close by, sending his hand leaping to his belt. Drawing his Webley service revolver, he spun, bringing the weapon to bear.

Two shadowy figures skulked into view through the waist-deep blanket of red. A thick web of dark veins writhed beneath their skin, groping for an exit from their fleshy prison. Thin tendrils of red weed snaked from bloody eye sockets tasting the air, sensing him.

He kept the pistol aimed at the nearest. The other moved, trying to flank him—not intelligent, more instinctive—and unlikely to give up an easy meal.

The Webley barked out two shots, breaking the silence, and the creatures slumped to the ground.

Wings thrashed behind him, and he ducked, hands protecting his face as he was buffeted by dark shapes. A couple of strikes to his leather gloves, painful but not enough to draw blood, then they scattered. A dozen crows faded into the pre-dawn darkness, their raucous laughter ringing in his ears. *Damned birds.*

One of the weed-ridden creatures was struggling back to its feet, tendrils whipping about in a frenzy. Simmons fired another round into the centre of its head, dropping it for good this time. *Damned bleeders.*

He needed to get moving and quick. Bleeders travelled in packs, and the gunshots would draw more of them. He'd ridden his luck enough for one night.

He returned to the girl and tipped the peak of his wide-brimmed hat. With a sigh escaping his dry lips, he lowered the pistol. "I'm sorry there isn't a better way, girl. But I can't let you become one of them."

A single crack echoed around the ruins, and he stepped back, reloading his revolver. He knew she was already dead, that she wouldn't suffer, but it didn't make it any easier.

Now he had to get to the city, to safety.

He clambered over the rubble remains of collapsed buildings, picking his way through the scorched and shattered stone. As much as he'd like to quicken his step, he couldn't risk it. A twisted ankle or a break here could prove fatal.

What was that?

He dropped to one knee, sinking into the eddies of scarlet around him. His breathing felt like a blacksmith's bellows, and his chest ached from the bad air, but he waited with the revolver aimed back the way he'd travelled.

He strained, listening for anything that might indicate pursuit.

A series of howls echoed in the distance, dull through the dense fog. *More bleeders.*

A sharp crack of splintering bone cut through the night air. With a shudder, he stood, turning to leave. He didn't want to hear any more—he had enough trouble sleeping as it was.

≈

Whitechapel Gate loomed above the thick fog ahead. Simmons trudged forward. It had been a long night, and his feet ached like hell. He couldn't wait to get back to his lodgings and out of his fog-gear. A relaxing soak in a hot bath and then, perhaps, sleep.

He hadn't found the man he was hunting, but the net was closing in. Eyewitness accounts of his target, a killer named Maddox, placed him amongst the Red Hands. The gang conducted their shady business in the flooded streets south of the river. He'd need to speak to the watermen who transported folk across the deeper sections to see what more he could learn. But that could wait till tomorrow.

The gate, a solid slab of metal wide enough for a dozen men, fused into the wall's outer structure which towered over fifty feet into the chill dark sky. He pressed the intercom button and waited.

A groggy voice sounded from the metal grille. "Papers."

Simmons thrust a sheaf of yellowed parchment at the lens. Energy crackled as an arc-lamp burst into life.

"Hold them closer," the voice said with a yawn. "Name and business?"

Simmons prodded his gloved finger at the wax seal at the bottom of the travel permit. "My name is Simmons, and I'm on official business. Now open the damned gate."

"Registered man catcher, eh?" The voice dripped with contempt. "Your paperwork seems in order. Stand back."

Light sliced through the fog as the lens swivelled, scanning, probing for hidden danger. Three metallic thuds rang like gunshots as bolts released, metal grated as the segmented steel door rolled up into the wall providing an entrance into the city.

Simmons ducked through, striding twenty feet to the midpoint of the tunnel. The dim lighting flickered from green to red, but he didn't need telling to stop. A familiar hum grew to a roar as turbine fans spun into action. The last remnants of fog fled the screeching gale to rejoin the vast red sea outside. He'd turned through a half circle with his arms out before the intercom crackled. "Turn around, arms—"

"I know the drill."

He completed his rotation, fingers reaching to slacken the respirator, as the outer door clanged shut behind him. The turbines slowed to a dull drone as he pulled the mask free. It surrendered with a loud sucking sound, and he scratched at his moustache and mutton chops—*Damn, that feels good*. The itch had been bothering him for hours. Maybe he should shave them off, but after thirty years, military habits died hard.

Green light flooded the tunnel again as the door ahead clanked open onto a dirty, cobbled street. A single streetlamp illuminated a lone uniformed figure, lounging with boots on the guard-post desk. The man's black uniform collar gaped at the neck. Simmons smiled. *Even the Black Guard let standards slip on the graveyard shift.*

If an officer caught the young man in that state of dress, his reprimand would be both sharp and severe. But it seemed unlikely any of the Black Guard's top brass would pull a surprise inspection at this hour. They were more likely sleeping off a skinful of whisky, cigars or something much stronger.

He held his papers to the grilled window, but the guard waved him through without a glance.

The usual mix of buildings greeted him—some intact, most ruined with rubble spilling onto the cracked cobbles. Spotlights scoured the streets for curfew-breakers, and in the distant centre, the great Inner-City walls thrust into the night sky. Lights zipped away as black carriages, reserved for the military and ruling elite, sped beneath rail tracks suspended high above the ground.

Only a few short years ago, that would have been me. Simmons suppressed a laugh as he crossed into the fortified city of London.

Home once again.

2

Simmons rented the rooms, and though they were far from what he'd been used to, they suited his needs. Number twenty-three sat on the corner of Wentworth and Commercial Street. The three-storey terrace dominated the end of the row in a better part of Whitechapel.

His lodgings, the entire top floor, comprised a large sitting room, two bedrooms and a study. He wasn't extravagant, but the reclining wingback armchair was a small indulgence he'd allowed himself.

As he fiddled with his key, the stairs creaked, and a soft yellow light crept upwards. Leaving the intricate lock, he reached under his jacket for the reassuring presence of his service revolver.

"Sir Pel?" came a whisper from the foot of the stairs, "is that you?"

He leaned over the mahogany bannister. "I'm terribly sorry Mrs C, I thought I'd been the soul of discretion creeping in."

"Oh, don't worry, dear. I was already awake." She lowered the lamp. "The fire's been on all evening, so there should be plenty of hot water. I know how you keep irregular hours. Have yourself a nice bath, and I'll bring you breakfast around eleven."

"That's ever so kind, Mrs C, but it's unnecessary."

"Nonsense," she replied, shaking her head. "It's the least I can do. I'll fetch you some nice kippers from the market first thing."

Before he could argue, she retreated into her room, returning the staircase to darkness. He suppressed a chuckle. Sometimes she acted more like an overprotective aunt than a landlady.

Mrs Colton lived on the ground floor and was a pleasure to deal with, but refused to address him as anything other than Sir Pel. He'd asked her to just call him Simmons but to no avail. Reluctant to give up the pretence she hosted a knight of the realm under her roof, she took every opportunity to let her friends know all about it.

Simmons returned his attention to the infernal lock that protected his rooms. Yes, it may be the pinnacle of modern security, but it was a pain in the backside to open. It didn't help that he struggled to remember the first turn. So, yet again, he endured the electrostatic discharge as he completed the final turn.

"Damn it," he said, shaking his right hand, trying to ease the painful jolt that shot up to his elbow. *How difficult can it be, you senile old goat? Anti-clockwise first.*

Once he managed the first turn, reflex took over and the other five followed in rapid succession. He smiled at the loud click, and as the door swung inwards, the complex mechanism whirred and ticked as it reset. In less than a minute, it would be ready to unleash another shocking blast against any unwarranted access.

～

"Sir Pel?" Mrs Colton's voice carried through the metal-bound entry to his rooms. "I've brought you breakfast, fresh kippers like I said last night."

"Just a moment, Mrs C." Simmons crossed to the door, his head thick this morning as if someone had stuffed it with cotton wool. The brass dial in the centre of the mechanical lock spun effortlessly at his touch. A series of cogs and flywheels whirred before they aligned and heavy bolts retracted with a dull clank.

He pulled the door open to find his landlady with a large tray. Wisps of steam rose from the silver teapot and covered plates, flooding his senses with the smell of buttered kippers and kedgeree.

"You shouldn't go to all this trouble on my behalf."

"Nonsense, it was nothing, whipped it up in no time." She smiled, tilting her head. "It's Darjeeling. I know it's your favourite."

"Where on earth did you find Darjeeling?" Getting decent food in the Outer-City was difficult. Fresh tea was a luxury only seen in the Inner-City coffee houses or the kitchens of the nobility. "You are a miracle worker, my good lady."

Her cheeks flushed, and she averted her gaze. "Oh, I don't know about that, Sir Pel. I can sniff out a good deal when new shipments arrive at the docks, that's all."

"There's a clipper in from India?" he asked, taking the silver tray.

"The market was full of news from across the ocean, and a good haul of fresh fish too. I got a few pieces of halibut to put into that refrigeration unit you bought last month too."

"You are a treasure, Mrs C." He placed the tray on his desk and turned to reach into his waistcoat pocket. Realising he was still in his dressing gown, he turned. "One moment if you please."

He rushed back to his bedroom, pushing the door so she wouldn't see the mess of clothes on the floor from last night, and found his wallet. Returning to the sitting room, he pulled two notes and thrust them into her hand. "Next month's rent."

"Oh no, sir. That's far too much. And it's not due for two weeks."

"Nonsense, I have it now, and so shall you. It's a little over our usual agreed rate, but treat yourself to something."

"Oh no, Sir Pel, please—"

"I insist. You have looked after me like a king during my

stay, and the food you conjure up is nothing short of divine. Please, buy something nice for yourself. Something frivolous, perhaps a new ball gown?" He felt the grin spread across his face. "Yes, then I shall take you dancing."

He seized the unsuspecting woman, waltzing her around the room and back to the door. She tried to speak as she laughed. "No, Sir Pel, stop. You'll have me swooning and tripping down the stairs to my death. What would my Arthur say?"

With a wink, he replied, "I'd think your dear departed Arthur would say 'Bless my Soul. Well, if that isn't the finest dressed landlady in all the Outer-City' and I would have to agree."

"You are wicked," she said, a frown creasing her face, "making fun of an old lady so."

"My dear woman, it's the truth. We *will* go dancing, and you shall be the belle of the ball once again."

"We'll see," she replied with a snort. "Now eat your breakfast before it goes cold, and enough of this silliness. *Some of us* have important things to attend to."

As she turned to leave, the frown changed to a sly smile. Simmons' mood lifted at the sight. The thought of Mrs Colton with a spring in her step through the day and the smell of the kedgeree had despatched any remnants of his headache.

He threw the thick velvet curtains aside, revealing a bright grey sky, motes dancing in the shafts of light flooding into the sitting room. Taking the tray from his desk, he laid his table and set his mind to destroying the excellent breakfast.

Turning right from his lodgings, Simmons followed Commercial Street to where it crossed Whitechapel High Street. The crash of hammers and the hiss of steam, from the quenching of near-molten metal, drifted from the Commercial Smithy. Intense flashes of controlled lightning pushed ozone through the air, and he wrinkled his nose as the sharp smell hit him. Welding was the new way of connecting metal, only the old-guard still relied on heated bolts and rivets.

He crossed the serpent-like mass of tramlines covering the High Street and continued along Leman Street to the H Division headquarters of Her Majesty's Metropolitan Police Force. It was approaching midday, and he wanted to catch up with any news or new jobs posted since his last visit.

Four steps led to the heavy double doors of the Leman Street Police Station which opened into chaos. Bodies milled about, and fists flew. A group of drunken dock workers were causing a commotion as two young constables struggled to restrain them.

"What the bloody hellfire is going on here?" boomed a voice from the stairs. A huge overweight fellow, his uniform jacket stretched to its limits, burst into the fray. "Jenkins, what have I told you if they get bothersome?" The three white stripes on the man's upper sleeve showed this was the desk sergeant Simmons was here to meet.

One of the younger constables jumped in shock. "Not to spare the rod, sergeant?" he managed.

"Not to spare the bloody rod," the sergeant replied. "You lot," he pointed at the dockers with his polished truncheon. "Shut it, or I'll give you something to complain about."

Three of the group backed away from the sergeant, but the largest squared up. "We don't take no orders from the likes of you, mutton shunter," he slurred. "You better watch—"

Two rapid blows from the wooden cosh cut the speech short, cracking hard across the big man's left ear and shoulder. He dropped like a sack of coal, face-first onto the polished wood with a crack. Blood streamed down his face and pooled on the floor.

The sergeant advanced on the three remaining dockworkers, truncheon raised to eye level. "Anybody else going to give me trouble?"

Whether it was the sergeant's tone, the felling of their leader or the thick smear of blood dripping from the weapon, Simmons wasn't sure. But, hands raised and voices lowered amongst a chorus of placating negatives as the fight drained from them.

"Jenkins, get this rabble downstairs. And for the love of God, remember what that weapon on your belt is for. It's not for poking the bloody fire now, is it?"

Two constables entered from the stairwell and hauled the collapsed man down the stairs while Jenkins and the other young constable ushered the remaining group to follow.

"Too bloody soft these days," the sergeant muttered as he rounded the front desk to take his position facing the main doors.

Simmons stepped around the pool of blood and approached the desk. "Sergeant Carter, I presume?"

"That's right, sir," there was a questioning tone in his voice. "What can I do for you?"

"They told me to ask for you about payment for the Rockwell case."

"Ah, so it was you what brought him in the other night?"

"Yes. The night sergeant said you handled all the payments now and that I should come back during the day shift."

"That's right. We've had a few changes. Need to keep things in order. Everything in its proper place." Carter retrieved a large leather-bound ledger from under the desk and flicked through the pages. "Pelham Simmons, isn't it?"

"It is, and just Simmons will do."

"Well, Mr Simmons, it seems you've done a fair amount of work for H Division."

"I like to keep busy."

Carter was an enormous fellow. Simmons felt his eyes straying from the bushy-bearded face down to the stretched uniform jacket, its buttons straining to hold back the man's bulk. One had already failed in its duty. Conspicuous by its absence, it exposed an expanse of white shirt between the gaping dark blue fabric.

"So it seems. Harris?"

A young constable poked his head around an office door. "Yes, sergeant."

"Two Guineas from the safe please."

The large man returned his attention to Simmons. "I take it you have your paperwork?"

Simmons pulled his permit from an inner pocket, unfolding it for the sergeant to inspect.

"Yes, this all looks fine. I'll make you a receipt." Carter scribbled in a smaller book, then tore a sheet and handed it to Simmons before copying the entry into the log book. "If you'd like to countersign that everything is in order, sir," Carter said, offering a silver fountain pen.

It was one of those modern ones with a self-pressured ink reservoir—the type Simmons hated ever since he'd ruined a long letter when the reservoir burst while signing. Since then he'd kept to what he knew and trusted, a quality nib and a good inkwell. He signed both documents without incident and returned the pen to its owner just as constable Harris stacked two gold sovereigns and two shillings in a neat pile.

"There you go sir, a pleasant day to you," Harris said before retreating to the safety of his office.

"And to you also," Simmons replied. He returned his gaze to Carter. "That seems to conclude my business for today, sergeant. I'll check the boards for anything of interest and then take my leave."

He turned towards the job boards but stopped, returning his gaze to the man behind the desk. "You appear to have lost a button from your uniform, sergeant." He motioned to the swathe of white cloth on the other fellow's chest.

"Bugger it—" Carter said. "I mean to say, thank you for drawing it to my attention, sir."

Simmons stifled a smile, imagining the massive fellow on hands and knees searching for the silver button which must have made its bid for freedom during the coshing.

He crossed to the notice boards by the main entrance. It wasn't quite the Wild West, with wanted posters plastered around to tear down for the rewards offered, but it wasn't far removed. Notices lined the wall for work the local force couldn't complete. Many involved criminals escaping Fogside, or requests to locate missing persons.

It reminded him of the walls surrounding Hyde Park, and the new Empress' residence at Kensington Palace. It was where people first posted photographs of their missing loved ones. Those poor souls now known as 'The Lost'.

After the invasion faltered, and the Martians succumbed to the earth's bacteria, people tried to reconnect with their scattered families. It started with pictures pinned to trees. Photographs or hand-drawn, they all had names and the hope that their loved ones would return one day. As time passed, and a high wall of black steel grew around Hyde Park, it became a focal point for those still searching.

Tales of tearful reunions were common in the press but much fewer in reality. It had been almost four years now, and through all the hardship, new pictures still appeared daily. Some replaced the old damaged notes while others sought aid in locating more recent losses.

Most of the notices here were typed on Met paper, but several, handwritten in a variety of scripts, remained pinned in the personal section. Simmons took notes of a few, even though these were pleas for help with little or no payment. *I know it's not much, Surita. But I am still trying to help them.*

He skipped the police notices. For now, he'd concentrate on finding Maddox. As with all police jobs, it paid well—in this case, better than most—the force looked after their own. Something felt good about helping them locate a killer of Maddox's reputation.

On his return to Wentworth Street, Mrs Colton presented a letter. "This came for you, Sir Pel. Delivered by hand, so I thought it must be important. The fellow said to give it directly to you."

"Thank you. This fellow, anyone you've seen before?"

"I didn't recognise him. Well dressed, a butler or valet to some city gent, I reckon."

Simmons frowned. *Who'd be sending me hand delivered post?* He flipped the envelope over, inspecting the front. It was quality paper, heavyweight and addressed to 'Pelham Simmons' in a flowing script.

"Thank you, Mrs C."

"It's always a pleasure," she said, hovering for a few seconds before realising he wasn't going to open it there.

Simmons continued to his room and sank into his armchair, reaching for a letter opener. The silver blade slid through the envelope with ease.

Simmons,

I find myself in need of your help in a rather urgent matter. I know that we have not been on the best of terms and your grievance is understandable. With hindsight, it seems I could have handled the situation better. But I hope that even if you hold me in your contempt, you will not ignore this matter which involves the safety of your goddaughter, Annabelle.

I do not wish to speak further of this by letter and so hope you will find it in your heart to meet with me to discuss matters further. You are the only person I can turn to who may be able to help Annabelle. If you won't do it for me, please do it for her sake.

Hoping to hear from you favourably,

I am, sincerely yours,
  Sir Edward J Pemberton.

"Damn you, Pemberton. This is just typical." Simmons cast the letter aside.

Pemberton comes begging for help when it suits him—where was he when I returned to London with Surita? Nowhere to be found.

They'd been friends once, many years ago. But with Simmons' appointment to India, they had lost contact. What made him think Simmons would help now? His damned daughter—that's what.

Simmons sighed, it wasn't Annabelle's fault that her father was an arrogant prig. In fact, he hadn't seen her since the christening, almost seventeen years ago. Now she was in some kind of trouble, and he *was* her godfather.

3

Nathaniel Bazalgette coughed up a lungful of putrid water, gagging at the stench. Shadows danced across the arched brickwork from the rolling arc-lamp, dropped when he'd tripped.

He retched, stomach heaving from the greasy muck burning his throat, and spat a mixture of water and mucus back into the slow-flowing stream of effluent. As he pulled himself onto the raised walkway, edging the sewage tunnel, he reached for the lamp.

Shifting shadows resolved under the intense glare of his prized invention. Countless hours of design, build and late nights had paid off. The lamp battery was the size of two house bricks which fit into a neat leather satchel. Its power output was what Nathaniel was most proud of, far better than anything he'd seen in the rest of the city.

Water dripped from him as he squeezed the liquid from his soaked beard and hair, careful to avoid it falling onto the battery pack. He found a cloth to wipe his filthy spectacles, but his efforts smeared more mud around the circular lenses than cleaned them.

Despite his sodden state, he loved the sewers. Part of it was family pride—his grandfather had designed the immense network of tunnels that ran for countless miles under the capital—that wasn't the only reason though. They were works of art. Even now, almost thirty-five years since their construction in 1865, they were a marvel of form and function. The sheer beauty of the ornamental brickwork lining them was staggering. Incredible when you realised nobody was ever expected to see the results.

He lay there, admiring the vaulted ceiling of the massive node. Perfect curves of red and yellow bricks melted into brass dividers. *No wonder they called them Cathedrals.*

He took his notebook from the leather satchel, along with his favourite mechanical pencil. With a few practised strokes, he completed a sketch of the cathedral, marking its location before returning the book to safety.

His effort to re-map the sewage system was progressing well, but it might take as long as it had to build the damned things. The original plans were lost during the war but, determined to complete the meticulous job of exploration, he visited whenever he could. It drove him in his plan to follow in his grandfather's footsteps, despite the tunnels now holding greater dangers than they ever had before. It could become a lifetime's work.

He checked his pocket watch, though damp, it still appeared to be working. It was just after eight in the evening, time to be heading back before the curfew. He consulted his map for the best route to retrace his steps. The sewers were a maze of similar looking tunnels and junctions, and he was running short on time. If the Black Guard caught him in the streets after nine there would be trouble, and they weren't known for their leniency. He'd heard the tales of people disappearing after being detained.

It only took fifteen minutes to locate the side tunnel into the main sewer. From there he could find a ladder to street level and be home well before the curfew. As he approached, a high-pitched shrieking and the skittering of hundreds of tiny clawed feet reached him. *Rats.*

The sewer ahead was full of them, the typical brown variety that lived there in their thousands. On their own, or in small numbers, they weren't too much of a threat. They could give you a nasty bite, and some carried disease, but when they swarmed, then they could strip a body of flesh in minutes. They were like urban piranha, and not to be trifled with. The best course of action was to keep your distance, retreat to high ground or hope they had recently gorged on something else. His gut clenched as he turned and fled back the way he'd come.

A small upward sloping tunnel caught his sight, just large enough for him to squeeze into. He'd mapped this part of the sewer and knew the shaft connected to a more extensive section via a ladder. *That should slow them down.*

The shrill squealing approached at an alarming rate as he scrambled up the incline. His rubber-soled boots gripped the shallow grooves in the floor, designed for these ascents, but water trickled down, making the surface slick and treacherous. He spotted the ladder and pulled himself onto the rusted rungs.

The ladder creaked, large orange flakes of metal fell where his gloved hands clung to the narrow bar. With a shrieking protest, it cracked and gave way. He grasped for a handhold but found only empty space. His boots hit the incline and slipped out from beneath him, dumping him face down on the slippery surface.

Air exploded from his lungs, fear rising as he slid back towards the screams of the swarm below. His right boot struck something soft, which squealed in protest, but his toe caught in a ridge while his heart thundered in his chest.

The vile creatures scrabbled around him, tearing at his boots and trousers as he tried to dislodge them. He slammed the boot tip down, feeling it skid off one with a sickening crunch, but the rubber sole stuck, and he threw himself forward, back to the corroded ladder. *Hell, why didn't I leave earlier?*

This time, the rungs held. He pulled himself away from the gnashing jaws. A few of the little horrors leapt at him, desperate to deny his escape. He kicked those still gripping him into the side wall, tumbling into the mass of fur and teeth that boiled below.

He collapsed onto a ledge six feet above, panting white clouds of breath into the frigid air. The squealing and scratching of the frenzied mob continued below. He turned the dial on the battery pack to full, and the arc-lamp flared, burning an incandescent after-image into his sight as he squeezed his eyes shut.

He thrust the blazing lamp over the edge, electricity crackled furiously, arcing into the ladder. Frantic squeals followed the smell of scorched fur as the rats skittered to rejoin the swarm in the safety of darkness.

As his internal count hit sixty for the second time, he set the arc-lamp to a more comfortable intensity. He opened his eyes, still blinking the bright image away. The lamp now crackled with blue-white arcs forming along the enclosed filament, a tiny raging lightning storm.

Above the heavy thumping in his chest was just the lapping of water against the edge of the narrow overflow. He descended past the charred remains of half a dozen rats, back towards the central tunnel. Everything had returned to the calm, peaceful silence he was used to as he retraced his steps.

The high sewer was a sheet of black glass, thirty feet across. Walkways lined both edges with a series of parallel supporting pillars in the main flow, their reflections in the low light seeming to dive deep into the void.

As there seemed to be nothing here to cause alarm, Bazalgette dialled the arc-lamp back towards full power. The light sliced through the blackness. Shadows fled the pillars like fingers grasping for the receding safety of the darkness beyond.

At the edge of his circle of light, he glimpsed colour between the brickwork and the dark water. A floating mass of red weed had somehow found its way into the main channel and wrapped around a solitary pillar.

Crossing the walkway towards the cluster of pale tentacles, he noticed the weed was brighter on the far side where it met the opposite bank. A slow pulsing from those strands looked a deeper vibrant red, the others grey and withered by comparison. He focused the beam on the healthier section where they wrapped around themselves, gripping several small brown and white lumps.

It was fur and bleached bones, the lifeblood leached from the creatures that had stumbled too close to the weed. He'd read the details released by the government about the alien plant. It clogged the Thames and grew wild out beyond the protective city walls. The Martians seeded it during the war, feeding it a vile cocktail of blood from both animals and captured humans. Now it spread unchecked, especially near water, and drained any living thing of its life essence. Blood, sap—it was all the same to the weed—just sustenance.

That's enough for today.

He would investigate where the red weed entered the sewer tomorrow when he'd come back prepared for battle—with fire.

4

Simmons rang Pemberton's Piccadilly number from the tele-phone at his lodgings, organising to meet with the man that afternoon. The maid he spoke to had been chatty and discussed the terrible time the family were having. He found it strange that a maid should express such open opinions. It reminded him how much London had changed in just four years. The Martian invasion had touched every aspect of society and must have made finding good staff harder now than it had ever been.

He left an hour before his meeting, heading to the Whitechapel High Street. Hansom cabs were plentiful, and soon he was skirting around the massive steel walls surrounding the Inner-City. Two Black Guard squads patrolled each of the gates, and they permitted access into the noble enclave only to those on official business.

Electrical discharge crackled above, followed by the clanking of carriages. Simmons craned his neck, watching the segmented black train as it passed high overhead, speeding between the walled districts that made up the Inner-City. This one was racing north from the Square Mile towards Regent's Park—where most of London's fresh food grew. Sparks flew as it crossed one of the pylons which suspended the track fifty feet above street level. Children stopped to point at the vehicle's passing, while the rest of the crowds ignored it and continued with their daily business.

Houses here were more intact than in Whitechapel. The further west you travelled, the better the size and quality of accommodation. The only exception was within the Square Mile itself. But entry there not only required significant wealth but also the correct social status.

It was rare that anyone crossed the rigid class divides, but it had happened occasionally. Tesla was one shining example, even though he was a scientist, and thus entrenched in the middle class. His inventions had paved the way for London to drag itself from the ravages of war, back into a new age of enlightenment. They said he had premises within the Inner-City's financial district where he conducted his research.

The fountain in Piccadilly Circus indicated that Simmons was drawing close to his destination. Its angelic statue poised with bow drawn was one of only a few landmarks that had survived the war intact.

The invasion had been hard on London. More than half the city's buildings were still empty shells and rubble. Though the government repeated their commitment to rebuilding, the process was slow and, like a ripple in a pond, emanated out from the centre.

Most of the people Simmons met day-to-day had little time for those in power, and less trust in their promises. Nevertheless, they still loved their young Empress, Victoria II, even though they never saw her in person.

The address was off the main street in Piccadilly. It was a different world to the East End, but it too had suffered devastation. Many of the once great houses lay in ruins.

The hansom pulled to a halt, and Simmons stepped to the cobbled street by the skeletal remains of a building. Boards surrounded the plot to protect the public from any escaping debris. Two workmen attacked an interior wall, grunts punctuating the harsh sound of hammers on brick.

Pemberton House occupied a road halfway along Piccadilly, on the northern side, but a stone's throw from the main thoroughfare. Simmons hustled, crossing the street to avoid the worst of the dust from the demolition work, and made his way to his destination.

He rang the bell and waited a few seconds before a short woman, wearing a maid's outfit, opened the door. "Good afternoon, sir."

She was in her late twenties, and he recognised her voice from their telephone conversation. "Good afternoon. I am Sir Pelham Simmons. I believe we spoke earlier regarding an appointment to see Mister Pemberton."

"We did, sir," she replied. "I'll show you to him. Please come in."

The wide hallway was furnished and decorated in the modern style—too ornate and more than a little gaudy. The maid led him into a room to the right of an elaborate wooden stairway.

Books filled the walls from floor to ceiling, and behind a dark polished desk, Pemberton stared through the large window that flooded the study with the mid-afternoon sun.

"Sir Pelham Simmons to see you, Sir," the maid announced, waiting by the doorway.

The man turned. "Thank you, Lucy. That will be all." The two men were of a similar age, but Pemberton's well-groomed thicket of black hair and handlebar moustache spoke of a much easier life. He waited a few seconds after the door to closed behind the maid. "I wasn't sure you'd come."

Simmons snorted. "That's the difference between us, isn't it?"

"What do you mean?"

"I take my responsibilities seriously. You said Annabelle was in danger and, regardless of how I feel about you, I won't see her come to any harm."

Pemberton stroked forefinger and thumb down his moustache. "You always were a bloody stickler for honour and duty. You were never happy unless you could ram it down someone's throat."

Simmons raised an eyebrow. "Is this supposed to be your attempt at making peace?"

Pemberton shook his head. "Sorry, Simmons. That wasn't an intelligent way to open this conversation. I am not myself—Annabelle is all I have left, and she's out there somewhere." He pointed out of the window behind him. "God knows what might have become of her."

Simmons took a deep breath and forced it out slowly. "What happened?"

Pemberton crossed to a wooden globe and rolled the spherical surface open to reveal an assortment of bottles. He returned to the desk with two crystal glasses and a decanter.

Simmons filled half his glass. A single sip told him this was a fine Lochnagar. It seemed their love of the highland spirit was one passion they both still shared.

Pemberton settled into a chair behind his desk. "I don't know where she is. She disappeared over two weeks ago, and there's no sign of her."

"Two weeks? Damn it, man. Why didn't you call me earlier?"

Pemberton's eyes narrowed. "Because I don't want to be indebted to *you* of all people."

"This is your daughter we're talking about. What the hell *have* you been doing to find her?"

Pemberton scowled. "I've not been sitting on my bloody backside if that's what you mean."

"All right, let's start again. When did you notice her missing?"

Pemberton sighed. "It was on the eighteenth of April. Anna went to the theatre with her governess—a Miss Porter—the stupid cow lost her at the intermission. Anna excused herself to use the facilities but didn't return. I was bloody furious. I questioned Porter then dismissed her on the spot." He paused, taking a sip, then sighed. "I suppose threatening to shoot her if I ever saw her again, and waving my pistol around like a madman, wasn't the wisest course of action in retrospect."

"Did she tell you anything else of interest?"

"She confessed that they hadn't been getting on well. Anna seemed to have rebelled against the woman trying to discipline her—she's too much like me in that respect."

A smile cracked on his grim face. "Anyhow it seems she somehow heard idiots spouting nonsense about workers rights and had asked Porter about it. 'Why the Inner-City was the first to receive new technology when those in the outskirts were the ones most in need'—that sort of thing. Anna let slip she'd seen a man named Silas Cooper give a speech in some filthy dockside public house."

Pemberton slammed his fist onto the desk and then stood, stalking back and forth behind it. "How could this woman allow my daughter to associate with people like that? Mixing with the lower classes. It's not proper, is it?"

"Indeed," Simmons replied, trying to sound agreeable.

"By now she was bloody crying and snivelling like some scullery maid. That's when I threatened her with the pistol. She ran out into the night bawling, and good riddance."

Simmons steepled his fingers before his lips. "So, what have you been doing since then?"

"I spoke to my contacts at the ministry. We notified the police, but they were bloody useless. After that farce, someone at the club mentioned you were making quite the name for yourself locating folk. I was too pig-headed. Instead, I paid three other fellows in your line of work, but they took the payments and either disappeared or said they couldn't find anything. So, here we are. It's probably too damned late now, despite how good people say you are."

Pemberton slumped back into the chair, head bowed. "I'm an idiot. I've doomed her to some terrible fate because of *my* pride."

Simmons sighed. "I won't disagree with you, but there is always hope."

"So you'll help? I can pay you. Name your price."

"I don't want your damned money. I am doing this for Annabelle, not you." Pemberton deflated under Simmons' gaze. "Give me everything you have on the governess—letters of reference, description, photographs. I'll need a recent like-ness of Annabelle too." *She was just a baby the last time I saw her.*

Pemberton rummaged through his desk drawer and retrieved a large envelope. "I thought you might ask for some-thing like this. Here are Porter's references. And there is a photograph of her and Annabelle together—it's a year old—but neither has changed since then."

Simmons accepted the small package as Pemberton rose, offering his hand. "Thank you, Simmons. I can't tell you what this means to me."

"I'm not interested how you feel," Simmons said, ignoring the gesture. "If you'd come to me earlier, I might have found her already. Now, it will be much more difficult." He sighed. "You're still the bloody same, Pemberton. It's always about *you* —*your* feelings—how people will think of *you* rather than looking out for those who should be dearest. If you recall anything else useful, let me know. Otherwise, I'll be in touch when I have more news."

Simmons strode from the room, not waiting for the maid to open doors for him, and burst onto the pavement. The late afternoon sun poured dappled light through the canopies of the huge oaks lining the street.

He stopped, body wound tight. *Breathe.* It was Surita's voice, and he struggled to recall her gentle words when he'd been boiling with rage. He sucked in a quick lungful of air, then let it out through his nose, a slow, steady stream of frustration ebbing from him. Another two breaths and he was thinking straight again.

Surita had that effect on him from the start, tempering his hot-headed reactions. It had been so hard these past four years, but at times like this, he almost felt he could open his eyes to find her smiling back at him, an impish twinkle in her gaze. But there was only the empty street, and he wiped mois-ture from his right cheek. *Damn it, Surita.*

Green Park was just across the Piccadilly high street, and

the day looked pleasant. A walk might be precisely what he needed to clear his head and plan his next move.

∽

The contrast between the greenery and the ruins to the southeast of the park was stark—there stood the blasted remnants of Buckingham Palace. They hadn't rebuilt it after the war, leaving it as a reminder of the horror of the alien invasion.

All that remained was the new Victoria and Albert statue —a giant tower of marble and gold—that honoured the great monarch and all who fell defending the Empire. The memorial rose like a sword thrust in defiance. The sculptured designs were masterpieces, right down to the smallest of details in wrinkles and folded cloth.

Simmons bowed his head, then headed west. The wall circling Hyde Park cast long shadows as they protected the royal residence at Kensington Palace. Fifty feet of matt black steel rose from the cobbles of Park Lane surrounding the whole estate.

Horse-drawn carriages fought with the newer vehicles for control of the road around Hyde Park Corner. Automobiles cut in and out between the slower traffic. Steam boilers hissed, and sparks flew as their horns blared. Cart drivers responded with angry shouts and shaking fists. It was a scene of utter chaos.

Simmons was unsure of this new technology. Locomotives seemed safe enough. If one of them ever exploded, you'd probably survive, if you were a few carriages back. But when you sat on top of the boiler? The results for the poor driver and passengers were horrific. Images of lobsters flooded his mind. He dismissed them before they got any worse.

He'd stay with what he knew and trusted. At least horses had a modicum of self-preservation. They wouldn't continue into danger at full gallop. That couldn't be said for those mechanical contraptions.

He hadn't expected to find anything in the park. It was a chance to clear his head and put his options into perspective.

The light dimmed as early evening approached, and he found a hansom cab in the busy Piccadilly traffic. The journey back to Whitechapel was slow, but he paid the cabbie an extra sixpence for his service before retreating to his rooms.

Simmons needed to change the filter in his fog-gear before venturing out again. He had unfinished business with Maddox. A trip south of the river to investigate his latest lead was in order and, with luck, he might find more about this Silas Cooper.

5

The Tower Bridge checkpoint was the usual farce of questions from the Black Guard. After what felt like hours, they relented, accepting Simmons' paperwork. With greatcoat flapping in the gale, he stepped from the covered bridge onto the southern shore as the protective gate crashed down behind him.

A motley crew stood along the jetty, swathed in a variety of fog-gear. Most of it looked serviceable, though a few wore nothing more than ill-fitting layers of sackcloth over their heads, held in place by goggles.

Their vessels bobbed on small swells as the river continued its rise. Wooden hulls hitting the stone quay with a dull, rhythmic thump.

Most of the boats were broad punts, poled along by their owners. A few, however, had engines allowing them to traverse the deeper areas of the submerged city on the south bank of the Thames.

He approached the first waterman. "I'm looking for a man named John Maddox, I believe he came through here a few nights past. Have you heard of him?"

"Sorry gov, no idea."

He repeated the questions with each of the others to no avail as he moved along the dock. He turned to leave but stopped as a gruff voice rose from below the quay. "I know Maddox. Runs with the Red Hands."

Simmons glanced over the edge. A thickly wrapped figure on one of the motorised vessels stared back at him. He'd been difficult to spot, but those sharp blue eyes were familiar.

"Isaac?"

The old waterman frowned. "Mr Simmons, isn't it? Long time no see."

"I've been tied up with jobs north of the river, but now it seems I need to explore the south bank."

"If you're looking for Maddox, I'd suggest starting in Greenwich," Isaac replied. "There's deep water between here and there. You'll need more than a regular pole pusher."

"Well, it's fortunate I ran into you then," Simons said with a wink. "Still sailing these waters for profit, eh? You old pirate."

"You know me," Isaac said with a chuckle. "I sail all the backwaters that these youngsters ain't never heard of. And I'll get you where you need to be. None of this 'I don't go there, sir, too dangerous, especially in the fog' nonsense. I set a fair price for the destination. If you want me to wait or pick you up later, I'll be there on time."

"Anything else I should know?"

"No. If that's all right with you, we can do business."

Simmons held out his hand. "Fine by me."

Isaac clasped it and helped him onto the vessel. "Welcome aboard, sir. So, Greenwich, is it?"

"In a moment. Just a few more questions if you don't mind?"

Isaac drew his pocket watch. "Right you are, Mr Simmons, but we'll be on the clock now we're working."

"That sounds fair. Maddox isn't much more than a name to me. Heard he was in trouble with the Red Hands." Simmons was lying, but he knew men like Isaac. They couldn't resist correcting a well-dressed stranger.

"Ha, you city folks got it all twisted. He's not in trouble with 'em, sir, he's their bloody enforcer. 'Mad Dog' they call him, though not to his face. Suits him down to the ground from what I hear, a real loose cannon. His reputation is well-known Fogside, and you won't find many ready to cross him over here. I thought even your lot knew that."

"I see."

"Mind you, it ain't just the law who'd like to get their hands on 'im. I'll tell you that for free, sir."

"I thought there was honour among thieves?"

Isaac laughed. "Not when it comes to Diamond Annie."

Simmons paused, thinking. "She's with the Elephant and Castle gang, isn't she?"

"More than just with 'em. She's fighting for the bloody leadership. She already runs the Forty Thieves, and a lot of the rank and file think the current leader's too soft."

"Really? I hadn't heard any of that."

"So they say, sir. The rabble see Annie as a breath of fresh air. Brutal, mind. She don't take no shit from nobody, and she's not one to bury the hatchet—unless it's in someone's back."

"So what does this have to do with Maddox?"

"Well, Maddox caused quite the ruckus on Diamond Annie's doorstep at her place in Lambeth. Not a wise move when there's already bad blood between them and the Red Hands."

"So, she has an axe to grind with him?"

Isaac produced a gap-toothed smile. "You could say that, sir. I can take you there if you want to poke around?"

Simmons nodded. "That sounds like a splendid idea."

Simmons watched as Isaac navigated them through the thickest patches of red weed with consummate ease. It wasn't until the half-ruined towers of Westminster appeared through the fog that the boat slowed.

Isaac tapped him on the shoulder. "We need to pick our way through the remains of the bridge. Most of it got destroyed during the war. The rest, gravity took over the years."

"Do you need me to do anything?"

"We should be all right, but you could stand at the prow and signal if it looks like we might hit anything."

"Right," Simmons replied, trying to keep his voice confident. He wasn't keen on the idea that Isaac might miss seeing debris from the collapsed bridge. The chances of surviving falling into the Thames seemed slim. If he didn't drown from the weight of his cumbersome fog-gear, becoming entangled in the vice-like grip of the weed would do for him.

"If you kneel in the prow so you can see forward, then signal with an arm to direct me left or right. Just hold it out straight so I can see. If we need to stop, hold both arms out like a scarecrow, you understand?"

"Yes, left or right and both for stop. Got it." Simmons spotted a bundle of folded canvas and laid it in the prow to make kneeling more comfortable. His knees ached enough in the damp weather as it was.

Water broke on the prow, sounding a lot less playful than earlier and the thickening curtain of fog parted, revealing the remains of Westminster Bridge.

Isaac seemed to do nothing more than lean on the tiller. But they were angling back from the centre towards the southern shore. Isaac pointed to his own eyes with two fingers and then gesticulated. Feeling chagrined, Simmons raised a thumb in acknowledgement before turning to resume his vigil.

Twisted rusty shapes rose from the dark water, and he signalled as instructed. Isaac avoided the obstacles, heading towards the remains of the southernmost arch.

A dark horizontal line appeared through the fog. The rope clipped Simmons' head, pushing it backwards. His mask pressed into his face, and as he twisted his body to free himself, the rope twanged past, taking his hat with it.

"Stop, stop," he shouted back towards Isaac, then remembering, held both arms out wide, waving them up and down hoping that would show Isaac that he should stop, right now.

A heavy thrum issued from the stern and the whole boat lurched as the engine went into reverse. Water bubbled, thrashing at the rear of the vessel as she slowed and came to a standstill. Simmons regained his balance and grabbed his rifle before making his way towards the stern.

Isaac was sawing at the thick rope that extended between the two piers they had tried to pass through.

"A bloody rope," Isaac said, thrusting the thick strands of woven fibres at him.

"Yes, it almost took me off my feet," Simmons replied. "It's a good job I was kneeling. Otherwise, I'd have been taking a swim."

"Who the hell would do such a stupid—"

"Drop that knife if you know what's good for you."

The new voice came from somewhere on the bank.

Simmons stopped and looked at Isaac. "You keep him talking while I sort this out." He flicked his eyes down to his rifle in its protective waxcloth case.

Isaac's head bobbed in a slight nod then he turned to face the shoreline. "What the hell's going on? Did you put this bloody rope across here?"

Simmons used his body to obscure the rifle, his fingers opening the buckles with a familiar rhythm.

"That's our rope, and we want whatever you got on there."

"What on earth makes you think I'd give you anything?" Isaac shouted back.

"Well, if you don't, then we'll just... sink your boat. Then what'll you do?"

"We've got guns," another voice added from the same direction.

A mumbled exchange drifted to them from the shoreline, Simmons thought it had started with 'Shut up.' He smiled to himself. *Clumsy opportunists.* "I'll tell you what, chaps," he shouted towards the shore. "Because I'm feeling generous tonight, I've decided to give you something."

"What's that?"

"I will give you... a head start."

"What?" came the confused reply.

"I'm going to count to three. Then I'll shoot you with *my* gun." He waited a few seconds to let the concept sink in. "Now,

I don't know what type of guns you have over there, but mine's very nice. It's a Holland & Holland .303 double chambered hunting rifle. I used it while I was in India. I was a great shot, bagged quite a few tigers and a couple of elephants. It's known as an 'Elephant Gun' because it's powerful enough to stop a charging bull elephant with a single shot through the brain."

He winked at Isaac through his goggles. He was having far too much fun to stop just yet.

"Well, there's no need to get excited now," called the voice from the shore.

"Oh, but I *am* excited. In fact, it's been a few years since I shot anyone. There was plenty of that in India, had to keep the locals and servants in their place. But, as an Englishman, it was only sporting to give them a head start. Oh, which reminds me. One..."

Silence descended, broken only by the soft lapping of the river against the boat.

"I can't hear any running," Simmons called. "Wouldn't be sporting to shoot stationary targets, even if you do have guns. Two..."

A splash, followed by frantic scrabbling came from somewhere on the shoreline behind the remains of the bridge.

"Three..." A deafening explosion cut through the night from a single barrel, followed by a resounding metallic shriek as the massive round struck the support he'd been aiming at on the bridge. Isaac almost leapt out of the boat in shock.

"Sorry," Simmons said, looking at the waterman. "Didn't realise you weren't ready."

Isaac clutched at his chest. "My heart, my poor heart. What did you go and do that for? I nearly shit myself."

"I told them I'd shoot when I got to three."

"Yeah, but I didn't think you would really do it. I thought you was just trying to scare 'em off."

"That *was* the idea. But if we want to keep them running all the way home, I thought I'd better show willing and make a bit of noise."

"A bit of noise? My ears are bloody ringing," Isaac said,

shaking his head. "Bloody kids. Don't they got nothing better to do?"

"Kids?"

"Yeah, no doubt they was trying to impress the Elephant and Castle with this *daring robbery*." He laughed, turning to Simmons. "It seems your Elephant gun was well named for tonight. Those little buggers probably thought you've shot members of the gang they're trying to impress."

"Do you encounter this sort of thing often?"

Isaac returned to cutting the rope. "Not really, there's an unwritten law that means watermen don't get troubled by the gangs. It's bad for business, for them and us. If word gets around that boats are getting rolled, the supply of transport will dry up or will get very expensive. Apparently, things are changing."

"I see," Simmons replied as the rope dropped onto the deck and slipped over the side. "So, you make yourself too important for them to upset you too much then?"

"That's the idea. Now, put that bloody cannon away and let's see if we can get you to Lambeth without any more excitement tonight."

≈

Simmons watched as the flaking red-painted arches of Lambeth Bridge passed overhead. "This used to be a horse ferry before they built the bridge," Isaac said. "But there was too much demand to get across from Westminster, so they built a permanent crossing in sixty-two. That were a farce though. The engineers didn't think about the cabbies that needed to cross, and the approach to the bridge was too steep. It was a right royal pain getting a horse-drawn cab onto the damned thing let alone across it. Most cabbies refused to use it and, after a few accidents, where two folk and a horse died, no-one would cross it other than on foot."

A run-down collection of close-packed buildings dominated the view eastwards. Occasional flickers of light marred the otherwise abandoned feeling of the whole area. "Here we are, Lambeth Palace." It was an imposing five-storey building —a large central gate squeezed between two square towers of brick. "That's Morton's Tower, the gatehouse. The rubble to the right is the remains of St. Mary's. I'll drop you there."

Each of the towers had a single window, one per floor. The diffuse glow in a few suggesting they had fogsheets up to protect them from any ingress of the vile stuff. Battlements ran along the top of the tower, and Simmons realised why someone would find a place like this useful. It was a miniature castle.

With a soft bump, the boat came to a halt. "Lambeth Road. That'll be three and six, sir." The amusement in Isaac's voice was clear.

"How about we add it to my tab?"

"Maybe next time, sir. Cash for now, if you please."

Simmons reached into an inside pocket and drew a handful of coins. "Four shillings, keep the change."

Isaac dropped them into a money belt at his waist. "Thank you, sir. I suppose I'll have to set you a tab up now then, won't I? You want me to wait?"

Simmons checked his watch. It was half-past six. "Yes, but if I'm not back by, shall we say nine, then presume I won't need your services further this evening."

"Right you are. There are steps on the other side of the church wall there."

"Thank you," Simmons said, disembarking.

He picked his way between the rubble of what had been St Mary's Church and crossed toward the red-brick tower. The Thames reached the sill of the ground-floor windows, and red weed clung to the brickwork above, trying to claw its way higher in a vile imitation of ivy.

A figure poked its head out between the crenellations of the central structure. "Oy, what are you doing down there?" It was a woman's voice.

Simmons noticed another dark outline with a rifle to the

left of the speaker. "I'm here to speak with Diamond Annie, about a mutual friend. Is she here?"

"Don't move. I'll send someone down."

A minute later and the wooden slats of a rope ladder clacked against the brickwork and made a wet sucking noise as they hit the ground.

"Up you come then. Nice and steady."

Simmons hauled himself up through the fog. It thinned as he passed the second storey, then he was looking up at a starlit sky. Pinpricks of bright light shone through the veil of deep black. As he reached the third-floor window, a fogsheet pulled aside to allow him access. He hooked a leg over the ledge and pulled himself into the small room—right into the barrel of a pistol inches from his face.

A well-built woman in her late thirties motioned with the gun for him to move along the wall away from the window.

"So what have we here?" she asked, pointing at his fog mask. "Take that off."

He reached up to the mask and undid the arrangement of buckles and straps that held it in place. "Gladly," he said as soon as the respirator had loosened.

"All right, let's have it. Who are you, and what the hell do you want here?" The woman's voice was loud and confident, as she calmly poked him with the pistol.

"Simmons," he said, placing the fog mask onto a nearby chair, proffering his hand. "I was hoping to speak with Diamond Annie."

She looked at the outstretched hand and grunted. "What have you got that Annie needs to know about?"

"It seems we have a mutual dislike of a certain Mr John Maddox. She may find what I have to say... beneficial."

The woman fell silent, her eyes intent on his. "Maddox, eh?" Her demeanour shifted. "Perhaps she will want to talk to you."

∾

Diamond Annie was tall. Taller than most of the men Simmons knew. There was an aura of confidence around her, a raw and ruthless ambition. It was in her eyes, an icy blue that spoke of a cold and grim determination. Her face was all sharp angles, and her nose followed an odd line, broken at least once before.

The dim light from two lanterns illuminated the opulent room, but what caught his eye were the myriad reflections from all the rings she wore.

"So, Mr Simmons," Annie said, breaking the silence. "Maggie tells me you want to talk about that walking bag of piss, Maddox."

"Yes," he replied. "I have a contract to recover him."

"Recover? And what exactly does that mean?"

"Dead, alive, as long as he's identifiable. I heard you had recent dealings with him, and as I'm looking for him, I thought we might be able to help each other?"

Annie sat in a plush armchair, she pointed to the other. "Sit. Let's talk details."

The aches and tension leaked from his body as he sank into the old cracked leather. "So, we have a common foe. What's your interest in him?"

The reflected points of light danced across the walls like stars through the heavens as she steepled her fingers in thought. Rings of all shapes and sizes covered her hands, at least one on each finger. "I want that bastard's head on a plate, for what he done to Gracie."

"That might cause me a problem. I have already given my word on that contract."

"A man of his word, eh? Now there's a rarity in these times." Annie reached over to lift a silver tankard from a side table. "How about you return what he took from Gracie, and you bring him back in one piece? I'll make sure you can claim your fee after I've finished with him."

Simmons pondered the options. "Provided there's enough for the sergeants to identify, I can do that. What did he steal?"

"A ring," she replied, her voice low. She seemed on the

verge of saying more, emotion welling behind those icy eyes for an instant, then gone. "A diamond ring, it was a gift. I want it back."

Surely you've plenty of those already, he thought, but he restrained himself. "How will I recognise it?"

Annie pointed to the first ring on her right index finger. "It's the spitting image of this one."

It was a large well-cut stone set in a plain gold band. "Fair enough. You'll get the ring once I've got Maddox. Do you know anything of his whereabouts?"

"He's meeting a man called Silas Cooper."

Simmons' eyes flared in surprise. "The political agitator?"

"Oh, aren't we well informed? You know him?"

"Not exactly," Simmons replied. "I'm aware of him from another case."

"Well, Cooper's gonna speak in the Whitechapel docks in a few days—the Britannia pub. That will be your best opportunity to catch them both." Annie took a long draught from her silver tankard then stood. The meeting was over.

Simmons pushed himself from the comfortable chair. "Thank you for your time."

Annie gripped Simmons by the hand. The single solid shake dispersed rainbows of light that danced across her chiselled features. Her pale eyes narrowed, drilling into his. "Just make sure you bring that bastard to me alive."

6

Woodruff struggled forward hand thrust before his eyes. The storm raged, snow tearing at his face, the icy particles biting into his soft flesh. He was lost, and couldn't even remember how he came to be in the mountains in the middle of the night. He was a financier from the Inner-City, not some bloody explorer.

The last he remembered, he was out slumming it in one of the seedier areas of Whitechapel. After a skinful of spirits, and still revelling in the opium haze, he'd spotted the woman. She was stunning. An English rose among the orientals and lascars who inhabited the dens. His eyes struggled to follow her, and he realised she was little more than a girl. That didn't bother him. The younger, the better.

She noticed his stare and sauntered back, half-naked, and dragged him off to a waiting carriage. More drink and drunken fumbling, then they staggered into a sleazy bordello and up narrow stairs to a room. It was all a blur of light and dark amidst the sickly perfumed pipe smoke.

It must be a dream. Either the smoke or the spirits had addled his brain. Another icy blast shook him back to the present, almost taking him off his feet. He slipped on the snow-covered path, his hand grabbing the jagged rocks as he fought to keep his balance. Pain tore through his palm, the frozen flesh burning. It was so cold, his skin hardly bled. This wasn't a dream—he really was stuck on a mountainside in a nightmare of a blizzard.

He cried out for someone to help him, pleading as he fell to his knees, tears freezing on his eyelids. Then she was there, the beauty he had met at the opium den, reaching out to him. He took her delicate hands, and she pulled him to her.

"Don't worry, Cyril," she said. Her palms burned, but her words were honey. "Are you ready for some fun?"

He was ready, all thoughts of the pain from the biting wind gone in an instant, consumed by lust. He reached for her, pulling her into a sinuous embrace as her two arms entwined around him, three, four?

What the hell was going on?

His eyes burst open, revealing the horror. Tentacles crushed him in a vice-like grip, their dead grey flesh squirming over his half-naked form. A scream froze as something slimy thrust itself into his mouth, clawing for his throat. Then he saw the eyes.

He stumbled back over the cliff edge, and the obscene creature fell entangled with him, its writhing appendages gripping him in a ghastly embrace. Air rushed past, ripping at his flesh as the vile cluster of eyes tore into his soul, and he howled.

The girl gazed from the shattered third-floor window. Two street lights shed a dull glow over the pallid body impaled on the railings. Iron spikes jutted through his chest, neck and shoulder while dark liquid oozed from the mangled corpse. Shards of glass sparkled crimson where the light caught sharp edges on the blood splattered cobbles.

She hawked and spat onto the disgusting figure. With a wry smile, she turned to leave the room, and the memories of her past, behind.

7

Simmons shot upright with a snort, not realising where he was for an instant. The paper draped half on his lap, the other half had somehow made its way onto the floor beside him. It was pitch black outside. He reached for the half-full cup of tea but realised it would be cold. It sat upon the silver platter, along with the sandwiches which Mrs Colton had left for him earlier in the day. He really had landed on his feet when he'd found this place.

His pocket watch showed a quarter past two in the morning. *Damn, I need to get back into a daytime routine*. The rapid turnaround his line of work required accustomed him to a more nocturnal lifestyle. But for now, he needed more sleep if he was to attend this meeting where Silas Cooper was due to speak. Then he'd catch up with Maddox—two birds with one stone.

The bare mantlepiece caught his attention, and he cursed, searching for his rifle case. It clicked open with the smooth action that spoke of expert craftsmanship, and he lifted a velvet-lined compartment revealing a teak shaving box.

The familiar gouges in the weathered surface scratched under his fingers as he opened it. Angling the hinged mirror, he began his evening ritual. As he retrieved items from within, he laid them beside it: a short candle, a teaspoon celebrating Victoria's Golden Jubilee and Surita's wedding ring. The last thing, a cracked photograph from Bombay, was the only image that remained of her. Water-stained and torn around the edges, he placed his wife into the mirror frame and lit the candle.

Images flooded his mind as he lost himself in the flame. He wasn't sure how long he sat there, fighting back the painful memories of their joyless return to London, but after a while, the dancing light fractured into starbursts. He wiped the tears from his eyes. "I'm sorry, Surita. I'm so sorry—"

His voice cracked, and he forced out a breath though his throat was tight. He held the flame between thumb and finger, heedless of the pain as his calloused skin blackened with soot. Then he closed them, snuffing it.

He returned the precious items to their allotted places, before grabbing his current bottle of whisky, and stumbled to his bed.

The Britannia public-house occupied two storeys at the corner of St Georges Street and Chigwell Hill. The clamour from the place echoed long before it came into sight. Laughter, shouting and the revelry of folk partaking of more than their fair share of cheap beer and gin.

A wall of sound struck Simmons as he entered the dingy establishment, followed by the sour stink of bodies pressed too close together after a hard day of work. The stale smell of ale and the bright tang of poor quality spirits reminded him more of hell-holes he'd seen in India, rather than a once civilised Britain.

"Stop bloody pushing, or I'll put you on your arse." The voice drifted from a stairway beside the bar. Simmons crossed to the stairs, the crowd murmuring consent and barking objections above. Cooper must have started his agitation a little earlier than expected. Simmons passed two rough-looking men squaring up for a fight, and into a large room which filled the pub's top floor.

All attention was focused on a small, wiry man in round-framed spectacles and a respectable brown suit. His jacket draped the back of a chair on an impromptu stage atop several pale wooden pallets.

Simmons found a comfortable corner with a little space from the mass of bodies all straining to get as close to the front as possible. He leaned against the wall by one of three large glass windows that overlooked a small yard behind the pub. It was past seven, and the light outside was fading. The fog would follow soon.

He drew his pipe from his inside pocket, lighting it while Cooper addressed the crowd. Four thugs stood before the stage to keep the throng from getting too close. They appeared practised in the act which comprised glares, snarls and the occasional raising of fists when anyone pushed too far forward.

"Now, let me tell you something I have found that will chill your hearts," Silas said. "Brothers and Sisters, we the underpaid, underfed and undervalued workers of the Outer-City have long toiled for little reward and less appreciation. While the toffs of the Inner-City drink their fine wines and attend parties where more food is thrown away than we could hope to buy for our families. They force us to work ourselves to exhaustion, so our young ones can share a crust and a sip of water that won't leave them wheezing with the taint."

He worked the crowd, deftly pulling their emotions first one way then another. "While we rush to avoid the curfew, they drink late into the night, free to do whatever they want, whenever it pleases them. To top it all, they send their filthy Blaggards to keep us down in the gutter begging at their tables for scraps, like the mangy curs they take us for. Isn't that right, my friends?"

The crowd jeered their approval. It took Cooper a few seconds to bring the tone back down as he motioned for calm with his palms outstretched. "I tell you that there is a conspiracy. A silent, malevolent plan made by the toffs behind it all."

He gestured with open arms, palms upward this time. "Now, all that's just talk, I hear you say. Where's the proof you ask? Well, that is why I have gathered you here tonight. To hear the evidence that links the Blaggards directly to murders of innocent workers such as you and me. And not just one or two, mind you. I have met witnesses to these heinous crimes who were there when they happened, spoken with these people who are too frightened to speak out in public. Too afraid for what will become of them and their families and what retribution they might face from these cowards and their black-uniformed hounds."

Cooper paused, allowing the message to sink in, letting the tempers rise to boiling point. "But it goes way beyond the mere murder of working folk like you and me. This evidence tells of why we see so little of our beloved new Empress Victoria. God bless her."

A murmur of assent came from the assembled crowd. Cooper changed his voice to that of a whining child. "But, she's unwell, sickly. The weight of loss hangs heavy upon her. I know you're all thinking it." Coopers mock-pity burned into sneering contempt. "Bollocks to that, I say. She isn't ill. They keep her under lock and key in her own palace. Not protected, but imprisoned by the Blaggards and those who hold their leashes."

With his fist in the air and speech rising in volume, he continued. "Now, I ask you, are we going to let these bastards imprison our Queen?"

A resounding "No." from the excited crowd.

Cooper raised his voice a touch more. "Our Empress?"

"Never," they shouted as one.

"Ruler of our great Brit—"

The oration crashed to a halt with a gurgle. Blood gouted from Cooper's neck hitting the roof. Stringy red droplets rained down onto the front rows. He sagged to his knees as another arterial spray pumped out of his rag doll form, then collapsed face first into the blood-soaked stage.

The place fell into chaos amidst screams and shouts of

confusion as the crowd jostled, pushing towards the single exit to the stairs.

Simmons stumbled back into the corner and let the madness flow past him. He'd encountered situations similar to this in the Bombay food riots. The sheer panic that could lead to people crushing their neighbours underfoot to escape. They reverted to their primal urges to fight or flee.

A man lost his balance, falling into the crush close by. Simmons raised his cane thrashing out in an arc in front of him, heedless of who he struck in the flow of bodies. "Go around, damn you. Out of the way."

It was like trying to cut through water as the crowd flowed by him: one moved away, replaced by another charging to fill their place. Between the shouting madman before them, and the whirling cane lashing out, the stream parted, pouring past as he got his feet either side of the body on the ground.

Once the crush passed, the room resolved into a semblance of order. Shouts and screams echoed from the stairs. No doubt falls had caused more fear and confusion in their rush down into the crowd below. That left just four people—two of the heavies from the stage, himself, and the fellow at his feet. Simmons reached to help the poor man up. "Are you all right?"

"Yes, I think so," the man replied, grimacing as he stood while holding his left side.

"Lucky I saw you fall. Could have been much worse."

"Thank you, mister?"

"Simmons." They shook hands, "and you, sir?"

"Bazalgette. Nathaniel Bazalgette. I think I might have cracked a rib."

"A few stiff drinks, strap it up and don't sleep on that side. Oh and take morphine if you have it. That's what my orderlies used to say."

Bazalgette stared at him. "Thank you. I'll see what I can do."

"Good man. Now, what the Devil is going on? Did you see that?" Simmons gestured with his pipe towards the body.

"Damnedest thing." He strode toward the two minders at the edge of the stage.

"You two," he said, reaching the confused-looking heavies. "This is Silas Cooper, correct?" He pointed at the body. Blood pooled around its upper torso. Drips still fell from the ceiling like rain from trees minutes after a downpour.

"Yeah. It were," one fellow said, his accent thick and uncertain. Streaks of blood smeared the side of his shaved head where he'd tried to wipe it. "I'm covered in this shit," he said, looking down at his clothing. Several dark stains were still spreading through the material.

Simmons waived his comment aside. "Yes, yes, but what do you know about Cooper?"

"We don't know nothing, do we, Reg?" the man said, turning to his comrade.

"Nah," Reg replied, nodding at the body. "He paid us to keep things in order. Make sure things didn't get out of hand. We don't know anything else about him."

Simmons studied the two men. "Do you know where he lives?"

"Damfino," Reg replied, "we met him here. It was supposed to be a simple job." He grimaced, glancing down at the corpse, and backed towards the exit. "I'm off, don't need no trouble with the crushers."

Simmons sighed. "Very well. I'll deal with the police when they get here."

As the men headed to the stairs, still muttering and cursing about the mess, Simmons looked up to find Bazalgette stood there. "Why are you still here?"

"I wasn't sure if I should leave before the police arrived. I don't want them thinking I absconded or had anything to hide. Besides, what on earth happened to Silas Cooper?"

"Good question. You wouldn't happen to be a medical chap, would you?"

"I'm afraid not. I studied a little anatomy at the Royal College of Science, but that's as far as it goes I'm afraid."

"It was a long shot," Simmons said. "An educated man though? So you'd be a good observer, take in fine details?"

"Well, I am a man of science…"

"In that case, can you tell me what you observed here tonight about Mr Cooper's demise?"

Bazalgette produced a small cloth from his pocket and started to clean his spectacles. "There was a large fountain of arterial blood from the left side of his head, and he dropped to the ground."

"And what of the wound?"

"I couldn't see clearly, but I presume someone shot him, though I didn't hear a gunshot."

Simmons beckoned Bazalgette over to the body. "All right, what do you make of this then?" He pointed to a two-inch incision at the base of Coopers' neck above the collarbone. It was oozing dark blood. "That isn't a bullet wound," Simmons said. "I've seen my fair share of those. This is a clean cut, the thrust of a sharp blade."

Bazalgette stopped his cleaning. "But how is that possible? There wasn't anyone else on the stage. Cooper was talking one minute, and the next he was showering blood over the front rows of the audience." He pointed up at the ceiling. "Look there, a clear trail of blood under pressure from the wound."

Simmons nodded. "My point exactly. It makes little sense, yet we both saw the same thing." He looked around the stage area and suggested Bazalgette check the rest of the room for anything unusual. After a few minutes, he was confident the makeshift stage held no new information.

"Simmons, look at this." Bazalgette stood by one of the three large windows nearest the stage. He was pointing at the window-ledge and a scuffed red patch on the otherwise grey stone. It was blood, but how had it found its way over to the sill? It was over fifteen feet from Cooper's body.

"How is that even possible?" Simmons asked.

"It's still damp. It must have rubbed off something, perhaps a boot?"

"Have you checked the window?"

48

Bazalgette looked at the large sash window. "It seems to be unlocked." He pulled on the lower frame, and the window slid up with the help of the counterweights.

"I need to check outside before the police show up," Simmons said, and turned towards the stairs.

"Wait for me. I don't fancy trying to explain this to them alone."

Simmons pushed through the door at the top of the stairs and almost walked into the barkeep. The man was getting on in years, his once solid frame now leaning towards fat, and the reddened face spoke of a life of sampling his wares. His breathing laboured from dragging his bulk upstairs, and the dirty stains on his bartender's apron told of untold spillages over the last week or more.

"Here, what are you doing?" the man said, his face wrinkled in irritation. "I thought everyone left?"

"Sorry my good man," Simmons said, "but you will need to keep everyone else out of here until the police arrive. They will, no doubt, want to investigate the scene."

"But—"

"Make sure nobody else comes up here till they arrive. All right?" He flashed his papers under the startled bartender's nose and continued down the stairs motioning Bazalgette to follow. Simmons had no authority here, but the bartender didn't know that—he probably couldn't even read the travel permit.

"So you're with the police then?" Bazalgette asked as they crossed the deserted bar.

"Something like that," Simmons said, a grin growing across his face. "Let's investigate the yard while we have the chance."

∼

The yard behind the Britannia was filthy and strewn with rubbish. The only light shone from the upstairs windows revealing old barrels and broken packing crates lying around the exterior of the space. It was barely large enough to fit a cart into, and the amount of refuse made Simmons think they must make deliveries to the front.

Bazalgette pointed up to the first of the three windows overlooking the yard. "That's the one with the bloodstain, isn't it?"

"Yes, let's take a closer look."

As Simmons moved to a point below the window, there was the unmistakable crackle of electricity, and a bright blue-white glow spread across the floor from behind. He looked back, Bazalgette had pulled a lamp from his leather satchel.

"Sorry," Bazalgette said. "I didn't intend to startle you."

"You didn't startle me," Simmons replied, eyes intense in the brightening light. "But yes, next time you pull some electrical contraption out of your hat, I would appreciate a little warning. What is that anyhow?"

Bazalgette perked up. "This is an arc-lamp. It's based on Tesla's street lighting in the Inner-City, but it's my design."

"You made that?" his voice sounded more surprised than he had intended.

"Yes. I use it in my work," Bazalgette said, his tone a little perturbed.

"Sorry, I didn't mean it like that," Simmons said, moving closer to inspect the artefact. "It's amazing that you've made it so small."

Bazalgette brightened. "Oh, yes. It took some work to find the right power source. I'm still having a few issues with controlling the luminosity though." He fiddled with a control on the lamp and the light dimmed. Simmons realised that he was squinting as the lighting became more bearable, but still bright enough to illuminate the entire yard.

"I thought it might be useful if we are looking for any signs of someone exiting that window," Bazalgette added.

"Good thinking." Simmons pointed to the foot of the building below the window. "Point it over here."

As the light passed across the broken remains of barrels, pallets and crates, something shifted beneath the pile.

"Hold it there," he told Bazalgette, reaching for the revolver inside his coat. He drew and aimed the pistol in the sound's direction. "Whoever's in there, you better come out before I shoot."

"Don't shoot. Don't shoot me," a child's voice came from behind the rubbish. A small, grimy figure emerged from the pile, hands held high in surrender. "I'm not doing nothing, just having a kip, that's all."

Bazalgette focused the arc-lamp on the child who narrowed his eyes in the brilliant light.

"Who are you?" Simmons asked. "What are you doing here?"

The lad looked no older than ten and dressed in a motley of worn and mismatched clothing, all of it filthy. "My name is Charlie, and I ain't stole nuffink."

Simmons lowered his voice. "It's all right, Charlie. I'm not accusing you of anything. I just want to know why you are here, and if you've seen anything unusual tonight. You're not in any trouble."

The lad seemed none too impressed with the offer, his eyes darting left and right seeking a route to freedom.

"How about we make a deal?" Bazalgette asked. "You tell us what Mr Simmons here wants to know, and I'll give you this shiny penny?"

Charlie cocked his head to one side squinting at Bazalgette, Simmons could hear the cogs whirring in the young lads head.

"How about sixpence?" Charlie asked.

"Oh," Bazalgette said. "I'm not sure I've got—"

"No, son. Not a sixpence," Simmons said. "Do you want the penny or not?"

"I've got thruppence," Bazalgette added.

"Deal." The young lad spat on his hand, thrusting it towards Bazalgette.

Simmons sighed. "After," he said before Bazalgette could deliver the coin to the cheeky urchin.

Bazalgette pulled his hand, and the thruppence, back to himself. "Yes, after you tell us."

"Right, Charlie. On the promise of thruppence from my friend here. Why don't you tell me what you saw tonight?"

Charlie relaxed and lowered his outstretched hand. "Well, I'd fallen asleep, but woke when summat hit the deck with a thump. So, I takes a peep, and it were one of them filthy Blaggards what was turning his coat inside out and putting it—"

"What? A member of the Black Guard, are you sure?" Simmons asked.

"Yes, sir, honest it was. I seen his sword on his belt. He wasn't wearing a proper uniform, but he was one of 'em. It were a Blaggards long coat when he turned it over, but it didn't have none of the buttons or stripes they normally have on 'em."

"If it wasn't a uniform, what was he wearing beneath the coat?"

"It were common work clothes."

Simmons' mind ran wild. "What about the sword?"

"Yeah it were a Blaggard sword, but it was under his coat, not like they usually wear 'em, and it were smaller. Once he put the coat on, you couldn't even tell it were there."

"All right, Charlie, that's good. Anything else you remember?"

"Well, he had this pocket watch what was in in his hand before he switched his coat about. It were a real pretty piece. A fancy gentleman's watch with silvery swirls and cut-outs in the case."

"Filigree?" Bazalgette prompted.

"If you like. Is that what it's called?"

Simmons nodded and waited for him to continue. "And then?" he prompted.

"That were it. He took to his heels toward the street. I stayed here cos I've heard things what happens to them what gets taken by the Blaggards." The boy shivered.

Simmons turned to Bazalgette. "Give him the thruppence —he's earned it."

With the transaction complete, Charlie disappeared down the alley, and Simmons returned towards the base of the first window. A boot print was visible among rotten straw which had spilt from a broken crate. "Yes, that's a military-style boot if ever I saw one," Simmons said, looking back at Bazalgette. "What the hell is going on here?"

"Well," Bazalgette started, not picking up on the rhetorical nature of Simmons question. "If we can believe the boy, the Black Guard murdered Silas Cooper and the killer somehow performed the act without being seen."

"Until the boy sees him out here," Simmons said.

Whistles sounded in the distance as the local constabulary flocked towards the area. Bazalgette shot Simmons a glance, eyes wide, like a rabbit caught in the sights.

"We best get our story straight," Simmons said. "I don't want to spend a night in a cold cell when I have a comfortable bed waiting for me."

"That sounds sensible," Bazalgette said, "but do you really think you'll sleep tonight after all this? I know I won't."

"It may seem somewhat overwhelming now, but give it a little time. You'll get used to it."

Bazalgette removed his glasses, rubbing the bridge of his nose between thumb and forefinger. "I'm not sure I want to."

8

Cargill beat at the flames with his jacket, but that only made them spread. Sweat dripped from his soot-stained brow. He was melting in the heat.

What had started as an entertaining evening, was turning into a nightmare. His attempt to douse the fireplace with a vase of water had been like pouring oil onto it. Flames leapt out along the wall to envelop the only door, blocking his escape. The wallpaper crinkled and burnt to hot ash as the wooden frame crackled, paint bubbling and spitting as it turned from cream to black.

He had to decide now. Should he throw open the large window and try to escape the blistering heat, or barricade himself from the rest of the room with furniture? The first option worried him. He was an educated man from the Inner-City and realised opening the window to the night air would feed the fiery beast. The resulting explosion of flame might cook him there and then, but at least he'd have a chance.

As he took a faltering step towards the large bay window, the red velvet curtains surrounding it fell in flaming tatters as the wooden rail snapped in the furnace-like heat, blocking his way. The ceiling rolled with thick smoke, and he coughed and sputtered for breath. He had to keep down, away from the billowing plumes of death. It was no less deadly to him than the Black Smoke used by the Martian fighting machines to eliminate entire sections of London during the invasion.

He screamed for help, for someone, anyone to hear him but to no avail. His skin was bright red, cooking in the luxurious furnace. He pulled a wardrobe and dressing table down around him, barricading himself into a small corner as far from the heart of the blaze as he could. There he sat hugging his knees tight to his chest and rocking back and forth like a straitjacketed inmate from an asylum.

"Help me," he yelled, clenching his eyelids shut, trying to stem the flood of tears streaming down his face from the acidic fumes. As he blinked them away, he noticed a change in the roiling smoke filling the top half of the once lavish room. Tendrils broke from it, reaching out, testing the surroundings. They leached colour from everything they touched, turning vibrant crimson to dull grey ash. Even the thick pile on the carpet was smouldering, an arc of black creeping ever nearer.

A weight slammed into him, holding him in place while peeling his eyelids open, forcing him to stare at the hellish scene around him. Smoke writhed, coiled tentacles reaching from the ceiling, pinning him to the wall with the strength of a dozen men.

The molten carpet was inches from his bare toes, the flesh blistering and charring. The intense agony tore through him as the flames licked his skin, and he screamed. His throat cracked as the torture intensified, and the fire crept up towards his ankles. As he thought the pain couldn't get any worse, it doubled, and he watched his flesh blacken and flake away to bright white bone.

Wood and glass exploded from the window, raining ash and streaks of flame to bounce off the cobbled street like a meteor shower. Huge flames leapt from the upper storey window, climbing high into the night air.

The dancing glow from the blaze illuminated the girl's grim smile down on the street. She savoured the last panic-stricken screams of the filthy bastard she had trapped up there. Cargill's voice cracked and then fell silent. She was a little disappointed it was over so soon, but two minutes of hysterical screaming was probably the most she could have hoped for. All that remained was the roar of the fire consuming everything in its path: wood, cloth and flesh.

The acrid smell of charred timber permeated the dark Whitechapel slum as she turned and left.

9

_____

The interview with the police soon wrapped up. It helped that Simmons' role as a man catcher required him to carry official paperwork. Things proceeded faster once he'd explained he was there to meet with Cooper to gain further information regarding a case.

The police questioned them both, and as agreed, they told everything except for what they'd gained from the young urchin. Constables scribbled their details into police notebooks, and then they were free to leave.

Bazalgette reached into his jacket and produced his card, offering it to Simmons. "In case you are ever in need of an engineer."

He took the card, noting the pertinent details—Nathaniel Bazalgette, Structural Sewage Engineer and Inventor—and returned the favour.

"And if you should need anyone tracked down, or just want to talk if you run into any further trouble from tonight," he replied.

Formalities completed, they parted, each making their way to hansom cabs waiting at the edge of the police cordon. A crowd of gawkers had formed around the area, held back by a line of constables. Simmons waited until the other cab left before climbing into his transport.

"Where to governor?" the cabbie asked. His voice muffled by the thick scarf and hood that gave a modicum of protection from the fog.

"Carleton Place in Spitalfields. Do you know it?"

"Yeah, up by St. Bart's, isn't it? Right you are, sir." The two doors slid shut encasing Simmons in a small protective bubble, out of the reach of the deadly fog. The cab lurched as the single horse reacted to the crack of the whip. Its impromptu fog mask wobbled, nothing more than a feedbag with eyeholes cut through, and the docklands receded behind them.

Simmons checked the card he'd rescued from Cooper's wallet when he searched through his jacket. It had held little of interest other than twenty pounds, a considerable amount of money for someone like Cooper to be carrying, and his calling card which provided his address.

The forlorn call of the foghorns started about halfway through the fifteen-minute journey from the south-east dock area. The docks were prone to flooding at high tide when the Thames came rushing back from the sea, trying to squeeze its way through the barriers constructed to prevent such ingress. With the water came the red weed said to cause the deadly nature of the fog.

The tempo of the hoof beats slowed, and the cab came to a halt. A thud sounded from above as the cabbie slid the hatch. "Here you go, sir. Carleton Place. That'll be sixpence please."

Simmons peered through the dirty glass at the darkness beyond. A single street light shed a dim glow behind them, the others either broken or, more likely, vandalised for their precious wiring. It was common in the regions nearer the outer wall where most police feared to tread. Even in the central areas, they patrolled in pairs.

He fished two coins from his pocket and held them up to the cabbie. "Here's a shilling if you wait here, and you'll receive another for the return journey to Whitechapel. I don't expect to be more than thirty minutes."

The cabbie took the shilling. "I'll be right here then, sir."

The hatch closed and a few seconds later, the familiar

clunk and hiss of the door mechanism released Simmons from his comfortable enclosure. He stepped onto the street, pulling his coat a little tighter. There was a chill in the air as he walked into a dark and abandoned Carleton Place.

The name was deceiving. He'd expected it to be one of the better areas of Spitalfields, but the reality was disappointing. Carleton Place was a narrow street without the space to drive a single hansom cab down. No wonder the cabbie made him alight at the corner. It continued into darkness the further he walked from the main street and the last remnant of subdued street lighting.

It ended in a cul-de-sac, with a collapsed building. The houses on either side looked to be back-to-backs and faced each other across the narrow cobbled road that had seen much better days. Number seventeen was on the left-hand side about three-quarters of the way down. Most of the houses were in a state of disrepair and most likely abandoned. There'd been no sign of life from any he had passed so far.

The door to number seventeen hung open, dangling from the ruined frame. Wood fragments lay on the ground ripped from the frame, and the door showed evidence of a brutal pounding and forced entry. He took his time listening and allowing his eyes to adjust to the darkness before proceeding.

Simmons stepped over the threshold and drew his revolver. His light footstep crunched on the remains of the lock mechanism. With a silent curse, he stopped, waiting in the darkness.

Once inside it was pitch black, and against his better judgement, he reached for his lighter and ignited it with a practised flick. The crackle and the low hum of the small device illuminated the area with a blue-white glow from the flickering crossed arcs of electricity. It had been a gift from his wife, and he pushed back a wave of melancholy, needing to focus on the job at hand.

The light was adequate for his needs, but compared with Bazalgette's arc-lamp, the contrast was startling. It was the difference between looking into the pleasant flame from a match and staring into the blazing heart of the sun. Through muted colours, shadows danced with constant movement. The hallway led to an open door on his right and continued onto stairs leading upwards. The room was a wreck, remains of drawers and seating smashed or ripped apart, pictures stripped from walls laying amongst other debris strewn across the floor.

With an experienced eye, he noted the telltale signs of multiple boot prints. Whoever was here had been searching for something. Where he'd hoped for a simple conversation with Cooper, those who had caused this mess had ransacked the place without a care for the owner's belongings or feelings.

There was something not right about the room. Simmons couldn't put his finger on it, but it lurked at the back of his mind leaving him with a sour feeling in his stomach. He'd learnt to follow his instincts in previous cases, and they usually panned out. Sifting through the refuse provided nothing of note. A writing desk in the corner of the room stood away from the wall, empty sockets where drawers should have been, and no trace of correspondence of any kind.

A glint of light caught his eye, a pale speck of fluff drifted in the air, perhaps from furniture stuffing. If that was still settling, it couldn't have been long since they turned the place over—a few hours at most. That coincided with the attack at The Britannia.

If this was a Black Guard operation, then they may have left a few surprises. They did that kind of thing, pleasant little devices that would take your leg off or any other extremity that got within a certain proximity. The wonders that Tesla developed for the good of the Empire also found use by those who protected it. In fact, the Black Guard utilised a fearsome arsenal of new weaponry based on Tesla's designs.

Damn, he needed to be more careful. He retraced his steps to the hall, stopping at the stairs. It didn't feel right, and as the lighter came closer, a dark metallic wire strung across the front edge of the step cast a flickering shadow.

That wouldn't be the only trap. He checked the next few steps finding another two tripwires. The dark coloured wires were almost too thin to see in the poor light. Without the lighter, he would have missed it and triggered the surprise left behind for the unwary.

He wasn't about to push his luck any further and retreated to the sitting-room door. As he looked in from the hallway, it clicked: the fireplace was a mess. Not through being disturbed and raked through like the rest of the room—it was still full of ash and soot.

Most people would have their fireplaces cleaned and raked out before they left for the day and re-laid with coal, ready to be lit on their return. Who could face having to clean out the remnants of yesterday's fire before being able to light a new one, especially when it was cold?

The fireplace looked like someone had made a half-hearted attempt to rake through the ashes, but then a soot-fall had put that to an end. He cracked a smile, imagining a furious Black Guard officer grubbing around with his pristine uniform covered in soot.

Nothing ventured. Simmons reached into the chimney, groping around the interior. Soot exploded as it hit the hearth and he coughed for the best part of a minute before recovering. With his scarf covering his nose and mouth, he tried again.

More soot fell, but his fingers brushed something smooth. He retrieved his discovery and, cleaning the worst of the dirt from it, exposed a small package wrapped in waxcloth.

What have we here? The fine soot brushed from the package leaving rough twine that held it together. After a few moments, he peeled back the waxcloth, revealing a red leather-bound journal. It contained writing on several pages in a precise and meticulous hand. A series of numbers and initials told a tale of money passing back and forth. It required more light and no doubt more time to divulge its secrets.

He folded the book back into its protective wrapping and headed for the exit to the street and, with luck, a cab waiting to drive him home.

After cleaning up back at his apartment, Simmons took the package and with the light on his desk turned up full, began his investigation of the ledger and its secrets. It was clear it contained several accounts in varying levels of detail. One page included money received by an 'SC'. *Could this be Silas Cooper? The initials fitted.* He then redistributed this to others in smaller quantities. Large sums went to an 'RC', but only over the last few weeks.

The remaining pages showed payments to other sets of initials. These were substantial amounts. Several hundred pounds at a time, enough to pay a butler's wage for years. Thumbing through the rest of the ledger, two pieces of paper slipped free. One was a collection of scribbled notes. Simmons opened the other which looked like a letter.

My dear fellow,

My humble thanks for the information you have provided us, it has already been of great use in furthering our cause. Our mutual friend continues to impress. As you suggested, she is a woman of remarkable talent.

Our time runs short while our list of tasks they still increase in number. I must ask you to double your efforts and find the other parties involved as we cannot allow them to get away from us. That simply would not do. I include with this missive payment of twenty guineas as agreed for your services rendered to date. Ensure the pressure is kept up on the authorities.

The time has come to close the net and squeeze it tight till we pop those wicked little fishes out onto dry land. Let them flounder and suffer as they gasp their last, their eyes glazing over, their lips turning black.

The message was signed with the letter J. The writing differed from the ledger, so small it was almost unreadable.

He returned to the other sheet that had fallen out. The

notes were in the same hand as in the ledger, but in various positions on the page. Each contained variations in the ink that hinted at their addition at different times.

Four names dominated the sheet. Checking the accounts, he found initials matching the large payments.

Cyril Woodruff - Funding
Alfred Cargill - Elocution and Deportment
John Addison - Clothing and Fitting
James Blakelocke - Planning and Recruitment

The top two names were struck through, as though resolved somehow. Next to Addison and Blakelocke were arrows leading to a note 'more for Rosie to sort out'.

Several references to 'The Watchmen' with another series of names that had lines pointing to a series of final questions on the page. 'Who are they, what do they watch? Could this be Dent's work? Need to check The Strand.'

So, Cooper appears to be a bookkeeper as well as a social agitator. Paid Twenty Guineas by this person who names themselves J, but to do what?

'Dent' had to be referring to Dents of London, the watchmaker. Simmons was sure the shop was on The Strand.

Hmm, let's see if Mr Dent can shed any more light on these Watchmen tomorrow, he thought before tossing back another glass of the peaty flavoured scotch he favoured. He refilled it, the amber liquid clung to the sides in greasy streaks, and he settled into his chair.

But what of this Rosie, what was her part in all this? How was she meant to 'sort out' these men?

Simmons reviewed his options. He focused on finding a medical explanation of Cooper's death to support his own ideas, then to learn more about these Watchmen.

10

Bodies always ended up at The London Hospital when retrieved by police investigations. Simmons set off after breakfast. It was a brisk half-mile walk from his lodgings following Whitechapel Road. The air was chill, dark clouds threatening to unleash torrents of rain at any moment. He hurried along, his greatcoat pulled around him, and made his way into the grounds just as the chimes for eleven were fading from Big Ben.

After a long wait, a nurse showed him to an office and introduced Doctor McKenzie.

"Doctor McKenzie," Simmons said as he offered his hand, "thank you for taking the time to meet me from your busy schedule."

McKenzie had a firm handshake, as befitted his massive build. "Erm, yes, very busy."

He leaned back behind a well-appointed desk, his chair squealing a protest at his sudden weight. "My assistant said you wanted to speak about a body?"

Simmons sat opposite the fellow and pulled his pipe from his inside pocket. "Yes, Silas Cooper. Someone brought him in late last night or early this morning. Died from a severe neck wound. Found by the Police in a public house in the Dock area."

"Oh yes, I'm aware of the gentleman, I did the autopsy myself, but your interest is?"

"Apologies, I'm Sir Pelham Simmons," he said, reaching for his papers. Though he didn't use his title often, it was useful on occasions such as these, cutting through the red tape like a surgical blade.

He waved his licence in front of the surprised doctor as he continued. "I'm investigating the issue with the Whitechapel constabulary. I need your medical expertise and insight."

"Of course," McKenzie answered. "Anything to help the authorities."

"Thank you. So have you found anything of interest with the body?"

"He died of a single stab wound to the left side of the neck which penetrated through the carotid artery and the aorta, then into the heart itself. He would have collapsed and bled out within a few seconds. Other than superficial bruising and a few minor abrasions where he fell to the ground, there's no evidence of other wounds or injury."

"Right, and how large would the blade have been that made the wound?"

McKenzie smiled. "Well the incision measured an inch and a half in width, so no wider than that. As for the length of the blade, it would be at least six inches to penetrate so far, maybe longer, it's difficult to be sure."

"So a long knife or sword, perhaps?"

McKenzie screwed his face up a little. "A sword blade would be long, but too unwieldy considering the angle of impact. The blade entered the side of the victim's neck almost vertically. A strike from above forcing the blade down, thus." McKenzie raised his clenched hand above his head and brought it down into his other palm with a slap. "If it had been a sword, I don't see how the attacker could wield it unless he was freakishly tall."

Simmons nodded. "So a long knife then. What about the attacker's position?"

"Oh, I would say he was behind the victim and a little to

the side. It would be the only way to strike the blow, presuming he was right-handed."

"And if he was left-handed?"

"Well, in that case, he could have been more central behind the poor fellow," McKenzie replied.

"Is there anything else about the victim that was unusual?"

McKenzie frowned for a moment, his eyes falling towards the floor in thought. "Perhaps just one other item of note," he said. "It seems an oddly precise attack. I've seen plenty of stab wounds in my time, ex-army you see."

Simmons nodded in agreement, allowing the doctor to continue.

"But in the heat of battle, it's more usual to find lateral, thrusting attacks with a bladed weapon. Much easier to stab into the back or chest, with an upward trajectory. This seems an awkward way of stabbing someone. It was effective, bypassing bones and heavier tissue to sever the arteries and heart, but tricky to make such a precise strike."

"Yes, I see," Simmons said. "What of the body, what's happening there?"

McKenzie looked up. "I believe it's due for collection later today or tomorrow. You would have to speak to my assistant for the details."

"I'll do that. Thank you, Doctor, you've been most helpful."

"Always keen to help, especially if it might lead to capturing the ruffian responsible. From your questions, I presume he's still at large?"

"I'm not at liberty to discuss that at the moment, as I'm sure you understand?"

"Oh, of course."

"But between you and me." Simmons tapped the side of his nose with a finger. "I think you've given us enough to be going on."

"Excellent. All the best, Sir Pelham. If you need anything further, you know where to find me."

Simmons stood and shook McKenzie's hand. "Thank you again, Doctor, your help is much appreciated."

Now he'd spoken to someone in authority, the assistant gave out the information without question. The undertaker was in Spitalfields, a G Pinkett and Sons. The body had been released into the care of the sister, a Miss Elizabeth Cooper.

That seemed quick, and something told Simmons it was a little too organised. A trip to Leman Street for a spot of further investigation into the family was in order. He just needed to find a way to sweeten the deal for his good friend Sergeant Carter.

≈

Leman Street was quiet as Simmons pushed the large wooden door open and approached the desk. "Good afternoon, Sergeant Carter."

"Good afternoon, Mr Simmons. What can I do for you today?"

The rogue button from Carter's uniform had rejoined its fellows in their ongoing campaign to contain his girth. "I need some information."

"Is that so?" Carter replied. "And what type of information would you be after?"

"I want to know about Silas Cooper's family and also any criminal record he may have."

Carter pursed his lips and sucked in a breath. "Now that's not material I can just give out. Legally privileged, that is."

Simmons gave the big man a knowing smile. "I thought you might say something like that. So, here's the thing. I found an item I fear someone must have lost and felt I'd best hand it in, being the law-abiding fellow I am."

"Oh, in that case, you'd better tell me all about it, sir."

"Well, as I was on my way, I happened across this bottle of Warriors Port. It says it's an 1870 vintage, which I believe was rather a good one. Anyhow, there it was alone and abandoned. It was then I remembered my good friend Sergeant Carter at Leman Street. He'll know what to do with it."

Carter held Simmons' eye for a few seconds, then shook

his head, a smile crossing his face. "If you hand it over, I'll see what we can do about reuniting it with its rightful owner."

Simmons passed him the bottle. "Excellent work, sergeant. And the other matter?"

"Yes, I'll look into it."

After minutes of searching, Carter returned with a brown card file. The sergeant thumbed through the contents. "Cooper had several arrests for inciting civil unrest, affray and some other minor offences. But it looks like he's never been charged with anything serious."

"What about the family?"

"Just one sister, Elizabeth. Ah, but she's dead."

"What?"

"Elizabeth Cooper - deceased August 1895. There isn't much else here. Keeping records wasn't a high priority during the chaos with those metal beasts on the rampage."

"Let me see," Simmons said, reading the line for himself. "Well, I'll be damned."

Had she been a victim of the aliens? Dragged off by their fighting machines to the labour camps where they processed humans like cattle...

Carter's jowled face scowled at him across the desk. "Are you all right, sir? You look rather pale."

"I'm fine, just tired," Simmons said. He forced his grip to slacken on the record file, his white knuckles returning to a more natural hue. With a visible effort, he released it and pushed it back to Carter. "Thank you for the information, sergeant, and I hope you find an owner for that port. I'd hate for it go to waste."

"Never you mind on that front, sir. Never you mind."

"Bethnal Green Road, sir."

"This will be fine. Thank you," Simmons said as the hansom slowed to a stop and he stepped down to the pavement.

G Pinkett and Sons stood on the left ten yards ahead, its traditional sign, silver script on a black wooden board hung above the shopfront. A bell chimed as he entered the small shop, walking between lines of ornate coffins to a wooden counter crossing the full width at the rear of the room.

"I'll be with you shortly," came a disembodied voice from the back office. The door swung open a moment later as an elderly gentleman pushed his way in, sleeves rolled up to his elbows and wisps of white hair plastered to his head.

"Apologies for my attire, sir. My son is unwell, so I'm minding the place on my own, and there's a devil of a lot of work to get through."

"That's fine. I wanted to ask you a few questions if that would be all right?"

"Certainly, sir. What can I help you with?" The older man brushed his sleeves back into position and buttoned them with two silver cufflinks.

Simmons reached into his greatcoat pocket and retrieved his papers again. He showed them to the undertaker. "I'm working with the Whitechapel constabulary about a murder. I take it you are the proprietor, Mr Pinkett?"

The elderly man's eyes widened a little, and he drew in a breath. "That's right, sir. How can I help?"

"I believe you were engaged to deal with the body of a Mister Silas Cooper who died yesterday evening. Is that correct?"

Pinkett swept his hand across his hair, trying to scrape it into a semblance of order. "I must consult my books, sir. The name doesn't ring a bell though my memory isn't quite what it used to be. I won't be a minute, sir." Pinkett went to a dark wooden bureau and fetched a worn brown leather journal.

Flicking through, he found the page he was searching for. "Mr Cooper to collect from the London for preparation here. Collection set for tomorrow morning. I remember now. A pretty young lady, his sister, Elizabeth."

"His sister? Are you sure?"

"Yes, sir. She was ever so upset. She was all alone and didn't know how she would manage. I felt sorry for her, I did. It was such a tragic tale. I gave her a discount, told her we'd sort everything out and that she needn't worry about a thing."

"Very kind of you," Simmons said. "So what about the arrangements, do things often happen this fast?"

"Well it is a little quick, but we can handle it. We're to collect the body first thing tomorrow, bring it back here for dressing, and then on to Highgate Cemetery in the afternoon. From what I hear, it's a single stab wound. There shouldn't be too much work required, and it's a closed casket."

"So what time are the proceedings at Highgate?"

Pinkett looked up from the book. "The ceremony is at three o'clock, so we'll leave from the North Gate at two with any cortege. Miss Elizabeth said she would make her own way to the service."

"Could you describe the young lady for me, Mr Pinkett?"

"Young, probably eighteen or nineteen. She was a touch shorter than I am and was wearing an elegant dark dress. Red hair, pretty face."

Simmons retrieved the photograph of Annabelle from his pocket and passed it to Pinkett. "Is this the young lady in question?"

"Yes, sir. That's her, though her hair is red as I mentioned, bright red, not like in that photograph."

"It is a few years old, so she may well have changed her hair colour, it's the current fashion among the young ladies."

"Is that so?" Pinkett said, "funny how fashion changes and all the youngsters must jump to its tune."

"Did Miss Cooper leave any contact details?"

"No, sir. She paid the bill and said she would meet us at the Cemetery tomorrow at three. Lovely she was, but I saw the depth of grief in her." Pinkett's eyes seemed to glaze for a moment, as if he were staring far into the distance, then his attention snapped back. "If that's all, sir, I'll be back to my work. Still got a lot to do before tomorrow."

"Yes, thank you for your time."

The mournful sound of horns blaring signalled an early start to the battle against the red fog. Pinpricks of light were visible down the street as the gas lights ignited for the long dark evening ahead.

Elizabeth, Annabelle. Just who are you, Miss Pemberton?

11

James Addison had never been a popular man. Others in the tailoring profession looked down on his creations as an exclusive ladies clothier. They considered it women's work, but he had a knack for it, producing some of the most elegant gowns within the Inner-City. Though he tried hard to gain their appreciation, the ones whose approval he desired most, laughed at him, and he felt out of place in their clubs.

It didn't help that his build and mannerisms seemed effeminate. Everyone thought someone in his line of work, looking and acting as he did, was less than manly.

He'd given up trying to impress the women he liked and taken to the less salubrious areas nearer the walls. There he could buy affection with no awkward explanations or convincing required.

So it was, he met the young woman in the Black Dragon opium den in Whitechapel. He noticed the quality of her crimson gown and his stare drew her approach. They talked for almost an hour, and she never commented on his appearance, voice or mannerisms. She was a rare find in such an establishment. Yes, she was a whore, but she had an air of refinement and education. Had she maybe fallen on hard times, perhaps even cast out of the Inner-City and left to fend for herself?

Whatever it was, she didn't want to speak of it and turned the conversation back to his endeavours. He gladly spoke of his achievements until she dragged him from the dismal place to head somewhere more private.

A hackney carriage drove them to a more pleasant location, though still on the fringes of Whitechapel. The large town-house with four floors was a brothel, but one on the verge of respectability, situated where it was.

The girl said she had a permanent room on the top floor, laughing as she led the way up the carved wooden staircase. They'd decorated the establishment with beautiful paintings on almost every wall. The carpets were plush, and lavish furnishing sat at each landing.

As she closed the door behind them, she pushed him towards the large four-poster bed. The drapes were gorgeous silk which complemented the flowing crimson gown that danced around her as she crossed the room. It had been the quality of the garment which had drawn his eye to start with.

He sank into the luxurious mattress and lay back as she passed him a drink while sitting beside him on the edge of the bed. He tried to rise, but she pushed him down, taking the glass from him. "Let me take that for you."

She leaned over him, running her delicate fingers through his thick mop of curls while resting the glass on his bottom lip. A drop of the fiery liquid trickled onto his tongue, the quality of the spirit astounded him. It was by far the best he'd tasted, even from his private supplier in Belgravia. To find this on the edge of London's slums was unprecedented.

"More?" she asked.

He nodded, eager to savour the spirit again now he knew what to expect.

A small gulp passed his lips, and he realised he didn't know what he was drinking. It was a spirit, but he couldn't place the fiery warmth as it ran down his throat and settled in his stomach. Another swallow, bigger this time, and he coughed, holding his palm up for her to stop. But she kept pouring.

He struggled to sit up, chest spluttering as it went down the wrong way, but she gripped his hair and forced his head back into the mattress.

He tried to move, but her grip was iron. Another hand grabbed his chin, forcing his mouth wide, and more spirit poured into him. How was she holding the glass?

He sputtered, droplets spraying into the air falling onto his face, his eyes burned as it seeped into them. His chest convulsed, body fighting to clear his airways, but the liquid kept pouring in.

Another hand gripped his nose, closing the airway. The mild panic of a temporary blockage in his throat blossomed into full-grown terror as the liquid flowed as if from a hose.

His whole body thrashed as his subconscious fought to find a means of getting air into his lungs but to no avail. The weight pressing down on him was relentless.

His eyes flew open, to see not the woman holding him down, but a vile grey-skinned beast vomiting blood into his mouth. Eight slimy appendages gripped him and forced him deeper into the mattress while a cluster of oily black orbs rested two inches above his, observing as his survival instinct failed. He screamed or at least tried to.

The young girl watched the last gurgle of brown sewage water as it leaked from the sagging edges of Addison's mouth. One pitcher was all it had taken. Then she'd watched him with glee as he struggled to comprehend the story unfolding in his mind, his body convinced he was drowning.

She stood to leave, satisfied another of her tormentors had met with a fitting demise. Just one left now. Then her icy revenge would be complete.

12

Rain fell from a leaden sky, striking the cobbles and leaving them slick. Simmons pushed onward through the downpour, pulling his greatcoat tighter to keep out the chill. The Black Guard seemed more tolerant at the Whitechapel gate during the hours of daylight. Within minutes he was striding towards the main road leading north toward Highgate Cemetery.

Almost everything Fogside was a ruin. Red weed riddled the few standing buildings, clawing and grasping its way up, over and through them. The alien menace leached the green from the pleasant land that had once been the London suburbs.

Mud ran like streams of blood between the decaying homes, cascading down the sides of infested stone and brick-work, settling to create small lakes. The landscape reminded Simmons of something more akin to what Dante described in his treatise on the Nine Hells. Thinking about it, it seemed an apt analogy.

The rain was still hammering down as he approached the cemetery. An imposing three-storey gatehouse guarded the entrance. His first impression was of a large church with an arched tunnel through the middle, wide enough to accommodate a horse and carriage with room to spare. A low wall, topped with rusted metal railings, extended from either side of the structure and skirted the overgrown grounds.

He knelt behind the cover of a rotting elm and unslung his rifle. The Holland snuggled into his shoulder, comfortable like a well-worn pair of boots. His eyes roamed the front of the building, skipping between the leaded windows for any signs of movement.

Satisfied the place looked empty, Simmons marched through the passage and emerged into a large rear courtyard with archways lining the far wall. Through the central arch, steps climbed towards a thicket of trees that edged the cemetery.

Peeling paint and discoloured frames spoke of rot and decay in the windows and doors at the rear of the structure.

He crossed to the nearest door. It was locked but gave a little as he pushed. He stepped back, then thrust his shoulder into it. With a protest of straining timber and tortured metal, it snapped open, striking the inner wall with a crack. He dropped to one knee, rifle aimed into the dark interior.

Other than a few strips of rotted wood that fell from the door casing and the slow whisper of water dripping from his drenched clothes, the place was silent. He waited a full minute, counting slowly to himself, but nobody came to investigate his incursion.

He wound between dusty shafts of grey light from the broken windows, careful not to disturb the rotting furniture scattered inside. Taking his time, he made slow, methodical progress through the building, but found nothing to show recent activity.

The room over the tunnel must have been breathtaking once with its glorious view through the double-height bay window. Now, water poured through a gaping hole in the roof, bouncing off the shattered slates littering the floor. Sodden debris and rotten beams lay collapsed among the stinking remains of carpet and curtains, all infused with slimy grey mould.

Simmons returned to the room above the door he'd forced.

All the windows remained glazed and intact. Yes, there were cracks, but it was dry.

It took a few minutes to find a solid chair which he placed by a table with a clear view of the rear courtyard. Next, he unbuckled a leather satchel and retrieved his prize possession, a Soyer's Magic Stove. Now, this little beauty had been a saviour during several campaigns around the globe, a marvel of brass and copper, worth its weight in gold.

He set the stove on the table and primed it with a small piston. A quick twist of a valve rewarded him with a low hiss of pressurised gas. With a flick of his ArcLighter, a purple flame erupted with a pop and soon faded to a pale blue as the gas settled. Simmons smiled and rubbed his hands together, already basking in the heat radiating from the miraculous little device. It wasn't called Magic for nothing.

~

The rain stopped soon after midday. Simmons sat holding his metal mug between both hands, savouring the warmth as much as the Darjeeling it contained. His coat was almost dry after his last outing an hour earlier.

He'd scouted the cemetery, learning his way around. The place held a tranquillity and natural beauty even among the trees and bushes peppered with the red weed. A series of beautiful marble statues lined the overgrown walkways silent in their eternal vigil. Their faces watched over the final resting places of beloved individuals and families. Some had names with new chisel marks, others weathered and faded by time.

Winged angels rubbed shoulders with all manners of ornate carvings, crosses of various size and style, eagles and even Egyptian needles thrusting into the overcast sky.

A sharp crack sounded outside. Simmons crossed to the nearest window, rifle in hand. It was nearing three o'clock, and a bedraggled group approached pushing the rear of the cart which had lurched sideways, one of its wheels stuck in a deep hole.

The driver jumped down to assess the problem, while another man, slighter in build, took the single black horse's bridle. Pinkett the elder, he surmised from the man's stature, though it was difficult to tell in the long coat and top hat he wore.

A few minutes of heaving and shoving ended with the wheel emerging from the ground, resulting in a small cheer from the group. It cut off after a moment as they realised why they were here on this awful day.

They continued their slow procession through the gate-house entrance. The cart stopped at the far side of the rear courtyard, beside the steps up to the hill. The group, organised by Pinkett, lifted a shiny black coffin from the cart and hoisted it onto the shoulders of four of the mourners. They moved with an efficiency that spoke of practice, and Pinkett led them up into the tree line and out of sight.

Years of training and experience fell into place as Simmons grabbed his gear, pulled on his coat and hat, and was heading downstairs within the minute. He waited at the door for a few seconds, surveying the courtyard, before making his way to the tunnel that split the gatehouse. The front of the building was clear and, once satisfied there were no stragglers, he crossed the rear yard towards the stairs.

The group wasn't hard to follow. They moved at the slow, respectful pace expected of pall-bearers, and Simmons took his time, leaving plenty of space between them and himself. He'd already scouted this part of the cemetery and knew there was a fork in the path ahead. He didn't even need to keep within sight of them. With the mud, it would be obvious which route they chose.

He stood there, concealed behind a tall angelic statue, and mused. It might have been more prudent to press Pinkett for the precise location of the burial. *Well, best-laid plans and all that.*

Simmons allowed plenty of time for the slow procession to draw ahead, then continued up to where the path split. Churned mud showed they had taken the left fork which led towards a massive wall with a gated tunnel at its centre. The ground rose at both sides, forming a hill twenty feet high, topped with thick bushes and trees.

The large double gate lay open, and the cortege was approaching the end of the passage beyond. He took a position to the left and heard the rasping of chains pulled across metal. A clang and slither as they dropped onto the stone, then the sound of slow footsteps resumed.

The columns had plenty of handholds, and he realised he could climb to the hill while keeping out of sight. With a few well-placed footholds and the help of a dangling branch, he was soon pulling himself into the dense foliage and under-brush atop the hillside.

He picked his way forward, avoiding the thickest tangles until he could see open ground. The tunnel exit led into a circular walkway below. Ahead of him was a gap of ten feet and then a massive plateau of overgrown grass and, in the centre of that, an enormous cedar tree. A double trunk rose skyward to a thick thatch of spiky green foliage.

He took cover behind a sarcophagus and peered past to where the funeral party came to a halt. They stood outside a white stone cube of a mausoleum. Carved arches and intricate latticework made up the walls of the structure. A tall obelisk thrust from the roof pointing up to the heavens. If this was a family tomb, it was far more ornate than anyone would have expected for the working-class man that Cooper seemed to have been.

As the group waited outside the elegant resting place, Simmons noticed movement from the northern edge of the cemetery beyond the Cypress circle. Rows of tombs lined the area, and from the side of one of these large grey buildings appeared three figures. Two burly looking chaps in ill-fitting dark suits, and a few steps behind them, a young lady in formal mourning attire, complete with a veil and a black umbrella. Though it looked the part, the dress she wore was short and without a trail. It exposed boots that rose above the dresses hem halfway towards her knees. *How shocking, but I suppose this is the verge of the twentieth century.* Since the invasion, fashion had veered from the sublime to the downright scandalous, in his eyes anyway.

As they reached the mourners, the two burly gentlemen stood to one side, allowing the woman through to speak with Pinkett. She raised her veil, revealing the face and bright shock of red hair he recognised as Annabelle Pemberton.

A few words exchanged, and she passed Pinkett an object. She stepped back towards her chaperones, who took up positions flanking her. She seemed a tiny figure between the two brutes, just reaching their shoulders in height.

Pinkett moved to the mausoleum entrance and unlocked it. The door swung open into the tomb, displaying a marvel of vibrant red and blue frescos amidst ornate carving of angels lining the walls. The flooring was a black and white checkerboard of marble. It was a stunning piece of architecture reserved for those no longer of this world.

They bore the casket into the house of black and white and out of sight. The pall-bearers returned and resumed their position with the mourners. Pinkett stood before the two assembled groups and spoke sage and solemn words about the departed. No doubt anecdotes of how, though he hadn't known the deceased, he had been a man of high moral fibre, and too early to depart this mortal coil. All the usual nonsense spoken of the dead regardless of their actual failings and depravities in life.

Quiet but steady footfalls echoed from the tunnel below and broke Simmons from his thoughts. The cortege was too distant to hear their stealthy approach, and Simmons winced as the unmistakable dark uniforms of the Black Guard exited the passage. They split to travel around the circular tomb. The officer motioned three of his men to move clockwise, while the other three followed him anti-clockwise towards steps to bring them up behind the gathered mourners.

A dull roar of distant thunder rolled across the dark sky, and the rain resumed its assault on those beneath. *Could this day get any more unpleasant?*

Simmons checked his rifle as an uneasy feeling filled his gut. One he always felt before a dangerous situation escalated into a deadly one.

He repositioned himself at the corner of his protective cover with a good view of the approach to the tomb. Several gravestones and statues nearby would offer protection if things got out of hand. The other group of guards reached a stairway to the north and positioned themselves in readiness. They now had a clear line of sight to the assembled mourners.

He focused back on the top of the stairs closest to the mausoleum as the officer lead his three-man team toward the group. The steady fall of rain slid down the tombs stone edge, dripping onto his hat's brim as he sighted down his rifle.

"Rosemary Carrington," the officer said. His voice carried across the distance. "You are under arrest for treason. Surrender now, and you will be treated fairly. Resist, and your punishment will be severe."

Several mourners turned and looked on the group of Black Guard with shock. The two thugs beside Annabelle moved their hands towards inside pockets but stopped as she said something, her palms lowered in a calming gesture. She took a step forward looking a little puzzled.

"I'm sorry, officer. I fear you've made a mistake. There's no Rosemary Carrington here. You must have the wrong cemetery."

The officer halted, his head looking at the ground as he tried to speak. All he could manage was a short stutter. "N-N- No."

He raised his face to look her in the eyes. "No, Miss Carrington," his voice strengthening further. "Come now. We know who you are. This attempt at deception is beneath you."

"I'm at a loss Lieutenant. My name is Elizabeth Cooper. We have gathered here today to pay our final respects to my poor deceased brother. Isn't that right?" She looked to the other mourners, who nodded and murmured their assent.

"Your name is…" the officer started, forcing the words out. "Your name *is* Rosemary Carrington, and you are coming with me dead or alive."

"Enough of this shit," yelled the large man beside Annabelle. He stepped forward, pulling a revolver and fired it at the officer.

The bullet missed but caught the guard behind in the shoulder, spilling him to the wet ground. The officer was a blur of movement, and quicker than Simmons could follow, he had a boxy looking pistol in his hands. Three rapid cracks burst out, and the thug stumbled. Blood blossomed on his damp clothes from two areas high on his chest, and a stream leaked down into his eyes from a shot to his forehead. He crumpled and collapsed in a spreading pool of crimson, the revolver tumbling from his twitching fingers.

Several things happened in rapid succession. Someone pulled Annabelle behind the mausoleum out of sight. Screams broke from the assembled cortege as they tried to escape. Two slipped on the muddy ground, others cowered by the tomb, but all sought safety from the madness unfolding around them.

A familiar hum crossed the distance, then bright arcs of power surged from the heavy weapons of the two guards behind the officer. Thick shards of stone burst from the edge of the mausoleum where Annabelle had retreated.

"Arc-rifles," Simmons said. "This just gets better and better."

13

Pinkett waved, shouting, trying to catch the Black Guard officer's attention. As he ran towards the officer, an arc of electricity struck him in the back flinging him through the air, impacting with a crunch against the white stone mausoleum. A red stain marred the pristine wall, streaking down to the crumpled form in the mud.

This has gone too far. Simmons aimed at the guard who had shot the old man. The thunderclap from the rifle echoed around the surrounding tombs. A large hole punched through the statue a few inches to the right of his target. *Damned weather.* He recalibrated his sight then peeked his head around to check if anyone had oriented on his location, but everything remained as it was. The guards to the north were still in cover and exchanging fire with an area to the rear of the mausoleum. The two with the officer moved towards the other side in a flanking manoeuvre, somehow ignorant of the shot Simmons had fired.

He aimed at the advancing guard, unleashing the second barrel. With the recalibration, his shot was true. The man dropped to his knees, clutching the stump of his severed right arm. It fell to the ground, blood spraying in bright arterial arcs, still gripping the arc-rifle. He collapsed forward never having uttered a sound.

This time there *was* a reaction. The other guard looked back towards his position and took cover behind a statue.

Simmons moved, keeping low and slid to an eight foot stone cross on a waist-high square base. He crouched there, reloading both barrels. *So much for not getting involved.*

His body swung around the base, sighting his rifle on the guard in a fluid motion. The wings of the angelic statue obscured his target, but that wouldn't be a problem for the Holland. He waited, gauging the timing and position, then holding his breath, squeezed the first trigger. The wing shattered, spraying razor-sharp fragments at the hidden guard. The man tried to protect his face, but without the angel's divine protection, he was exposed and the second shot punched through his chest, dropping him.

That last shot had been a risk, and Simmons felt a kick in the chest as his cover crumbled. The cross protected him from the brunt of the arc-rifle blast, but now, only a small stump remained of the upright jutting from the charred base.

His left arm burned, and he sucked in a breath, his entire body spasming. A long gouge tore his jacket down to the smouldering remains of his glove. The buckles at the cuff were molten slag, dripping and hissing onto the damp ground.

Damn fool, he thought, the first guard shot by Annabelle's associate wasn't dead after all.

The distant sound of thunder roared from arc-rifles. The clouds above replied with interest as they added their own flashes of lightning to make sure no-one forgot who really owned the largest guns.

Simmons pushed himself along on his back, trying to rub sensation into his left arm, making his way back to his original position. His body had ceased spasming, leaving him with an occasional muscle twitch. The feeling returned in his hand, but his wrist was sore as hell as if he'd caught it on a hot brazier.

Behind the protective cover of the sarcophagus again, he reloaded. *Damn, but it was a beautiful weapon.* The side-by-side twin barrels had saved his skin on more occasions than he cared to recall. It wasn't a standard issue. He'd chosen and paid for it himself, custom made to fit his dimensions by Holland & Holland. Many might have said the price was ridiculously extravagant, but how much value could a man place on his own life?

A glance around the sarcophagus showed the guards from the northern stairs had advanced but lost one of their group in the process. The officer now crouched at the far edge of the mausoleum exchanging fire around the corner, and there, behind the stone steps was the blighter who had shot him. The arc-rifle lay propped on the balustrade pointed in his direction, but the man appeared to be struggling with his right arm.

Simmons aimed for the man's centre of mass, ignoring the stone railing, relying on the force the Holland would impart. Gently squeezing the trigger, Simmons felt the mechanism engage just as the figure slipped on the muddy ground.

The shot was accurate and would have hit the guard square in the chest. Instead, it punched through the stone, missing its target, sending shards and splinters flying. In his slip, the guardsman held onto his rifle, pulling it back over the balustrade and into the path of the rapidly moving stone fragments.

Metal shrieked, followed by a scream of electrical discharge and a massive explosion. The concussion wave hit Simmons like a punch in the stomach. Boxing had never been his thing, but he imagined this is how it would feel taking a blow from a regimental champion.

He lay on his back gasping for air and turned to see a steaming crater six feet across and a gaping hole in the stone staircase. His chest hurt like hell, but he surprised himself with a laugh. *Modern technology is all well and good, but you can't beat the reliability of a solid wood and steel rifle. Who in their right mind would want to carry something they were worried about dropping?*

The cemetery fell quiet after the explosion, no signs of movement. Bodies lay scattered around the mausoleum amid rubble blown from its once beautiful facade. The pristine white tomb now stained with black scorch marks.

A woman's scream split the air from the far side of the mausoleum, and Simmons raced towards it. A figure shuffled around the corner almost stumbling into him. He stepped back, raising his rifle. Her eyes widened, wincing as she moved the hand from her side. Lifting a gloved finger to his mouth, he motioned for her to get behind him.

She frowned, weighing up her options, then did as he suggested. The officer's voice called from around the edge of the building.

"Come now, Rosemary, you can't escape. Surely you would prefer to live? I have my orders, and it makes little difference to me, but you should think of the Empire."

Simmons stepped around the corner, rifle pointed at the man just ten feet distant. The officer's smile slid from his face as he evaluated this new situation.

"Ah, the accomplice. Dragged from your hidey-hole to fight like a man at last."

"Stay where you are and keep your hands in sight."

"I'm not sure how she found you, and I don't care. You know you are being used, don't you?" he gave Simmons a knowing smile. "She will discard you like she has all the others once she is finished with you, when you've played your part, and are of no more use."

"Enough talk. Didn't anyone—"

The officer vanished. One moment there, the next gone.

Simmons stood for a second, dumbfounded, then every fibre of his body told him to move. He hit the ground, rolled and came up facing the other direction, expecting the cold steel embrace of a duelling sabre in his neck, but everything was silent.

The scream shook him from his confusion, he rushed toward it to find the officer holding Annabelle from behind, her head pulled back, and his pistol pressed against her temple.

"Oh shut up, you troublesome witch." The officer thrust her left side into the wall, and Annabelle gasped in pain. "You," he said, looking at Simmons, "put down that weapon, or I will kill her, here and now."

Simmons was stuck. Between the Devil and the deep blue sea, wasn't that what they said? This kind of man wouldn't keep his word. As soon as he dropped his rifle, the man would shoot him, another problem removed from the equation. If he didn't drop it, he would shoot her, and then try to kill him.

As good as Simmons was, the officer held Annabelle way too close to make shooting him a realistic option. So he did the only thing he could.

"All right," he said. "I'm putting it down. Don't hurt her."

He dropped the rifle then stood, holding his hand out in a placating motion. The officer smirked as he oriented the pistol on him. "Bloody idiot."

"Simmons, duck," came a voice from behind him and he took the advice, throwing himself to the ground.

A shot rang out from the pistol towards the dark shape rounding the corner behind them. There was a brief hum, and a bark of electrical discharge as an Arc-Rifle fired.

The beam of intense energy missed both the officer and Annabelle by two feet.

No, Simmons thought. *No, No, No.*

The shot hit the tomb behind the officer and rebounded, striking the centre of his back. He and Annabelle flew forward and landed hard on the muddy earth. The officer's back was a smouldering ruin of charred flesh and burnt clothing, his body still spasming from the electrical discharge. Annabelle lay sprawled a few feet away, but with a pained moan, she seemed to be trying to rise.

Simmons looked up at the familiar face offering him a hand.

"Bazalgette? What the hell are you doing here?"

"Well, I came to pay my respects to Mister Cooper. Thought it only right," Bazalgette said matter-of-factly. "Truth be told, I couldn't get the idea of his murder out of my head. How someone could remain unseen while killing him. The pocket watch stuck in my mind, and I've been trying to work out how it's all connected. It's got to be some form of time distortion—"

"All right," Simmons said. "I don't need your entire thesis. What happened to you *here* at the ceremony?"

"When all hell broke loose with those Black Guards, I slipped towards the back of the mausoleum. I thought I better lie low till all the excitement finished."

"And the arc-rifle?"

"Well, one of the soldiers cornered me. I told him I was just paying my respects, but he wasn't having any of it. He cuffed me with the butt of his rifle and then threatened to shoot me if I didn't tell him the truth. So I did the only thing I could think of." He rubbed the right side of his face, which had an angry bruise forming.

"Which was?" Simmons prompted.

"I jabbed him with the arc-lamp. I thought if they can use arc technology with their rifles then so can I."

"You electrocuted him with your lamp?"

"Well, I wouldn't say electrocuted," Bazalgette said, "more of a severe shock, enough to knock him unconscious."

"By hell, next you'll be telling me you intended to miss with the arc-rifle."

"Well," Bazalgette looked a little hurt. "It's physics. I didn't want to risk injuring the young lady, so I reasoned that the angle of incident would be the same as—"

Simmons laughed. "Stop there. You're a damned marvel. A strange but brilliant marvel."

"Well, it's nothing really. I didn't expect it to preserve quite so much force from the reflection. Should we perhaps see if the young lady is all right?"

Simmons smiled and shook his head as Bazalgette pulled him to his feet.

"Yes, I suppose we should."

Annabelle's eyes rolled, and she almost fell as Simmons helped her to her feet.

"Whoa there," Simmons said. "How are you feeling?"

She took a few seconds to steady herself. "Like I was kicked in the back by a horse."

"Sorry about that," Bazalgette said, "but it was rather a difficult situation."

She brushed at the mud on her dress but must have realised it was futile. "Who are you?" she asked.

"My name is Simmons, and this fellow here is Bazalgette." Bazalgette tipped his hat and shivered as the rain washed down the back of his neck. Simmons smiled. "You're my goddaughter. I'm here to help you with whatever problem you have become entangled in."

"Goddaughter?" she said. "I don't remember you."

"It was a long time ago—you were just a baby. I've been in India for the last seventeen years, but I'm here now. We'll sort this out."

The girl narrowed her eyes, taking a step back. "I don't know what you're trying to achieve here, Mr Simmons, but..." Her voice changed, returning with a harsher edge to it. "You should tell me exactly who you are, and why you are looking for me."

"I'm Pelham Simmons, a registered man catcher, sent to investigate your disappearance. Your father, Edward Pemberton, asked me to find you." The words were out before Simmons realised what he was saying.

Annabelle paused, processing the information he'd blurted out.

"What just happened?" Simmons asked.

The girl ignored the question. "I don't know who this Pemberton is, but he's not my father. He died a while back."

"What? Are you sure?"

"I should be," she replied. "I dissected the old bastard."

In the stunned silence, Annabelle surveyed the broken and charred remains of the Black Guard officer and the carnage around the tomb. "Perhaps we should seek shelter? It doesn't seem that the rain will let up any time soon." She gave the body a solid kick which elicited no response. Satisfied, she stalked away.

Simmons looked over to Bazalgette. "Could you escort the young lady to the mausoleum, see if the roof is still watertight? I need a moment."

"Of course," said Bazalgette and jogged to catch up with her.

Simmons thoughts were whirling. He pushed them to one side and knelt to inspect the officer's body, trying to focus on the present. He rolled the face-down corpse over, the sickly-sweet smell of burnt meat diminishing as it flopped onto its back with a wet thud. From the man's jacket hung a delicate silver chain to an ornate pocket watch which was open and caked in thick mud by his hand. The filigree work peeked out through the layers of grime, but it was recognisable from the urchin's description at the Britannia pub. If this wasn't that same timepiece, then it was a stunning copy.

Simmons unhooked the chain, transferring the watch to his inside pocket. He inspected the man's pistol. The angular design identified it as a Mauser, German-made and a very new design—the latest desirable firearm for discerning young officers. A box magazine in front of the trigger guard fed the semi-automatic weapon and, as Simmons had witnessed, it had a remarkable rate of fire. The officer's belt held four vertical strip clips, each with ten rounds. Simmons took them all.

He was about to stand, but there was something in the man's ear. A closer look revealed an earplug, similar to those worn by artillerymen. Simmons checked the officer's other ear, but it was empty. He moved to another of the guardsmen and found the same style of grey plugs in both ears. *What's that all about?* He rose, moving to meet the others inside the mausoleum.

The exterior of the structure had been impressive, but the interior was breathtaking. Intricate black patterns covered a central circle on the floor, surrounded by a checkerboard extending to the edges of the room. Raised plinths stood on the walls, each designed to house the caskets of the Cooper family. Above them, bass relief angels carved in pristine white marble, every curve and crease captured in astonishing detail. The one on the far wall showed an ascending angel with a child cradled in a protective embrace.

His eyes tracked up to the vaulted ceiling where more carvings lined the inside of the Egyptian style needle forcing its way up and away from the realm of mortals.

"Ah, Simmons," Bazalgette said. "There must have been some misunderstanding. Let me introduce Miss Elizabeth Cooper, Silas Cooper's sister."

"That might be a little difficult," Simmons said.

A frown passed across Bazalgette's features. "How so?"

"Do you want to answer that?" Simmons asked the woman, "or should I?"

She stared back, eyes intense, but remained silent.

"Very well," Simmons continued. "Elizabeth Cooper was indeed our dear departed Mr Cooper's sister, but she died during the invasion. I've seen the files."

Bazalgette turned back towards the young lady. "But you said—"

"Does it matter what I said?" Her manner was cold, clinical.

Bazalgette looked a little flustered. "So, who is she?"

"Now, that's the right question," said Simmons. "Pray enlighten us, Miss Cooper. Who are you, and what are *you* doing here at this funeral?"

Simmons drew the photograph from his jacket, opening it to show her image. "This is you, isn't it? Annabelle Pemberton."

She gazed at the image, a slight frown growing across her brow. "Well, it looks like me, but that's not my name."

"So, who are you? This Rosemary Carrington, the Black Guard were looking for?"

"No, no, NO!" There was hatred in her voice as she almost screamed the last syllable. "Not that filthy bitch, pulling tricks that would make the sleaziest whore blush, just to keep up appearances for those Inner-City gentlemen." She spat the last word, real venom in her. "By special invitation only, of course. What would her father say? Well, perhaps he'd say nothing and let it continue while he cowered upstairs out of earshot. Let them prod and poke her while they strapped her to that infernal machine. Burn and brand, cut and slice, oh their fun went on for hours, days sometimes. And their slimy limbs pawing at her and those eyes, so many eyes boring into her soul, unable to break contact from those blackened pits. The screaming. Oh the screaming, she thought it would never stop. Never."

Her voice caught, and she faltered, almost sobbing. Her face hardened, and she wiped the unshed tear from a watery eye. "But she's gone now. Gone, far away. You should call me Rosie."

Simmons and Bazalgette stood there in stunned silence, the heavy pattering of the rain beating the ground outside.

"So, Rosie," Simmons said, voice gentle. "What are you doing here? Who is Silas Cooper to you? Do you have any idea of the danger you are facing?"

"Oh, I'm well aware of what is going on," Rosie replied with a smile. "The question is, Mr Simmons, *are you?*"

"We need to get out of here," Simmons said. "When the Black Guard find out what's happened, there will be hell to pay."

"You'll have no argument from me," Bazalgette said.

Rosie looked at the coffin on the right-hand side of the mausoleum, then up at the two men. "I'd like to say a few words before I go."

Simmons nodded.

"In private?" It wasn't a question, but an invitation for them to give her some space.

"Of course," Bazalgette said, stepping into the torrential rain. "We'll leave you to it." Simmons followed.

Dark clouds filled the heavy sky, but at least the thunder seemed to have receded into the distance. The howling wind drove the rain into their exposed flesh, and Simmons looked down at his left hand as it gave a painful twinge.

The leather of the glove near his wrist had all but melted away, leaving an angry, raw burn that the icy droplets stabbed at like a thousand tiny needles. He'd seen what the arc-rifle had done to the Black Guard officer and thought he should count himself lucky he still had a hand to worry about.

He pulled a silver hip flask from his belt. After taking a mouthful, he poured a splash onto his wrist, sucking the damp air in through his teeth as the burning intensified, then offered it across to Bazalgette.

"Are you all right?" Bazalgette asked.

"Yes, it's nothing, just a burn."

Bazalgette approached to get a closer look. "I don't know—it looks rather unpleasant."

"Thank you, Doctor, but I think we established your lack of medical credentials the other night at the Britannia."

"Well, there's no need to be like that."

Simmons sighed and reached into a belt pouch, producing a strip of bandage. In this light, it almost looked clean but was more grey than white. He peeled the last remnants of the melted glove from his tender flesh, most of it lifting and pulling at the oozing wound. Gritting his teeth, he pulled it clear in a single swift motion, thinking it better just to get it done with.

The pain was intense. He gasped, blood welling around the edge of the raw and angry flesh. He tried to wrap the bandage, but with his other gloved hand, it was a farce.

Bazalgette reached towards him. "Let me do that."

"I'm fine," Simmons said through clenched teeth.

"Yes, I can see that." Bazalgette grabbed the strip of material from Simmons' grasp and placed it over the wound, winding the rest around his wrist. He finished tying it in a very reasonable attempt at a field dressing.

"Thank you," Simmons barked, almost sounding thankful.

"You're welcome," Bazalgette said with unreasonable civility.

Simmons wasn't sure if Bazalgette was trying to annoy him. *Damn, but he was infuriating.*

"So, did you ever get into combat during your military service?"

"Of course I did," Simmons replied, the indignance in his tone harsh even to his ears.

"So how is it you're so bad at looking after yourself, did you never get wounded?"

"That's what bloody corpsmen are for, and medical orderlies, isn't it?"

Bazalgette turned a stern gaze on Simmons, then burst out laughing. "Yes, I suppose it is."

"Sorry, Bazalgette. I'm a misery when I can't sort simple problems out. I've had people to do all this for me for so long, that sometimes the smallest thing irritates me if I can't do it myself."

"We each have our moments."

"We need to get moving," Simmons said, looking up at the dark sky. "Even if we make good time back to the city, the fog may already be rising."

Bazalgette cast his eyes over the scene of destruction. Crows were picking at the corpses, their brethren egging them on from the treeline with caws and croaks. "I don't believe this..."

"It will be all right," Simmons replied, tapping Bazalgette on the shoulder. "We'll sort things out."

"How? These are the Black Guard. They're dead. We killed them." Bazalgette's voice dropped to a whisper. "I killed them."

"Well, they didn't give us much choice, did they?"

Bazalgette's shoulders slumped, and he sighed. "Is that supposed to make me feel better about it?"

"Oh hell," Simmons said, his eyes widening, and he took off towards the rear of the mausoleum.

"What is it?" Bazalgette shouted, following.

Simmons stood behind the structure, the rain beating down on him in waves.

"Simmons. What's the matter?" Bazalgette called as he

rounded the corner almost running into his stationary comrade.

Simmons' voice was low. "Where's the one you stunned with your arc-lamp?"

"He was over—", Bazalgette gestured to the back of the next tomb. Towards the bare ground behind it. "Oh, bugger."

Simmons pushed Bazalgette and Rosie to make good progress as they left by the northern exit. It took a little longer to cut around to the east, but it kept them off the most direct approach to the cemetery. One that any Black Guard reinforcements were likely to take.

The rain continued its steady drumbeat on his hat as they moved over the cracked cobble remains of what had once been a primary thoroughfare towards the capital.

Bazalgette was quiet, but Simmons noticed he'd liberated an arc-rifle and fashioned a makeshift cover from one of the Black Guards long jackets. It hung over his shoulder as he traipsed along behind them.

"So, Rosie, what *is* your association with Cooper?" he asked as they walked.

"He was a friend when I needed one," she replied. "And yes, I am sad that he is no longer with us, regardless of what you think of me."

"I'm not judging you," he said. "I don't even know you."

Most of the mud that coated the front of her jacket had vanished under the constant downpour. The sodden hat she wore dripped into her bright red mop of hair, leaving thick strands clumped together. "Well, there's an interesting thing. Where did you get the photograph then?"

"An ex-army colleague called Pemberton. We were friends years ago. He said it was his daughter, my goddaughter."

"And the other woman?"

"She was your governess."

Rosie laughed. "Do you honestly think I'd have a governess?"

"Her governess," Simmons said. "It seemed reasonable. I hadn't seen Annabelle since she was a baby and she..." He stopped again, correcting himself, "*you* looked the right age."

"But why would he give you my portrait? Where did he even get hold of it?"

"I'm still trying to work that out."

She paused for a second then turned on Simmons, her gaze growing fiery.

"They followed *you*. It was the bloody Black Guard. Lured you in and waited until you led them to me. Damn you, Simmons."

"Now wait a minute. The Black Guard killed Cooper, and if they knew you were connected to him, it's reasonable to guess you'd attend the funeral."

"But we were there," Bazalgette said, his voice low. It was the first thing he'd said since they left Highgate.

"What?" Simmons said.

"We were there at the Britannia; you were there. What if Cooper's murder was a ploy to get you to find Rosie?"

Simmons shook his head. "No, but that would mean—"

"It means," Rosie interjected, "that they followed you to their little performance at the Britannia. Killed poor Silas to hook you further and then trailed you until you brought them here."

Simmons felt his fist's tightening, and as his eyes lowered, he blew out a long breath. "Damn them. Damn them to hell." It all fit into place. Pemberton, leading him to find the girl who had run off, fixated on Silas Cooper. "I'm a damned fool. It's my fault Cooper's dead, and Pinkett too. Now, I've even got you involved Bazalgette. What was I thinking?"

"Maybe you weren't," Bazalgette said, "but this *is* the Black Guard we're talking about. They specialise in information and deception. To be honest, I was as intrigued as you."

"Perhaps I'm just getting too old for this, going soft in the head?"

"Look," Rosie said, "there's no point mulling over this now. We need to get away from here somewhere safe, somewhere out of their reach."

Bazalgette shook his head. "Where's safe from the Black Guard?"

"South of the river," she said. "We'll go to Josiah."

"Who?" Simmons asked.

"He's a man who knows almost everyone. Silas worked for him, and I suppose I do as well."

Simmons flicked his eyes towards Bazalgette and back to Rosie. "We don't have a huge number of other alternatives. Where do we find him?"

"Greenwich," she replied, picking up the pace.

14

The towering city walls cast a deeper shadow than the rest of the jagged ruins as Simmons surveyed the view ahead. Icy gusts tore through their clothing as they picked their way between the remnants of old buildings. Bazalgette pulled his coat tighter around himself, but the wool wasn't designed to withstand a prolonged soaking. His teeth were chattering while he thrust his hands deep into his pockets.

Rosie showed no outward signs of the chill conditions. She plodded on, one foot in front of another, oblivious to the water that had soaked her dress and jacket.

"We need to get under cover, or we'll freeze," Simmons said. Bazalgette nodded.

"I know people," said Rosie, pointing further to the east. "We can rest there for a while."

Simmons was unsure, but what choice did they have? They couldn't stay out much longer in this weather. If they delayed too long, they would be at the mercy of the fog rising from the Thames. *Oh, and the constant threat from the bleeders.* "Very well. Lead on."

Rosie led them to an old warehouse on the dockside; its doors and windows boarded up. A dim red haze rose on the river, and the lapping of its waters wove a steady rhythm on the stone steps leading to the waterline.

She stopped. "I'll go ahead. We wouldn't want any unfortunate misunderstandings."

"If you're sure," Simmons said.

"It's for the best," she replied, striding off towards the warehouse.

"How are you holding up?" he asked, turning to Bazalgette.

"I'm freezing."

"Well, let's hope these *people* are the friendly sort, with plenty of space."

"And blankets," Bazalgette said, his whole body shaking.

"Stamp your feet," Simmons said. "Get things moving. It will keep you warmer."

He took the lead, showing what he meant. Stamping his feet and clapping his arms back and forth around his torso in a strange, vicious hug. "Go on," he said. "Don't worry how stupid you look, get the blood pumping."

Bazalgette stood for a few seconds, then gave in to his demands. The pair of them must have been a pretty sight stomping and flapping their arms about.

"Can you two make any more noise?" Rosie's voice cut through the darkness. "Let's get inside."

They wasted no time, covering the distance to the front of the warehouse in moments. As they approached, a dim yellow glow from a small coal brazier illuminated three rough-looking fellows in thick clothing. Rosie stood next to them, her hand on a large wooden door.

"Come on," she said, ushering them through, "mind the fogsheets."

Simmons pushed his way through the layered blankets that lined the doorway. They were a mix of wool and canvas, with a strong chemical smell. It was common practice Fogside to have this type of protection. It trapped most of the fog between the different layers as folk entered or exited the premises, any remaining wisps dissipated harmlessly.

A few gas lamps lit the dim interior, along with open fires in metal drums providing warmth to small groups huddled around them. Black smoke hung above them but drifted to exit through a series of makeshift grills in the high ceiling. A ragged band of hard-looking men and women occupied floor space between the barrels. Their eyes tracked the interlopers through their territory, and Simmons knew they weren't the friendly sort he'd been hoping for.

Bazalgette turned to him. "Are you sure about this? It doesn't look—"

"It's fine," Rosie said. Her voice was calm, but she kept it low. "These are members of the Black Canaries."

"The gang?" Bazalgette blurted.

"Yes. They are associates of Josiah, and thus friends to us."

Bazalgette seemed to relax. "Oh. Well, that's all right then."

Simmons kept a wary eye on the hard faces. There were perhaps fifty bodies he could see, each with the telltale black and yellow about their clothing advertising their brotherhood. Most sported sashes at their waists, others bright waistcoats contrasting with dark shirts or jackets.

As Rosie led them to the rear of the large building, the occupants lost interest in their new visitors. They soon found themselves in a secluded spot near a makeshift brazier, flames painting shifting light on the wall. Four of the Canaries lazing in the vicinity stared up, eyes dark with suspicion, hands moving towards belts.

"Here," said the nearest, "why don't you bugger off somewhere else? This is our fire."

Bazalgette stumbled to a stop, turning to Rosie.

"We're all family here," Rosie said, a great smile beaming from her petite face, "there's plenty of space over there." She pointed out another burning barrel, twenty feet away. "So, no need for any trouble here is there? You don't want to upset my friends or me, that's not a good idea, is it?"

"No, no trouble," the mouthy one replied standing and raising his hands. "Come on lads there's room over there." He nodded towards the other area, and they sloped off, nervous looks on their faces.

Rosie sat and rubbed her palms by the fire. Simmons watched as the four gang members made their way across the floor to join their brethren around the other barrel. He turned to see Bazalgette had joined Rosie, and steam was rising from their wet clothing. Regardless of his apprehensions, and their precarious alliance with the Black Canaries, at least they were out of that damned rain and safe from the fog.

A short while later, clothes drying by the fire, they huddled in blankets the four earlier residents obviously hadn't needed.

Simmons turned to Rosie. "What exactly is your relationship with these... people?"

"Josiah has links with all the gangs, except the Elephant and Castle, but he's working on that. They know I work for him, so we get along fine."

"Right," Simmons said, shifting his coat a touch further from the fire. It didn't do for it to get too dry. If the wax cracked, it would ruin the waterproofing.

"So they work together?"

"Josiah has information and skills useful to them. They do favours for him in return. It's a good arrangement, everyone benefits."

"So what of Cooper? What was his role in this?"

"Silas was a go-between. He organised and distributed money. Disbursement I think he called it. Josiah paid for people to do certain things, and Silas made sure it went to the right places."

"Ah, that explains it. I found a ledger, at Cooper's house, full of payments. It mentioned an RC. I presume that was you, plus there were a few others."

"Oh, who were they?"

"I was rather hoping you could tell me. Woodruff, Cargill, Addison, Blakelocke?"

"Oh yes, I remember them well..." Rosie seemed thoughtful for a moment. Then her eyes lit up. "I killed them."

"You what?" spluttered Bazalgette.

"I killed them," she repeated matter-of-factly. "Well, most of them. I've still to find Blakelocke, he's proving to be a slippery one."

They sat in stunned silence. Bazalgette, opened his mouth

as if to speak, then closed it again. Simmons stared at Rosie, who had reacted with no more emotion than if she had told them how much sugar she preferred in her tea.

"Why did you kill them?" Simmons asked.

She looked him in the eyes. "Because they deserved it, of course."

She sat back against the wall, still warming her hands.

"Is that it?" Simmons asked. "That's all you have to say, it's that simple to you?"

Rosie shrugged. "Oh, I wouldn't call it simple. It took considerable time and effort to locate them and plan how it needed to happen. One by fire, one by air and one by water. It was only fair."

"Huh," Simmons snorted, "and the last, no doubt, by earth."

"Oh, yes. Perhaps buried alive? Can you imagine the clawing desperation? The sheer despair trying to dig his way out with cracked and broken fingernails, his mouth slowly filling with dirt and filth?" Rosie smiled, her eyes intense. "Delicious, isn't it, almost poetic?"

Simmons checked how Bazalgette was faring. He had distanced himself, eyes downcast, chin resting on his hands and fingers interlocked with bright knuckles as if in silent prayer.

"But why?" Simmons asked, trying to keep his voice calm.

"They brought it on themselves," she replied. "They came to see *her*. She knew them all, in every way you could imagine, and then many more you couldn't even conceive. Ask Josiah, he knows the truth."

Simmons left it there, unable to bring himself to delve deeper into her fractured past and instead moved over to Bazalgette. "Are you all right?"

Bazalgette lifted his eyes to meet Simmons' gaze but raised his right hand. "I'll be fine. I need time and rest, perhaps." He returned to contemplating the rough wooden floor.

≈

Regardless of the strange surroundings and Rosie's revelation, Simmons slept. He awoke in darkness, a low furnace-like glow cresting the top of the steel drum they huddled around. Bazalgette lay to his right, wrapped in one of the blankets left for them. To the other side, a crumpled mess of material, but no sign of Rosie.

Simmons checked his watch. By the dull red glow of embers, it was just before seven-fifteen. A figure resolved from the darkness. Rosie's black mourning dress swishing as she moved past a couple of wooden chairs.

"Time we got moving," she said. "Is he all right?" she nodded over towards Bazalgette.

"I'm sure he'll be fine," Simmons replied. "A good night's rest does wonders."

"If you say so. Best wake him then. There's a boat waiting for us."

∾

Bazalgette jumped like a startled animal caught in torchlight.

"Sorry, it's just me," Simmons said, keeping his voice low. "Are you ready to leave?"

Bazalgette stifled a yawn. "Yes, I'm fine." He stretched and flexed his shoulders, then pulling the blankets to one side, rose yawning again. He took the arc-rifle and slung it over his shoulder. "Well, lead on, old chap."

The three of them picked their way through the darkness, mindful of the grunts and snorts of those still sleeping. Amidst muttered obscenities from the residents, they crossed to the doorway and out into the bright, morning sun.

The fog had burnt off and, as they moved to the dockside steps, Simmons noticed a familiar-looking vessel moored there. Isaac doffed his cap as Rosie approached. "Morning, Miss Rosie."

"Good morning, Isaac," she replied, "early as ever I see?"

"It don't pay to be late."

As Simmons and Bazalgette got closer, Isaac's face lit with

recognition. "Ah, Mr Simmons, a pleasant surprise, sir. Are you well?"

"Yes, and yourself?"

"Mustn't grumble," Isaac said, his voice sour, "or so the missus always told me."

Rosie turned to follow the exchange. "You two know each other?"

"Yes," Simmons said. "Isaac took me over to the south bank a few nights ago, quite the adventure. Red weed, a near capsize and gunshots fired. He was the consummate professional."

"I'm sure he was," Rosie said, "he's something of a legend amongst the other watermen, isn't that right, Isaac?"

The older man hung his head, mumbling. A little louder, he added. "Well, I don't know about that, Miss Rosie, I'm just a humble transporter of goods, mercantile or flesh-and-bones. Mister Simmons did the dangerous work the other night, weren't none of my doing." He pulled his cloth cap down onto his balding head and started a slow rolling walk towards the stern and the sanctuary of his canvas tent.

"Come now," Simmons said. "Don't be playing down the role you played in that evening's endeavour, Isaac. You handled this vessel with expertise I've rarely seen in these waters."

"It's no big deal, sir. I ply my trade and keep things tidy. Get folk from A to B and sometimes back again if that's their pleasure." His voice trailed off as he retired from the uncomfortable limelight into his private sanctuary among the fumes of the clanking boat engine and the steam of the tea kettle.

"Small world," Simmons said to Rosie.

"So it seems," she replied, "but as he's the best in the city, not too surprising you've used his services before."

Bazalgette, conspicuous in his silence, surprised Simmons as he asked Rosie. "So Greenwich and this Josiah then I presume?"

"Yes. Nathaniel, isn't it?" she asked.

"That's right. I must apologise, in all the chaos of yesterday, I don't think we were properly introduced."

She looked somewhat shocked for the briefest moment. "I'm Rosie."

"Nathaniel Bazalgette," he replied, taking her proffered lace-gloved hand and bringing it to his lips, "at your service."

Simmons glanced from one to the other, a mirthful but confused expression on his face. "Well, if everyone is finished with the introductions, I believe we have somewhere to be?"

"Ready when you are, Isaac," Rosie called.

"Aye," came the muffled reply behind the canvas. A soft splash announced the lines casting off, and with the growing roar of the engine, the vessel pulled forward against the incoming tidal waters of the Thames.

≈

Isaac steered them out into the centre of the river heading east past the once great London dock. Massive tangles of red weed bobbed on the water. The high tide made it difficult to tell where the different piers and jetties ended.

Simmons watched as the docks faded behind them as they continued south around the loop towards the Isle of Dogs. The dilapidated buildings became more ruin than dwelling here. Many of the poor folk called the appalling slums home. It was a shanty town of makeshift bricks and wood scavenged from the ruins of the other structures. Their shoddy construction spoke of being thrust together in desperate hope rather than built, and most were prone to ingress by the red fog with a high risk of collapse.

Bazalgette waved, and Simmons headed over to him. "Everything all right?"

"I've never been south of the river, this close to it, I mean. I've seen it from the outer edges of the city walls, across the Thames, but never like this."

"You've not missed much," Simmons said. "It gets worse the further south you go. The flooding is widespread over there, especially at high tide. But even through all that, some people call it home."

"Really?"

Isaac piped up from his position leaning on the tiller. "Yeah, most of them have no choice, but there's them what choose to live there."

"Who in their right mind would live that way?" Bazalgette asked.

"You never heard of the Golden Dawn?"

"Who?"

"They're a group devoted to magic and the occult. You must know of Aleister Crowley?"

"The wickedest man in the world?"

"So the papers would lead you to believe. Anyhow, Crowley is a member of this Golden Dawn cult, and he moved their main temple to somewhere in the depths of South London."

Bazalgette looked stunned. "Why on earth would he do that?"

"Well, I hear he believes they can reach the spirits through the fog, and that's why they live in those stinking waterlogged ruins."

"You believe in this magic? You didn't strike me as the superstitious type."

"Don't be so quick to dismiss it, Mr Bazalgette. I seen plenty of strange things in my travels. Perhaps one man's magic is another's science?"

Simmons smiled as Bazalgette lapsed into silent contemplation. As they chatted, the vessel ploughed on, and Greenwich soon hove into view on the southern shore through a misty haze. This part of the Thames looked more like an inland sea than a river. Buildings of every shape, size and in all states of repair perched on islands. Ruined walls shed brick and stone into piles where the water lapped against them and crept toward the upper-storey windows.

Isaac steered between the ruins, and they emerged onto a vast open area with water as far as the eye could see through the low mist. He popped his head out of his canvas hidey-hole, a steaming metal mug of tea in hand. "Almost there," he called forward.

"What is this place?" Bazalgette asked.

"It's what remains of Greenwich Park," Isaac said, lifting his hat and scratching through wisps of coarse white hair. "If you look there," he continued, pointing to the south, "you'll see the ground rising as it goes up the hill towards the Observatory. That's where I'll drop you. It's not a long walk, but it's way too shallow for this fat old girl."

Isaac tapped the side of the boat. There was a strange sense of tenderness in how his hand seemed to linger as he caressed the wood. He turned to Rosie as she emerged from the stern, she also had tea, but in a china cup, complete with a saucer. "I'll wait as you asked, Miss Rosie. If you haven't been in touch before the fog sets in this evening, then I'll return in the morning for you. Is that all right?"

Rosie finished the remains of her tea in a single mouthful. "Yes, that will be fine."

She passed over a single coin. Simmons couldn't be sure of the denomination, but it looked big enough to be a gold sovereign. *I'm in the wrong line of business*, he thought. Isaac steered the boat, so it drifted sideways into a low wall with a soft bump.

"After you, Rosie," Simmons said, offering his hand to steady her, which she accepted with a smile.

Once she had alighted, he and Bazalgette followed.

"It's only a few minutes to the Observatory," Rosie said. "Josiah will expect us, and he's not a man you want to keep waiting."

15

As they climbed, the Observatory came into view between the trees. Its red and white brick facade had four domed turrets. Two large ones stood on either side of the main building with two smaller ones atop the front corners of the roof. The nearest had a bright red ball perched on a flagpole.

Simmons nudged Bazalgette, pointing at the strange sight. "What is that?"

"That's the Greenwich time ball."

He looked at Bazalgette, none the wiser.

"It's how they measure Greenwich Mean Time and have done for years. I believe they installed it in the eighteen-thirties."

"They measure it how exactly?"

"The ball rises to the top of the pole just before one pm, then drops on the hour. You can see it from the Thames. It's how the navy and the workers on the river and docks set their watches."

"Not that there's much of a navy anymore."

"True," Bazalgette said, "but I've heard talk of new construction in the shipyards that survived in the North East and Scotland."

"Really?"

Bazalgette nodded. "Some of the labourers from the meetings that Silas Cooper organised talked about a better life up there, but there's debate about whether it's true. Even if it was, how would they get there with travel restricted as it is?"

"Fair point. The Black Guard has a lot to answer for."

"It's not just them though, is it? They take their orders from the council."

Simmons frowned at him. "Robertson you mean."

"Well, I suppose so, he leads the council, doesn't he?"

"Hmm," Simmons grumbled. "I met him once, before the war, didn't like him. There was just something about 'General Sir George Frazer Robertson' that disturbed me. He struck me as particularly ruthless, couldn't stand not getting things his way. And he's one of those types to hold a grudge."

Ahead of them, a massive white dome stood atop the third storey of a long brick frontage. It angled towards the turreted building they had seen earlier, and another wall met it at a rusty iron gate leading into a courtyard. At their approach, two figures detached themselves from their position leaning against the wall. "Oy, who are you and what the hell do you want?"

"My name is—" Simmons started before the big man interrupted.

"Do I look like I give a damn who you are, Mister la-de-da? Piss off before I plant my boot up your posh—" the man broke off halfway as Rosie made herself visible.

"Oh, Miss Rosie. I—" he stuttered as she glared at him. "I didn't know you, you was coming. If these fellows are with you, then I suppose—"

Rosie lashed out, her tongue like acid. "You suppose? Well, there's a first. That would seem to indicate that you can think. What with little more than a walnut between those ears of yours, I'm surprised you manage to breathe and walk at the same time."

He stood there, eyes cast down, unwilling to meet her gaze.

"I had a pig of a day yesterday, so I suggest you open this gate before I get annoyed and inflict my foul mood on someone within arm's reach."

He jumped to it, unlocking the padlock and swinging the rusty gate outward.

"I'm sorry Miss—"

"Shut up." Rosie strode into the courtyard while Simmons and Bazalgette followed. The man was breathing hard, and Simmons wondered if he was holding his anger in, or letting his fear out; perhaps both. The other guard watched, his face a mask of calm indifference to their passing. Rosie moved towards the building across the courtyard, her boots crunching on the packed gravel.

Bazalgette stopped. "The Prime Meridian," he said, his voice carried an air of awe.

Simmons looked down at a dirty strip of corroded brass crossing the courtyard. "That's the meridian?"

"Well, yes," Bazalgette said. "Granted, it's seen better days, but it's the principle of the thing."

Simmons hadn't meant to sound so negative. "I suppose if it were polished... It would be quite something to see?"

"Oh, it was," Bazalgette said, his enthusiasm back. "I came here when I was a lad. My grandfather brought me, and it shone like fire when the sun caught it. It's a remarkable reminder of our maritime heritage. Longitude zero degrees. I remember standing astride it, one foot in the east and the other in the west, don't you feel it?"

Simmons felt something, but it wasn't the enthusing that his friend had for this scientific marvel, or natural phenomenon, or whatever it was to him. It was a gnawing rumble in his gut, reminding him he'd not eaten for the best part of twenty-four hours.

"Let's catch up with Rosie," he said. "I'm sure there will be plenty of time to explore later."

Bazalgette stood astride the meridian a moment longer, then followed.

Rosie waited beside a dark wooden door into the building, watching them with an expression that spoke of incomprehension. Her velvet tones fluttered across to them. "If we are ready, gentlemen?"

They both stepped a little sharper to cover the distance. Rosie watched, her mouth slipping into a quiet smile, and shook her head as they reached the two steps up to the door.

"Right," she said. "Josiah will be waiting in the octagon. It's where he spends most of his time. He's, let's call it, unusual in appearance. Try not to stare." This last bit seemed focused at Bazalgette, but he was oblivious, eyes still darting around the building and courtyard.

≈

The interior was an Aladdin's cave of all things clockwork. Clocks, watches and timepieces of all shapes and sizes lined the walls, taking pride of place within their protective glass housings.

Every clock face showed the same time. Second hands were so synchronised they each clicked, ticked or swept at the same moment—an orchestra of precision instruments playing to a hidden conductor's tempo.

Bazalgette stood awestruck. "Look at it," he said, his voice a hoarse whisper.

"Yes, very impressive," Simmons replied. "But perhaps we shouldn't keep this Josiah waiting."

Deaf to his words, Bazalgette moved to inspect the largest display case. An array of brass and steel pipes and cogs swung back and forth, almost silent. The only sound was a quiet ticking as mechanisms engaged and disengaged from the pendulous collection of weights and pulleys.

"It's a Harrison sea clock," Bazalgette murmured, staring at the intricate mechanism. "No," he added, "it's *the* sea clock, his first design. Simmons, it's beautiful. A masterpiece of engineering."

"Yes, it's very impressive, but—"

"He was a genius, years ahead of his time. He made this over one hundred years ago and look at it. They might have built it yesterday."

"Very interesting—"

"That's just the start. This clock worked on a naval vessel and kept time to within the second. No electricity, just clockwork, precision engineering, springs and escapements—"

"Bazalgette." Simmons placed his hand on his friend's shoulder. The mesmerising effect of the sophisticated timepiece's spell broke. "Bazalgette, we need to meet Josiah. You can come back later. All right?"

"Yes, of course."

Simmons turned and hurried to catch up with Rosie. A narrow stairway opened onto a small hall where off-white plaster awaited a new coat of paint.

Rosie approached the large double doors, thrusting them inward. Dark wooden panels covered the walls of the octagonal room with double-height windows occupying each wall. The bright plaster continued above the wood, and light flooded in painting them whiter than their yellowed brethren outside.

More timepieces adorned cabinets on the walls which drew their eyes to a figure seated at the opposite side of the lavish wooden floored chamber.

To say Rosie had warned them of Josiah's unusual appearance, it was a shock to see the man in the flesh.

Leather, brass and steel replaced skin and bone on the left half of his face. The different elements fused with heavy stitch marks along the edges where they met flesh. Though shaped to mimic the original aspect of his features, they were bulky and angular. Mechanisms whirred, producing an eerie sense of constant motion. Pistons hissed, expanding and contracting to power his arm as he turned his bald head to greet his visitors.

Simmons felt his eyes drawn to the movement and the strange, sharp angles of Josiah's entire left side. *Don't stare. She said not to stare.*

"Rosie, my dear," Josiah said, his voice low and gravelly. "I see you have brought guests with you."

"Josiah, let me introduce Sir Pelham Simmons and Mr Nathaniel Bazalgette."

"A pleasure to meet you both, gentlemen."

"And you too, Josiah," Simmons said with a nod.

"Yes, a pleasure indeed," Bazalgette added, his eye wandering around the room to yet more marvels of mechanical artifice.

"So, time is short," Josiah said. "I'm sure you have questions."

"Quite a few," Simmons said. "Let's start with Rosie and the Black Guard—"

Josiah held up his right hand, stopping him. "Let us hold that thought, Mr Simmons. Rosie, these gentlemen must be famished. Would you be a darling and pop over to the kitchens and get them to organise tea? I could do with a drink, and I feel there is plenty to discuss this day."

Rosie returned her view to Josiah, her face blank for a few seconds. "I'll be back in a jiffy."

"No rush. Take your time, my dear."

≈

Josiah waited till Rosie left the bright octagonal room. "Sweet girl. Still, a little *troubled,* shall we say?" He focused on Simmons. "I'm aware of your investigations into my associate Mr Cooper and the rather unfortunate events that transpired at the public-house. You no doubt also have questions about the names mentioned in his journal."

Simmons looked Josiah straight in the eye. "You seem to know an awful lot about my activities and findings."

"I am a man of means, Mr Simmons. Information is the lifeblood by which I thrive, the procurement and distribution of that knowledge is how my empire grows and expands."

Bazalgette turned from his perusal of a large floor standing clock. "Rosie said she killed the men on that list. Three out of four, anyway. Why would she do that?"

Tiny clockwork mechanisms clicked into frenzied activity for a few seconds as Josiah turned to face Bazalgette. "They undertook a great project and were sworn to secrecy. You could claim, they made her what she is today. But I do not wish to bring the tone down so early in the day. Our time may be short, so suffice it to say, Rosie was the daughter of a brilliant, but evil and cowardly man."

Josiah tapped on the table, a rhythmic click from his reconstructed index finger marked perfect tempo with the clocks as he seemed to consider how to continue. "He allowed them to experiment on his only daughter. In return, they promised him great rewards in the years to follow. It was after the war, and they had discovered many artefacts. These were dangerous and sinister things from a world very different from our own. I have seen information that leads me to the conclusion that Doctor Carrington recovered a live sample. One of the alien creatures. He used it to create something that was more, and sadly, also less than human."

"What are you suggesting?" Simmons asked.

"Having spent a little time with young Rosie, you may have noticed she has, shall we say, a few *peculiarities*? She finds it easy to get on with people and to turn them to her way of thinking, all part of her father's experiments with alien brain tissue. The ordeals they put her through seem to have been too much for her fragile mind to cope with. It fractured, trying to protect itself, hiding elements away deep within her psyche. Things that return to the surface in times of stress."

"You expect us to believe this man blended alien and human tissue?" Simmons asked. "If it's true, why are we not overrun with these creatures?"

Josiah smiled, the left side of his face creaking with the movement. "She was the prototype for the many *Hybrids* they commissioned Carrington to produce, but his daughter's suffering haunted even his callous nature. He freed her—his last attempt to redeem himself for the horror he had inflicted upon his own flesh-and-blood. She repaid him with the only kindness she knew. They say his body was unrecognisable when they found him. Alien symbols carved into what little skin remained, his vital organs positioned around him on the floor, removed with a surgeon's precision."

"Dear God," Bazalgette said.

"I am not here to judge Carrington. I tell you this as a pretext to why the four men from the journal are involved, of what they hoped to create. Their task was to produce someone capable of passing themselves off in high society, accomplished at debating and gaining great concessions from powerful negotiators. Of ruling an Empire."

He let the information sink in. "Yes, they sought to replace the young Empress with a tool of their choosing, who they thought they could control. Instead, they unleashed a monster which, through pure luck, keeps itself locked away, most of the time."

"How did she come to your attention?" Simmons asked.

"Fortune shined down upon me when young Rosie came into contact with a trusted associate of mine, Silas Cooper, and I saw her potential and learned of her strange story. Thus it was that with their plan foiled, these four men, and those who pull their strings, required a replacement - and quickly. They needed to find an interim until they could recover Rosie, and their payments matched the urgency of the task. From the information we have gathered, it seems their plot is already in motion. That our good Empress Victoria is an imposter, groomed and trained for her role and kept as far from the public as possible."

"What?" both Simmons and Bazalgette said together.

"Cooper discovered the truth, but against my advice, he shared that information with the people. And so, here we are. The Black Guard are unforgiving, and once the hounds are unleashed, there is often only one outcome."

"So you're telling us that Victoria is an imposter as Cooper was preaching, but what of these Watchmen and Dent?" said Simmons.

"The Watchmen are but tools of the Black Guard, officers selected for their loyalty and skill in the field."

"And you know who is behind it?"

"Come now, Mr Simmons. You already have the answer to that question. He who owns the Black Guard controls the Watchmen."

Simmons spat the word. "Robertson."

Josiah gazed out of the nearest window for a while, the room falling into silence. "As for Dent's work, clever? Perhaps, but flawed. They are cheap copies of his father's achievement. Those were real masterpieces. Yes, these trinkets tweak the time and space continuum and may seem useful, but they are the product of an amateur, not a true Horologist."

"Horologist?" Simmons asked.

Bazalgette half whispered to him. "The study of time and chronometers."

Josiah continued. "Ever was the young Dent keen to take on his father's trade, but his heart wasn't truly in it. Granted, he is a superb artificer and can produce pieces of exquisite beauty and precision, but that isn't enough. A Horologist dedicates his entire being to his craft, must make great sacrifices and let nothing stand in the way of his quest for knowledge. Dent focused too much on chronometers, while I have transcended that limited view and opened my mind to everything a true Horologist may accomplish." He motioned to his mechanised body for emphasis.

Simmons inspected the assortment of cogs, flywheels and miniature piston pumps. "So you are such a person as you describe?"

"Yes. Horology is the study of time in all its intricate beauty and how it transcends mere chronometry and opens our eyes to the surrounding universe. Why else would I be *here*?" he gestured around the room, "in this place. Can you not feel it? The energy that runs through it even now as we converse?"

Josiah dropped his hands back to his lap with a significant clunk. "We stand upon the very spot that gives London its power, which fuels the greatest empire in the world. A point at which both time and space are physical assets to manipulate as we wish."

Bazalgette looked at Josiah, his eyes wide. "Yes, I think I understand what you mean. I thought it was just the memory of having been here before, but it's much more than that. Something tangible."

"You are a man of learning, Mr Bazalgette," Josiah said. "Let us see if you can open your mind to the endless possibilities, to revel in this new golden age of discovery. Few are the true visionaries, who unlike the sheep, refuse to shy away from the cliff's edge and instead plunge ahead choosing the mystery of the abyss."

"Can we get back to business?" Simmons said. "If I'd wanted to talk about auras, I could have gone to a cheap back-street seance."

Josiah frowned. "You wound me, Mr Simmons. Our conversation is not about the supernatural, but about super-nature and science."

"Yes, but let's return to the here and now, please? What about the Black Guard and the Watchmen?"

"It seems Dent is making copies of his father's original work," Josiah said. "No doubt he is under duress from the Black Guard, seeing as they are the ones carrying and utilising them. So the question becomes, why are the Black Guard involved in this? What is their ultimate gambit?"

"Well, Robertson controls the Black Guard, so he must be directing things."

"Robertson long sought to enforce military rule, and our young Empress rebuked him for it. Now here we are in a state of Martial Law, so for which side does he play?" Josiah stood, the repetitive clicking and whirring changing to a more subtle tempo. "If the Black Guard get their hands on the original schematics, then these current watches will seem like children's playthings. The originals are an order of magnitude greater in power and complexity. The Black Guard is already a fearsome force; give them true control over time, and they'll be unstoppable. Who knows the bounds of Robertson's ambition?"

Bazalgette turned to Josiah. "So what can we do?"

"An excellent question, Mr Bazalgette. Dent must know where the originals are, the schematics produced by his father. It's only a matter of time before he breaks and gives the Black

Guard what they want, the means to locate them. So we need to find them before they break Dent."

"You mean to kill him?" Bazalgette asked.

"If we can't release him, then yes. We cannot leave him for their torturers to extract the information. With the best will in the world, no-one could withstand them indefinitely. It appears he serves a purpose, providing them with what they think are the original specifications. But when they discover the truth, they will force the secrets from him."

Simmons turned on Josiah, his face a deep frown. "How do you know all this? About the original watch schematics?"

Josiah laughed. Leather and flesh rippled and stretched against the course stitches. "Mr Simmons, as I told you earlier, my business is to know all the mysteries of this once great city. Every whispered conversation in dark meeting places. They are how I maintain my position in society."

His face settled into a less grotesque mask. "I am told stories of the original watches. Yes, there was more than one. They were a gift for our old Empress before the war. Two exquisite timepieces, priceless gifts, one each for Victoria and Albert. When Albert died early during the invasion, they never recovered his body. Victoria found looking at her watch became unbearable; they were identical, you see. They say viewing it brought her too much heartache, and so she gave it away. Not to a family member as you might expect, but to her bodyguard, to one of the ArcAngels."

"ArcAngels? You mean the Black Guard elite?" Simmons asked.

"Yes, but they were more than just elite soldiers. The ArcAngel power armour made them near indestructible. It was Tesla's crowning achievement, well according to what we know. But he wasn't working on that project alone."

"Dent," Bazalgette said. "He worked with Dent, didn't he?"

"Yes, Mr Bazalgette. Dent and Tesla produced a marvel of electro-mechanical artifice. The likes of which we may never see again. Imagine someone capable of battling and defeating a full division of foot soldiers. Next, imagine that same person with the power of time at their command."

"That's how they did it," Bazalgette said. "How they fought for so long after the destruction of the rest of the armed forces. The defensive and offensive capabilities of the armour along with the watch. I remember reports many times of their destruction only later to hear of an ArcAngel reappearing elsewhere in the city and battling with the Martians there."

"Yes, they kept the aliens off balance for months," Simmons added. "Time and again they drew the bulk of the fighting machines away from the camps so the resistance could try to free survivors."

"But ultimately, they failed," Josiah said. "A huge fireball crashing to earth, the destruction of the great Angel-One airship. But perhaps not the end for the watch."

"What do you mean?" Bazalgette asked, a puzzled look on his face.

"It's possible it might have survived. Nobody knows precisely where Angel-One crashed outside the city. If we can get hold of the schematics, we may discover a way to track the watch's location."

"How could it survive?" Bazalgette said. "The airship fell from the skies. It exploded and burned like a comet, leaving shredded ruins of twisted and molten metal, if even that much survived the impact."

"I fear you may be correct," Josiah said. "But I am not willing to pass up the remote hope that something might have endured. It could provide us with a starting point to recreate Dent's masterpiece and give us an advantage against the Black Guard, and to free our Empress."

Simmons held up his hands. "Whoa, whoa. Just a minute there. How did we get from finding schematics to rescuing the Empress?"

"Surely that is the logical extrapolation of our conversation, Mr Simmons?"

"What?" Simmons shook his head, pointing at Josiah.

"Hold on. You're coming out with all this talk of conspiracy, and I've yet to see any real evidence that supports any of this."

"But Simmons." Even Bazalgette had turned on him now. "You must see this makes sense. Your involvement with locating Rosie, leading to Cooper and his bizarre death. The watches and Dent, and those four fellows trying to create an imposter to take over from the Empress? I agree, it's not empirical, but by God, if it isn't true, then it's the biggest coincidence I've ever come across."

"Et tu, Bazalgette?" Simmons said, but the fight had left him. Deep down, he felt responsible for Cooper's death and Pinkett the undertaker. If what Rosie had said was true, then the Black Guard had duped him into leading them to her. Cooper had been just more impetus to force his investigation on, to draw them closer to their real quarry. They had taken him for a prize fool.

"Damned Black Guard," he said under his breath. "Don't make me regret this."

16

A maid served refreshments, pouring the tea before leaving. Rosie rejoined the others at the octagonal table as they continued their discussion.

"So," Simmons said, "do we know where Dent is being held?"

Josiah's gears and cogs whirred. "Yes, he's in the Tower."

"There's nothing as exciting as breaking into a stronghold of the Black Guard," Simmons said, his sarcasm seemed lost on the others. "So how do you expect us to break into a royal prison that's protected by half of the military in the city?"

"Perhaps you will need to rely on your wit and guile, Mr Simmons. I am a master of knowledge gathering and artifice. I fear I am lacking in the arts of breaking and entering."

"Do you have information about Dent's location within the Tower? It's a large place, all but impossible to locate him going door to door."

"Quite so. My sources have informed me there has been mention of the Black Cells. Now I must be straight with you. I have not heard the name before, and so far details elude me as to their whereabouts."

Simmons sighed, looking across the table to Bazalgette for any hint of inspiration, but he shrugged his shoulders, unable to add to the conversation. It was Rosie who perked up. "What about the Ravenmaster?" She looked at Josiah. "He might know something."

"Indeed he might," Josiah said. "Well done, my dear, he may be exactly who we need to crack this particular nut."

"Who is this Ravenmaster?" Simmons asked.

"He is a man of uncommon talents and surrounds himself with birds of every variety," Josiah said. "If you pardon the pun, they flock to him in their hundreds, be they crow, bloodshriek, razorbill and even the ravens themselves. He has a talent, and they seem to follow him."

"What? All of them?" Simmons asked. "Most of the birds around London are a menace, and the ones Fogside can be deadly."

Josiah's eyes narrowed. "That may be true in most cases, but he's not called the Ravenmaster without reason."

"I was wondering about that," Bazalgette said, "especially when you mentioned the Tower."

"Ah, yes, Mr Bazalgette. It is not merely a name he has taken a fancy to. It was his role. Before the war, he was a yeoman warder at the Tower of London, responsible for the royal ravens, and hence the name. He has an affinity with the great birds, and they, in return, appear to keep their avian brethren in line. Well, for him at least."

"So as an ex-yeoman warder, he would be privy to the inner workings of the Tower," Simmons said, "and may have information about the Black Cells. So, where do we find him?"

"He's taken up residence at St Olaves, the old asylum on the edge of Southwark Park," said Rosie. She screwed her face up. "It's not a safe place to visit. The whole park is swarming with birds and making things worse, it's disputed territory between the Red Hands and the Elephant and Castle gangs."

"Why isn't anything ever easy?" Simmons asked.

Rosie continued. "Well, the gangs used to fight over the area, but it's quiet now. Too many fights spilt over close to the asylum, and the birds didn't take kindly to it. The body count got so bad that both gangs gave up on it and avoid the park now. If they want to have a bit of a do, they go further north or south of the place."

"What, the gangs ran away from a few crows?" Bazalgette asked.

Rosie smiled. "Those razorbills are aptly named. I've seen a flock of those bastards tear hard men to shreds in seconds, all while the other birds laughed and cawed from the trees."

"So what's the best route to Southwark Park from here, boat?" asked Simmons.

"Yes, you'll need someone good. The waterways are treacherous around there."

"Like Isaac?"

"Yes," she replied with a smile, "someone exactly like Isaac."

While Rosie went to organise the waterman, Bazalgette had taken the time to view the clocks. Simmons didn't mind Bazalgette's obsession with the place. It allowed him to speak with Josiah alone.

"How may I help you, Mr Simmons?" Josiah asked as Simmons entered the octagonal room. The door had been ajar, and he wasn't one to wait for an invitation. "It's funny you should ask. I've been thinking."

Josiah smiled. "Always a tricky business that, leads to all kinds of trouble."

"Yes, but as I am helping you with this endeavour, it only seems fair..."

"Ah. Is it that time already? Do you not feel it is your duty to help our beloved Empress?"

"Of course it is," Simmons replied.

"I did not mean to impugn your honour, Mister Simmons. It was just my twisted attempt at humour. It would seem reasonable I offer you something in return for your generous aid. What is it you wish?"

"I'm looking for a man named Maddox," Simmons said. "He has been elusive."

"And you thought I might know of him?"

"You pride yourself on your network of information, you said so yourself."

"That I did. Yes, I know John Maddox."

"I have a contract for his capture."

"In what state do you intend to recover him?"

"He killed three police officers, so the constabulary is understandably upset. They'd prefer him in one piece so they can stretch his neck in public. But they won't shed too many tears if I come back with his head in a bag."

A long silence filled the space between them. The only sound came from the slow ticking of the clocks around the room and the occasional whir and click of Josiah's complex mechanisms.

"As you wish," Josiah said, breaking the tranquillity. "I will give you the information you desire when you return with the schematics. It is but a small thing compared to what you are undertaking for me."

"Right," Simmons said. He'd expected it would require more hard bargaining. "With that settled, I'll be on my way then."

"Good luck, Mr Simmons."

As he left the room, he almost barged straight into Bazalgette stood just outside the door. "What the—"

"Sorry," Bazalgette said, moving to the side, "but you've got to see this, it's amazing."

"Have you been eavesdropping all this time?"

"No," Bazalgette said. "I arrived a few minutes ago and could hear that you were in discussion with Josiah so I thought I'd wait until you finished.

"So, how much did you overhear?"

Bazalgette dropped his eyes to inspect the floor like some schoolboy caught red-handed with his fingers in the biscuit tin. "All of it really. This Maddox fellow doesn't sound like a pleasant chap. Who is he?"

Simmons chuckled. "He's a nasty piece of work who needs bringing to justice. I've been trying to track him down for some time."

"Oh. Fair enough. So you'll bring him back alive then?"

Simmons didn't answer. "So what was all this I needed to see so urgently?"

Bazalgette opened his eyes wide, mouth equally so. "You'll never believe what I just found. Come on, it's incredible."

He scuttled down the stairs, beckoning Simmons to follow.

∾

"Southwark Park," Isaac said as he guided the boat west through the narrow streets. "Now that's a place I don't get to visit often."

"Do you know anything about the asylum?" Simmons asked, warming his hands on the stove they all huddled around at the stern.

"The Infirmary you mean? St Olaves."

"They described it to us as an asylum," Bazalgette said.

"Folk might describe it that way. But they called it The Infirmary, probably to avoid the stigma *asylum* brings. I suppose it's the same thing. It was for those who couldn't cope with the realities of life. There was quite a few servicemen took there in its heyday, struggling with what they'd experienced while at war." Isaac fell quiet for a second. "Along with all the other lunatics, of course."

"We need to get inside to see this Ravenmaster," Simmons said.

"Good luck with that. I've heard he's well suited to that place, if you know what I mean." Isaac's tone was conspiratorial, and he took a quick look around before whispering. "They say he speaks with the birds, and they tell him secrets from across the city."

Bazalgette stifled a short laugh and whispered. "Why are you whispering?"

Isaac tapped one finger to his nose. "They're bloody everywhere, ain't they? They might be listening."

"Good God, man. You're not serious, are you?" Simmons asked.

"Shh." Isaac's voice carried a slight tremor. "There's no point upsetting them, is there? The ravens abandoned the tower during the war and look at us now - the kingdom's fallen just like they said it would. And where did they all go? To him, weren't it?"

Simmons shook his head. "Superstitious claptrap. They left because the damned Martians were blowing the hell out of London."

"Yeah, but it don't matter now, do it? You can believe what you want, and I'll believe what I want. But the kingdom, in my humble opinion, is well and truly knackered, and the ravens seem to be doing just dandy. So I'm hedging my bets."

Isaac picked up his tin mug of coffee and skulked away to lean on the tiller. Simmons pondered on where he found such excellent beans. Perhaps he had the same contacts as Mrs C?

"Don't be too harsh on him, Simmons," Bazalgette said. "Everyone has been through a lot, and they take comfort in what they can. Superstition, Religion, Family. I lose myself in my work."

"I understand that, we've all lost someone," Simmons said, his voice dropping to a whisper. "Does it even matter anymore?"

"Look, we weathered the storm and survived against all the odds during the invasion. Britain is slowly getting back on its feet. Now's the time to put our support in the right places and not let corruption rot the hearts of good people. If someone has replaced Victoria, then we must do something, whatever we can to restore her to power so she can lead us into a bright new future."

Simmons sighed, he seemed to do that a lot recently. "You're right, Bazalgette. I know it deep down, I'm just so tired. Sometimes I wake and wish it could go back to how it was before the war, but that's a foolish man's dream."

"It doesn't have to be foolish. If we stop dreaming, we cease to explore the boundless possibilities. It's like Josiah said, we need to walk up to that precipice and leap in, feet first. If we are unwilling to take great risks, then we can never expect to achieve anything of true value."

A smile crossed Simmons' face. "Spoken like a true visionary, my friend." He clapped Bazalgette on the shoulder. "Now shut up and put the tea on."

∼

Isaac steered them through the narrow streets as they approach Southwark. "The park is a few minutes away, gentlemen."

Bazalgette looked over towards Simmons. "So how are we going to get past the birds and into the infirmary?"

"We'll have to play it by ear, I suppose," said Simmons.

Isaac perked up from the stern. "You should check the bandstand."

"The bandstand?" Simmons asked.

"Yeah. They say while St Olaves still had residents, there was an escape. A load of them made it through a tunnel they'd been digging for months—came out under the bandstand. I'm sure the authorities blocked it all up, but I wouldn't have thought they would collapse the whole thing. Just an idea."

"Well, it's as good a plan as we have," Simmons said.

Bazalgette nodded in approval. "What about the birds though?"

"Well," Isaac said. "I've heard them say as long as you do nothing to upset them, then you should be fine."

"And what defines upsetting them?" Bazalgette asked.

"I suppose getting too close to their territory. Maybe you should try to look inconspicuous?" Isaac said with a shrug of his shoulders.

"Yes, thanks for that pearl of wisdom," Simmons said. "Let's see the approach to the bandstand and take it from there."

"Right you are, Mr Simmons."

Isaac cut the engine and drifted across the final open stretch of drowned street. He'd insisted the lack of noise would make them less of a focal point for any birds in the area. The boat bumped against the railed wall surrounding the park. "The main entrance is over there," he said, pointing along to a gap visible between thick trees. "It's not deep, only a few inches, but if you keep hold of the railings, you'll avoid the worst of the weed. Then head due south, and can't miss the bandstand."

Simmons waited while Bazalgette climbed onto the wall. The boat shifted as he transferred his weight, and the makeshift bag for the arc-rifle swung from his shoulder like a pendulum. Simmons followed, and the pair traversed the nearly submerged wall. They alternated, shifting their grip on the railings with their foot movements, treading carefully to avoid the red weed as they made their way towards the old park entrance.

Isaac waved at them, trying to catch their attention, then gestured to a gap between the buildings. He pushed the vessel off the wall with a long pole, punting back across the street. Simmons gave him a quick salute as the boat drifted away in silence towards the submerged alley.

There were gaps in the railings where patches of rust had eaten into the metal. One section was tricky where they bent out away from the park. Bazalgette slipped as he placed his foot onto an area slick with moss. His body leaned back at a precarious angle, but the railings supported his weight, and both men made it to the entrance. Five feet of water stood between them and the muddy, waterlogged ground of the park itself.

"Should we try to jump across?" Bazalgette asked.

Simmons surveyed the area. There was no clear route to get to the parkland. The overgrown foliage of the trees fought a losing battle with the red weed which swarmed up from the water's edge, strangling everything in its reach. Dead twigs caught in its deadly embrace led to larger decaying branches, the weed sucking the life from the natural flora.

"We could try to use the branches overhead," Simmons said. "But the weed may have left them weak, and I don't fancy falling into the damned stuff."

"Yes, you're probably right. Take my hand, and I'll launch you across."

Simmons looked at Bazalgette, trying to keep the scepticism from his face.

"Very well," he said, taking Bazalgette's hand and leaning back as much as he dared. "On three then?"

"Agreed," Bazalgette said tight to the railings on the other side. He gripped the end railing while clasping Simmons' gloved hand around the wrist.

"One, two... three."

Simmons shifted his weight forward as he pulled hard against Bazalgette. The other man did the opposite, throwing his body back towards the park, launching Simmons.

With a loud splash, his trailing foot caught the water, and he slipped in the muddy shallows where the weed reached the new shoreline. His arms wheeled as he tried to maintain his balance but to no avail. He landed in an unceremonious pile on the bank and felt movement as the weed flailed its sinewy strands in his direction.

Simmons scrambled on his backside further onto drier land, away from the red foliage reaching for him like an odd assortment of disembodied veins.

"Are you all right?" Bazalgette called across to him.

Before Simmons had a chance to reply, a mass of flapping wings burst from the trees further into the park, filled with raucous arguments of crows as they took flight. Simmons froze in place, his eyes turning skyward.

The black shadows of twenty large birds circled above, rising into the air. Their alarm calls received curious replies from their brethren further around the park. Simmons lay there still and silent. The birds headed eastward, and as

Simmons' eyes followed their path, he saw several angled roofs poking up beyond the tree line at the park's edge.

Birds covered the roofs all standing in silent vigil. The trees on that side shifted as the creatures sitting on the branches shuffled and cawed their warnings.

He got to his feet and headed back to the encroaching weed at the water's edge. It had returned to its dormant state, not having found anything to latch onto during its few seconds of frantic thrashing.

Keeping his voice low, he called to Bazalgette. "I'm all right, but how are you going to get across now?"

"Don't worry," Bazalgette said rummaging in his pack and producing his arc-lamp. "I have an idea."

Simmons shook his head, holding his hands out before him. "Wait a minute, let's not do anything rash."

Bazalgette seemed oblivious as the familiar low hum of power built, and a glow lit the right-hand side of his coat.

"Bazalgette," Simmons hissed, "what the hell?"

Sparks exploded from the railings. Bright arcs of electricity dazzled him as they danced across the water and leapt through the tangle of weed into the leaves and branches of the trees in its stranglehold. Pops and hisses erupted from both the weed and the trees, and small flames burst from the dry twigs like kindling.

The lightning arced from the end of the lamp, enveloping Bazalgette. It looked like he'd thrust it into the water's edge ahead of him.

"Bazalgette," Simmons shouted, heedless of the consequences.

"I'm fine," Bazalgette replied, "insulated."

"What?"

Bazalgette pointed towards his gloves and boots. "I'm insulated," he repeated.

Simmons stood there his mouth agape. The electrical arcs around Bazalgette subsided. A large section of the railings cracked and fell behind him. It hit the water with a violent hiss like iron quenched in a smithy. Bazalgette waited a few seconds, then leaned out and jumped forward, landing with a splash amidst the red weed a few feet from the bank.

"Bazalgette!"

Swathes of red weed surrounded him, tangled around his long boots, but he ploughed on towards the bank regardless. The weed remained limp and unresponsive in the muddy water.

"What the hell were you thinking, man?" Simmons said through gritted teeth. "That could have killed you. The red weed, why didn't—"

His voice fell away as he struggled to reconcile what he'd witnessed with all the tales of what should have happened when someone fell into a patch of weed.

Bazalgette stared at him. "Science," he said as if it were the most obvious thing in the world.

"But—"

"The weed doesn't like high voltage or current. Water is an excellent conductor, and I'm insulated. It was a logical extrapolation when I realised I wasn't able to leap the distance unaided."

"A logical extrapolation?" Simmons said, trying hard to keep his voice under control, and failing.

"Yes, a deduction or assumption?"

"I know what it bloody means. What if it hadn't worked?"

"But it did."

"But—"

"It worked, Simmons; I knew it would."

"But—"

"Look," Bazalgette said, pointing past Simmons, "that must be the bandstand."

"What?" Simmons said, still incredulous.

"The bandstand that Isaac mentioned. It's right there. Come on, old chap."

Bazalgette strolled past as if he were out on a sightseeing trip. Simmons stood for a few seconds unable to either move or form any coherent reply. As he turned to follow his friend, he felt something twist in his gut. The birds fell silent.

17

"Bazalgette, stop," Simmons whispered. He moved to catch up as his friend turned.

"What is it?"

Simmons nodded toward the nearest trees. "The birds."

The branches were thick with them. All observed the trespassers, their eyes staring with unnerving intensity.

"Should we run?" Bazalgette asked.

"Let's keep it slow. If we take it steady, maybe they won't get upset."

"They seem upset enough as it is."

"All the more reason for keeping things calm then."

Simmons took a hesitant step, and Bazalgette followed. Feathers rustled as several crows chose that moment to flex their wings, but remained perched.

The bandstand was around a hundred yards distant. Its large circular structure rose ten feet, topped with a conical copper roof. Verdigris discoloured the metal, but it seemed in excellent condition despite the blue-green streaks that ran between areas that glowed like red fire where they caught the sun. The wooden facade had once been white, but now it stood yellowed with age and neglect.

Simmons edged another few steps closer to their target, keeping an eye on the sea of dark shapes watching them. A loud croak burst from the nearest tree, and the floodgates opened.

"Run," he yelled, pushing Bazalgette forward.

The scream of birds and thrashing wings erupted around them. Simmons glanced back and wished he hadn't. Streams of black bodies boiled from the trees, the sky turning dark. The first wave crashed over them, beaks and claws raking, seeking exposed flesh to rip and rend. Then they were curving up and away to circle for their next assault.

Bazalgette flapped his arms around, trying to protect his head and face from the second flight as they dived past. Simmons grabbed him. "Keep moving, man." He tried to ignore the constant battering from the bird strike and dragged Bazalgette along as they fought their way to their destination. They bounded up five steps to the raised floor of the bandstand. A square trapdoor sat in the centre secured with a rusted padlock. The screeching of the birds increased. Metallic pings rang from the copper like a hailstorm where some misjudged their dive, bouncing from the angled roof stunned or dead, such was the ferocity of their attack. Several of the damned things still managed the narrow gap above the railings to tear at them. Others crash-landed, the survivors dancing towards them pecking and shrieking their fury.

"Get it open," Simmons yelled.

Bazalgette produced a small crowbar from his bag and went to work. Within a few seconds, there was a crunch as the lock burst free.

Simmons kicked at the mass of birds around them, and they scattered with angry caws. Bazalgette grunted with effort and strained with his full weight on the trapdoor. With a crack of splintering wood, it surrendered, revealing a void below. Bazalgette hit the ground and dropped in, and Simmons followed. He slammed the door shut, locking the birds outside, still pecking and screeching above them.

The smell of rot and decay surrounded them. Bazalgette fired up the arc-lamp and thrust it ahead, surveying the area. "It seems to be a storage space."

With the adrenaline fading, the aches and sharp pain from the minor wounds and scratches caught up with Simmons. He took a moment to check himself over, only scrapes and a little bleeding—the worst was from his right ear.

"Let me look at that," Bazalgette said.

"It's nothing."

Bazalgette ignored him, moving the arc-lamp to the side of his head to get a better view. "You've got a nasty tear near your earlobe. It could do with stitching."

Simmons pulled away. "I'll live. What about you?"

"A few pecks, but other than that, I think I avoided any long-term injury."

"All right, let's see if this tunnel of Isaac's is fact or fantasy."

Brown canvas-covered shapes filled the central area out to the circular walls. The ceiling height was under five feet, and they both had to duck their heads standing in an uncomfortable hunch.

Bazalgette lifted the corners of the material and found wooden boards, paint, brushes and an extending ladder. "Makes sense, I suppose."

"Yes, beats having to transport spare materials for repair." Simmons turned towards the rear of the space. His stomach dropped as if by reflex as his head grazed a low beam. "Damned beams." He rubbed the spot. "You would have thought they could afford to build it a few inches higher."

"I think they made them to a specific standard." Bazalgette walked with a practised stoop while scanning around the damp space. "Over here," he called, beckoning Simmons to several crates near the wall.

"What is it?"

Bazalgette pointed. "Do you see? These are the only ones packed this close to the edge. The rest are more central, and this is the area nearest the Infirmary."

"Ah. Let's get them moved."

It took the pair a few minutes to move enough to find an iron grill in the floor that concealed a drop of around six feet.

With the aid of the arc-lamp, they could make out a tunnel which led off eastwards at the bottom.

Unlike the trapdoor above, the bars were a permanent fixture, set in concrete. Bazalgette determined the easiest way to bypass it was to chip away at the edges where they recessed. Once weakened, the crowbar popped them out, leaving a hole large enough for them to squeeze through.

"There are footholds down here," Bazalgette said with a grin. "They reinforced them with pieces of wooden planking."

"Well, lucky for us that the authorities couldn't find the time to fill it all in then."

"Yes, though I should prefer to check to see our escapees showed such diligence in propping and reinforcing the rest of the tunnel before we go any further."

"That sounds like a plan. I don't relish getting trapped down there in any kind of collapse."

One by earth, Simmons recalled the grim insights from Rosie about the fourth conspirator, Blakelocke. A shiver ran down his spine as he watched Bazalgette descending into the ground, a strange square shaft of light painted on the ceiling above the hole.

Bazalgette shuffled about below, the glow from the arc-lamp growing and fading as he shifted position. After a few minutes, the room lightened, and the makeshift ladder creaked with his return. "Whoever organised that escape knew how to support tunnels," he said, popping his head over the ledge.

"Where did inmates in an Asylum get hold of wood to build pit props?"

"I'm not sure. They seem to be a mixture of bed slats and wall or ceiling panels."

"Interesting, perhaps not so mad after all?"

"Well, it isn't just the insane they put into places like St. Olaves. There have been many cases of people unable to cope with life for short periods then getting lost in the system. If they didn't have friends or relatives to bail them out, they'd leave them to rot. You must have known men in the military traumatised after combat who couldn't manage?"

"Not really, we shot cowards back in my day."

"Surely not?"

Simmons smiled. "Not me personally, but it happened. We live in different times now, I suppose. What with the Martians and the work camps, I saw my fair share. I sat on the precipice for a while myself after my wife died." He sighed, realising he'd said too much.

The room fell into silence. It seemed Bazalgette didn't know how to deal with the revelation. "I'm sorry," he replied after a while, "for your loss."

Simmons turned the sigh into a cough, raising his hand to cover his mouth. "Yes, well let's be making a move, we haven't got all day. Do you want me to go first?"

"No," Bazalgette said, "it would be best for me to lead so I can check the supports. We'll be on hands and knees down there so it won't be easy."

"Off you go then. Let's not keep this Ravenmaster waiting."

Simmons followed a few feet behind as Bazalgette led the way through the rough-hewn dirt tunnel. Improvised wooden props lined the walls at regular intervals supporting the tons of earth above them. As they progressed eastwards, the ground became wet.

Instead of the occasional muddy patches they'd encountered at the start of their journey, now they crawled through inches of standing water.

"Bazalgette," Simmons called forward, "are you sure this is safe?"

"It's only mud. I checked the props as we passed them. They are all sound."

Simmons bit back a retort. *He's a structural engineer, if he doesn't know if it's safe, who would?*

"Very well," he replied at length, continuing their slow progress. *At least we have good light. I wonder what the poor blighters who made this escape route had?*

After half an hour, Bazalgette came to a halt. The tunnel was dry again, and the place hadn't collapsed around their ears. "I think we're through," Bazalgette whispered.

Simmons stretched. His knees and back protested the effort he'd put them through with two loud cracks. Bazalgette disappeared, a dim glow of light lingering in the shaft ahead leading up out of the hellish crawlway. He returned after a few seconds. "There's another grille at this end. I've given it a shove and a good prod with the crowbar, but it appears to be solid."

"So, what next?"

"Not sure," Bazalgette replied, unbuckling the arc-rifle bag he'd dragged along tied to his boot to make travelling with the bulky device a little easier.

Simmons felt a clenching in his gut. "Wait a minute. What are you doing?"

"I thought I might try the arc-rifle, see if that can loosen anything."

"Is that a good idea in such a confined space?"

"Well the bars are iron, so it should draw the arc towards them and contain the reaction as far as I can see."

"And how far is that?"

The quip soared over Bazalgette's head. "What?"

"Never mind," Simmons replied, trying to keep his voice calm, just about managing it. "If you're confident it won't cause us any danger."

"Danger? Nothing to worry about, old chap. I'll get it set up, and with luck, it might produce enough flex in the bar via conduction to crack the housing. Then we can use leverage to force the grille."

"I'll stay down here then shall I?"

"It's probably for the best. In case of anything untoward."

With that, Bazalgette disappeared upward with the rifle. Simmons mused for a moment. *Well, he's a scientist and bright, he wouldn't do anything too dangerous, would he?* Instinct got the better of him, and he pushed forward looking up into the vertical shaft. "Bazalgette—"

An ear-splitting explosion shattered the silence, and a

massive shock-wave knocked him flat onto the tunnel floor. An ominous creaking sounded from behind as dirt rained down around him.

"Bazalgette," he shouted, grabbing the sides of the vertical wall forcing himself to his feet. "Bazalgette, are you all right?" The tunnel remained silent as he thrust his way up the shaft. He reached the top rung and poked his head into a swirling dust storm. One boot lay exposed on the ground, the rest of his friend's body covered in a mixture of grey dust and raw brown earth. Five feet ahead stood a gaping hole where the grille Bazalgette described must once have been. All that remained was a ruin of concrete and plaster where a ragged hole opened out onto the splintered remains of a dust-enshrouded cupboard.

Simmons grabbed the boot and pulled Bazalgette's body from the mound of earth. As his friend's head emerged, he fell into a fit of coughing.

"Are you hurt?" Simmons asked.

Another couple of coughs, then a hoarse voice replied. "No, I'm fine. Just a little winded. It was a touch more energetic than I expected."

"What the hell happened?"

"It was difficult to see much with all the dust. The iron heated in an instant, the arcing between the rods was amazing. They must have expanded faster than the surrounding concrete could absorb and exploded."

"So just as planned then? Nothing for me to worry about?"

"Well—"

"Bloody hell, man. You could have drowned under a sea of dirt."

"Suffocated," Bazalgette said.

"What?"

"I would have suffocated," he said. "Drowning is the process of asphyxiation by inhaling liquid. I would suffocate in a tunnel collapse—" He stopped when he noticed Simmons red-faced glare.

"Are you really going to quibble over semantics? Right here and now?"

"Yes, you are probably correct. This might not be the best time—"

"Damn right this isn't the bloody time. I wonder how you are still alive at all?"

"Well, I took precautions. I was a good five feet from the grille—"

"I don't mean now, I mean in bloody general," Simmons' eyes were wide with disbelief. "You play with high voltage electrics, and God only knows what other dangerous compounds. How the hell have you survived this long? Everything around you seems to explode."

"It's not the voltage—"

"If you tell me it's amperage, I'll bloody swing for you."

Bazalgette remained silent. Simmons could see he was biting his tongue.

"Perhaps we should make our way through the *bloody great hole* I blew in the wall before anything else—"

A loud thump echoed from below, and dust particles leapt into the air around the edge of the vertical shaft. They both watched the lazy motes drift for a second. Simmons hung his head in disbelief. A few dull rumbles followed along with accompanying tremors through the packed earth.

"Collapses," Bazalgette finished.

They dragged themselves through the hole into a mess of splintered furniture. The explosion had launched the wooden cupboard, that stood before the grill, right across the shabby room. It looked to have been a hospital ward, but the furnishings were old, rusted and rotten. Six beds lay scattered around along with mouldy mattresses strewn in the corner. A simple desk took pride of place before them with a doorway beside it.

The building smelled of mildew and neglect mixed with the dry powdered dust from their extravagant entrance. Barred windows lined the wall on the left. Shafts of dusty light pierced the broken shutters where a few wooden slats had fallen free.

Bazalgette remained a dirty grey colour, despite trying his best to brush it from his coat. Instead, he made a cloud of the fine particles which engulfed him, leading to yet more sneezing and coughing.

Simmons dusted off his clothes, checking his rifle for any problems. Content that the weapon was undamaged, he shouldered it and crossed the room past broken chairs towards the door.

Bazalgette packed the dirt-encrusted arc-rifle back into its makeshift case. "Perhaps I'll leave it until I've had time to get it cleaned up."

"Yes, that might be for the best," Simmons said. His voice had a weary, resigned tone, which he didn't like. Bazalgette's eyes darted away when he looked his way. *Damn, why do I feel like I just kicked a puppy?*

"Look, Bazalgette. I didn't mean to be so harsh back there. It's—"

"No, you're right. I can get a little distracted and sometimes act before thinking through all the consequences. It was too dangerous doing what I did while you were still in the tunnel. You could have... *drowned*."

Simmons stifled a laugh. "What am I to do with you? I've dragged you into this mess and now berate you for having ideas on how to help."

"I'll be more careful, Simmons. Sorry about—"

"Don't go there. It's not your fault. You've killed a man because of me."

"Yes, but he would have shot you, and Rosie. No doubt I would have been soon after if he'd had the chance."

"That's true. Let's find the information we came here for."

Simmons turned the handle and found the door opened into a long hallway. Several others lined the corridor, some of them were open into similar rooms. At the far end stood a pair of oversized double-doors.

Faded paint fell away in thick flakes with a strong odour of damp and decay. A lot of the furniture was rotting, and when tested, it crunched like dry paper. Splintered wooden panels and picture frames lay cracked on the scratched tiled floors. Apart from their soft footsteps and the low hum from the arc-lamp, there wasn't a sound.

They continued through the eerie silence. Elongated shadows grew and shifted as they travelled along the corridor. Patches of pale green paint showed in bright squares where photographs once lined the walls. They now stood conspicuous against the dull grey of the wall after years of exposure to the elements.

Simmons tried the handle on the double-doors, hoping they too would open without resistance but found them locked. They were heavy with a large circular window at eye level. It was intact but opaque from dust and grime. Simmons peered through, trying to make out what lay beyond, but it was too dark on the other side. He rubbed at the dirty glass, his gloved fingers clearing a small spot.

There was a flash of light from outside, bright enough to see, but the dirt obscured any detail. It looked like rays of sunlight cutting through the grimy darkness, a voice followed it.

"Bertie, is that you?" It was a child, a young girl if he wasn't mistaken. He raised one finger to his lips as he motioned for Bazalgette to move back.

The girl approached, singing something as her footsteps skipped along the tiled hallway. "Rachel, Rupert, is that you in there?"

She stopped outside. As Simmons stared at Bazalgette, unsure what to do, a quiet rasping noise accompanied the slow turning of the handle.

≈

It pushed down and held there for a few seconds. A soft rattle of the door, then a second, stronger shake. "Huh, not in there," the girl said with a tone of disappointment. The handle sprang upright with a loud clack. A slight pause, then skipping and the singsong voice receded. "Bertie, Rachel, you'll soon see, you can't hide that long from me."

Simmons hadn't realised he'd been holding his breath until he heard Bazalgette exhale beside him. He looked over at his friend. "What was that?"

"A young girl at play?"

"In an abandoned asylum?"

"Maybe she discovered a way in somewhere with her friends, and they are playing hide-and-seek."

"Doesn't that seem a little strange, with the birds being so territorial? If they are enough to scare away two sets of gangs, what are children doing here?"

"When you put it like that, I'm not sure," Bazalgette replied.

"Found you. Oh."

Simmons spun to find a small figure peeking around a door on the corridor wall behind them. The girl looked about ten-years-old, perhaps younger. She wore a simple short-sleeved green dress down to her knees, showing her dirt-stained legs and filthy bare feet. Her hair was a shoulder-length tangle of black and stuck out at odd angles as if it hadn't seen a brush in months. She waited, surprise painted across her grimy features, but not an ounce of fear in her dark eyes.

"You're not Bertie or Rachel," she said. "Who are you?"

Bazalgette turned to the young girl. "I'm Nathaniel, and this chap is Mr Simmons. What's your name?"

The girl squinted at the two men. "Lily."

"Hello, Lily. What are you doing here?"

"Playing."

"With your friends? Bertie and Rachel?"

"That's right. Do you know them too? Have you come to play with us?"

Bazalgette shook his head. "No, we're looking for someone called the Ravenmaster. Have you heard of him?"

The girl peered back, a frown creasing her young forehead. "Do you mean father? Some people call him that, but it's not his real name."

"Father?" Bazalgette said, shock clear in his voice. "So, you live here?"

She beamed him a smile. "Yes, this is my house."

"So, who else lives here?"

"There's father, Bertie, Rachel, Carrie-Anne, Rupert, Geoffrey, Alice—"

"So quite a few of you?" Bazalgette asked.

"Lots, I can't remember all their names. Not all of them have them yet."

Bazalgette looked a little confused. "So these are your brothers and sisters?"

"No, silly," the girl replied, "they're my friends. We play together all the time. Oh and there's Ravenna - but she doesn't join in much, she likes to watch, and she looks out for all of us, keeps everyone safe."

Simmons crossed to where his friend was standing. "Lily, you mentioned about your father. He's sometimes called the Ravenmaster?"

"That's right," the girl replied. "I'm not allowed to say his real name. Ravenna said it was dangerous."

"So where is he now?" Simmons asked.

"Oh, he'll be in his lab-ora..." Lily struggled with the word. "Lab-rat-or... La-boro-torium." A satisfied grin crossed her face. "He spends most of his time there. That's when I play. Are you sure you wouldn't like to join in, you could be my friends too."

Bazalgette smiled at her. "That would be lovely Lily, but we need to speak with your father rather urgently. Could you take us to see him, please? Then perhaps you could find us later?"

"All right," she replied, a big smile spreading across her face again, "follow me."

She led them back into the room from which she'd emerged. The door was metal, strips of peeling white paint and three heavy security bolts lined the outer side. Inside, the filthy grey padding hung from the walls, rotten, torn and damp. In the far corner, the wall was bare brick which had fallen away, leaving a small hole.

Lily squeezed through the gap then stuck her head through to peer back at them. "Can you fit? You look too fat to get through."

Bazalgette laughed. "Yes, I suppose we are a little large for that. Let me check."

He bent to inspect the bricks around the opening and soon found some loose enough to remove. With the help of his crowbar, he enlarged the hole allowing both men to crawl out to the hallway. Lily skipped on ahead, past the locked double-doors, oblivious to the discussions of her two new friends.

"So we follow her to her father and hope he is this Raven-master then?" Simmons asked.

"I suppose so, who better to introduce us?"

Simmons shrugged, and they quickened their pace to catch up with the Ravenmaster's daughter.

18

Lily led them through the maze of dark corridors. The gloom was broken only by occasional gleaming rays from cracks in the ill-fitting window shutters.

The young girl skipped and sang throughout the journey. She spoke of her friends and how they played together. As far as Simmons could tell, there was no sign of anyone else passing through the old abandoned hallways of the asylum.

Their footfalls echoed through the place which held a dry but musty smell. Lily knew it inside-out, able to name every room and where each corridor led. She told them of particular areas of interest as they passed, most of them were her friends' favourite hiding spots, the places she always searched first.

"Here we are," she said at the top of an ornate staircase. "Father's study and workshop are through there." She indicated a set of double-doors before them.

"And should we just knock and enter?" Simmons asked the girl.

"Oh no," she replied. "I'll let him know you are here. Come on." She skipped over to the doors and flung them open with dramatic flair.

"I'm home," she called ahead, walking through the opening, leaving them to bounce from the walls. "Father, I've found some new friends, and they want to speak with you."

Floor-to-ceiling cabinets lined the office. Each housed an extensive collection of leather-bound volumes, set behind a protective layer of glass. A solid wooden desk sat in the middle of the room, several books lay piled on it, stacked and ready to compare notes between them.

A figure turned towards them, affixing something to his face. Lily's father was a tall man, a little over six feet, though it was difficult to tell due to the dark hooded robe he wore. A leathery beak of considerable length protruded from the hood. The table lamps lit enough to show an old-style plague-doctors mask. Constructed of black leather, with brass edgings and circles of light reflecting from the glass eye-sockets, it made him look like a strange bipedal bird. *Fitting*, Simmons thought.

Light reflected in the glassy orbs as his view shifted between Simmons and Bazalgette. The thick stitching along the beak was precise in its style and spacing. A gentle voice issued from the figure, hardly muffled by the leather mask. "My daughter forgets that I prefer a little more notice before receiving visitors. She can be somewhat dramatic." He spoke with a down-to-earth, but cultured tone. A man of learning, but not of the gentry.

"Sorry if we are interrupting anything," Simmons said. "We wished to talk with you, presuming you are The Ravenmaster?"

"No, it is fine. Please forgive me, I don't receive many visitors. Lily dear, you should go play. I'm sure these two gentlemen and I shall be awhile in discussion."

"But what will I do, father? Without my new friends, there isn't anyone to play with."

The beaked mask tilted and held itself at an odd angle for a few seconds as if waiting for something. The girl shuffled her feet looking downward. Her features scrunched up in a mixture of thought and petulance. The room fell silent, and she seemed to look in every direction but at her father. With a soft tone, he prompted. "Lily?"

She scuffed her left foot on the thick rug while trying to

seem casual as she swung it back and forth. "All right," she said, resigned to her fate. "I'll talk to her if I must?"

"You know there isn't anything you *must* do," her father replied in the same low, calm voice. "There are just things you should and should not do. You are old enough to understand the difference, and it is up to you to choose the path to follow." He paused, waiting for the young girl to decide.

When she spoke the negativity had left her. "You are right, father. I shall go to see Ravenna. She'll teach me lots of new and wonderful things, and I will enjoy it as much as playing with any of my friends." She looked up, and a grin crept across her tiny features. "Maybe we'll talk about the taint again." With that, she turned and skipped out the way they had entered.

"Did you forget something, Lily?"

She stopped at the doors, her face a picture of demure innocence, a huge smile, eyes wide. "Goodbye, Simmons. Goodbye, Bazalgette." She executed a precise curtsey and pulled the double-doors shut behind her as she backed out into the hallway before any of them had the chance to reply.

"Manners maketh man," her father said. "Now how can I help you two gentlemen?"

Simmons inspected the Ravenmaster. He seemed an ordinary enough fellow if you ignored the birdlike mask. "We hear you might know how to get us into The Tower and the location of the Black Cells."

"The Tower of London is the most secure prison in the realm," he replied. "Well, it was before the invasion. Why should I divulge its secrets to you?"

"Because the future of the Empire is at stake," Simmons said.

"How do you come to that conclusion?"

"There is a man named Dent being held in the Black Cells. He's a skilled watchmaker, and the Black Guard are trying to use him to recreate his father's work on a very intricate time-piece. This is something that could tip the balance even further in their favour and bring more than just curfews to the streets of London, but a complete military lockdown."

Simmons caught the man's eyes through the mask, his voice grave. "Please tell me you harbour no love for the Black Guard and their masters."

The Ravenmaster, silent for a moment, shook his head. "No, they killed the last of the yeoman warders when they seized control of the Tower. I saw many good friends fall that day, but I was powerless to stop it from happening. I swore I would do whatever it took to repay them in kind."

Simmons smiled and with a conspiratorial lowering of his voice asked. "Perhaps that day is today?"

"Perhaps it is."

"You're saying there is no way to get to the Black Cells via the main Tower courtyard?" Simmons said.

The Ravenmaster looked him in the eye. "There's a full garrison of the Black Guard stationed there, with elaborate alarm systems. You'd never make it through without being detected."

"So is there no other way? No secret door always kept locked, and you know where the key is? An unknown entrance, something simple for once?"

The Ravenmaster shook his head, the beak on his plague mask wobbled almost comically, but Simmons wasn't in the mood for humour. They had talked for thirty minutes, discussing options and details of the Tower and its grounds.

"What about the sluice gates leading to the cistern?" Bazalgette said, breaking his five-minute silence, lost in thought. "There must be a connection to the main water outlet, and from your description of the entrance to the cells, it would appear to be in the same vicinity."

"You mean the water storage area?" the Ravenmaster asked.

"Yes. The inflow comes from here," Bazalgette said, pointing to the mass of hand-drawn maps he'd pulled from his satchel, now laying on the desk. "This is where the water enters the Tower grounds and into the collection area in the cistern."

Simmons sat up, having slouched somewhat in the uncomfortable chair. "Could we get in through there?"

"No, it's far too small," his friend answered. "The inflow enters through a wide pipe but then reduces in diameter building pressure to fill the cistern—the large water container."

"I know what a damned cistern is." Simmons let out a deep sigh. "Right, so where does this leave us? Why is this inflow so important?"

"Ah," Bazalgette said. "It's not the inflow I'm interested in." Looking towards the Ravenmaster, he continued, "Though there might be mileage in..."

Simmons waited for the conclusion, which he realised would not be forthcoming. Bazalgette had a habit of doing this, trailing off in the middle of a sentence when another idea struck him.

"Yes," Bazalgette continued, "Yes. If we can devise a means to drain the cistern and stop it refilling, then the outflow would empty. But that would need a pressure release to open the sluices—" He looked up realising that his voice was the only sound in the room. "There may be a way to gain entrance through the outflow."

"Excellent," Simmons said, "though why do I feel there's a 'but' coming?"

"They secured all the old outflows when my grandfather built the new deep sewers. If I remember this one has a series of locked gates."

"There are three gates." The two men looked to the Ravenmaster. "Each sealed with high-security locks."

"And you know this how?" Simmons asked.

"I was one of the team that oversaw the securing of those sewers back in 1865."

Simmons tilted his head, smiling. "Ah. So what else can you tell us about these locks?"

"Only they were the best that money could buy. It wouldn't

surprise me to find them in the same condition as when they installed them, even after being submerged for the last thirty years. There is more," the Ravenmaster added, "but it is both good and bad."

Simmons looked back up. "Out with it, man."

The Ravenmaster reached under his long jacket and pulled out a strong but ornate chain from around his neck. The metal was a dull grey with three ornate keys attached.

"Those are the keys to the locks," Bazalgette said, the wonder no secret in his voice.

"Aye," the Ravenmaster said. "It was my duty, and I was honour-bound to keep them safe. I never thought there would come a time when the old words would ring true."

Bazalgette reached out towards the chain, "May I?"

The Ravenmaster nodded as the thick metal links slid through his fingers.

"It's so light," Bazalgette said his eyes widening. "I can't believe how light this is. Simmons, you have got to feel this."

Simmons raised a hand to stall his friend. "What did you mean about the old words?" he said, looking back to the masked figure behind the desk.

"You will have heard it," he replied. "If ever the ravens are lost or shall abandon the Tower of London, the crown shall fall and Britain with it."

"Yes, even I know that fairy tale, and I've lived most of my life out of the country."

"It's no fairy tale, Mr Simmons. Even during the invasion, the ravens remained within the Tower grounds. It wasn't until the war was over, when the Black Guard took control, that they left. Every single one. I was Ravenmaster then, tasked to care for the birds, to see to their needs and whims. They are incredibly intelligent creatures, and they have something special about them, a mystique of their own with distinct personalities. Some are playful, others serious, and then there's Ravenna. She controls the other ravens, and all the other birds that make London their home roost."

Bazalgette's eyes widened. "Ravenna? Ravenna is a raven?"

"Not just a raven, Mr Bazalgette, she is *the* raven. Brood-mother to them all."

"But that means—Oh."

Simmons glanced towards Bazalgette, a question unsaid but painted across his anxious face.

"Don't you see, Simmons? It's Lily."

"What about her?"

"All her friends she plays with, the names are other birds, and Ravenna doesn't play, she teaches." Bazalgette looked at the man behind the desk. "She can understand them can't she?"

The Ravenmaster inclined his head with a slight nod.

"What?" Simmons asked.

"It's her," Bazalgette said, he was almost bouncing with excitement. "Lily is the Ravenmaster. She understands them, speaks to them, plays with them."

"And they do what she asks," Simmons finished. "She tells them to play, and so they play."

"Yes, and Ravenna teaches her how to do it all, through games, something a young girl can understand. That's it, isn't it?" Bazalgette turned to face the man in the beaked mask. "So what is your role in all this? Who *are* you?"

The man reached up and unbuckled the plague mask, exposing a much older looking face than Simmons had expected. Liver spots ran down the left side of his wrinkled and blotchy skin between his eye and jawline. He reached out to the chair and collapsed into it.

"Are you all right?" Bazalgette asked, reaching out to steady the suddenly frail-looking figure.

"Yes, I'll be fine. I'm tired, and this pretence of youth drains me, but Lily is not yet ready to look after herself." He pushed his back into the chair, rolling his shoulders in what seemed a painful movement.

"As to your question, Mr Bazalgette, I am who I said I was, a yeoman warden of the Tower. Skaife was my name, and as a younger man, they tasked me with looking after the ravens." He sighed. "Nobody else wanted the job. The man who handed me the title of Ravenmaster told me this. 'Lad, I don't envy you this task. They're vicious little brutes who take joy in playing tricks on folk. Don't take your eyes off them or they will be up to mischief, or will have your eye out if they take a particular dislike to you.' It seemed he was taking it all too seriously and just didn't enjoy the task. I loved it, and the birds, well they seemed to like me after I realised not to suffer any nonsense from them."

"What about Lily?" Bazalgette asked. "I take it she isn't really your daughter?"

"No. Ravenna led me to her when I escaped from that bloodbath in the Tower. She was in a half-submerged ruin on the south bank. God knows how long she had been there. I found her crumpled in a heap of collapsed timbers amidst the most incredible sight I have ever seen."

He paused for a moment, taking a deep breath before continuing. "A ring of dead rats. Hundreds of the little sods, blood staining the floor around their remains. She looked so tiny, weak and pale. At first, I thought she was dead for sure, but Ravenna croaked at me. That's what they do when they want your attention. She made me inspect the body."

Skaife's eye glistened with moisture, and he took a second to wipe it dry before continuing. "As I got closer, I saw black feathers among the rat carcasses, and then I saw all the dead birds. There were crows, bloodshrieks and razorbills, their mangled bodies lying amongst the rats, and stood around the girl's body, four great ravens. Injured, but still alive. The birds had protected this little girl from all these rats, a full-on swarm. When I reached her, she was still breathing. Dried blood caked her face, and there were crumbs around her mouth and in her hair. They'd fed her blood and biscuits."

"Blood and biscuits?" Bazalgette asked as Skaife paused.

"Yes, it's what I used to feed them in the Tower. They wouldn't eat the biscuit on its own, much too bland for their refined pallets. So I mixed it with blood when we didn't have enough raw meat for them, and they wolfed it down. They must have been hoarding them somewhere and then brought them to feed the girl. Must have found a way of getting her water too, not sure how, but she seemed to have been there a while from the look of the surroundings. Anyway, Ravenna and the other ravens had a big conversation croaking and cawing, and then the others left. I carried the girl, following Ravenna until she brought me here. And here we've stayed, almost four years."

Skaife leaned back and exhaled. The noise rattled in his throat, and he coughed, covering his mouth with his sleeve. He looked the part of a tired old man now.

"So we have the keys," Simmons said. "That I presume was the good news. What was the bad you mentioned?"

"The sewer outlet flooded after the war. The Thames has risen so much since then. You'll never get in."

"About that," Bazalgette said in a way that Simmons knew was begging for a dramatic revelation. He had a knack for making the ordinary into a spectacle. "The outlet may still be accessible at low tide. If, as I mentioned earlier, we can block the inflow. There should be enough airspace in the outflow for us to get through, and with the keys, it should be a simple matter of waiting for low tide."

Skaife smiled. "It's a little more tricky than just putting the keys in and turning them. There's an order to follow, and if it's not done in the correct order, then the locks will seal, permanently."

"Typical," Simmons said. There had to be something else to make it more complicated than it needed to be.

Maybe, when all this was over, he could head back to India. Life had been much simpler out there. His hardest decisions revolved around where to take afternoon tea or whether to have whisky or port after dinner. Simmons longed for the joy of simple choices again. Which type of biscuit to have with his tea, and if he could get away with dunking it in his cup as he'd seen the enlisted men do.

One day all that will be mine again.

19

The hull of Isaac's boat scraped as he poled it alongside the wall on the north bank of the Thames. It was an hour after midnight, and the fog was thick, swirling around the three densely wrapped men like a sinuous living entity. Simmons sat with Isaac at the stern while Bazalgette leaned forward at the prow scanning through the darkness with the arc-lamp's intense beam.

They had spent the last few days at St Olaves, drawing up their plans. Bazalgette had pored over the forecasts of the tidal flows of the Thames to calculate when the waters would be at their lowest. When he wasn't doing that, he was babbling on about volumetric pressure, fluid dynamics and other such things that went way over Simmons' head.

Bazalgette's plan for blocking the cistern inlet had been brilliant in its simplicity. After hours of searching for the correct pipes, it only took a few minutes to plug them with waxed cloth, ramming it in and securing with sewer mud. Well, Simmons had thought it was mud, and didn't want to consider any other alternative.

"There," Bazalgette said, pointing the intense beam at a section of wall.

Simmons moved forward. The top of an arch of stone stood

a few feet above the filthy river water. "We're getting in through there?"

"There are another fifty minutes before we reach low tide."

"Will it make that much difference?"

Bazalgette pointed up twenty feet above them. "The tide reaches the top of this wall at high tide, and it drops rapidly too."

"Crikey, I'd not thought it dropped that far."

Isaac turned to Simmons. "Yeah, there are areas on the south bank where the water sits above ground level even at low tide. Those places are submerged once the tide rolls in. Makes for interesting currents and navigation."

"By my calculations," Bazalgette said. "I'd expect another three to five feet before the hour is out. Then we'll have our work cut out to get in and back out before it rises again."

"How long do we have?" Simmons asked.

"I wouldn't want to leave it over two hours. The quicker, the better."

They waited as Bazalgette suggested. The water level had dropped, and the metal gate seemed to thrust itself upward from below the waves as the tide continued outward.

"This will be about as good as it gets," Bazalgette said motioning at the murky waterline. Simmons followed his friends gaze towards the base of the gateway as the red-tinged Thames lapped against the wall and between the bars.

"Are you sure it's safe?"

"Yes, the mud isn't usually too thick. We could get Isaac to check if that would reassure you?"

"Well, it might be prudent, don't you think?"

Isaac approached with the long pole he used for manoeuvring his vessel. "Here," he said, pushing it into the dark waters. "Mister Bazalgette's right. It won't be deep." It dipped under the waterline and stopped as it met the mud. Isaac leaned his weight onto it, and the wooden shaft descended a short way before meeting more solid resistance. "There you go," he continued releasing the pole with a subtle twist of his wrist and pulled it back out showing six inches of thick brown sludge.

"Fair enough," Simmons said, looking to Bazalgette. "We best be off then."

Isaac steadied the vessel near the wall while Bazalgette and Simmons dropped into the freezing river with two quiet splashes.

The water reached halfway up Simmons' boots, and he felt the slick mud below sliding around his sole and heel, gripping his foot. It took a moment to steady himself before he tried to cover the few feet to the entry point they needed to breach. After three failed attempts, his boot pulled free with a thick slurp from the muddy river bed before splashing down ahead of him, a little stronger than he'd intended.

Bazalgette stood at the wall watching him. Was that chastisement in his eyes? Simmons awaited the pithy comment about keeping quiet, but it didn't come.

"If you twist before lifting, it's much easier. Try to get onto the ball of your foot."

He transferred his weight forward, trying what his friend had suggested, and found his boot lift from the riverbed with much less effort.

"There you go," Bazalgette said, smiling at him. "It's a technique you learn after you've had more than your fair share of mud baths."

"Sounds like you're speaking from experience."

"Hmm." Bazalgette returned his attention to the gateway. He searched his pocket and pulled out the metal chain, which was the same dull grey even under the intense glare from the arc-lamp. Three keys and three locks as the Ravenmaster had described. Bazalgette turned them in the order Skaife had instructed. A metallic thunk sounded as the mechanism activated and thick steel bars retracted into the walls. The solid gate swung inwards as if newly installed rather than having been underwater for years.

They proceeded through the arched tunnel of brick and sludge. The water level dropped to ankle height as they stepped into the construction and was little more than a trickle.

"Seems blocking the inflow did the job," Simmons said as he turned to push the heavy gate closed behind them.

"We need to move swiftly if we are to get out this way before the tide turns." The arc-lamp lit the damp passageway as water dripped from walls and ceiling with soft splashes into the stream they trudged through.

"Was this constructed at the same time as the sewer systems?"

"Yes," Bazalgette said. "It's the same brickwork they used, apart from the area around the grates."

As they approached the next grate, Simmons thought he detected less discolouration where the mechanism recessed into the tunnel wall. "Are you sure you have the sequence memorised?" he asked as Bazalgette pulled the keyring from his coat.

"Yes," his friend said. "It's only two digits to recall in three sequences."

Simmons felt chagrined but chose not to show it. It had been a stupid question. Bazalgette had often proved that his memory was incredible.

Through the shifting grid of shadows created by the current grate, the tunnel ahead twisted out of sight. Simmons waited, suppressing the desire to tap his foot, while Bazalgette turned the keys in the mechanism.

The smell was a little less pungent now. Either it was diminishing as they continued further from the river, or he was becoming accustomed to the life of a sewer dweller. That it had come to this, wading through the muddy waters of other people's filth. The bars holding the grate in place slid back with a clunk.

"Just one more to go," Bazalgette said, voice eager with excitement.

"Excellent," Simmons replied, trying for enthusiasm to make up for his earlier brusqueness.

They rounded the corner in the tunnel, losing sight of the

dim glow from the distant entry point. The floor below became rougher and ridged underfoot. After a short while, the strain in his calf muscles told Simmons they were on a slight incline. They slowed as they neared the final grate and he tapped Bazalgette on the shoulder.

"What layout are we expecting ahead?"

"The Ravenmaster wasn't clear. It's not somewhere he frequented, but I expect we shall emerge into a holding tank area. There should normally be overspill from the inlet that washes everything through from the cistern, and we will have a few sluice-gates to bypass."

"Sluice-gates?"

"Yes, large wooden sections with rubber seals around them that stop backflow." Bazalgette brows creased as he fought for the right words. "Erm, they don't allow the sewage that has gone through to get back in. As the Thames retreats at low tide, the pressure inside the system is greater than outside, and so it can flow through the sluice. But when it returns, the water forces the sluices closed. Ingenious really."

Simmons chuckled. Bazalgette had been so careful in phrasing his answer. "So it stops all the... *waste* coming back into the cleaner areas?"

Bazalgette beamed at him. "That's it. Simple but effective."

"So the next question is, how do we get past?"

"Ah, brute force, I'm afraid."

"Brute force?"

"Well, that and plenty of leverage."

It took half an hour to open the sluice-gate. Most of that was to satisfy Bazalgette that the wedge was secure if they needed to get out in a hurry. Even with that done, it was still a squeeze pushing past the massive section of dark-stained oak. The flow of water was a touch stronger once it opened though only enough to nudge it a few inches before it thudded back against the wooden chock.

The last grate surrendered to the final key combination, and they were into the inner workings of the Tower of London. They stood in a collection area where the waste outlets emptied.

A rusted ladder led up to floor level from the far side of the pool and pipes entered the room, seemingly at random. They ended in the central vat, some form of water processing Simmons thought. Grilled metal walkways, edged with steel barriers, lined the vast chamber, and across from them was a single doorway. The exit was an impenetrable-looking grey monstrosity: seven feet in height and half-again as wide as a typical door.

As Bazalgette crossed to inspect it, and a soft click sounded as it swung inwards.

"What do you know?" Bazalgette said, surprise evident in his tone. "Unlocked."

"Isn't that strange?"

The engineer glanced over his shoulder. "Well, I don't think they expected to have to lock anyone in here, so not too unusual. Maybe it's just the element of luck we need?"

Not convinced, but unwilling to get into a further debate over it, Simmons crossed the gantry to peer out onto a dark stone cut stairway leading both up and down.

He listened for a few seconds at the edge of the stair. Satisfied they weren't about to walk straight into members of the Black Guard patrolling outside, he motioned down the stairs.

As Bazalgette took the lead with the arc-lamp lighting their way through the blackness, Simmons pulled the Mauser from his coat and checked the magazine. The time he'd taken to make sure it was in good shape, during their stay in the Infirmary, had been well worthwhile. He held it low as he proceeded with slow, precise footsteps.

The stairwell descended and turned left ninety degrees every twenty steps. They were on their fourth full rotation when Bazalgette stopped. The light dimmed, and the arc-lamp dropped to a quiet hum.

"I think I heard something below," Bazalgette said, his voice a hoarse whisper.

"Turn off the lamp."

The stairs plunged into blackness. They waited. The only sound - Bazalgette's slow breathing two steps below him. As his eyes adjusted, a faint glow emerged, almost indistinguishable, but enough to show the reflected light from below. A scraping noise echoed to them, followed by a murmur of conversation.

"Let me take the lead," Simmons whispered. He made his way past moving towards the next turn of the stairwell. "Oh," he added, "and whatever you do, make sure you secure your equipment. This isn't the time for a spanner to go tumbling down there."

As he stopped at the corner, he held his hand up to his friend, hoping he'd recognise the universal signal to wait there. Peering down, the light was stronger, but there were still a few more turns of the stairs below them. He beckoned Bazalgette forward and pointed at his position on the stair then moved with deft footsteps down to the next corner.

There were voices ahead, the back and forth of idle conversation, guard chatter. Yes, definitely the sound of two guards trying to kill time until someone relieved them.

He continued, moving to the next corner while Bazalgette took his previous position. After a few turns, the bottom of the stairs opened out into a small room illuminated by at least one lantern. The faint smell of smoke drifted past, reminding him of his old paraffin lamp.

"It's bloody freezing," said a gruff voice from within. "How can you stand it, you're not even wearing a jacket?"

"It's not that bad, you soft git. Anyhow, in or out?"

A pause and then a grumbled reply "Call. Two pairs, jacks and sixes."

"Oh, sorry my friend, but that won't cut the mustard. Three tens."

"Whoa. Wait a minute. Two pair beats three of a kind, don't it?"

"Really? You're having a laugh, mate. One pair, two pairs,

three cards, straight. As it has always been. Now stop your belly-aching and cough up."

Simmons moved closer, hugging the wall for a clearer view into the room. Two guards sat either side of a small folding table, their rifles leaning against the wall behind them. He grasped the opportunity, striding in with his pistol aimed at them.

"Good morning, gentlemen," he said. The men reached for their weapons before the realisation struck them of the pistol pointed at them.

"Oh, I wouldn't do that if I were you. Now we can do this the easy way, or the hard way. The easy way entails you being bound and locked in a cell until someone misses you at the next guard change. While the hard way..." He paused. "Well, let's just say you won't enjoy the hard way."

They stared at him, their faces a rictus of loathing. Both wore Black Guard uniforms, and Simmons pointed to the one wrapped in his greatcoat. "You, sit on the floor there," he indicated a spot a few feet in front of the table, away from the rifles. "Hands behind your back. And you, my good friend," this time gesturing to the guard in his shirt, "you can join him, back to back."

"You'll regret this," the second guard said through gritted teeth, eyes narrow. He was a little older and slighter of build.

"Not as much as you, if you don't shut up."

The man manoeuvred himself into the requested position. His eyes flitted around the room, looking for something, any advantage he could use. Simmons repositioned himself to stand ahead of the second guard. The one in the coat had resigned himself to captivity, and he wouldn't be a problem.

"Now from here," Simmons said with the pistol aimed at the guard's chest, "the round will pass right through you and into your colleague. So, let's be sensible, and no-one needs to get hurt."

The older man laughed and spat to the side, a smile growing across his face. "And what next? How do you expect to tie us while keeping that gun in our faces? That'll be a tricky and dangerous manoeuvre, won't it?"

"Only if he was alone," Bazalgette replied, stepping into the room. A crackle of blue sparks and a deep hum issued from the arc-rifle focused on the two captives.

The smile dropped from the short man's face.

≈

It took little to convince the younger guard to give up the keys to Dent's cell. His older colleague cursed and threatened him until Simmons applied a dose of percussive therapy. With the senior man slumped unconscious, the other spilt everything he knew.

Dent was in the last of five cells that led from the guard-room. Simmons pulled the door open a crack into a dark interior with several tarps laid over the floor. An array of metallic components sat on them, clockwork, gears and various lengths of wire. Pushing further inwards, he saw movement from a simple cot at the far side of the cell. A man lay huddled beneath two threadbare grey blankets on the hard stone—his clothing, once elegant, now worn with rips and loose stitching.

"What is it? It's not ready, it's the middle of the night," the man said, his voice slurred from recent sleep.

"Mister Dent?" Simmons asked.

"Yes? What's going on?" His eyes darted between the two men in his cell. "Who are you?"

"We're here to free you from this place, Mr Dent," Bazalgette said, taking a step further into the cold room.

"But. The guards?"

"They won't be a problem," Simmons said. "Come on. Time is short, collect anything you can't live without and let's be going."

Dent looked up from the filthy cot. "I can't leave."

"What do you mean?" Simmons asked. "Don't you understand, we're here to rescue you, to get you out of this Godforsaken hole."

"Simmons," said Bazalgette, his voice was distant. "Look at his legs."

Dent pulled the damp woollen blankets aside, exposing the ruined remains of his lower legs. They both bent at an obscene angle below his knees. It was more severe than the worst-case of rickets or deformity Simmons had encountered in all his time in the subcontinent.

"They broke them," Dent said, "when I refused to co-operate. Said I didn't need them for what I had to do."

"And they didn't splint them?" Bazalgette's face was a mask of horror.

"No, they left them to heal like this. Told me that if there were a next time, they'd take an axe to them."

"Damn it. What now?" Simmons kicked the wooden door.

"We carry him," Bazalgette said matter-of-factly. "Between us, we can get him out of here."

Simmons snorted. "It's impractical, he'll slow us down, and what would we do if we encountered any more guards?"

"We can't just leave him here. Look how he's suffered already."

"Well we can't take him, so what do you suggest?"

"Mr Bazalgette?" Dent's voice, like his frame, was frail. "Listen to him, he's right. I'd only slow you down."

"But—"

"No, please listen. I have important information that needs to get out of here. If the Black Guard tear it from me, then all is lost."

"I'm sorry Bazalgette, it's the only way," Simmons said.

Bazalgette stared at his feet unwilling or unable in that moment to meet the gaze of either Dent or Simmons.

"Who are you? Why should I trust you?" Dent said. "You might be from them trying to trick me into telling what I know."

Simmons walked further into the cell. "A man who told us of your father, and his work as a Horologist, sent us. He revealed secrets that only he knew and that you tried to follow but didn't fully understand."

"Who?"

"He's a strange fellow. His name is Josiah."

"What?" Dent asked, his face ashen. "Josiah is alive?"

"Well, yes," Simmons said, "he said was a Horologist like your father. You know him?"

"Yes," Dent said, a catch in his voice. "He's my brother."

"Brother?" Simmons said, turning to Bazalgette. "Why didn't he say?"

"I'm not sure, perhaps..." Bazalgette shook his head. "I have no idea."

Dent was suddenly more animated. "What did he tell you of father's work?"

"That it was to do with the schematics for the original pocket watches," Simmons said. "And he thought you were making copies."

"Yes, that's what they wanted me to do. The Black Guard needed them, but I realised they'd know if I was lying, so I made one, but it's inferior—by design. I limited the mechanism so it will only work for a short period and then require a long time to recharge." Dent's eyes dropped to his ruined legs. "It was my miserable attempt at defiance."

"How long have you been here?" Bazalgette asked.

Dent's brow furrowed. "Around six months, as far as I can tell. They marched into my store and dragged me off on charges of treason."

"And how many of these watches have you made for them?" Simmons asked.

"Six. One per month. It's as slow as I can make it seem reasonable, but they're finding it harder to locate power sources."

"Power sources?" Simmons asked.

"Yes, the power comes from certain... artefacts. It's an electrical component of some form, but nobody fully understands it. I believe they're from the remains of the alien fighting machines, from the war."

Simmons leaned back against the cell wall. "How are the Black Guard getting hold of these components?"

"They have caches of alien salvage. The government organised the dismantling and collection of it all when the Martians died. Didn't want it falling into the wrong hands."

"All right," Simmons continued. "Let's take a step backwards. Why did you think Josiah was dead?"

"It was during the invasion when the aliens were approaching London. We were at home, and when they hit the house, it collapsed around us. Josiah and I were in the cellar. A beam gave way, and the whole roof came down, Josiah pushed me back, but he..." Dent let out a long sigh, shaking his head. When he raised his view, his eyes held a haunted look. "Well, I thought he must be dead. Everyone else died in that collapse except me."

"Didn't you check?"

"Not at the time—I ran. Then I got caught up with the others fleeing their homes. The Martians doused the whole neighbourhood with the Black Smoke and then fires rampaged. When I made it back a few days later, there was nothing left but charred remains."

"Fair enough," Simmons said. "I can see why you thought as you did. Your brother also mentioned the ArcAngel project or network and to cut a long story short, he thinks one of them—"

"Gabriel," Bazalgette interjected.

"Yes, that one, possibly Gabriel, received an original timepiece from the Empress. And that it might somehow have survived when the airship crashed. Is that feasible?"

Dent grunted as he tried to shift his position to lean against the wall. "Well, the ArcAngels were tough. I mean really tough. Tesla provided the blueprints for their power sources. It was unfathomable, but yet beautifully simplistic in design. My father worked with him on the project, and the pocket watches used several of the same components that made the armour near indestructible. So, yes. It's at least possible parts could have survived."

Bazalgette seemed to perk up at this. "And with the schematics, it could be possible to find the ArcAngel?"

"ArcAngels," Dent corrected.

"Yes," Bazalgette said, "but they destroyed the other three before the fall of Angel-One. Gabriel was the last survivor."

"That may be true, but as I have stated, they made them of stern stuff," Dent said. "If you find the schematics, then you might discover a resonant frequency to locate the watch."

"Where are they?" Simmons asked.

Dent paused, then nodded. "They are in the basement at my store at number sixty-one, The Strand."

"Are they hidden? In a safe or something?"

"Ah. That's trickier. You'll need to find Otto. He's a mechanical toy father made for us when we were children. Within, he holds the schematics on microfilm. But he's a little skittish around people he doesn't recognise."

Bazalgette frowned. "What do you mean?"

"Well, he is an elaborate device but only has a simple machine intelligence. So his default action is generally to run away if he's confused. He's got a few hiding places which are difficult to get at, so your best option is to lure him out."

"And how do we do that?" Simmons asked.

"He likes music—especially uplifting works. His favourite was the 1812 Overture by Tchaikovsky. I know it sounds crazy, but it was my father's favourite too. He must have written something into Otto to recognise it."

It was Simmons' turn to screw up his face. "So we find the music and Otto will just come marching out for us?"

"Well, yes. I had a good selection of recording tubes, Tchaikovsky should be among them if they are still there."

"It seems possible," Simmons said, looking towards Bazalgette for confirmation.

He stood there, silent, the cogs whirring. "We can't leave him, Simmons. There's got to be a way."

Dent shuffled trying to move his mangled limbs into a more comfortable position. "Mr Bazalgette. Please, listen to your friend. I know too much. It's only a matter of time before they realise I've been lying to them, then they will rip what they want from me. We can't let that happen."

"I can carry you. Simmons could take the Arc-Rifle and—"

"Please, leave me. You have to retrieve the schematics. Every second you waste arguing about how to save me could be time getting to the information you need." The crippled man looked up to Simmons, a pleading look in his eyes. "Do you have a spare pistol?"

Simmons retrieved one of the guard's weapons and handed it to him.

Dent looked over towards Bazalgette then back to Simmons. "I can make a stand when the next guards come down. A final act of defiance." He called over to Bazalgette. "Please tell my brother I'm sorry. It should have been me pushing him to safety, not the other way around. I was the elder brother—I should have saved him."

Bazalgette nodded. "Of course."

"Yes, Good luck," Simmons said. He turned to leave, knowing the charade had all been for Bazalgette's benefit. "Come on," he said, placing his hand on his friend's shoulder. "We need to get moving."

As they began the long climb back up the dark stairs, there was a single quiet crack from the pistol below.

20

Simmons and Bazalgette made their way through the darkness into the West End. They moved between the shadows avoiding the arc lights lining the silent early morning streets. With Simmons leading they bypassed the main checkpoints, keeping to the less travelled routes.

The droning of the foghorns masked the chimes of Big Ben as the thick fog continued its attempts to breach the city walls. In response, the whirring fans atop the barricades whispered their ceaseless song as they pushed it away, back towards the Thames.

They arrived at an intersection with The Strand. The dark alleyway opened into a blaze of light which crept along the main thoroughfare. Simmons held up his hand to warn his friend to wait as he inched his way toward the corner of the alley.

The luminous circle scaled the walls of the buildings across the street, and he tracked it to the watchtower atop the Inner-City wall. He reached under his jacket and retrieved his pocket watch, flipping the gold cover open to inspect the wedding gift from his late wife. He almost laughed, recalling Surita's insistence that his timekeeping must improve, but the lump in his throat made him swallow back any signs of mirth. With the grim determination he'd come to rely on to get him through the day, he checked the time. The glowing digits bright in the darkness, four forty-seven am. The glow was from some chemical elements, phosphor or something similar—no doubt Bazalgette would know.

Simmons motioned for his friend to approach, his attention locked on the progress of the searchlight. There was a rustle as Bazalgette sat on the ground next to him. It took five minutes for the spotlight to complete its circuit and return its stark light to scanning their side of the street.

"We'll wait until they illuminate the shops over there, then we can cross to that alleyway," Simmons said pointing. "From there, we have four minutes of darkness to move further toward number sixty-one."

Bazalgette pointed along the dark street. "That's it, past that collapsed shopfront with the green sign."

They waited as the bright light inched across the cobbles. As it hit the edge of the building opposite, Simmons stood. "Ready?"

"Yes," Bazalgette said, taking the outstretched hand and allowing the older man to pull him up.

They crossed and squeezed into the alleyway. The recess was only three feet before rubble and old wooden supports filled it, sharp edges poking at them.

"Do we wait here for the next cycle?" Bazalgette asked.

"No, let's make progress while we have the chance."

They moved out onto the street and along the storefronts. Number sixty-one was a mess. Instead of the elegant exterior he had expected, rough wooden planks boarded over the door and windows. Several lay shattered on the pavement.

Stepping around them, Simmons checked the sweep of the spotlight. It was transitioning back down the shopfronts on the other side of the street. They had about two minutes before it would illuminate them.

The remains of the sign proclaiming 'E. Dent & Co. Master Watchmaker by Royal Appointment' hung at an odd angle, weathered but still showing signs of quality. The background was a lustrous black and the writing in vibrant white cut through the gloom.

Not enough time to break into the doorway, boarded as it was, they needed another option. The ticking of the second hand on his pocket watch screamed at him as he continued further down the street. They had less than a minute now. *Calm*, he thought, scanning for somewhere they might gain cover from the approaching beam.

There. An alley entrance led between the buildings a few shops ahead. They could take shelter there. Simmons broke into a run, looking back to see Bazalgette peering between the boarded windows of Dent's store.

"Bazalgette, hurry."

His friend's feet hit the cobbled roadway as he hustled to catch up. Simmons rounded the corner into the passageway between the shops and glanced back. The light streaked up the street towards them like the first rays of the morning sun cresting the horizon.

He's not going to make it.

He grabbed Bazalgette by the arm, dragging him into the alley and out of the beam that rushed past them. They both stood, hands on knees, breathing hard.

"That was closer than I had hoped," Simmons said, pressing his back into the cold brick.

"Sorry, I thought I saw movement in the shop."

"Someone inside?"

"I don't think so. More like a reflection."

"We need to get in if we are to find these schematics. We might as well be direct about it."

Bazalgette seemed to have caught his breath, so Simmons pushed further along the alley which opened out to a series of shabby backyards behind the stores.

A rickety fence prevented them from seeing the rear of

Dent's store in the dimly lit space. Simmons found a section where the slats hung loose and peered through.

The back of the shop was much like the front, barred windows obscured by poor quality boards. The stains, cracks and warping spoke of them being around for some time. A metal sign swung by the doorway stating 'RESTRICTED AREA - STRICTLY NO ADMITTANCE - BY ORDER OF THE BLACK GUARD' in large white stencilled letters.

As he pushed his way in through the wooden gate, a damp, musty smell reaffirmed the age of the material used to board up the building. Dark shadows shrouded the yard as they headed toward the rear entrance. Simmons reached a gloved hand to try the handle, but it didn't budge. "Any chance you know how to open a locked door?"

"It depends on the quality of the lock, old chap," his friend replied. "Let me take a look."

Bazalgette moved past, pulling something from his tool-belt and tinkered with the mechanism.

Simmons turned his gaze back to the area behind the building. All was quiet. Every few minutes, searchlight beams passed over roofs, shadows stretched and danced for a few seconds before the place returned to its natural blackness.

A dull glow and the telltale crackle of the arc-lamp sundered the darkness. He spun. "Do we have to announce our presence to everyone?"

"Sorry," Bazalgette said. "I didn't design it for secrecy. I need light to see more detail of the mechanism."

"Very well. Are you making any progress?"

"Yes, I think so." A metallic clink signalled something breaking. "Ah."

"What is it?"

"The pick broke in the lock. It's tougher than I thought."

"Can you fix it?"

"I'm not sure I have anything else to use."

Simmons poked his head out of the gate, scanning up and down the alley. All remained quiet. "So, what now?"

Bazalgette let out a deep breath. "I could try to remove the fragment and see if I can botch something together."

"How long will it take?"

Bazalgette checked the tool-belt. "I couldn't say. Thirty minutes? An hour perhaps?"

"We don't have time. Move over."

Bazalgette had removed the boards so there was clear access to the lock and the door looked to open inwards.

"What's your plan?"

Simmons smiled. "The old-fashioned heavy boot method."

He aimed, just below the handle, then launched his right boot. It made a loud crack as it struck the solid wood, but remained intact. "Damn, that's tough."

Bazalgette inspected it. "I don't think kicking it will be sufficient."

"Okay, let's move to Plan B."

Bazalgette gave him a quizzical glance as Simmons shrugged his rifle from his shoulder. "Oh, I see."

The wood shredded from the double barrel blast, the sound echoing through the silent alley like thunder. With a clunk, the shattered lock mechanism fell to the floor.

"Inside," Simmons said, kicking the ruined door inwards.

"Won't someone have heard that?"

"It's possible, so let's make haste. Though they might not identify where it came from."

The room beyond was a kitchen, lit only by the arc-lamp's diffuse soft glow from outside. Simmons scanned it for any sign of danger before moving further into the building.

The doorway on the opposite wall opened onto a dark hallway. From there, stairs led off to his left both rising and descending into gloomy darkness. The only other exit was a fractured doorframe leading to the shopfront. Shards of wood and glass littered the corridor. Simmons stepped over the splintered remains of the door that once occupied the frame, lying battered and twisted on the plush carpet.

A check of the storefront showed a scene of carnage. Not as much wanton destruction as Simmons encountered at Cooper's house, but the search had been brutal and efficient. Cabinets lay devoid of any items to lure the wealthy and discerning customers of the West End. Glass shards crunched under his feet as he moved across the room.

He returned to the hall and stood in silence, straining to pick out any sounds of life in the building, before moving back to Bazalgette. He beckoned, miming for him to close the door behind him.

"The Black Guard searched the place," Simmons said, keeping his voice low. "There are stairs up and down, but no sound of anyone about."

"What now?" Bazalgette said, scanning the kitchen with the arc-lamp. "It looks abandoned. Look at the mess."

The light picked out the remains of breakfast plates piled beside the ceramic sink. Filthy grey mould grew over them all.

"Yes. Dent said it was about six months ago when they arrested him. We need to find that basement and the toy with the microfilm."

They descended the stairs which opened out into a workshop, two long benches lined the shelved walls, but it was a shambles—ransacked like the front room.

Tools littered the area. Tiny brass cogs and complex silver workings lay strewn across the floor, crushed underfoot. Intricate gears and mechanisms, some not much larger than a pinhead, twisted and ruined on the dark hardwood flooring.

"This must have been amazing before they wrecked it," Bazalgette said, his eyes wide as he scanned the tools and fixtures around the room.

"I'm sure it was," Simmons replied. *Heaven knows how long Bazalgette would moon over the mess given free rein.* "How do we find the schematics?"

"Well, Dent spoke of the mechanical toy. Perhaps we should focus on finding that?"

"That makes sense, but where do we look?"

Bazalgette mumbled something to himself and scanned the room, moving this way and that until stopping near the wall opposite the stairs. "Aha."

Simmons waited for the usual explanation that followed outbursts like this, and waited.

Bazalgette dropped to his knees, looking below a section of workbench. "Here it is."

"All right, I'll bite," Simmons said, crossing to get a better view. "Here what is?"

"A vent."

Simmons spotted the small grill in the wall an inch above floor level. "So what's so exciting about it?"

Bazalgette looked at him as if astounded that he should have asked such an absurd question. "The interior is metal. That's strange."

"And?"

"Did you hear that?" Bazalgette said.

"Hear wh—"

"Shh."

"I beg your pardon."

"You're forgiven. Now, listen."

As gob-smacked as he could ever remember being, Simmons stood trying to work out how to respond. A soft metallic tapping and scraping started within the vent.

Kneeling beside Bazalgette, he peered inside. There, about three feet in, was a flash of red light caught in the beam from the arc-lamp. "What is—"

As soon as the words left his mouth, the scuffling disappeared around an intersecting passage. He spotted a glimpse of brass and silver as segmented legs propelled the thing out of sight.

Bazalgette smiled at him. "I think we've found Otto."

After some time trying to coax the mechanical beast back into the light, they couldn't get Otto to make another appearance.

Something drew it towards the arc-lamp, but it never came close enough to capture, preferring to lie out of reach beyond the corner of the intersection. They caught sight of the glittering red eyes, but it retreated as soon as they tried to open the vent.

"This is useless," Simmons said. "What's the point of having a toy that hides from you?"

"Well, it's incredibly intelligent for a construct—"

"Yes, yes, but how do we get the *incredibly intelligent* little construct out *here*, where we can grab it?"

"We need to think of something to coax it out."

What I wouldn't do for a few ArcRounds—that would sort the little sod out. "Why don't you prod it with the arc-lamp?"

Bazalgette looked mortified. "I'm not doing that. It might damage it. It's shocking you'd even suggest such a thing."

Oh, so now I'm the bad guy? Typical.

"Right," Simmons said. "If you haven't got a better idea, then I'll shoot at the little devil to scare it out. You get ready at the next vent to catch it."

"We can't do that, Simmons," Bazalgette said, and he sighed. "All right, I'll try the arc-lamp if that's what you want, but we'll do it my way, on the vent."

"What's that going to achieve?"

Bazalgette's voice was quiet, resigned. "It's conductive and won't be as dangerous as directly shocking its frame. Maybe that will be enough to overload its systems."

Simmons blew out a breath. "Fine. Let's get this done."

Touching the lamp to the metallic interior seemed to work as expected. Blue waves of electricity flowed onto the surface and rippled through the vents. Otto emitted a high-pitched scream and leapt into frenzied motion. Its legs skittered as it disappeared, the sounds receding as the creature escaped upwards.

Simmons sat ready to grab the beast if it fled in his direction. A strong electrical surge arced into his gloved hand, jolting through the fingers into his palm. The muscles contracted to produce a claw-like grip he couldn't release.

"Damned thing," Simmons hissed through gritted teeth. His hand soon recovered, turning to cramp as he regained feeling. He stretched and rubbed his fingers, sharp flickers of pain rushing down into his wrist. *Thank the lord I'm wearing gloves.* He turned his eyes towards Bazalgette, just waiting for some intellectual quip.

"Perhaps we should try something else?" was all his friend had to say as he stood and moved toward the stairs.

They found the creature on the top floor after an extensive search for its telltale clicking. It had rammed itself deep into a section well out of reach and cowered there. Red light reflected from its eyes, and an occasional tremor made one leg tap wildly for a few seconds.

Simmons stood and stretched. Looking around the bedroom, he noticed something amongst the tangled bedding, which now lay on the floor by the window.

There in the twisted sheets was a broken phonograph horn. *Idiot,* he thought, *Music, Dent said it liked music.* "Bazalgette, there's a battered phonograph over here, do you think you could fix it?"

Bazalgette studied the remains for a moment, then brought his hand up to slap his forehead, eyes rolling. "How could I be so dense? We need music." He returned his attention to the device. "Hmm," his tone spoke of concern. "It's taken a beating, but might be repairable. Can you find any Tchaikovsky?"

Simmons made room for Bazalgette to work and began the search for record tubes. Half an hour later, it was playing, albeit manually. The clockwork mechanism was far beyond repair. With the device ready to wind and a wax tube recording of the 1812 Overture, they set forth to lure the reclusive beast.

Bazalgette wound the phonograph. After the initial crackles

and hissing, music burst forth. A little slow at first, but he soon had the tempo adjusted to produce a recognisable tune.

There was an instant change in the noise from the vent, all the tapping stopped, and the mechanical device seemed rooted in place. As the overture reached its crescendo, with bells and cannon echoing around the room from the patched speaker cone, a corresponding clanking began. The creature tapped out a steady marching rhythm with all eight legs. At first, it marched on the spot and then propelled itself forward.

"It's working," Bazalgette said with unbridled joy in his voice.

"Yes, but what now?" Simmons replied, watching the thing approaching down the narrow metal corridor.

"Open the vent, let it come out here."

Simmons took a screwdriver from the tool-belt and unscrewed the metallic plate as he had seen his friend do downstairs.

The grille swivelled clockwise once he'd removed the third screw and the intricate silver and brass automaton dropped a few inches to the carpet and continued towards the phonograph. It marched to the edge of the repaired wood and metal device, and stopped in place, legs still rising and falling to the music.

Bazalgette reached out with his free hand, lifting the spider. As soon as it left the ground, it ceased moving. "Oh, I wasn't expecting that."

He rotated the torso to reveal the underside. The limbs hung loose like a bicycle chain no longer under tension, victims to gravity.

"It has several small screws holding the thorax in place. I'll need the jeweller's instruments we saw in the basement," Bazalgette said scrutinising the item with a glow of wonder on his face as he rose.

Simmons followed him downstairs to the workshop. Bazalgette carried the device in reverent silence and deposited the spider on the workbench with great care. Simmons cast his eye over the room again at the destruction wrought by the Black

Guard in their search for evidence, and Dent's arrest. It seemed the schematics no longer interested them now they had the designer.

Returning his gaze to Otto, Bazalgette was already into the guts of the machine. He prodded with tiny prongs and screwdrivers that looked like someone designed them for a doll to use. As he watched his friend making minute adjustments, it reminded him of the precision of a surgeon.

The interior was a hive of wires, cogs and pulleys. Bazalgette pressed on something inside, and a leg jerked in response. A moment later, he had another of the creature's limbs twitching. "Astounding."

"And the microfilm?" Simmons asked.

"Oh yes," Bazalgette said. "I think there must be a special combination. The wires take the place of ligaments but look to have an excessive amount of play. They seem to be over-designed. Perhaps if I..."

He appeared to be looking off into the distance. A few seconds passed. "Yes," he continued, changing tack. His hands left the instruments in position, and he spread the limbs out, making something resembling an eight-pointed star. He reached and pulled on two opposite legs with a resounding click. Continuing the process with the three remaining pairs, each lengthening, he returned his attention to the body cavity.

"Yes, look," he said, motioning Simmons to peer into the recess.

The spot, previously packed full of wires and mechanism, now exposed a tiny octagonal box. They must have recessed it behind the leg mechanisms. Bazalgette reached in with long nosed tweezers and lifted the ornate container out onto the workspace.

"Is that it?" Simmons asked.

"I believe it is," Bazalgette replied. He'd found a pair of jewellers spectacles and was adjusting the multiple lenses. Arms rotated on their housings, moving in front of each other to create the correct magnification for the task at hand.

His friend fiddled with the silver octagon for a few minutes before a small lid popped open revealing a brass cylinder. It looked like a sewing spool, for holding thread.

"This is it," Bazalgette said, lifting it to the light from the arc-lamp. "There are hundreds of drawings on here, the schematics as Dent suggested."

"Excellent. Let's get out of here and find somewhere safe to hole up."

"My house is not that far from here. It would be quicker than getting back to Whitechapel. That is where you're based, isn't it?"

"Yes. To the mad scientist's laboratory then?"

"I don't know what you mean," Bazalgette replied, his face a mask of innocence.

He replaced the microfilm in its protective octagonal case. Once safe, he reassembled Otto and placed the mechanical spider in his leather satchel, along with the tools he had collected to work on it later. "It seems an awful shame to leave such a beautiful workshop to rot."

"I suppose it is, but let's find somewhere to safely plan our options, then you can concoct a strategy to steal all this stuff."

Bazalgette narrowed and twisted his mouth as if he'd eaten something distasteful. "Well, we could re-purpose it. As its previous owner is dead, it has no legal ownership, so it wouldn't *really* be stealing."

"However you want to look at it," Simmons said. "As long as it means we can leave now."

Bazalgette took one last glance around the workshop before following Simmons upstairs. They stepped into the back yard, the faintest glimmer of pink tinging the dark sky, and Bazalgette drew the watch from his inside pocket. "Almost six o'clock," he said while Simmons opened the gate into the alley.

A harsh voice thundered from behind them. "Halt. You are violating a restricted zone after curfew. Raise your hands and submit to inquisition."

21

As Simmons turned to face their accusers, four Black Guard troopers emerged from the dark alley followed by another man in a long trench coat. Two crossed silver daggers high on his collar denoted his officer status.

The guards each carried an arc-rifle burning with a soft blue light along the length of the barrel. Sizzling white sparks danced at the muzzles, casting shifting shadows over the refuse-laden walkway.

The officer scanned his face. "I know you. Simmons, right? I said you were trouble from the start. We should have arrested you earlier. Now it seems you've confirmed my suspicions."

"Get ready to run," Simmons whispered.

"When?" came the low reply as Bazalgette stretched his shoulders.

"You'll know when it's time. Have the arc-lamp ready."

Simmons turned back to the officer. "I think there must be some misunderstanding."

The man sneered at him. "Don't act the innocent here, Simmons. You are a confirmed sympathiser with opponents of the Empire, and we look harshly on those who murder our brethren. Or did you somehow forget that trip to Highgate the other day, traitor?"

"I didn't forget anything, except—"

Two staccato shots rang out, and the officer dropped to the cobbled street, blood spreading beneath him.

"Was that the signal?" Bazalgette asked, his voice somewhat higher than usual.

"Yes, damn it. Run!"

Simmons bustled past his friend as the whine of the arc-lamp's ignition sequence grew. Light blossomed behind him, the rapid burst casting long, stark shadows all around. Turning, he fired another two shots into the area occupied by the other guardsmen. Bazalgette followed, along with the telltale wail of arc-rifles discharging.

The flash from the arc-lamp must have damaged the guards night vision as three arcs of charged particles crackled past them into the railings lining the alley. Sparks flew, and small explosions of mortar and brick sprayed them as they turned the corner back towards The Strand.

Through the dark alley between the buildings, Simmons saw the two guards knelt, aiming at them from the street. He dug his heels in trying to arrest his forward momentum. *This isn't going to go well.*

Instead of slowing, his right boot slid out from beneath him, his weight already dropping as he slipped on the slimy rubbish in the alley. Everything seemed to fall into slow motion. As the hum of the arc-rifles ahead built to a crescendo, a shadow of something flew above him on the brick wall.

Electricity exploded before him, deadly tendrils of white light grasping to scour the flesh from his bones. A second larger explosion followed with shrapnel whistling by, rebounding from the alley floor and walls. A sharp pain tore into his right leg above the knee, sizzling and burning. Ozone filled his nostrils as everything crept back into rapid motion. Someone was tugging at his arm. His head felt full of knives, maybe this was what that dockworker enjoyed before passing out in the police station?

"Get up."

"What?" His vision swam, and his stomach clenched, threatening to heave.

"Simmons, get up, we have to leave." It was Bazalgette. The other man pulled him to his feet. The face coalesced into the familiar bearded form he had grown accustomed to though it seemed to have an unusual look of concern. "Can you walk? We need to go now."

Everything was a little fuzzy, like when Simmons awoke in the middle of the night after one too many bottles of poor whisky. He moved his legs under him, but they were unsteady.

Pain lanced through his thigh as he tried to support his weight. He gasped, almost collapsing until Bazalgette's shoulder intervened lifting beneath his arm, half supporting, half dragging him across the road.

The familiar but distant whine of a siren cut through the ringing that filled his head. He recognised it instantly—the Black Guard were mobilising troops. *Damn, we have to get off the streets.*

"Wait here," Bazalgette told him, his footsteps receding into the gloom of a side street.

Simmons reached down to his leg, his vision was still blurry, and his hand came away slick with blood.

Metal scraped in the darkness, followed by a solid clunk. He searched for his Webley, but the holster was empty. Hadn't he been holding it a few seconds ago? Realising he must have dropped it when he fell, he instead reached into his jacket for the Mauser. It was reassuringly sturdy in his hand, and he aimed it down the dark alley.

Footsteps approached, and he recognised a form emerging from the darkness.

"Whoa," Bazalgette said spotting the pistol pointing at him. "Are you all right? It's me, Nathaniel."

"I know who you are. Don't leap out of the shadows like that when I'm injured and jumpy."

"I've opened a sewer grate to get us out of sight. It sounds like we've caused a ruckus with the Black Guard."

"Fine, let's get moving, then you can tell me what the hell is going on."

It took Simmons a while to descend the iron rungs into the

blackness below. He realised he couldn't support his weight on his right leg after almost passing out the first time he tried it. Instead, he used his good leg and both arms to position himself and then hopped down to each new rung.

A loud scraping of metal above reassured him Bazalgette had repositioned the manhole cover, blocking the way against pursuit.

Simmons misjudged the distance, his foot slipping and fell the last two feet to collapse in a heap on the sewer floor below. Pain shot up his leg as he foolishly tried to break his fall, and tears filled his eyes.

A rapid clanging descended above him as Bazalgette dropped as quickly as he could, a soft halo of light following from his lamp.

"Bazalgette," Simmons said, it surprised him how pained it sounded. "Perhaps you should check my leg, I think it's bleeding again, and I feel—" His gut heaved, and he coughed out a stream of hot, acidic liquid. He waited for more, and though his stomach wrenched, thankfully he had nothing left to bring up.

Bazalgette helped him sit, using his pack as a makeshift backrest. "Let me have a look at you."

The light brightened as Bazalgette twiddled with the arc-lamp, and the full extent of the damage became clear. A spreading circle of blood-soaked cloth centred on a puncture hole two inches above the knee. A short length of metal protruded from the wound, smeared in crimson.

"What is that?" Simmons asked, pointing at the offending article. "Shrapnel?"

"Yes, I'd guess it's the remains of Otto."

Simmons furrowed his eyebrows. "The toy from Dent's place?"

"Yes," Bazalgette replied, gently probing around the damage. "I threw it at the guards before they shot at us. I thought if I could get it far enough ahead, it might disrupt the arc-rifles, which it did. Both arcs diverged to strike the device, much like a lightning conductor. However, it exploded rather spectacularly. I think this is one of its legs."

"Well, it feels like I rammed whatever remained of Otto's leg further into me when I landed, and it hurts like hell. What's the medical opinion, Doctor?"

Bazalgette looked Simmons in the eye, and his face showed concern. "I'm not a doctor, well, not a medical one."

"Yes, I know that," Simmons replied. "I was trying to make light of the situation."

"I'm not sure how to remove it, or even if I should. Though there is blood oozing from it again."

Simmons grasped Bazalgette's arm. "I can't move with this bloody lump of metal stuck in my leg, and we can't hide here forever. The Black Guard aren't stupid. They *will* work out where we went, so that leaves one solution." He grimaced at the thought. "Pull the damned thing out, patch me up as best you can and hope I can hobble my way out of here."

Bazalgette wiped the sweat forming on his brow with the back of his hand. "I can do this. It's just engineering—with soft materials."

Simmons decided he needed anaesthetic. His trusty hip flask held the aid he required, and he took two deep swigs as his friend began the extraction.

There was blood. A lot of blood, but it looked like he had been lucky, no major blood vessels seemed damaged. It oozed through the bandages Bazalgette had wrapped around the wound, but the second layer remained more white than red when applied over the top.

It was good anaesthetic. Simmons had accrued enough from the hunting jobs to ensure he had access to a few luxuries, and quality spirits were something he wasn't willing to scrimp on.

Bazalgette inspected the articulation below the knee to check on any movement that might interfere with the dressings and decided that immobilising the limb was the best option. It was a straightforward job of applying a makeshift splint to lock Simmons' leg straight, and now he could hobble about.

"Damn, that hurts," Simmons said, eyes watering as he applied too much weight to his right leg.

"We'll take it slow, but you'll live."

Simmons wrinkled his nose. "You come down here often. How do you stand that stench?"

"You get used to it after a while. Are you ready to move?"

"Which way?"

Bazalgette smiled. "Just follow your nose."

Simmons had grown accustomed to the constant dripping and gurgling of the sewer waters. Even the smell was but a distant memory.

Bazalgette led, guiding them through the twisting sewers. They alternated between travelling beside the sewage on wide walkways and climbing on hands and knees through side-passages leading to more tunnels. The place seemed endless. Simmons was sure he couldn't find his way back to their entry point without his friend's directions.

The arc-lamp shed brilliant patterns across their field of view, reflecting from the muddy waters and illuminating the arched walls and ceilings. It was difficult in places with his leg splinted, but he managed, only complaining a little. Bazalgette seemed to hang about waiting for him to ask for help, which of course he wouldn't, but he was there anyway.

Simmons kept his shrapnel in his waistcoat pocket, the last remnant of the fantastic machine Dent created for his sons. Bazalgette had cleaned it up as much as he could, but it still retained a red sheen and specks of congealing blood on the interior. It would make an excellent souvenir to add to the two bullets fragments he'd saved from his military service.

The slap of his friend's footsteps through the shallow water ahead slowed then stopped. Simmons waited for Bazalgette to move again, or to tell him what he was waiting for. After thirty seconds he was about to continue forwards when Bazalgette turned and headed back towards him.

"I heard something up ahead. Not sure what, but it didn't sound like rats. I think there were footsteps."

"Was there any conversation or multiple footfalls?"

Bazalgette shrugged. "I couldn't make it out, but there was movement and, if I'm not mistaken, more than one of them."

"Can we go around?"

Bazalgette rummaged through his satchel which held the massive battery powering the arc-lamp. "I'll check my notes."

Simmons strained for any clues from the darkness ahead but heard nothing other than the slow feculent waters and occasional drips from the tunnel roof.

"Hmm," Bazalgette said, leafing through a sheaf of papers. "It won't be easy. This is the most direct route to get us to the East End. There are other options, but they will require squeezing through narrow joining passageways between the main sewer and some smaller tributaries."

Bazalgette studied Simmons with a critical eye. "I don't think that makes sense with your leg."

"Perhaps you're right. It looks wide enough here. If we keep to one edge and make our way forward carefully, maybe we can find out a little more about what we're facing. We might have to switch the lamp off, or have it emit as low a light as possible."

"I can do that," Bazalgette said, reaching down to dim the lamp hanging from his belt. "We best wait a few minutes for our eyes to adjust before we move on."

Simmons followed him to the edge so they could use the tunnel wall to steady themselves. The light dimmed and dropped them into the utter dark only appreciated fully by those who explore deep caves or underground sewer systems.

He realised the low hum, which had accompanied them during their travels, had changed to a quiet ticking, more like a pilot light trying to engage. The glow floated away from him as Bazalgette advanced, and Simmons followed, trailing his gloved left hand against the curved brick wall.

They progressed with slow deliberation, listening for anything that might carry towards them, but all remained quiet.

After a while, the roar of rushing water echoed from ahead, and there was something else: soft shuffling noises and occasional splashes.

Simmons waited, taking in the sounds. "I think it's bleeders," he whispered. The two men crept forward to a weir, the source of the cascade. It was only a drop of a few feet, but enough to aerate the water, bubbles forming in the dark murk below.

For five minutes they viewed the area, spotting three figures in the blackness. There might have been more, or they may have seen the same ones several times, but they all wandered around aimlessly.

"What now?" Bazalgette asked.

Just how many are there? Simmons thought. *If I shoot one, it's likely to draw more within earshot, and down here in the tunnels, that will carry a significant distance.*

"Simmons?"

"I'm thinking."

Bazalgette lapsed into silence.

"I could probably drop all three, especially with this weir between us. They aren't very bright, but the sound might attract others in the vicinity."

He looked back to Bazalgette. "You're sure there's no other way around?"

"No, this is the only easy route to continue eastward."

"What about other options further on? Is there anywhere we can get to a higher level? Ladders are good—those things are too stupid to understand how to use them."

Bazalgette thought for a moment. "Well, there are regular access shafts between levels, I'd have to check to see where the nearest ones are."

He took the notes from the waterproof satchel, flicking through and holding them close to the dim glow from the arc-lamp. "There should be a ladder around two hundred yards ahead of us, on the left. From what I can tell, there are other chambers off to the right, but I have no details where they lead."

"Let's hope it isn't more bleeders," Simmons said. He checked his pistol. The Mauser looked fine, no damp or dirt in sight and loaded with ten rounds. He snapped the mechanism shut, trying his best to minimise the noise.

"Ready with the lamp?" he asked. Bazalgette nodded in the near darkness.

With the pistol aimed in the general direction of the stumbling sounds ahead, Simmons covered his eyes with his left hand. "Now."

Light erupted around him, even through the soft leather covering his view. A thrum accompanied it, rising in pitch behind him.

He squinted as he pulled his hand aside, the bright red brickwork seemed illuminated by a small sun. It cast his elongated shadow down onto the tunnel floor below. Four shambling figures turned their heads, shielding ruined faces with arms draped in ragged cloth.

His first shot took the nearest creature in the face, the sound echoing from the walls of the enclosed space. It collapsed with a loud splash. The other three staggered towards them, still covering their bleeding sockets from the arc-lamp's intense glare.

Two more shots rang out, felling another of the fiends. The last pair stumbled onwards, oblivious of the weir they would need to climb. His next shot hit the nearest in the forehead. It slumped as if it were a grotesque puppet and someone had cut its strings.

"Simmons," yelled Bazalgette.

The final creature was only a few feet away, stepping into the main flow of effluence where it cascaded over the lip of the weir. It moaned, a pitiful noise issuing from its ruined face. Tears of thick blood oozed between writhing tendrils of red weed, painting streaks from its eyes, nose and what remained of its tattered lips. Yellowed, fractures of teeth gnashed together as the thing lunged to grab at Simmons.

Two rapid shots and the creature fell into the churning weir. Its broken-nailed fingers slapped onto the stone inches from his good leg, then slumped back into the bubbling red froth, its body flipping and turning in the undertow.

"Are you all right?" Simmons asked, reaching to reloaded his pistol. It was a reflex, but he paused, realising it wasn't necessary. He'd become used to reloading his six-shot Webley revolver. He would have to adjust to the Mauser's ten-round magazine.

"Yes," came Bazalgette's breathy response from behind him. "That was a bit close."

"Well, I thought I was running low on ammo. Wanted to make those last shots counted."

"But it almost—"

"Yes, yes. It all sounds quiet for now. Let's see if we can find this ladder while we have the chance."

Simmons drew one of the stripper clips from his coat and replenished six rounds into the Mauser. It was a surprisingly simple task, and he always preferred having a fully loaded weapon.

The arc-lamp flooded the area with light. Narrow steps led down either side of the weir and Bazalgette offered a hand for Simmons to negotiate the slippery stairs

It seemed much more pungent here. *Was it the churning sewage water?* Simmons was about to mention it, but Bazalgette beat him to it. "Is it just me, or is there a different smell here?"

"I was going to ask the same thing," Simmons said as a low howl issued from the dark recesses on the southern wall opposite them. Others joined it—many others.

"Run, Bazalgette. Run!"

~

Figures shambled from the dark alcoves, echoing each other's morbid song.

Bazalgette pointed. "The access way is up there."

"Go," Simmons said.

"But what about you?"

"Bleeders are slow. Even I should be able to keep ahead of them." Simmons turned to face the growing crowd of tainted bodies lumbering towards him. He stepped backwards, making sure his footing was secure. *This should be fine.* Yes, there were a lot, and the thought of struggling to climb a ladder with them approaching was a little daunting, but it was doable.

A throat-tearing roar reverberated through the tunnels.

Bazalgette stopped in his tracks, turning back to Simmons. "What was that?"

Simmons felt his stomach drop. He had only heard a sound like that once before, and he hadn't hung around to see what made it.

Bleeders exploded into the air as something immense burst through between them. It scattered half a dozen of the weed-infested creatures who bounced from the walls, bones splintering as they fell. The enormous beast bellowed, spittle, blood and brown ichor sprayed from its vast maw.

"Bloater," Simmons shouted, turning and trying to run despite the splinted leg slowing him. "Bazalgette, get the hell out of here."

Bazalgette sprinted for the access point, and Simmons did his best to follow. Something whistled past, impacting on the wall a few feet away. A sickening crunch exploded off the brickwork, leaving a sack of broken bones and a spray of God-awful ichor that made him gag.

He coughed, fighting to stop the bile from rising further in his throat. With a shake of his head, he struggled to grasp what was happening. *That thing is throwing damned bleeders at me.*

The glow from Bazalgette's arc-lamp bounced as he sprinted to their destination. Behind, the sloshing of bleeders pushing through the stream of sewage seemed closer. Simmons dare not look back for fear of tripping. The bloater roared again, and by instinct, he dodged to the side. Just as well, another rotting body shot past clipping him and sending him sprawling onto hands and knees in the dirty water.

He strove forward, pain burning in his leg. Not far now. He was almost to the exit, to safety. He clawed his way upright, willing himself to make progress. The bleeders were catching up, but it was all fine, it was only another twenty yards—he was going to make it.

"Simmons," came the distraught call from ahead.

"What, are you all right?"

"There's no ladder."

22

"What do you mean?" Simmons asked. He heard the disbelief in his voice and fought to keep calm. *How can there be no ladder? This was the way out—the only way out.*

The bloater showed it hadn't done with them as another body exploded against the wall. Simmons ducked around the corner and glanced back. The mass of creatures shambling towards them split as the monstrous beast broke into the edge of the lamplight.

It was enormous, head and shoulders above the sea of bleeders. Its swollen torso looked ready to burst, a huge barrel-chested monster, over-inflated like a giant airship.

Black gore oozed from rips where its grey flesh could no longer contain the strain. A web of dark veins covered its skin and writhed where thick cords of red weed erupted from the wide gashes in its body. Thinner tendrils probed the air from the blood-stained eye sockets, sniffing out its prey.

Bazalgette was frantic. "It should be here, this is the access way to the upper levels, but it's gone."

Simmons grasped Bazalgette by the shoulders. "All right, calm down. Where could it be? It can't have just disappeared."

He held his friend's wide-eyed gaze until he saw the terror retreat. Bazalgette's breathing slowed a little. "Let me look again."

They both rounded the wall into the small antechamber that contained a circular hole in the ceiling. Bazalgette rushed over and projected the blinding beam of the arc-lamp upward.

"My God. It's there, about ten feet up."

~

Simmons limped across the tunnel, leaving Bazalgette frantically reaching for the rusted ladder with a crowbar. "Bazalgette, shine the light on me now."

"What are you doing? We've got to get out of here."

"Just do it, man."

The bright beam cut through the darkness, casting a large shadow of movement as Simmons ripped his rifle from its case and brought it to bear.

The mass of stumbling creatures was less than twenty feet away. They still headed toward the source of the light until the .303 shell shattered the dark with a gout of flame from the end of the left barrel.

It slammed three of the shambling crowd back, their uncaring brethren trampling over them. They turned to focus on Simmons and the ear-splitting scream from his hunting rifle.

A roar of anger and vile hatred burst from the group and reverberated from the sewer walls. *Well, that's got its attention.*

Simmons aimed at the nearest cluster of bleeders and unleashed the second barrel into their midst. He took another step back, a little further from the safety of the escape route his friend was still struggling to provide.

"Come on, you filthy blighters," he screamed at the mass of writhing flesh, ensuring he stayed in the arc-lamp's beam. He snapped the rifle open, ejecting the spent cartridges with a soft popping sound, and replaced them from his bandolier in a swift, practised motion.

Checking behind, there was room to retreat further into a side tunnel, but if he made it that far, there would be no getting out. Even with their stumbling progress forward, the creatures were moving as fast as he could withdraw. *Damned leg,* he thought, waddling his way back along the line of Arclight.

"Over here. Over here," Simmons yelled at the horde. A chorus of groans, moans and guttural sounds, wet and fleshy, turned towards him. A loud crunch nearby released a spray of rancid smelling gore, splattering his coat. *Damn, that was too close*. The corpse had flown through the darkness, striking one of the many pillars lining the sewage channel. It had shielded him from the rotten mass that would otherwise have floored him.

His mind raced as he calculated the most likely trajectory back to its origin and fired both barrels in rapid succession. The first shot hit the wall somewhere in the darkness, skittering off into the distance. The second, however, rewarded him with an enraged roar of pain and the wet sucking sound of flesh ripped from its frame. *How do you like that, beastie?*

Instead of the crash of the massive creature hitting the ground, an even louder bellow thundered around the tunnel walls. Heavy footsteps followed, splashing through the muddy sewer water, picking up speed.

Oh good, I've made it angrier, he thought while he repeated the instinctive reloading action. A clang from across the passage and the shriek of rusted metal announced sections of the ladder releasing their ages old embrace to slide apart.

"Simmons," Bazalgette shouted, his foot alighting on the lowest rung.

"Get out. I'll draw them off."

"No."

"It's the only way. Please, just go, save yourself."

The beam from the arc-lamp wavered as Bazalgette picked it from the ground and started the ascent to safety.

As the light leaked away, Simmons felt the weight of the darkness pressing in, suffocating. The unbearable stench of rotten flesh made him gag, and the sound of their slow shuffling gait was lost in the splashing approach of the behemoth beyond.

He stepped back, feeling the tunnel wall press against him. *End of the line.* He rammed the rifle butt into the brickwork, supported by just his right arm, and pulled the trigger unleashing both barrels.

The muzzle-flash illuminated the full horror of the crowd of bleeders all around. Their arms groped for him, tendrils of weed writhing mere inches from his face. Bodies exploded, clearing a small area before him, replaced by the massive shadowy bulk of the bloater barrelling towards him.

A soft click and the scene hung there illuminated by the dying glow from the rifle rounds. He pulled his left hand from within his jacket, revealing the ornate silver filigree of the time-piece he had taken from the Officer at the cemetery. The pocket watch was ticking backwards from thirty seconds—twenty-nine, twenty-eight.

He pushed through the macabre statues and headed for the glow where the arc-lamp still illuminated the base of the ladder. Though disgusted by the grim mass of inanimate horrors, he forced his way through, expecting at any moment for their greedy hands to pull him down into their grisly embrace.

The watch continued its smooth and methodical count-down—twenty-two, twenty-one.

Blood and gore smeared his garments as he squeezed past the tightly packed nightmarish mob. One last row of the creatures ahead of him and then an open space clear to the ladder. He would make it with time to spare.

His eye, ever-present on the second hand of Dent's time-piece, noted it approaching fifteen seconds as his foot caught, tripping him. Struggling to regain a stable footing, he stamped down onto something mushy and felt his injured leg slip from under him. He flailed, trying to restore his balance, clutching for anything to break his fall. But only ruined flesh and tattered garments slipped between his grasping fingers.

He hit the ground with a thump, not even noticing the smell as the sewage water splashed into his face. The all-pervading stench of the creatures masked everything.

No, No, No. Get up. Get to the ladder before time runs out.

Scrambling forward on hands and knees, he crawled between the final rotting bodies blocking him from the hope of escape.

He drove two of the remaining bleeders to the ground, their soft flesh breaking his fall. The last thing he needed was being winded and struggling for breath.

With the butt of his weapon as a crutch, he pushed himself to his feet and hobbled towards the ladder, like some crazed marionette.

The pocket watch was relentless. Five, four, three. Simmons secured the rifle-strap across his shoulder as his foot reached the bottom rung and he pulled his aching body upward.

A strange sensation filled the air, and his ears popped. Chaotic sound shattered the silence from the central tunnel. Moans, screams and bellows reverberated through his skull as he dragged himself up the ladder, two arms securing his weight before hopping up a rung onto his good leg.

Light burst into his view from above. "Simmons?" came the shocked voice of his friend ten feet above him. "My God, you're alive."

Simmons stared up into the blazing heart of a thousand suns, shading his eyes. "Keep climbing, and get that damned lamp out of my face."

~

With the terror left far behind, they made good progress through the upper levels of the sewer and eventually popped up near Oxford Circus.

It had taken them over three hours to get here from the ladder ascent. Streaks of grey light flooded into the tunnel as Bazalgette lifted the cover, which protested with squeals of metal long left untouched.

"There is activity," Bazalgette said. "But it doesn't seem out of the ordinary, street vendors and workers by the look of them."

Simmons thought for a while. "We need to hole up for a while and work out where we go from here."

"We're a long way from Whitechapel."

"That's true, and as the Black Guard knew me by name, we have to assume they will have found out where my lodgings are. Too risky, we need somewhere else."

"My workshop is close," Bazalgette said. "We could walk there in around thirty minutes."

Simmons grimaced. "In my state, it's likely to take somewhat longer and might attract too much attention. We should try to get a cab."

Bazalgette nodded. "Right. I'll go see what I can find then come back for you."

Darkness enveloped Simmons as the cover lowered with a dull metallic clang. A tiny crescent of light played on the wall beside him, cast from the gap where the lid didn't entirely seal. He sat, leaning against the curved brick, yawned and closed his eyes.

~

Simmons snapped awake to the grating sound of the cover being pried open. Blinding light flooded in, bathing the filthy sewer in colour. A silhouette appeared against the dull morning sky.

"Sorry, there wasn't much traffic about," said Bazalgette. "I had to make my way to Oxford Street, but I've got a cab waiting for us."

He reached down, and Simmons gladly accepted a helping hand up from the ladder to ground level.

Bazalgette led him through a maze of narrow alleys teeming with rough-clad figures. Men, women and children followed their passage with wary eyes then shied away as the smell hit them. If their stench offended these dregs of society, God alone knew how they would fare in polite company.

Simmons hobbled onto the main street to a waiting hansom cab, the driver ready with reins and whip in hand. The cabbie grimaced as they approached. Bazalgette opened the side door, helping Simmons up into the plush red leather seating.

"It's all right. I've paid him for the mess," Bazalgette said. "Though to be honest, I'm not sure he understood the full extent of how filthy we would be."

"Give him two extra shillings and tell him we don't want to be remembered. That should do the job."

Simmons collapsed into the cab, pain flaring in his leg. Bazalgette climbed into the seat beside him ,and within seconds, they pulled away into the busy traffic heading north.

Bazalgette had told the cabbie to drop them two streets away from his workshop. Simmons was surprised at how pleased he was that Bazalgette hadn't announced his exact address as he might have done just a few days before. *Perhaps he's learning not to trust people at last? Now there's real progress.*

After a short journey through the backstreets, Bazalgette pointed to the three-storey building ahead of them. The double doors were of sturdy metal construction and looked large enough to drive a cart through. The structure seemed a little worse for wear, discoloured brickwork alongside peeling paint drew a picture of silent neglect.

He opened the complex lock on a door that led into a cellar. Several loud mechanical clacks and it pushed open. "Welcome to my humble abode," Bazalgette said and gestured for Simmons to enter.

In stark contrast to the messy exterior, the interior was both lavish and pristine. *Damn, he must have an army or servants keeping it tidy.*

"It's," Simmons paused, struggling for the right word, "lovely." He cringed, was that the best he could come up with?

Bazalgette didn't seem to mind. "I often feel I should

show the same care to the building itself, but it would only draw attention to the place being different to the rest of the street."

As the door closed behind them, motors and gears whirred until thick metal bolts returned to secure it with a slam. Simmons turned to see a similar device to what he had at his lodgings. "That's a Starling lock, isn't it?"

"It's based on one. I made minor alterations to the design. It has a solid enough structure, but I've added a little extra finesse to the locking mechanism, and reinforced the locks and bolts."

"Is there nothing you can't turn your mind to?"

Bazalgette seemed to ponder for a moment. "Well, not as yet. It's a simple matter of analysis and redesign. Some things take longer, like the clockwork, and the fact I had to override the security to access the internals. They don't want people to reverse engineer their designs, you see."

"So you are telling me you bypassed the most secure locking system available, just to find out how it worked?"

"Well, yes. When you put it that way, it sounds like a profound achievement, but it was reasonably straightforward."

"Bazalgette, you are talking about the company that provides security for the Inner-City elite as if it were nothing. How many people do you think could have done what you did and then treat it as if it's a simple matter any of us might have achieved?"

Bazalgette stopped, his own gears and cogs whirring. "Well, now you mention it, yes I suppose there aren't many who could do it. Starling would go out of business rather sharply if the other security manufacturers produced improved versions of their designs."

"Oh," Simmons said, realisation dawning on his face, "you know what this means, don't you?"

"No, I'm not sure I do."

Simmons laughed. "*You* can bypass a Starling lock."

"Well, yes. That's what I said."

"You don't get it, do you? These are the systems used by the

Nobility, the Black Guard and the Empress herself. Damn it, man. We have a way of getting into the Inner-City."

"Oh," was all the response Bazalgette managed. He looked back to Simmons, and down at his splinted leg. "Well, before we get too excited, perhaps we should get you cleaned up. I'd hate for you to die from infection or contract the taint."

∾

They spent a while cleaning their filthy clothing in an area of the workshop reserved for scraping the muck from Bazalgette's many sewer visits. Hoses sprayed chemical formulations, then rinsed, and resprayed. Once set in motion, it continued to scour the garments while Simmons went to soak in a hot bath.

Bazalgette found a spare robe for him and advised him to keep his leg out of the water until he could clean and redress the wound. He also passed Simmons a bar of red carbolic soap and insisted he use it.

The soap left Simmons' skin tingling and a little sore in places. The fragrance though was a glorious contrast to the stench he'd grown accustomed to while making their escape through the sewers.

Simmons lounged with a glass of fine malt whisky, and his pipe, which he'd refused to subject to the cleansing his clothing was undergoing. He'd just scrubbed it in the sink with warm water and soap.

He dozed in the relaxing heat of the bath, drifting in and out of consciousness. His mind drifted back to the hot Indian summer and the colonial mansion from where he oversaw the running of the interests of the Crown.

Simmons had quickly acclimatised to the constant noise and bustle of an army of servants, and a life of ease. He even came to enjoy it when required to intervene when some stupid English fop thought they could treat the locals any way they wanted. They were soon put right on that score, and the people loved him for it.

He'd been the colonial governor in Bombay and had grown

to love the beautiful British outpost. Like almost all western travellers, the poverty, heat and smell of the place had appalled him when he first arrived. But after a short period of adjustment, he came to understand the natural flow of the people living their daily lives. He realised he'd discovered a tiny piece of heaven and loved every moment of his time there. So much so, he never imagined ever returning to his country of birth.

It was still difficult to believe it was only five years since his dramatic fall from grace. Simmons had fallen in love with an Indian girl, a servant in the colonial household. Against the advice and warnings from friends and family, he'd courted and then married her. Surita was beautiful, intelligent, and brooked no nonsense from anyone.

It was how they'd first met. He'd stood there under her withering tirade of how to maintain the residence in a state of cleanliness becoming an ambassador to the Empress. Little did she realise that *he* was that ambassador.

The government recalled him to London once they got wind of the scandal. They stripped him of both his title and commission. He'd expected nothing less from the jumped up bureaucrats in Whitehall. What hurt more was being ostracised by his former friends. They distanced themselves from him and his new wife. Even his club closed their doors on him stating they 'could not entertain a fellow of such low moral turpitude'. That was the real London, and his fall, in the eyes of the ruling elite, was complete. *Well, damn them. Damn them all.*

At first, they struggled to find servants who didn't look down their noses at the dusky skinned mistress of the house. But their worries settled and their small home in the country proved more than adequate for their needs. Ironic then, that the Martian invaders chose their timing to coincide with a period where he thought things were working themselves out.

The memory of those first weeks after the aliens invaded their peaceful life was still as vivid as if it were only yesterday.

Simmons had dragged Surita halfway across the globe to face his accusers in London, the 'so-called' heart of the great

British Empire. He'd torn them away from the country they both loved, and for what?

He'd tried to ignore his wife's final plea, that he should continue, that he needed to be strong. Surita told him he must help those unable to fend for themselves, the children, the poor, anyone who couldn't survive alone against the alien menace.

She'd died in the first month of the Martian invasion. Simmons, the great white hunter, the great colonel of Her Majesty's forces, the great coward, hid at the bottom of a whisky bottle. Instead of following his wife's dying wish, he drank himself into oblivion.

A clock chimed outside the bathroom. His eyes opened to a greasy film covering the surface of the now tepid bathwater, a mixture of the soap-scum and grime that had washed from his skin.

Enough lounging in my own filth and self-pity. His right leg hung out of the tub, an attempt to keep the knee and the filthy wad of bandage dry. *Time to get this cleaned up too.*

As Simmons made his way downstairs in the fluffy white gown, he heard movement in the living room and went to investigate. A trolley sat to one side with an assortment of bandages, gauze pads and several brown bottles of liquid. It looked like a regular field surgery unit.

"Ah, there you are," Bazalgette said. "How are you feeling?"

"Better," Simmons replied, "and a lot less pungent."

"Yes, I took the best part of an hour scrubbing with soap. The sanitiser completed its cycle, but I've run the clothing through again. I wanted to make sure, what with all the other fluids from those horrors."

"Sounds like a good idea."

"So how's the leg? Any more bleeding?"

Simmons shook his head. "No, it's fine. Still hurts like hell, and I struggle if I put too much weight on it. Had to hang onto the handrail on the way down, but I suppose it's early days."

"Let me have a look and see what we need to do with it."

Bazalgette motioned Simmons to a chair beside the trolley. A set of surgical instruments sat in a drawer on the far side of the table.

"I thought you said you weren't a doctor? You seem well equipped."

"I'm not qualified, but you never know when implements such as these might come in useful. I've done a spot of reading, and hopefully, all you require are a few sutures to secure the muscle and then we can close the wound."

Simmons swallowed, hoping it hadn't been too noticeable. "So we don't need a surgeon then?"

"No, it seems a straightforward task."

"And you learned this from a book you read while I was upstairs?"

"Yes, *Anatomy: Descriptive and Surgical, by Henry Gray*. It's a fascinating read, extremely well observed. Oh, and there was a text on field surgery, that was helpful too."

Simmons looked Bazalgette straight in the eye. "You're sure you can do this? Are you confident?"

"I am. It's a simple process of inspecting then stitching the torn muscle. Then I'll deal with the exterior wound. Ensure there is no foreign material in there before closing it, and that's all there is to it. The books were very precise."

"What about anaesthetic?"

"If you want," Bazalgette said with a shrug.

"What do you mean, *if I want*? I think a shot or three of good malt is in order, at the very least."

"I have ether."

"No. Whisky will be fine. I prefer to keep an eye on what's happening."

"If you're sure?"

"Well, now I'm not."

"Come on, Simmons. Trust me."

"You damned well better not say 'I'm a doctor'," Simmons said, settling back into the leather of the armchair.

Bazalgette retrieved the whisky Simmons had sampled earlier and poured him a fresh glass. He offered it to Simmons, who took it with a nod. "You might as well leave me the bottle."

Simmons wasn't sure if it was the medicinal properties of the single malt or Bazalgette's skill with needle and thread, but the whole process was complete in no time. There had been a little discomfort with the initial stitching of the muscle, but that soon passed after polishing off a few glasses.

"So," Bazalgette said. "You need to keep your weight off it as much as you can over the next day or two. The tear was minor, so a good night's rest should do you a world of good, and we can see how things are in the morning."

Simmons vaguely recalled heading back up the broad stairway with Bazalgette supporting him. His leg felt stiff, and it was slow going up the steps. But with the remains of the bottle clasped firmly in his left hand, he finally reached the landing and stumbled off to bed.

23

Foghorns blaring in the distance woke Simmons. The room was unfamiliar, dark, and he took a few moments to recall where he was.

A steady ticking from above the fireplace drew his attention. As his eyes adjusted, the clock face brightened, roman numerals sharpening into focus—five-twenty am. Fleeting memories flooded his alcohol fuddled mind from the previous day and the escape through the sewers. His leg protested as he tried to stand, making him think twice. It was splinted again. *Had Bazalgette done that after stitching him back up?* He must have, when else would he have had the opportunity?

The long wail of the foghorns sounded again from the city walls, and with a decisive motion, Simmons pushed his legs out from under the covers and sat up. He was wide awake, all vestiges of sleep had fallen from him, and it left him with the familiar dry mouth that spoke of excess from the night before.

As he searched the darkened room, his eyes alighted on a washbowl on a bedside cabinet. There was no sign of a glass anywhere, so he hoisted the pitcher to his lips, feeling the cool refreshing water hit his parched throat. In his eagerness, a stream spilt down his face. The chill made him shiver, and he coughed returning the jug before wiping his neck and chops.

Slowly, carefully, he pulled himself to his feet, trying to

balance most of his weight on his good leg. The cabinet helped as he pushed up and supported himself using it as a makeshift crutch.

Intending to head across to the curtained window, he let his right leg take some of the strain. It surprised him how much better it felt than he'd feared. The new splint seemed well constructed, and he only contended with the discomfort of his restricted movement, rather than any of the sickening pain he had encountered before. He inched around the edge of the room, making sure he could support himself if the leg gave way.

Pulling the plush velvet curtains to one side, he peered out into the darkness. Street-lamps dotted the East End, many of them vandalised for the raw materials, saleable if you knew the right people. The imposing slabs of the Inner-City wall jutted up silhouetted against the creeping pre-dawn light. Colours deepened the closer you got to the outer walls surrounded the Capital, increasing to a bright crimson glow where the fog reached out from the Thames.

Shadows shifted in the yellow haze around the gantries topping the walls—the Black Guard. Now they knew his name, the search would be on. Branded as a traitor and murderer, London was no longer a safe place for him.

What now? The logical thing was to get the schematics to Josiah as soon as possible, but Simmons' heart pulled him back towards his lodgings. He had to know what had happened to Mrs Colton, that the old girl was unharmed.

Simmons headed for the house on Wentworth street as soon as the curfew ended at six. He left a note for Bazalgette on the kitchen table and went in search of a cab.

There was still damp in the air, the last remnants of the fog clung to the vegetation. The dew held a subdued red sheen that twisted in swirls and reminded him of playing marbles as a child.

Simmons told the cabbie to drive him past Wentworth Street so he could see if there was any unusual activity. Though, knowing Mrs Colton frequented the fish market first thing, he asked for Dock Street instead. He thought he might intercept her as she returned home.

Workers scurried along the busy track heading to the Western Docks. Wives and mothers passed them on their way to the New Billingsgate Market. They had moved the original when they built the Inner-City.

Simmons left the cab as they neared the Thames, where large warehouses replaced the street-housing. Turning right, he followed Upper East Smithfield to St Katherine's Dock thankful for the help of the walking stick he'd found at the workshop. It was a sturdy thing, more functional than his sword cane, which was back in his lodgings.

The stink of tanneries, breweries and smithy's waned, replaced by fresh fish and the scent of the river. The tangy iron smell of red-weed spores filled the air. Red rivers flowed as if hell had opened its gates, and the gutters ran with blood flooding back to sate the desires of its vile denizens.

He stopped near the main entrance to the covered warehouses. A constant stream of people rubbed shoulders as they went to pick up whatever they could afford to feed their families.

Simmons leaned against the slimy brickwork of a recessed alley beside a seedy public-house as he cleaned and repacked his pipe. All the while he kept an eye on the passers-by, seeking his quarry.

Fifteen minutes passed before he spotted her. The long brown coat pulled tightly about her small frame as she strolled between the two central warehouses skirting the market entrance. Clutching a woven basket, she made her way back towards Dock Street, and Simmons moved to intercept.

He adjusted his pace, allowing himself time to check if she was being followed before speeding up to meet her at the intersection.

He bumped into her, carefully taking her left arm to ensure

she didn't fall. "I'm so sorry, madam," he said in an exaggerated East End accent. "I'm such a clumsy ox," he continued, whispering "Shh," when she caught his eye.

"You nearly knocked me off of my feet," she replied, playing along. Then in a whisper, "Sir Pel, are you all right? The Black Guard are searching for you."

"I wasn't looking, here let me help you." He bent as if retrieving goods fallen from her basket. "Are you well, Mrs C? I never intended for any trouble to come your way."

"I'm fine. They roughed the place up and kicked in your door. The one what done it got frazzled by that lock of yours, but they broke in, and have people watching the house. They gave me a hard time about knowing where you were, but I'm just a simple landlady. How should I know the comings and goings of my residents, especially at all times through the day and night?"

"As long as they haven't hurt you?"

"No, I can look after myself. My Arthur taught me that."

"Good. I'll get money to you for repairs," Simmons whispered grasping the frail looking old woman by the hand. Back into the charade. "I'm ever so sorry to have caused such a mess. I hope you'll forgive me, but I must be on my way."

"It's no problem, Sir Pel," she replied, "all the best." She wiped a single tear on the back of her hand then turned and scurried away.

His breath caught for a second. *Damned Blaggards*. He'd have this out with them. He stifled a laugh, realising what a crazy idea that was. This wasn't some frail elderly lady. Mrs Colton was tough as old boots, and no doubt had given the Black Guard officer as hard a time as he was ever likely to receive from a civilian. He smiled at the thought and left to catch a cab to an overdue meeting in Piccadilly.

Simmons watched the house with the red door from across the street. The thick trunk of the oak provided plenty of cover as he waited. It was approaching midday, but the streets were empty of pedestrians, just the faint sound of traffic from the main thoroughfare.

He crossed the road with a purpose in his steps and banged three solid knocks on the door with his walking cane. It opened. The maid he'd met before started. "Oh. I'm sorry, but the master is not at home."

"Yes, he is," Simmons replied. "Whatever, he's told you about not seeing anyone doesn't apply to me. I have news of his daughter. Urgent news."

He strode along the hallway towards the library, leaving the girl lost for words in the doorway. He thrust the door open and entered the room.

"What the hell," Pemberton shouted, looking up from his desk. "Oh, it's you."

"Good afternoon," Simmons said, taking a seat opposite the man.

"What are you doing here?"

"I bring important news about your daughter. I've found her."

Pemberton's eyes narrowed before he pulled on a new face, natural surprise with a touch of fear. He paused a moment. "Wonderful. Is she all right?"

"Your lack of parental concern is astounding. But it's hardly surprising when the photograph isn't of your daughter, is it?"

Pemberton's hand crept towards the edge of his desk. He screamed as the cane cracked down onto it, pulling it back cradled to his chest. "Bloody hell! What are you doing? You've broken my wrist, you bloody lunatic."

Simmons smiled at the man. "Probably. Nicely weighted, isn't it?"

"What?"

"The cane. It has a good weight."

Pemberton winced, eyes watering. "I'll have you bloody well shot."

"We're not in the army now, Pemberton. I heard it was one of your great pleasures, doing the shooting yourself. As it seems, is lying about my goddaughter. Let's have a nice private conversation about that."

Simmons stood and moved around the desk, pushing the man back with his cane. He pulled the drawer open, revealing a Mauser pistol, just like his own. He frowned. "Well, this is disappointing. I come here to tell you of your daughter, and your first reaction is to pull a gun on me? What am I supposed to think of that?"

"I don't care what you bloody think, get out."

"After you explain what's going on here. Why did you say Annabelle was in trouble then send me looking for someone else? Where is she?"

Venom filled Pemberton's features, and he spat the three words out. "She's bloody dead."

This time it was Simmons' turn to stare in shocked surprise. "What?"

"She died during the invasion. Are you happy now you've uncovered the truth, that's what you do isn't it?"

"But how?"

Pemberton stared at the floor, clutching his injured hand.

Simmons was breathing hard. "Where were you?"

"At a safe location."

"What about Annabelle?"

"There wasn't room."

"HOW COULD YOU?"

Pemberton shuddered, tears dripping from reddened eyes. "They pulled me into a coach and pushed her back. There was nothing I could do."

"Nothing you could do? You bloody coward."

"She was banging on the window, trying to open the carriage door as we drove away, she almost fell under the wheels."

Simmons stared at the broken man before him. Cold fury filled him as he moved towards Pemberton. "Who were they?"

"Robertson's men."

"Black Guard?"

"Yes, his own elite unit. They took me to a secure bunker

somewhere under London, and we waited there for five days. When I returned, the house was intact, not a mark on it. I hoped she'd stayed inside, which she had, with the rest of the staff. But they were all dead."

"How?"

"The Black Smoke. One of the approaching war machines laid down a volley of canisters into the area. Nobody survived."

"Dear God. Annabelle, what did you do to deserve this?" Simmons blinked back tears, teeth grinding. "Damn you, Pemberton. My goddaughter. I swore I'd do anything to keep her from harm."

"She was my bloody daughter."

"And look what you did to protect her. I would have given my life for her."

"Well that's typical Simmons, isn't it? Always holier than though. Defying the powers that be for your own personal crusade, giving up everything for love. How did that work out for you?"

Simmons raised the cane, fire in his eyes, and Pemberton flinched. The blow never landed. "Damn you, Pemberton. If there is a hell for the worst cowards and traitors, then what do you think awaits those who sacrifice their children?"

"I couldn't do anything. It wasn't my fault."

"It never is, is it?"

Pemberton's body heaved, a wave of sobs consuming him.

Simmons emptied the rounds from the Mauser and returned it to the drawer. "So, you sold me out to the Black Guard?"

"They said they would ruin me unless I complied."

"Pity, that would have been fitting. What about the girl? Some phoney photograph so they could find her?"

"Yes. They've lost her, and she's important to them. They found out about my link to you through Annabelle and someone came up with the plan to use you to locate her."

"What is she to them?"

"I don't know."

"You didn't ask?"

"You don't ask questions of Robertson. That's a sure way to lose fingers."

"You'll never be free of them. You know that, don't you?"

Pemberton sighed and nodded. "What now?"

"I should bloody shoot you for cowardice. But I'm not like you." Simmons dropped a single round for the Mauser onto the desk. It rolled in a slow half circle to clink against Pemberton's cup and saucer. "There's the gentleman's way out if you can find an ounce of courage or remorse. You don't deserve it, and I fear you'll end up living the rest of your miserable life with the memory of what you should have done. Good luck with that."

He turned, leaving the Piccadilly house for what he knew would be the last time.

When Simmons returned, Bazalgette was waiting. "Where have you been? I was worried. How's the leg?"

"It's fine, I found this," he waved the walking cane. "I presumed it would be all right to borrow."

"Of course, whatever you need. Do you want tea? The kettle has just boiled."

They retreated into the house, Bazalgette leading them to the rear of the ground floor and a large kitchen table. True to his word, a black kettle sat on his electric range. Simmons hadn't noticed before. He'd assumed it was coal or wood burning. "Your range is powered by electricity?"

"Yes, everything here is. Can't abide gas, much too dangerous. Just one leak undetected could end up blowing the entire street apart. Electricity is the future: safe, clean power. I heard Tesla is working on producing such vast quantities he can give it away, for free."

"I don't see that happening," Simmons said. "Why would anyone do that? It's got to be a trick or scam."

"No, it's the truth. One reason he left America was around the companies over there and how they were trying to earn from his inventions. He's a true scientist and philanthropist. He thinks it's his duty before God to make this world a better place for all of humankind."

"Sounds like too much electricity arced between his ears, to me."

"Were you always such a cynic, Simmons, or do you have to keep in practice?"

"I've seen the darkness in men's hearts too often to believe in such nonsense. I hope I'm proved wrong someday, but nothing makes me feel it will happen anytime soon."

Bazalgette sighed. "What do you prefer?"

"What?" Simmons said, looking up.

"Tea. Do you like anything in particular? I have a few blends, how about Indian?"

"Yes, that would be grand."

Two streaming mugs thumped down onto the table, along with a milk jug and sugar bowl.

They discussed their options and agreed on the plan to get the schematics back to Josiah as soon as possible. Then they could quiz him about his brother and father's work. Bazalgette suggested they inspect the microfilm before handing it over. So they knew they had the correct information if nothing else.

Bazalgette led the way down to the basement level workshop with Simmons in tow. He'd got used to the cane, and it improved both his balance and relieved the pain in his right leg. At this rate, he might be up and about without it by the end of the week.

The stairway opened out into a broad area which must have covered the entire floor space of the building. Several workbenches lined the walls, each with a variety of components and mechanisms in various stages of completion. Or at least looked near complete to Simmons.

Massive coils of copper pipes, tubes and wires ran around the place and fell from regular cable runs from the roof, to drop to selected workspaces.

Simmons pointed over to one bench where a series of

familiar blue tubes rang alongside a large barrel. "Ah, that's the arc-rifle, isn't it?"

"Yes, I've been stripping it down to look at the internal mechanism and the power source. It's a very complex piece of work, and there are parts I'm still not sure I understand. It should keep me out of mischief for a while." He gave Simmons a wry smile.

"Not for long, I bet."

"Over here," Bazalgette waved for Simmons to join him where several intricate devices stood, one of which looked very much like a microscope.

Producing the small octagonal box from his pocket, Bazalgette removed the circle of dark film from within. He opened a panel on the device, placed the spool inside then pressed it closed. The machine whirred, and light shone from the eyepiece.

"Let's see what we have," Bazalgette said peering in while rotating a short handle on the side.

Bazalgette pulled himself away from the machine after a few minutes. "There are hundreds of schematics," he said. "Overviews of the mechanism, then lots of diagrams of a tiny section hidden deep within the watch. It's remarkable work, and the power transfer system," he seemed breathless, lost for words. "I don't understand how it works, let alone how it interacts with the other components. It will take time to study this in enough detail."

"That, my friend, is something we are short on."

"Yes, you make a valid point, but there's more here than just the watch schematics."

"What do you mean?"

"There are additional designs hidden amongst the ones for the watch. I thought they were blemishes in the film, but some appear in repeated locations between the other schematics, so I zoomed in, and there they were."

"So not so secret then, if you could find them so quickly."

"I'm not sure that's entirely true. My equipment has significant upgrades and magnifies over ten times more than a standard viewer."

"Another of the re-engineering projects you seem so fond of?"

"Well, yes. But the level of detail is incredible, getting it onto the microfilm in the first place is a work of genius. I feel that almost anyone else would overlook the blemishes as just that, scratches or faults in the film."

"So what do these secrets designs show?"

"It looks like a battle suit."

"The ones Dent described?" Simmons asked, his voice low.

Bazalgette nodded, his eyes wide. "Yes, these must be the original schematics for the ArcAngels."

24

Simmons led as he and Bazalgette wound their way through the maze of tight alleys that formed the outskirts of The Devil's Acre. It owned a reputation as one of the foulest slums in the city. Not only from the squalid living conditions but also the reception you were likely to receive from its residents.

Simmons exited the dark alley into Pye Street, stepping over a comatose figure stinking of cheap gin and excrement. "Try not to stare at anyone. They can be an unsavoury lot, with short tempers."

Bazalgette nodded and mumbled that he understood. *Damn, what a cesspit this place is*, Simmons thought, but they needed a way out of the city, and this was where to find it. He'd been here before in search of items difficult to get on the open market.

Simmons was to meet his contact at one of the gin palaces in the area. How they could liken anything around here to a palace was beyond him. People spilt out of the filthy ruins of buildings and sat or lay on the broken cobbles propped against the brickwork. Half-naked women leant from rotting windows calling lewd comments to the men below, while young children sprawled in doorways, draining the dregs from dirty bottles passed between them.

The smell was rank, worse than in the sewers. Musty

odours of bodies that hadn't seen soap in some time, if ever, assaulted them. It mixed with the raw sewage in the gutters, flung from the morning's chamber pots into the street. All this within sight of Westminster Palace.

The shadow from the clock tower, housing Big Ben, spread over the slate-roofed drinking establishment. The contact, lazing in a dark backroom, pointed him a few streets away to The Widow's Arms.

As they reached the intersection with the next street, a large figure appeared out of the shadows ahead of them blocking their way—a thick-set fellow wearing a filthy green and yellow check jacket.

"What do we have here?" came a deep Irish accent, loud pops echoing from the walls as he cracked his knuckles.

Simmons left his hand resting on his pistol. "We don't want any trouble. We're here to meet someone."

"Is that so, gents? Look, lads. They're here to meet someone."

Two further figures emerged from the dark recesses of the alley. "Looks like they've met someone, Jack." This came from a smaller man in a similar jacket to the first. His eyes ferreted between Simmons and Bazalgette while an uncontrolled twitch distorted the puckered scar between his eye and mouth.

"I'll keep this simple for you," Simmons said. "To make sure it gets through that thick skull of yours. We are here to see Ratter. If you don't get your sorry excuse for a brain to move that slab of fat out of my way, I'll put a hole through it. And that follows for your two lackeys."

The veins in the huge man's neck bulged, his yellow-tinged eyes widened, and Simmons waited for the swing of one of those meaty fists. But it didn't happen. He squinted back at Simmons. "Where are you meeting this fella then?"

It was a test. He was checking that Simmons hadn't just come across the name to put the fear of God into them.

"Backroom at The Widow, as usual."

Suddenly the big man was all smiles. "Right you are, sir. Sorry for any misunderstanding."

Mumbled words of disagreement echoed from the other group members as they retreated into the alley, followed by a sharp slap, then silence.

"Erm," Bazalgette whispered. "I thought you said not to upset anyone?"

"Sometimes you need to break the rules a little. As long as you know when to do it."

~

The Widows Arms was a mess of dark wood at odd angles, speaking of constant repairs. The sign above the door depicted a severe-looking woman in black with arms crossed, one brandishing a bloodied kitchen knife. It hung at a crooked angle and creaked from the slight breeze that blew in from the southern end of the street bringing the stink of the Thames with it.

The raucous squawking and harsh laughter spilt onto the cobbles, along with the smell of hops and gin. Simmons walked straight in, Bazalgette following swiftly behind.

Dim reflections from pewter tankards and stained glasses shed shards of light up the walls. Heavy black wooden beams crossed the low ceiling, making Simmons duck as he entered.

People packed the place, standing shoulder-to-shoulder and, from further within, the sound of fiddles and singing permeated the smoke-filled air.

Simmons pushed through the mass of bodies to the bar and caught the barman's attention. "Ratter?"

The bartender looked them up and down, seemed to think for a moment, then with a curt nod, he motioned them to follow him. He led them to a room at the back of the building, which was strangely quiet. Four men and a woman sat around a table, the rest of the area was empty, and a palpable atmosphere filled the space.

These weren't patrons, even though they had beer and cards in play. This was the group that kept things in order for the man called Ratter. The black market used intelligent people, not slabs of dull-witted muscle, as he'd encountered on the street. These were hardened killers, fast and deadly.

The barman walked in and tapped twice on a wall panel, then pulled it aside onto narrow steps leading up. He turned to Simmons and Bazalgette, nodding towards the new doorway then left without a word.

Halfway up the stairs, the wooden panel clicked back into place below them, and they emerged into a dim room with sloping eaves. A single lantern stood on a table at the rear of the attic. Simmons crossed to the figure sat there who finished writing then looked up.

"Simmons, my old friend. What can I do for you this fine evening?"

Ratter had a strong accent that elongated his vowels. He'd been a penniless Russian immigrant some years back. Now he was *the* man to go to if you needed something unusual.

"Ratter, this is my friend, Bazalgette."

Ratter nodded to Bazalgette, then returned his gaze to Simmons.

"We need to get out of London."

"Ah, Yes." Ratter relaxed into the leather chair. "I received some disturbing news earlier, regarding you and your friend."

"We ran into a little trouble with the Black Guard," Simmons said.

"Hmm, that seems a significant understatement. The whole garrison is on alert, a full patrol dead, murdered by a cowardly trap is how I heard it. Didn't sound like your work."

"I only shot one officer as I recall."

"Oh," Bazalgette added. "The other two in the street might have died too. The arcs from their rifles and the shrapnel caused their weapons to explode."

"Mister Bazalgette, welcome to the conversation," Ratter said.

"Thank you," Bazalgette replied.

"I meant it sincerely. I prefer we have an open discussion, so there are no misunderstandings. That way, everybody knows what they are getting into."

"Understood."

"Please, gentlemen, take a seat." Ratter motioned to where two chairs stood to the side in the eves.

Simmons dragged the seats to the table, and he and Bazalgette sat. "So, can you help us?"

"You know me, Simmons, always ready to help a friend."

"What's it going to cost?"

"Oh dear, as ever, straight to the point. No discussion, no preamble, but why should I expect you to shed that skin?" Ratter smiled, a glimmer in his eye.

"We are in somewhat of a hurry. The Black Guard are on our heels, and my travel documents are useless."

"And you have no other ways out, a man of your reputation? I'm disappointed, Simmons."

"Unfortunately, the Black Guard saw our return to the city. So, that access point is no doubt sealed and patrolled by now."

"Unfortunate, indeed." Ratter weighed the price in his mind. "In that case, one hundred guineas."

Simmons' eyes bulged. "How much?"

"I'm sure you heard me. I speak very clearly when discussing monetary transactions."

"That's true, but I am struggling to comprehend the sum involved," Simmons replied.

"We have a network to support. Work like this is challenging, especially when helping known criminals escape the Black Guard. Do you realise how hard it is to find people in that group willing to aid us?"

"You have members of the Black Guard in your employ?" Bazalgette asked.

Simmons turned to his friend. "They don't so much help as are forced to comply. Bribes, blackmail, threats and other forms of coercion. Once they let one thing slip, like letting certain goods through a gate without a full inspection, then they're trapped, caught in our friend's web. Isn't that right, Ratter?"

"Well, I wouldn't put it in such crude terms myself, but you have the gist of it covered. I am sensing opposition to my generous offer. Is there something you would like to discuss further, or shall we conclude our business and go our separate ways?"

"Look, Ratter. It's too much—simple as that. Come on, be reasonable. We've worked together before. Am I not a good customer, payment up front or well within agreed timeframes?"

"This is true, but the price remains. I hope you continue your excellent repayment schedule. But unless you have another way of navigating the sewers, there is nothing more to discuss."

Bazalgette's face lit up. "I think we can come to an arrangement."

After speaking at length, they came to an agreement. Bazalgette's sewer maps held information even the black market was unaware of. It seemed this knowledge was more important to them than cold hard cash. Simmons topped up his supply of rounds for both his rifle and the Mauser and received a substantial discount as part of the deal.

Ratter told them it would take a while to organise everything and they should return the following evening to meet their guide who would escort them out of the city.

They left the way they had entered and made it back to Bazalgette's workshop with plans to lie low and relax for the next day.

The following morning, Simmons found no sign of Bazalgette in the living room or kitchen, but soon the telltale sounds of activity from below became apparent. *I have to tell him to stay here, where it's safe.* Simmons descended the stairs. *The Black Guard only know my name, so why should he risk his neck for me?*

"So I was thinking," he began as he stepped down the final step into the workshop.

"Simmons, excellent timing. I've cracked it."

"Cracked what?"

"The frequency of the original watches."

"How—"

"Well, I couldn't sleep," Bazalgette said, still sitting by the microfilm viewer. "So I thought I'd come down here and see if I could find anything further from the schematics."

"All right. How long have you been working on this?"

Bazalgette flipped open his pocket watch. "Since three this morning, give or take a few minutes."

"So, what have you found?" Simmons said.

"Sixteen point eight megahertz. That's the frequency Dent's father used in the watches. He devised a crystal that controls the precision of the device using high-frequency oscillation."

Simmons stared at him. "I don't have a clue what you are saying. You sound very excited by this, but I can't understand half the words you are throwing at me."

"Well," Bazalgette said. "I suppose the technical stuff isn't that important. I've found a way to locate the original timepieces."

"Right," Simmons said, realisation dawning on him. "So we need to detect that frequency?"

"Exactly."

"Can you build something?"

"I believe so. I have everything required, and with a spot of tinkering, I should be able to power it from the arc-lamp battery."

"How long will it take?"

"Well, a few hours for a working prototype, then it's a matter of refining the design."

How do I tell the man I don't need him, and he should remain here? He was a pain in the backside on occasion, but less often than when they had first met, but he was a genius all the time.

"Bazalgette?" Simmons asked.

"Yes."

"I wanted to say thank you. For all you've done."

"It's no trouble," Bazalgette said, his mind already speeding off on a new track of thought. The present, a station fading into the foggy distance behind him.

∼

True to his word, Bazalgette had a prototype within the hour. The device was a clunky but functional contraption of wood and brass. It was the size of a pocketbook, but thicker to house all the workings. Intricate wound coils at the front led through a series of electrical gizmos to a dial.

Simmons had struggled with the patience to understand theoretical science. He didn't feel the need to know how things worked, just how to use them if they were useful.

Bazalgette's detailed explanation revolved around a few key points. These were, connect the device to a power source. In this case, his battery pack for the arc-lamp. He had already constructed a pair of leads that clipped between the terminals and the scanner.

Second, twiddle the knob below the dial to set the desired frequency. It sounded simple enough, but that wasn't enough for Bazalgette. He added a tiny cone that acted as a speaker horn from which they could hear a sound representing the strength of the signal.

Bazalgette demonstrated his invention. He tuned the device until they heard an audible click which matched each twitch of the needle on the dial. As he moved towards the watch, the clicking became louder, increasing in tempo as he got nearer.

They tested it with Simmons hiding the watch somewhere in the upstairs rooms of the house while Bazalgette waited below in the workshop. It was a resounding success. Each time Bazalgette located it after a few minutes, even when it was at the bottom of a wardrobe wrapped in a sock and stuffed into a boot.

The trial established the machine to have an effective range of around thirty feet. It was possible to pick up a weak signal beyond that, but it depended on the obstacles in the path to its target. The denser the material, the trickier it was to locate. This had seemed evident to Simmons, but Bazalgette still wanted to test each type of obstacle. Wood, stone and brick of varying thicknesses.

When satisfied, Bazalgette retreated to the kitchen to prepare tea and food before their evening jaunt to meet their black market guide.

"You don't need to come along, you know," Simmons called, trying to broach the subject as gently as he could. "I'm sure I can operate the device."

Bazalgette popped his head around the corner. "Nonsense. Do you think I'd let you have all the fun locating that watch on your own? I want to be there when we find it, see it in person. Anyhow, if there are any issues with the detector, you'll need me to fix it."

Simmons shrugged, *well, that's told me.* He went to check his gear ready for the long evening ahead.

25

Shards of icy rain blew almost horizontally, biting at exposed skin. Simmons raised his coat collar trying to deflect the worst, to no real avail. He and Bazalgette shivered and water sluiced from them as they searched for a cab to take them towards Westminster. Dropping bags onto the floor, they took their seats for the bumpy ride west back to the Devil's Acre.

The constant patter of rain on the glass created streaks that refracted the street lights into starbursts of colour on the grease-stained windows. Bazalgette reached to check his canvas bag for what must have been the fifth time since they'd left the workshop.

Simmons leaned across and caught his friends arm. "Did you pack everything you wanted before we set off?"

"I think so."

"And was it all in order the last time you checked?"

"I suppose so."

"In that case, it will still be all right now. Rely on the knowledge you've done this already. Anything we've left behind or forgotten, we'll need to work around or find from here on."

"That's easy for you to say."

"Yes, it is. Sit back and relax. There is no benefit in getting anxious about what may or may not occur. We planned as much as we can, now we follow the plan until we have to change it. Even the best-laid plans never run as expected. You need to accept that."

Bazalgette slumped into the hard leather seat, clasping his gloved hands together. Simmons leaned back, closing his eyes as the staccato beat of the rain danced over the cab's exterior. As the vehicle shifted in the heavy gusts, he let himself drift off as they covered the final minutes of their journey. He opened them as the cab came to a halt. They needed to brave the elements again, which tonight seemed to have it in for them.

He paid the drenched cabbie the shilling they had agreed earlier and jumped to the rain-battered street. Puddles grew and shifted as the raging night air swirled. The vortex caused by the tightly packed houses buffeted them towards the entrance to The Acre which looked surprisingly empty. *It seems even the drunks and low-lives find somewhere undercover in this weather.* Simmons led the way again towards their meeting at The Widows Arms.

Light spilt from several of the buildings en route. The shouts of merriment identified them as places of entertainment, whether it be of the flesh or a more liquid variety.

As they crossed Pye Street heading for the pub, a figure detached itself from the shadows stepping into their path. Simmons' hand was already on his pistol, and he felt no inclination to remove it.

A soft glow illuminated the underside of a wide-brimmed hat dripping with rainwater and revealed a woman's features as she drew on a thin stemmed pipe. "Mister Simmons? Ratter sent me, said you needed a guide. So you can follow me or stay here getting soaked. No difference to me, I get paid either way."

She turned and strode into a side alley that ran beside The Widow, fading into the darkness, a dull orange glow illuminating the slick walls as she departed.

Bazalgette looked to Simmons. "Do we trust her?"

"No, of course not. But we have little choice other than to follow."

They caught up with the woman, splashing through thick puddles in the alley. The rain bounced from the roofs, cascading down the rough brick. It created small rivers that meandered and formed lakes they each tried to avoid.

"So you decided you fancied a walk, eh?"

"So it seems," Simmons replied. "Do you have a name?"

"Most everyone does."

Simmons waited for her to continue, but the slow splash of her feet on the wet cobbles and the rain pounding on his hat was the only reply.

"So, are you going to tell us?" he asked.

"Does it matter?"

"Well, it's a little easier than shouting 'hey, guide', don't you think?"

"I'm not sure what all the fuss is about." She exhaled a large plume of pungent blue-grey smoke which billowed off the tight alley wall. "Call me Molly, if you must."

As much as he wanted to be flippant, Simmons held his response in check. "So, Molly, how far do we have to travel this fine evening?"

"Well, I hope you brought your best walking boots 'cos we have a fair trek ahead. I see you have fog-gear, that will be useful, if you want to avoid spewing blood from every orifice, that is."

"Now we've got you talking, you don't say much of use, do you?"

"That'll be right. So, if you'll kindly shut up, we can get moving and out of this pissy downpour. Unless you prefer to keep me yapping, so I can't hear if we're being followed?"

Simmons bit back another response. "Very well. Please, lead the way." He checked behind over his shoulder.

Bazalgette adjusted his pack to a more comfortable position then shrugged, water dripping from his hair and beard. "It would be rather nice to get out of this dreadful weather."

Molly led them through the dark confines of the Devil's Acre. The narrow streets squeezed inward, and on two occasions, she doubled back, ensuring nobody was following them. Finally, they stopped at a dead end in one of the many alleys between the walls of sooty red brick.

She rapped on the wooden doorway three times, a short pause then twice more. The conditions that evening hadn't improved. They were all dripping wet and shivered from the harsh windblown rain gusting through the winding rat warren.

A creak accompanied the door as it opened into a dimly lit interior. Molly wasted no time in pushing her way in, out of the torrential downpour. Simmons nodded for Bazalgette to follow as he checked over his shoulder before ducking into the welcome warmth of the hovel.

Three gruff-looking fellows glanced up from around a table, seated as they had been the previous evening at The Widow's Arms. The door closed behind them with a solid thunk as the security bar slammed into place.

"Molly, you look like a drowned rat, love," the woman at the door said. She made shooing noises at the three men with the cards. "Move up, you lazy buggers. Let poor Molly get some warmth from that fire."

There were squeals of wood on the stone floor as they shifted over, and Molly didn't wait for an invitation, moving to the dancing flames. Simmons and Bazalgette followed as the wave of heat hit them from the crackling logs glowing red and white before slowly charring.

Molly looked back to the other woman. "Damn it's cold out there tonight, Lizzie. Thought I'd catch my death. Tell me again how it is you get to stay in this cosy little hole while I trudge about getting piss-wet-through?"

"Good judgement, my love, and someone needs to keep an eye on this sorry lot." Lizzie nodded her head towards the gamblers at the table. The men hadn't missed a beat with the clink of coin followed by the flick of cards on the stained tabletop.

Simmons removed his hat, trying not to pour too much water from the dripping brim. "Is there somewhere we can put these to dry?"

"This ain't no bleeding laundry, darling," Lizzie replied with a laugh. She moved to the side of the small room and unhitched a line from the wall leading towards the ceiling. Above her hung a rectangular frame of wood to hang clothes on. She released the cord bringing the airer down to chest height. Molly looked at her. "Well, stone me if you ain't running a laundry after all, Liz."

A fit of cackling laughter echoed off the rough plastered walls. Simmons smiled, trying his best not to scowl at the witches. He removed his dripping coat and looped it over the frame. Bazalgette and Molly followed Simmons' lead, and Lizzie hoisted the airer back into place. Simmons couldn't have said Lizzie was pretty, but she wasn't ugly either. Her face was square around the jaw, and her features a little too sharp. But who was he to judge beauty? He was no Adonis.

He returned to the fireplace, alternating between rubbing his hands together and holding them out till they felt like they were melting. The crackle and pop of the splitting logs filled the room, interrupted by the sizzle of drips from the clothing above.

∼

The constant chatter of the two women catching up grated. After what seemed hours, Molly stood. "Right gentlemen, shall we?"

Simmons leapt to his feet, and Molly led them into a back room, laughter and faint music reverberated through the wall ahead of them. Instead of continuing that way, she took them to the left and a trapdoor in the floor. After opening the metal lock, she struggled to free the thick wood and iron panel.

Bazalgette stepped forward. "May I be of assistance?"

"Aren't you a darling?" she said, stepping back. Bazalgette wasn't a big man, but he knew how to lift things. *Must be all that practice with sewer grates*, Simmons thought.

Steps led down and out of sight into the blackness below.

Bazalgette lit the arc-lamp with a now familiar crackle and hum followed by the intense cone of light.

"Well, would you look at that," Molly said. "That puts my poor oil lamp to shame it does."

The light flooded the stairs illuminating the first ten steps as Bazalgette led the way.

"Straight down to the bottom, then you should see a cover ahead," Molly said following after Bazalgette. "Close the trap behind you, Mr Simmons. One of those worthless immigrants will lock it later."

The thick trapdoor was heavier than he'd thought, and it dropped with a resounding thud. Dust leapt into the air around his head, causing him to cough.

"Mind the last few inches. I once nearly brained myself dropping that."

"Thanks for the warning," Simmons replied, coughing as he turned and followed the others into a cold cellar.

Wooden barrels lined the walls, and true to her word, a grilled opening appeared in the floor a few feet beyond the final step. An odour wafted up, reminding Simmons of his last trip through the sewers.

Molly was fishing inside her coat for something and pulled out a large key-chain. She thumbed past a few smaller keys before settling on one.

"Here we go," she said, kneeling to unlock the heavy padlock. In a few minutes, they were descending a wood and rope ladder. It looked frayed at points, but though it stretched a little, it soon felt sturdy and supported their combined weight. Bazalgette took the lead with the arc-lamp lighting the way as they descended twenty feet.

Simmons headed down second at Molly's instruction. She had stopped to lock the padlock, and with a clang of metal on stone, it closed behind them.

Halfway down, the wall changed from rough rock to broken brickwork, and stepping down the final few rungs, he recognised the familiar arched walls of the sewers.

Light from the arc-lamp played across the tunnel roof as

Bazalgette surveyed the area. "It looks like they dug down to intersect with this part of the sewer," he said, still looking at the entry point as Molly descended into the beam.

"Do you mind not staring right up my skirt?" she asked.

The light pulled away to illuminate a section of tunnel to their left, but even as darkness fell around Bazalgette, Simmons saw the glowing crimson on his face.

"I'm ever so sorry," he blurted. "I was just admiring the view."

"Really?"

"Of the sewer roof. Where the tunnels break into—"

Amusing as it was, Simmons decided he couldn't let his friend flounder any further in this deep water. "I think you should quit while you're ahead."

"While I'm ahead?"

"Yes, you know? Move on, onto subjects new."

"I suppose that would be prudent."

Molly stepped down from the ladder with a splash. "Oh, doesn't that top it all?" she complained. "If it isn't young men trying to look up your skirt with torches, it's wet feet."

Bazalgette turned to face her. "It was an accident. I am terribly sorry."

"It's all right, dearie. If you'd just asked, I'd have shown you for a shilling."

"Wha—" Bazalgette stammered, he stuttered making a series of croaks and clicks in his throat before turning and moving forward covering some distance to be alone with his embarrassment.

Simmons looked at Molly, and they shared the joke at poor Bazalgette's expense. "Well, Mr Simmons, that were a funny do. But the same goes for you if you've got a spare shilling." She winked at him and sauntered down the tunnel after the diminishing light.

Simmons swallowed. *Did she mean? No, that was just another joke, at my expense this time. Wasn't it?*

Bazalgette hardly said a word, especially when Molly was near. He'd mentioned they were heading southeast and should be close to an outflow to the Thames soon if they continued at their current pace. He busied himself, adding extra details to his notebook.

Simmons checked his watch. He flicked the casing, which clicked open as faithfully as ever. It was approaching ten o'clock.

Molly looked at her map, counting to herself. "It's two junctions further on the left." She pointed to continue down the central tunnel, rather than taking the smaller tributary and continued their slow and steady pace through the ankle-deep sludge. It was hard going, and Simmons could feel the ache growing in his leg. As the others continued, he took the opportunity for another swig from his flask—for medicinal purposes.

They moved across to the wall and clambered onto a narrow ledge. It was less than a foot wide, but was a welcome relief for aching muscles, and removed the threat of getting their boots filled with water.

"Not far now," Molly said, looking up from her map. "Another two turns, and we should be there."

With spirits lightened, they made good time, and following the arching bend of the smaller sewer, saw a sizeable grilled gateway across the width of the tunnel, barring their progress.

The sewage level had risen and now lapped at the edge of the walkway, about waist deep Simmons guessed. It had picked up speed a little too, dirty grey froth bubbling up where it pushed through the gate.

"So, what next?" Simmons asked, "is there some secret lever that opens it?"

"Hardly," came the tired reply from their guide. "But I have the magic key."

She pulled the chain from inside her coat and rattled through several keys in the bright light from Bazalgette's lamp.

"There she is." Molly pushed a small key to the top of the

metal chain that kept the tangle of jangling objects clasped together.

"There's a lock on a grille at the base of the gate, low enough to be concealed, even at the lowest tide mark. You'll need to open it and push yourselves through."

Simmons looked at her as if she were mad. "What? You want us to go under that?" he said, pointing at the dark churning water.

"Well, unless you have a better plan?"

"No, it's fine," Bazalgette said. "We best undress, we can pass the clothes through the bars, so at least we'll have something dry on the other side."

"What?" Simmons said again, a little more concern in his tone.

"Oh, what a great idea," Molly said. She rubbed her hands together, a wicked grin spreading across her face. "Shall I hold the lamp this time?"

≈

Bazalgette stripped down to his cream-coloured long johns.

"Aren't they coming off as well?" Molly asked.

He ignored her and slipped into the water which rushed around him above his waist. "It's not too bad," he said through chattering teeth. "Once you get used to it."

Molly passed him the key-chain. "You be careful with that. I'll bloody kill you if you lose it. The padlock is down near the bottom of the grille which hinges along its top edge. It's two feet square."

Bazalgette moved to the gate and knelt in the flow, the water rising towards his neck. He extended his hand below the waterline and fiddled for a few minutes. "It's tricky, not being able to see the lock and all. Just a minute, got it." He retrieved the padlock and clipped the arm around one bar of the gate, holding it in place above the rushing water.

"Right," he said. "I'll try to get my shoulders through, if they fit, it will be a doddle for the rest of me."

"Good luck," Simmons said while his friend took a series of long deep breaths. He continued his breathing, signalling to Simmons with a raised thumb. Then ducked below the dark surface.

Simmons could hear nothing beyond the gurgle and splashes around the gate, then a mop of black hair surfaced on the far side. "Are you all right?"

Bazalgette wiped the water from his face. "Yes, but I wouldn't advise you open your eyes in this stuff."

Simmons grimaced. "Fine, let's get this gear through the bars and move on."

Bazalgette crossed to the walkway, and between them, they moved all their equipment except the canvas bag he'd brought, containing the arc-rifle. "It won't fit through, will it?"

"No," Simmons said, "the barrel is far too thick. Is the bag waterproof?"

Bazalgette sighed. "I fear we're about to find out. Let's get it through as quickly as possible."

It was an easier job than either of them had thought. Simmons carried it on his shoulder to the side of the gate, while Bazalgette waited on the other, holding the grille open with one hand. On the count of three, Simmons shoved the bag under the water and launched it forward. It was submerged for only a second or two before it broke the surface. Bazalgette lifted it into the air, drips beading and dropping back into the frothing stream around him.

Simmons made his way through the grille with much less trouble than he had feared. He had never felt comfortable swimming, even when in clean water. This was more akin to slithering along the bottom of an enormous filthy bathtub, and his relief to break the surface without drowning was palpable.

Bazalgette locked the grill before crossing to the walkway. He used his undershirt to rub himself dry, then discarded the discoloured and soaked long johns, and Simmons followed his lead.

Molly roared with laughter at their half-naked attempts to evade the roving arc-lamp beam, and she seemed sad to relinquish it. She lit her oil lamp, shedding a pale glow compared to the light from Bazalgette's electrical device. "This is where our paths go their separate ways, my dears. I'll be heading back to my cosy fire."

"Where do we go from here?" Simmons asked.

"Follow the stream for another hundred yards, and it opens into an outflow to the Thames. Someone will meet you there."

"Thank you for your help, Molly," Simmons said.

"Oh, don't thank me. You already paid good for this, and thanks for my generous tip."

"Tip?" Simmons said.

"Yes, I definitely got *my* two shillings worth," she said with that same wicked smile. "Possibly even two-and-six." She winked then turned, cackling, and headed off into the darkness, leaving both Simmons and Bazalgette lost for words.

A dull red glow grew in intensity as they approached the exit tunnel. They both reached for their respirators, but as they had assumed, there was little fog, just a light swirl of vapours on the surface of the dark waters beyond. The familiar shape of a patchwork wooden boat with a square tarpaulin tent at the stern came into view as the rounded the last bend. "Well, bless me if it ain't Mister Simmons and Mister Bazalgette."

"Isaac, you old dog. I didn't know you worked for the black market."

"Any port in a storm, as they say, Mister Simmons. Now get yourselves aboard, we've got a fair way to go to where you are staying tonight."

26

"If I'd known it was you two, I might have found a better safe house," Isaac said as he leaned on the tiller. "What's the rush to be out here by the old sewer gate? You fallen out with the Black Guard?"

Simmons smiled. "Something like that. How far is it to this place?"

"It's a fair trek, are you planning on heading back to Josiah? Cos if you are, it might be as well to sod the safe house and get you to the observatory instead."

Simmons looked towards Bazalgette, who nodded. "Greenwich it is then, Isaac, full steam ahead."

Isaac turned to Bazalgette. "Don't he know this is a diesel engine?"

"No, he'll probably ask you to hoist sail if we're not moving soon."

Simmons walked to the prow, letting them enjoy their little joke. It felt good to hear humour from Bazalgette.

They cut through the dark waters under the steady thrum of the motor. Even though the fog was more like thin red steam rising from the surface, they all wore full fog-gear.

The rain bounced from the deck, and myriads of droplets danced on the Thames. The splashes evoked strange patterns on the river as circular ripples expanded and merged. It created a weird soundscape as drops struck wood and water, the sounds muffled and distorted by their protective fog masks.

Searchlights from the north bank reached into the darkness from the city walls. It was nothing for them to worry about, most scanned the streets hoping to capture those breaking curfew. Their jaunt along the Thames was likely to go unnoticed by anyone.

As they passed under Tower Bridge, a cough from the stern and the whine of motors struggling to continue their rotations signalled the engine failing. It spat twice then fell silent.

"Oh, that's bloody typical," Isaac said, emerging from his tarp. He grabbed a pole and thrust it towards Simmons. "Here, take this and make sure we don't hit anything."

"What's wrong?" Simmons asked before Isaac headed back to the stern.

"A blockage or shitty fuel. I'll have a look." With that, he disappeared to start his repairs.

The vessel found a large patch of overgrown red weed that clung to one of the bridge stanchions and halted. Its rise and fall made it seem like the alien plant was gently rocking them to sleep before crawling aboard to strangle them in the dark.

The rain continued unabated though the bridge sheltered them from most of it. Curtains of water fell a few feet ahead of them where it drained from the edge of the road. The mesmerising waterfall split and shifted in its relentless thundering drop into the depths.

It took Simmons back to the first raindrops appearing on the windows, signalling the start of the monsoons. The small drops twisting their way down the pane, joining with fellows to plummet out of sight. A prelude of what was to come with the deluge of rain that turned dusty earth into torrential rivers of mud.

He looked up at the sharp pop and rumble of the engine bursting into life for a few seconds, then fading. More discussion followed from the stern before another series of cracks and splutters reverberated under the bridge. *Hell, they must have heard that the other side of Whitechapel.* Simmons hoped the rise in the fog-level over the last half-hour helped in masking the sound.

The engine continued to sputter and cough for a while, before changing in tone, returning to a throaty but stable growl. Simmons leant on the pole, forcing them from the support, and away from the thickest of the weed.

As they breached the sheets of cascading water, Simmons held his hat and pulled his coat tight. He only just kept his footing as the deluge sluiced over him, bouncing from the deck with a heavy thrum. He turned and watched with fascination as the waterfall proceeded back along the vessel's length.

"Bazalgette, Isaac, look out," he called, but it was too late as the torrent beat down onto the canvas cover at the stern.

Above the noise of water striking wood and tarp, there came a new sound, something between a shout and a squeal as the downpour caught his comrades unaware. Two figures appeared from the gloom, drenched and with hair plastered to their skulls between the straps of fog masks which looked somewhat off-kilter.

As much as he tried to keep his face straight, an exterior of professional calm and order, he failed miserably. He burst into peals of laughter. Even the seals of his respirator couldn't contain his mirth. A fact made clear by the dirty looks he got from both Isaac and Bazalgette.

When he finally pulled himself together, he stood before the two drowned rats. "I'm sorry chaps. I tried to warn you, but what with the masks and the fog, it seemed a forlorn task."

Their stares could have killed men at twenty paces. As he was close to that distance, he thought better of finishing the sentence with 'but at least we're underway again'.

With the fuel situation resolved, they arrived in Greenwich close to midnight. A plume of steam mixed with thick smoke from the engine where Isaac and Bazalgette had dried off, having spent the final leg of their voyage huddled by the stove.

As the boat headed inland towards the south bank, Simmons recognised familiar outlines in a few of the larger structures. The Queen's House and the Naval Academy Barracks stood out. Both were now under the ownership of the Red Hands.

Isaac steered them between half-submerged ruins and sunken remains as they made a slow approach to the landing point. "I'll drop you two gents here again if that's all right?"

Simmons strode to the rear of the vessel. "Fine. Thank you, Isaac," he said, giving the old man a wave.

"A pleasure, Mr Simmons."

Isaac took Bazalgette by the arm and shook his hand. "Are you sure you've never worked on a diesel engine before?"

"No. It was the first time, but a thoroughly enjoyable experience. I must look further into this Diesel fellow's work."

"Well, she's purring like a kitten now, thanks to your help."

"It was nothing," Bazalgette replied. "As you said, it was mainly poor fuel that clogged the injectors and not enough air through the intake to compress for combustion."

"Yes, but your idea of a filter on the feed lines. That's inspired. Let me know if you get anywhere with it. I'll be happy to test it for you."

"I will do. Take care, Isaac."

"You too, Nathaniel."

Bazalgette stepped down from the boat to join Simmons. As they crossed to drier land, the engine growled behind them as Isaac backed out into deeper water.

"You two seemed to get along well," Simmons said as they trudged up the hill towards the observatory.

"Yes, I never realised Isaac was a mechanic. And that diesel engine is something to behold."

The downpour eased to gentle rain, but the ground, still soaked from earlier, made footing treacherous. They each slipped several times before reaching the stone pathway which led the last hundred yards to the building. Two pinpricks of light issued from upstairs rooms. Other than that the place looked abandoned to the night.

They passed the meridian line and the strange twenty-four-hour clock face, and arrived at the wooden gate, locked up tight.

"There's a bell on that side," Bazalgette said as he pointed to the left of the wall.

"How do you know that?"

"I saw it when we were here last time, behind the guards we spoke to. It might be our best option to raise attention."

Simmons nodded his agreement as Bazalgette walked over to inspect it. The man continued to amaze Simmons with his off-hand comments and recollection of minute details. Bazalgette pulled the chain, and a harsh clang echoed through the darkness. A flock of crows made their views clear with loud caws from the roofline, flying toward the nearby trees in the hope of a more peaceful roost for the evening.

They waited for a while with no sign that anyone, other than the birds, had heard their signal. Bazalgette rang it again. A crack of light spilt from a doorway in the main building. It opened further owing a back-lit figure with a rifle in hand.

"Enough with the bloody bell already. Who the hell are you, and what are you up to coming here at this time of night?"

"Simmons and Bazalgette, we're working for Josiah. We need to discuss our findings with him," Simmons said.

"Old Tick-Tock himself, eh?" said the man approaching the gate. There was a sharp clack as a wooden viewing panel slid open. A pair of beady eyes peered through before pulling back with a hand shielding them from the bright glow from the arc-lamp.

"Bloody Hell. What you got there, a bloody lighthouse?"

Bazalgette reduced the brightness. "Sorry, but if you hadn't noticed it is pitch black out here."

"Nearly bloody blinded me."

"This is all very pleasant," Simmons said, "but are you going to open up or not?"

There was no reply, just the sound of bolts sliding to free the entrance mechanism, and with a soft creak, the gate swung inwards.

The guard told them Josiah saw no-one overnight, no matter how important they thought they were. Instead, he organised a room for them until the morning.

The rain stopped at five am. Simmons had slept a little but had spent more time thinking through their current situation and where they went from here.

Could they trust Josiah? He hadn't been forthcoming about his relationship to Dent, either junior or senior—but did that make him untrustworthy? He *had* put them in contact with the Ravenmaster, and that led to finding the schematics, so what was his problem with the man? Why did he have this nagging feeling that things weren't right here?

The glimmer of first light crept in through the curtain-free windows, and Simmons realised he wouldn't get back to sleep now. The birds were awake and made sure everyone else knew what a beautiful morning it was regardless of how tired or hung-over they were.

Simmons sat with Bazalgette in the same octagonal room where they last met Josiah. Light streamed in from the bright morning sky, glinting from the display cases and the polished brass and silver clocks within. The single entrance door opened, followed by the clicks and whirs of Josiah's mechanical enhancements. "Good to see you two again, back so soon after your previous visit."

The hydraulic pumps down the left side of his body shifted in time with his movements as he made his way to sit behind the desk. A slight hissing noise faded as his weight settled into the large wooden chair.

"So, what have you learned that you return here in the middle of the night, Mr Simmons?" he turned his attention to Bazalgette, exposing his stitched leather profile, and nodded. "Mr Bazalgette."

"We found what you were looking for, the schematics for the watches," Simmons said. "We met Dent in the Tower and listened to his tale of their original construction and where he hid them."

"Which was where?"

"In the workshop at the Strand."

"Impossible," Josiah spat out. He took a deep breath and then let it out again slowly. It seemed to calm many of the devices which had burst into frenzied motion at his outburst. "Apologies, gentlemen, that was unwarranted. I have been under some considerable strain with my work and perhaps should take a little more rest. Please, go on."

Simmons shared a sidelong glance with Bazalgette. "We located the microfilm hidden within a toy spider. After Bazalgette performed some technical wizardry, he found it held hundreds of detailed schematics of the pocket watch as Dent had suggested."

"Excellent work, my friends. You brought these designs with you?"

"Yes, but don't you want to hear what else we learned from Dent?"

"If you feel it's important," Josiah said, failing to keep the annoyance from his voice, and followed, once more, by a flurry of clicking dials and gears. "Please complete your tale, but perhaps remember, time is pressing."

Simmons stretched his shoulders, the muscles having grown tense. "Dent had a younger brother, who he thought was dead, killed in a collapse during the invasion. We weren't able to rescue Dent, he took the honourable way out, but he identified his brother's name as Josiah."

Josiah's leather face rippled and creased, accompanied by a frenzy of whirs and clicks before he replied. "By your attitude, and how you told this tale, you think I am that younger sibling? That I should somehow be a broken and weeping wreck for losing a brother?"

He held Simmons' eye for a few seconds, then continued. "I know nothing of this brother you speak of. Even if I did, it makes no difference to the task at hand, to the direction we must travel to achieve it. Dent's death is—unfortunate—but time marches on, and so shall we. Now is there anything else before we get to the business of deciphering the schematics?"

Bazalgette stood. "You can't believe it's mere coincidence, can you? We mention your name, and he mourns that his younger brother, Josiah, saved him from a collapsing building, and was crushed doing so. Everything fits. Are you saying you learnt your skills of horology in total isolation from the Dent family?"

The hissing and whirring faltered for a second before bursting into high speed. "I have told you I know of no connection, and that should be enough for the both of you. I have no care for what happened to Dent. His part in this was complete once he informed you how to retrieve the damned schematics from Otto. To be honest, I don't give a damn if he shot himself or you butchered and fed him to the rats."

Josiah rose, surpassing Bazalgette's height by six inches, the leather skin on his face twitching. "You, Nathaniel, of all people should understand the importance of avoiding distraction from your work. I do not have the time to waste on these idiotic fancies. Now, where is the microfilm?"

All was silent, Bazalgette looked from Josiah to Simmons, a frown growing across his forehead. "We didn't mention the toy's name."

"What?" Josiah said. The whirs and clicks increased as his eyes widened.

Just let it go, Bazalgette, Simmons thought. But, of course, he couldn't.

"You called him Otto. We never mentioned that."

"What do I care about this contraption? Where are my schematics?"

Simmons inched his right hand towards the holstered pistol. He hadn't thought to leave it unclipped. Now it would need the toggle flipped to release it from the holster. The sound from all the clocks around the room seemed to drown out everything else as they ticked in perfect unison. Tick, Tock, Tick.

"Do you think I don't know what you are doing, Simmons?"

Josiah asked, his voice had darkened, dripping with contempt. "Do you really believe you can draw and fire that pistol before I reach out and snap Bazalgette's neck?"

Josiah's mechanical arm flashed across the space, grabbing Bazalgette by the throat. Thick metal fingers tightened as he raised Bazalgette into the air with the ease of lifting a toddler.

Bazalgette croaked something as his hands thrashed to grip either side of Josiah's wrist. Simmons had only just pulled the Mauser from its housing, but continued his draw and aimed at Josiah's face.

"Release him," Simmons said, cocking the weapon.

"Now, now," Josiah said. "There's no need for incivility. Didn't your mother teach you manners?"

Bazalgette's feet scrambled for purchase, dancing a foot above the beautiful wooden flooring.

"Put him down *now*, before I blow that freakish head from your shoulders."

"Tsk, tsk, Simmons." A loud click issued from the mechanical arm. "That sound means, the arm is on lockdown, so it cannot release unless I instruct it. Even if you tore it from my body, it couldn't open without fully constricting first. With dear Nathaniel's oesophagus and spine in the way, that could prove unpleasant for him. Well, look at him," Josiah turned his attention from Simmons to Bazalgette. "He's already going red, next comes purple, then black. No air, you see? Now be a good little soldier and give me the schematics. Or would you prefer to watch him struggle for breath, his brain dying from lack of oxygen and the pain in his lungs burning till he bursts?" Josiah laughed—a harsh grating noise. "His eyes are bulging. They might pop out if we're lucky."

Simmons faltered. What could he do? The arm was a biomechanical mass of wires, pipes and clockwork. If he only knew which controlled the hydraulics, but that was Bazalgette's field. He lowered the pistol. "It's in his jacket pocket, the inside one. Just let him go."

"Drop the weapon."

Simmons knelt and placed the Mauser on the floor and

stepped back, arms raised. Bazalgette had ceased kicking. A weak twitch came from his left foot, and his hands slackened, falling from Josiah's arm, leaving his face a horrifying purple, darkening by the second.

"Take the damned thing and leave him be."

Josiah's other hand darted into Bazalgette's pocket and retrieved the octagonal box, flicking it open. His ruined features creased with a grotesque sneer as he saw the microfilm. "Now, that wasn't hard, was it?"

Another loud click and Josiah launched Bazalgette the full length of the room. His limp body crashed through a bookcase near the doorway and fell in a crumpled mess, wood splinters and shards of glass dropping around him. Simmons hung his head. *What have I done? If I'd just handed the film over at the start, Bazalgette could have—*

A whoosh of something cut through the air from his right. By instinct, Simmons ducked away but was too slow. Sharp metal cogs tore into his cheek, and the full impact of the arm followed behind it. Unbelievable pain flooded his mind, and it felt as he imagined being hit by a train might. Brilliant white filled his head like a thousand arc-lamps, then sudden all-consuming darkness.

27

William, son and heir of Lord James Blakelocke, wiped the mud from his boots. A liberal application of polish and elbow grease brought them to the level of shine he expected of both himself and his men. *Now, where did I leave that damned pistol?*

"Willie, come back to bed," a muffled and sleepy voice called from under the bedcovers.

"Got things to do, Chloe," he replied. "This damn city doesn't patrol itself."

"Suit yourself."

She pulled the silky covers tight and rolled over, hiding her naked form from his gaze. He never tired of looking at her, the curve of her hips and breasts etched into his memory.

Blakelocke rose from the velvet-lined four poster bed and crossed to the nightstand where he grabbed his uniform jacket. His hand brushed the fine material at the shoulders just below the collar where three silver daggers marked him as a captain of the Black Guard.

He pulled a brush through his tangle of short dark curls and applied a liberal amount of hair cream to tame the unruly strands which refused to stand in line. It took several minutes before his appearance was that befitting an officer of his reputation. He nodded at his reflection in the mirror and moved to the door.

The bell from the nearby clock tower rang out four times in the darkness. Angry cawing erupted from its roof where a handful of disgruntled birds leapt into the air, their disagreement with their early alarm fading into the distance.

Blakelocke took the steps two at a time and almost bowled another of the madam's girls over at the first landing. "Look where you're going, stupid whore."

He knew it was his fault but wasn't one to apologise to commoners like her. She scurried past mumbling apologies, but he was already moving down the stairs as if she never existed.

"Excuse me, sir."

"What the bloody hell?" Blackelocke turned to rebuke the girl for interrupting him again, riding crop raised. She seemed a little different, though he wasn't sure. These damned whores all looked the same.

No, this one wore a wave of red hair cascading down the left side of her face, matching the fetching crimson satin dress.

"Who the hell—"

Blakelocke stumbled backwards, his ears ringing much like the bell he'd heard earlier. His nose throbbed as blood gushed from it. She'd bloody hit him. Before he could react, something pulled over his head, cinching tightly at the neck. A crunch sounded, and he tried to scream as agony flared from the pressure on his face. An acrid chemical scent invaded his senses, and his world melted into darkness.

Blakelocke awoke. God knew what time it was, but the sky held a dull grey pallor. A narrow tunnel with a rectangle of light dominated his view. He struggled, realising his limbs were bound. The scene still made no sense, and with his head throbbing, he looked to the side, and almost threw up there and then.

"Awake then?" a woman's voice called, one of two silhouetted heads peering from the light six feet ahead. It was the redhead from the brothel—he was sure of it. The other was a heavy-set man who stood behind her.

Blakelocke struggled with his bonds. "What the hell do you think you're—"

"Shut up," the woman said.

"What? How dare you. Do you know—"

"Who you are? Yes," she said. "William Blakelocke, second son of Lord Blakelocke, and murderer of your older brother, if I'm not mistaken."

That stunned him—he was lost for words. His surroundings came into closer focus as the pain in his skull subsided. Packed earth walls led to the bright rectangle—he was in a bloody hole.

"A user of illicit substances, banned throughout the Empire," she droned on. "Sadist, torturer and a perverted arsehole of the first order."

"I'll not take that from the likes of you. Get me out of here at once, or—"

"Or you'll what? Have me arrested? Torn limb-from-limb in one of your dark cells while your cronies watch, or perhaps subjected to more interesting torture?"

He could hear the hatred and bile within her, and his bowels turned to water with recognition. "Oh God. It's you, isn't it?"

"Respect at last. Please tell me you're not going to cry and plead for your worthless hide?"

His gut clenched and when he found his voice, it quivered. "I didn't realise what they would do. I had no part in it, just organised the people they required. I was never there. You'd remember me if I were. Wouldn't you?"

She hawked and spat: it was a good shot. The splatter of viscous liquid hit him below the left eye and snaked down into his ear. He moved his head, trying to wipe it on the cushioned lining. Realisation struck him—he was in an open coffin. "Please no, Rosemary. It doesn't have to—"

"Don't speak as if you know me," she roared.

He shrank back from the ferocity in her voice and felt warm liquid dribbling down the inside of his immaculate pressed uniform trousers. "I didn't know. I swear I had no idea." He broke, great sobs heaving from him. "Don't kill me like the others. They were the ones who tortured you, not me. I—"

"Had nothing to do with it?" she sneered at him. "You were complicit in making it happen. You brought them together to have their sordid little game at the behest of my father. That vile, degenerate bastard,"

Rosie stood at the lip of the grave, her breathing ragged with fury. "Carrington got what he deserved." She looked over at Maddox and nodded once.

"It wasn't him," Blakelocke shouted. "He didn't organise it."

Rosie motioned for Maddox to wait. "What are you trying to say?"

"I can tell you who was behind it all, who orchestrated everything. But if I do, you let me go."

Maddox shook his head at her, a shovel full of dirt waiting, but there was something that intrigued her.

"I'll think about it," she said, "but this better be good."

"It is. I promise."

"Out with it then."

"It was Robertson."

"What? Your great Lord Commander?"

A spray of earth fell over Blakelocke. He screamed in shock. "You said you'd free me if I told you."

"John, stop," Rosie said. "What are you doing?"

Maddox dumped another shovelful of dirt into the grave. "He's fucking lying. There's no way Robertson would speak with someone like him."

She held her hand out to calm the situation. "Wait. I want to know what he has to say."

"Robertson doesn't deal with mere captains or even majors," Maddox said. "He only speaks with the upper-brass. They do his dirty work for him."

"No, it's true," Blakelocke said, his voice frantic. "I spoke with him myself. He gave me the task to recruit the people he needed. Cargill, Addison, Woodruff."

"Bollocks," Maddox said. "Utter shite. He never deals with underlings. That's not his style."

Rosie watched as Maddox poured two more shovelfuls of soil onto Blakelocke's face.

"Please. You've got to believe me," Blakelocke said between spitting dirt from his mouth.

"No, I don't think I do," she replied. "Maddox is right. General Sir George Frazer-Robertson is too up his own arsehole to deal with small-fry like you."

"No, it's true," Blakelocke screamed, his voice cracking. "Said he'd sacrificed as much as anyone for this task."

"Enough of this shit," Maddox yelled, shovelling more dirt into the hole. The man coughed and gagged, trying to wriggle a way to clear his mouth of the soil, but the weight of it was already pushing him down.

With each new load Maddox piled in, they heard less of Blakelocke's muffled coughs and screams, until all Rosie could see was a single bloodshot eye, wide with terror. Then earth covered that too.

She perched on a gravestone watching as Maddox finished the job. He worked tirelessly, never once stopping to rest, powering the dirt back until it filled its original home. He threw the shovel down, wiping the sweat from his brow. "So, where now?"

"I shall head to Greenwich. I have to speak with Josiah. What about you?"

"I have a few loose ends that require tidying up around the city. I'll be at the usual place when you need me."

Rosie kept her face calm as she walked away, but something was wrong. Something deep inside her screamed. She should be rejoicing at the end of her long journey of revenge. The four perpetrators and her father dead, all by her hand. So why, instead of relief, did she feel like a whole new bag of trouble had burst open? Blakelocke's frenzied attempts to convince her of Robertson's involvement were nonsense. Weren't they?

But why did it seem, in his last frantic piss-drenched moments, Blakelocke had been too afraid to lie?

28

Agony blazed through Nathaniel's body, and his throat was raw. Shooting pain followed every breath, ragged fingernails tearing down the soft fleshy interior. He reached for his neck, pulling his fingers away sharply at the gentlest of probing touches.

In the darkness, he struggled, trying to recall how he ended up here. Other than thrashing about unable to breathe and being lifted from the ground to dangle from Josiah's grasp, he remembered nothing more.

He checked his inside jacket pocket, but the microfilm wasn't there. As he searched further, he winced. *Broken ribs*, he thought, or severe bruising—*how had that happened?*

The pain lessened as his breathing slowed. If he kept still and concentrated, he could see shadows in the room resolve to patches of lighter and darker grey. They formed ideas of shape, but he couldn't identify them. Maybe given a little more time to recover.

His legs felt odd, crammed under him, and fearing them broken, he shifted position to test his hypothesis. Though they burned up as he tried to straighten them, it was the sharp, biting pain of blood flow rushing back to relieve cramped muscles. He grimaced for a second, but it faded into dull pins and needles with movement.

Focus on your breathing. In through the nose seemed less painful than via the mouth. He wasn't sure of the precise anatomical difference, the nasal passages joined the oesophagus, but who was he to argue with his body. Perhaps he could look it up later when he had the chance.

He checked for any major injuries. But, other than feeling like he'd gone five rounds with a street fighter, the pain seemed superficial, and with extreme care, he lifted himself to his feet.

Where was Simmons? The thought rushed into his mind unbidden, but then rattled around refusing to budge.

The schematics were missing, so what did that mean? Had Simmons handed them over? Was he part of Josiah's plan all along? No, he wasn't willing to believe he would do that. Simmons was a man of honour, a man of his word. Everything he had experienced screamed that his friend wouldn't turn on him.

So what happened? He felt something slick under his boot and reached down to investigate. As he brought his fingers up to smell the slimy substance, he already had a good idea of what it would be. Blood, thickening a little, so it had been a while. Back on hands and knees, he followed it. If this was from Simmons, he could be bleeding out as Nathaniel fretted about their friendship.

How could I be so self-absorbed when Simmons might be hurt?

He crawled between stacks of furniture following the bloody trail which led to a body, unmoving, on the other side of the room.

It had to be Simmons, a pool of blood puddled around his head, hair matted with clots stuck to the right of his face.

Probing in the dark, Nathaniel felt up the neck and identified the telltale mutton chops his friend wore with pride. He repositioned himself with his ear to Simmons' mouth and listened for a sign of breathing. Anything that would indicate life.

It was faint, but there was a breath, shallow and almost silent, but it was there. Simmons was alive.

Nathaniel pulled away, a vast feeling of relief washing over him. *What now? I need light.* He'd always had his lamp, so it had never been an issue. He searched Simmons' pockets, and after a few seconds located a lighter. The striker flashed, producing a thin arc of blue flame that crackled into being.

Simmons' face was a horrific mess. Blood seeped from a ragged gash that ran up from cheek to forehead. Well, the scalp wound explained the volume of blood, which made Nathaniel a touch more comfortable. It flooded down Simmons' face, pooling in the hollow around his eye and nose. Small streams bubbled under his nostril from his shallow breathing.

Nathaniel tore strips from his shirt and used them as makeshift bandages, applying a little pressure to the head wound which seemed to stem the remaining flow of bleeding.

As he moved Simmons to drain the blood, it soon became clear the socket was empty. Whatever caused the gouging wound from his cheek had ruptured his right eye, leaving just a few strands of shredded flesh and gristle.

Nathaniel's breath caught in his throat. *I can do this.* Fearing his lack of medical knowledge, he erred on the side of caution. He placed a pad of material over the remains of the eye, then tied it in place with longer strips and secured it with his tie.

"Come on," Nathaniel said, "you need to fight. I promise I'll get you out of here, somehow."

Rosie sneaked through the observatory as raucous laughter filtered up from below. Josiah's men enjoyed their time off-duty and out of sight of their demanding master. She passed through the deserted upper levels—the stairs fading behind as she crossed to the southern edge of the building. Josiah was most likely locked away with his toys deep in his research. She needed more information—where were Simmons and Nathaniel?

The idiots at the gate told her most of what she feared. It didn't take much to learn what transpired earlier that morning. She'd known Josiah could be unstable, but this confirmed her fears. She couldn't trust him. If he'd lied to her about the two men's fate, then what of his promises to her? Was she another tool to be used by him, then cast aside? She wouldn't let that happen.

The strange pair were her best chance to finish this, now Josiah was off on his own crusade. She had better things to do with her time, more pressing matters in which Josiah would not interfere. If Simmons or Nathaniel opposed her, she could always bend them to her will.

Rosie tried each door as she passed them on the upper floor. So far, all opened onto rooms full of junk, no sign of the odd pair thrust into her life by the machinations of the Black Guard.

Simmons, she had expected. Old fashioned and good at his job, but too easily led towards what he wanted to find. The other one though, what was it that fascinated her so?

Nathaniel was a handsome man, but that didn't impress her. Perhaps it was his mind—there was no doubt he was brilliant, but no, there was more to it. In a flash, it came to her, and she recoiled at the thought. It occurred when she told them that she'd killed those three beasts. Simmons had looked surprised, but he seemed to understand. But it had shocked Nathaniel.

Why should that bother her? Her revenge was justified. Who was he to be disappointed in her, he wasn't her—

A shiver ran down her spine, and she almost collapsed, clinging to the wall for support as she bit back the taste of bile in her throat. No, he was nothing like that. What she'd done had appalled Nathaniel, that she was capable of it, but the next morning, he presented himself as if meeting at a society event. As if he'd forgotten her past, put it aside, or as she now feared, forgiven it.

Why was it so easy to control the minds and emotions of others while hers were a mystery even to herself?

She pushed herself from the wall and continued down the corridor. Another couple of rooms proved fruitless, but as she reached the next handle, it refused to budge. The door straining against the thick wooden frame, and something shuffled within, then all was quiet. Kneeling at the doorway, she bent and placed her eye against the keyhole, seeing only darkness. She cupped her hand around to block the light from the filthy windows.

"Nathaniel, Simmons?" she whispered.

"Rosie?" came a soft reply.

"Nathaniel, I've come to help."

After a short delay, he replied. "Simmons is hurt. He's still unconscious, and I'm not sure we should move him."

"Well, it's that, or we go without him," said Rosie.

"No, I can't leave him."

"Then help me work out how to get this blasted door open."

"If you can locate my toolkit, then we'd be in a better position."

Rosie thought for a moment. "It's probably in a guardroom downstairs somewhere. I'm not sure I want to leave you here if there's another option."

"Do you know how to pick a lock?" Nathaniel asked.

"Strangely, no. Do you?"

"Well, yes," he replied, "but I don't have any tools."

"Oh, and because I'm a woman, you expect me to have the required hairpin for such a task?"

"No, I didn't mean that. Though a hairpin might be helpful, but I'd also need a sturdy blade."

Something pushed under the doorframe and Nathaniel retrieved a narrow-bodied wooden haft and a length of wire ending in a rounded glass bead.

"But I thought..."

"Never speak about hairpins again," Rosie said, "and be careful with that knife."

He found a metal switch on the handle and six inches of steel shot out as he pressed it. "I seem to have located the blade," he said, tracing the razor-sharp edge protruding from the end of the device.

"Good. Still have all your fingers?"

256

"Yes, thank you. More by luck than judgement, though. Where did you get this?"

"Is that important right now?"

Nathaniel bent the hairpin, both shaping and strengthening it for its new purpose. "No, I suppose not," he said as he focused on opening the door.

It was a standard lock and clicked open with little effort. The rasping noise as the blade turned the mechanism sounded like it would wake the dead. But there were no ghouls in the corridor as he pulled the door inwards, just Rosie's silhouetted form as sunlight flooded the room, banishing the veil of darkness.

He placed his hand before his eyes, trying to shield them from the sudden brightness, then turned back to where Simmons lay slumped in the corner.

Rosie stepped past. "Dear God, what happened to him?"

In the light, the blood smeared about his friend's face looked worse than Nathaniel had expected. The makeshift padding over the eye was messy with dried streaks of bloody tears running down Simmons' cheek.

"It must have been Josiah," Nathaniel said. "He wanted the schematics and throttled me. I'm presuming as leverage to force Simmons to hand them over."

Rosie knelt beside Simmons and, after looking over his prone form, returned her gaze to Nathaniel. "His face?"

"He's lost the eye, and I think the lower orbit around it is shattered. It's hard to tell with all the swelling, but I couldn't feel any resistance when I checked it."

"There's a lot of blood," she added, pointing to the congealed mass of dark liquid staining the wooden floorboards.

"It looks worse than it is. Most is from the scalp wound where something tore the skin across his forehead. He needs professional medical treatment for his eye."

"Shit. I'd hoped I could just break you two out of here and we could make for the river. Now we'll have to carry him."

She looked him up and down. "Were you injured?"

He smiled. "No, I'm fine. Battered and bruised, but nothing to slow me down too much."

"I'll go see what I can organise. It will be later this evening before I return. We need the cover of darkness to get out of here in one piece."

"You had best lock us back in here in case any of Josiah's men check."

"Close the door, but leave it unlocked." Rosie reached into her pack and produced a water canteen, handing it to Nathaniel. "Here. I'll speak with the guards and try to put the fear of God into them, tell them Josiah wants you to rot for a while. That should keep them from poking about. You need to be ready to move when I return after dark. Take care, Nathaniel."

"You too," he replied.

Rosie left, pulling the door closed with a soft click.

Simmons alternated between short incoherent fits of consciousness, until the pain overcame his threshold, and then restless sleep. Nathaniel gave him a little water, but after a coughing fit, where he feared he'd half drowned his friend, he was more careful. He found pouring it onto a cloth and dribbling it over Simmons' lips was a slower, but safer solution.

Time dragged while waiting for the thin crack of light under the doorframe to dim until it disappeared in the early evening. Nathaniel scavenged together a few rugs to prop behind Simmons, making him as comfortable as he could in their cramped confines.

Though there had been a few noises below, nobody checked on them. So it seemed Rosie had been successful in her attempts to deter the guards from disturbing them.

Footsteps approached along the corridor, two sets as far as Nathaniel could tell. He pushed himself to his feet and took a position beside the doorway, Knife gripped in his fist, not knowing what he hoped to achieve with it.

Rosie's low voice followed a quiet tap on the door. "Nathaniel, it's me. I've brought a friend to help us, so don't be alarmed."

The door inched open with a soft creak. Dim lamplight seeped in illuminating the small room and outlining Rosie. Beside her, a much larger figure dumped an armful of clothing and gear with a heavy thump onto the floor.

"Careful," Rosie said.

"What's the worry, love?" The man spoke with a thick London accent. "It's not like there's anyone down there what can hear us now, is it?"

She sighed before passing a bundle to Nathaniel. "Here's your equipment. How's he doing?"

"He's drifting in and out of consciousness. But even when he *is* awake, I think the pain is too much for him to bear for long."

The large man proffered his hand. "This should help."

Nathaniel accepted a small pouch. In the dim light, he saw a red cross on the canvas material. "Medical supplies?"

"Yeah, Black Guard field kit. It will have morphine in there. They're sealed units, so it don't need a medic to measure out the dose. Break the seal and jab it into him. That should sort the pain for a while."

Nathaniel rummaged through the bag and pulled out a glass vial. He snapped the top and rotated a small needle into place. Jabbing the makeshift syringe into Simmons' right arm, he squeezed the rubber plug, forcing the drug into his bloodstream.

Turning back to the figure, Nathaniel thrust out his hand. "Thank you. Mister?"

The larger man gripped him in a firm shake. "Maddox. John Maddox."

∾

Nathaniel and Maddox carried Simmons' limp body down the narrow stairwell. Rosie led, with the arc-lamp lighting their way. As they reached the ground floor, Nathaniel stopped. Three bodies lay sprawled through an open door. Maddox looked across. "They're not going to be causing any more trouble."

Half-carrying, half-dragging Simmons, they moved on. Rosie cast the bright lamplight into a room with a doorway to the courtyard beyond. Two unfinished bottles of beer sat on a table between stained couches. Empties littered the area and, after carefully picking her way through, Rosie pushed the door open into the cold night air.

She motioned for them to remain inside, while she checked the other buildings, crossing the dark yard. She reached between the metal bars of the gate and pulled a chain through a heavy padlock, placing it on the ground without a sound.

It swung wide in silence, and she beckoned them to join her. Maddox closed the door behind before they traversed the short distance to stand with Rosie outside the observatory.

"Get him down to the river. Isaac is waiting there," she said.

"What about you?" Nathaniel asked.

"I'll lock up here and then meet you at the boat. The longer we can keep this quiet, the better. There will be hell to pay when Josiah finds out. Go." She shooed them away like obstinate children and returned to the gate.

Nathaniel followed Rosie's advice, and with Maddox helping, it was a simple task supporting his semi-conscious friend.

"So, Mr Maddox," he said, trying to keep his tone calm. "How is it you became involved in this endeavour?"

"Well, Rosie asked, and she's a difficult lady to ignore."

"That is true, but you do know who we are, don't you?"

"Course I do. What of it?"

"Nothing, I wasn't sure if you knew..."

"What? That Simmons was after my hide? And he intended to leave it with more holes than it had before? Yeah, I know all of that."

"And it doesn't bother you?"

"Look, Rosie told me all about this, and how they manipulated Simmons. As far as I'm concerned, he's just been playing for the wrong team and didn't see it until now. I'm a lot more like him than he knows. I'm also on their most-wanted list."

"Well, let's hope *he* sees it that way when he comes around."

As they crested a small rise, the scarlet glow of the fogbound river was visible below.

"We need fog-gear on before we get into that," Maddox said, pointing at the sea of red that swept between the packed buildings on the river's edge.

"Agreed," said Nathaniel.

They lowered Simmons to the damp grass and pried him into his greatcoat and respirator. After long minutes struggling to fit his gear while he seemed to twist from them, Nathaniel was content Simmons was adequately protected. They made much better progress with their own clothing, then hoisted Simmons back to his feet and approached the wisps of fog crawling towards them.

The boat was right where Rosie had told them it would be, and as expected, Isaac was his usual cheery self, shouting through his protective gear. "Good evening, Nathaniel. Gods, what's happened to Simmons?"

"A disagreement with Josiah," Nathaniel said.

"Best stow him in the stern. I'll give you a hand."

Isaac took over from Maddox, who returned ashore. The waterman was remarkably strong, considering his small stature and advancing age and seemed to ignore the aches and pains he must have been feeling. Either way, Nathaniel let out a sigh as they laid the body down under the tarp.

A bell rang out in the distance from up the hill.

"Shit," said Maddox from the shore. "This tub better be ready to shove off."

Isaac leapt into action, heading for the engine. "Pull the mooring ropes, fore and aft," he shouted. The small man's commanding voice took Nathaniel by surprise. These were orders, not mere requests. As Nathaniel scuttled towards the rear line, he heard Maddox clamber aboard heading forward, his heavy footfalls thumping on the wooden deck.

Nathaniel tugged on the thick rope. "Can you see Rosie?"

"No sign," Maddox said, "but she'll make it. Either now, or she'll catch up with us later."

"Nathaniel," Isaac called. "The *other* line."

"What?" he replied, looking back to the waterman, as the engine roared into life.

"Pull the other line," Isaac shouted, pointing to his right. "It's on a short slip, it just pulls loose."

Inspecting the tangle of ropes again Nathaniel saw his mistake. With a change of grip and a sharp tug, it unravelled, slithering into the black water like an eel returning to the Thames.

A gunshot cracked in the darkness, followed by two more.

"Pull those lines aboard now," Isaac called, the thrumming of the engine vibrating through the deck. "We can't afford to get tangled. We can stow them later."

Nathaniel gathered in armfuls of wet rope. "What about Rosie?"

"We can't wait for her here," Isaac said. Water churned, bubbling around the stern as the vessel lurched into reverse, pulling away from the makeshift jetty.

"You can't leave her," Nathaniel shouted. "Not after she risked everything helping Simmons."

"If we don't get out into the channel, we'll all be dead. We're exposed between the buildings. It's too narrow to make any speed. They'll board, or pick us off with pistol fire from a few yards away."

Nathaniel froze, uncertain as what to do.

"You need to choose now, but I'm leaving with Simmons. I'll find him a doctor, but if you and Maddox are staying, you'd best disembark."

Nathaniel looked to where Maddox scanned the fog. Dark shadows shifted between cover as they swarmed forward. Another muffled gunshot rang out between the dilapidated buildings. Maddox discharged two rounds from a heavy pistol Nathaniel hadn't even seen him draw.

"Maddox, what do we do?"

"We leave her."

"What?"

Maddox shouted to the rear of the boat. "Isaac, get us out of here."

The engine growled in response as Isaac swung the vessel, drifting around a tight corner. Sway on the deck almost toppled Nathaniel, and he grabbed the low rail to keep from plunging overboard.

They rounded the last of the buildings, heading out into the dense fog. A shadow darted over the rooftops, as a black-clad shape launched itself into the open amidst a hail of gunfire. The coat billowed behind as they seemed to hang in mid-air before thudding onto the deck.

The impact jarred and sent the figure toppling and slipping across the damp surface. Nathaniel glimpsed a flash of red hair as Rosie flew past, splinters flying as she shattered the wooden rail. He threw his arm out, desperate to grab anything to arrest her momentum. The sleeve of her coat, slick with the residue from the fog, slid through his fingers. Cloth, buckles and straps rushed past, none catching in his grasp.

His hand closed on her wrist for a moment—then she was gone. It left him holding a torn red leather glove as bubbles broke the surface and slow ripples spread out on the Thames.

29

The cold seized her as the dim light above faded to pure black. Rosie tried not to gasp in shock but failed, a stream of bubbles erupting from the filter on her mask.

The thick clothing that protected her from the fog, now fought her, impeding her movement and drawing her into the depths. She fumbled with her coat, searching for the belt and a way to release some weight. But her right hand was too numb, the fingers slow and unresponsive in the icy dark.

The pressure built, squeezing her like a ripe orange. She kicked, trying to slow her descent, but her legs wrapped in the long coat. It was futile. Drips ran down her face like dark tears. The charcoal filters worked well in fog, but she knew it was only a matter of time before the water crept through to steal her breath.

It had been better when she just followed her base instincts for revenge. Now, even that tasted bitter in her mouth, or was that the Thames?

Something bit her in the left shoulder, then was off. Her heart stuttered, the sound of pumping blood filled her ears. She'd heard tales of giant eels in the river, feral and vicious— like all creatures tainted by the weed.

Rosie gasped, and black water leapt into her throat. A fine mist of spittle sprayed inside the mask as she fought to keep her cough reflex from drowning her. She coughed again, this time holding her lips closed to prevent inhaling more of the foul water. The stink of the brackish river—a mixture of sewage and the strange iron taste of the red weed, made her stomach roil.

Her heart raced, water bubbled under her nostrils as she panted. Desperate, she tipped her head back, gasping to find more air. She gained a moment's respite, drawing one last breath—then the river gushed over her face as the mask's seal failed.

The creature hit her again, and bubbles of precious air burst from her mouth as it drove into her chest. She grasped its spindly body in her gloved left hand, intent on wringing the beast's neck. Instead, it jerked and fled upward.

She held on for dear life.

∾

Cracks of gunfire echoed through the thick fog from the shoreline. The hiss of a bullet cut through the air beside Nathaniel, sending splinters from a wooden crate flashing past his face.

Yanking the pole, he felt continued pressure and hauled it hand over hand. The additional weight required him to brace his legs against the shattered rail, mere inches from where Rosie had burst through. It creaked ominously, as he reeled his catch towards the surface.

A red glove surfaced, clamped around the pole and his heart sang in joy. He'd saved her. "Maddox, help me get her on board."

Heavy footsteps followed a booming gunshot from the prow. A meaty arm reached down and clasped Rosie by the wrist, hoisting her up through the weed which clung to her, writhing and pulsing.

Between them, they lowered her to the deck, her body convulsing. Before Nathaniel could react, Rosie tore the fog mask from her face.

"No," he shouted, reaching for her, but it was too late. A

265

stream of water gushed over the deck as she hacked and coughed. The mask dropped, hitting Nathaniel's boot with a soft thud, and rolled into the river.

The weed thrashed as it tried to break through the protective layers between it and its prey. Nathaniel ripped at the stuff but with little effect. It was tough as old leather.

"Leave it," Maddox said. "Out of the way."

Nathaniel flinched as a heavy blade crossed his vision, and Maddox sawed at the alien plant with relish.

Rosie coughed again, disgorging a lungful of black water, then cried out in pain as a strand of red fibres wrapped around her gloveless hand. Her body shifted, inching towards the river as the thing refused to give up its hard-won prize.

Nathaniel grabbed her coat lapels and braced against the incredible pressure building as the weed fought back. "It's pulling her in."

Maddox sawed through one strand of the vile alien flora with a squelch, only for another to thrust out of the water to grasp onto its fellow. The individual fibres writhed and twisted, forming thick muscle-like tentacles.

"Faster," Nathaniel shouted. "It's gaining strength."

Maddox looked up, still cutting through the thinner strands. "They're getting tougher. I can't keep up."

Nathaniel lurched forward as the weed gave a mighty tug. It was like trying to hoist a grand piano onto a roof. His feet slid further towards the splintered gap. "It's too strong," he shouted. "Isaac, get some fuel into the water and ignite it." He locked his knees rigid, the muscles in his legs solid and screaming with the strain.

Something flew by, hitting the surface with a splash. A yellow barrel bobbed in the weed-ridden river, dark liquid gurgled from the unstoppered cap.

"Close your eyes," Isaac shouted as an arc of red light leapt into the writhing mass.

The force of the explosion rocked the boat, and an almost animal shriek tore at their ears. The pull on Rosie weakened, then with several wet pops it reduced further and released.

They floated in a sea of fire, spreading over the weeded surface of the Thames. The weed popped and sizzled as it sank. Knots of muscle that had been drawing Rosie into the river ended in ragged, bubbling masses which slipped overboard with a slurp. The tangle of weed, still attached to her body, twitched then fell immobile, burning and smoking at the severed ends. It was a scene as near to hell as Nathaniel had ever encountered, and he would be glad never to see the like again.

"Get that fire out," Isaac screamed, pointing at buckets along the deck. The vessel powered away from the blazing inferno lighting the Thames in a hellish glow. Black plumes of greasy smoke rose from the red weed. The smell of oil mixed with the tang of iron and tallow, hanging thick in the night air.

Floodlights from the city walls oriented onto the river, scanning the area where it still blazed. Shots continued from the shore but now fell short, ploughing furrows into the water's surface.

Maddox threw buckets of sand, dousing the last flames while Nathaniel pulled the remaining strands of weed from Rosie's prone form. Blackened and burnt at the ends, tar-like ichor oozed from them onto the deck. The rest turned from grey to almost translucent at the tips and, in contrast to their earlier strength, the remnants crumbled at his touch, and he threw them overboard.

Rosie opened her eyes, groaning as she tried to push herself up, slipping on the blood leaking from her gashed left hand. "I'll need to look at that," Nathaniel said, "but first we should get you undercover and back into a mask."

"Am I really such a sight you have to hide my ghastly features?"

He tore his eyes from her. "No, it's not... Just stop talking. You're overexposed to the fog as it is."

Rosie smiled as he lifted her to her feet then supported her as they travelled to the stern and into the canvas tent.

"You should get out of those wet clothes," Nathaniel said.

"Whatever you say, Doctor," she replied, a twinkle of wicked humour in her eyes.

Nathaniel fled—his face a mask of crimson.

30

They travelled around the loop of the Thames, to a point north-east, beyond the Isle of Dogs.

"Silvertown," said Isaac, pointing across the flooded area on the northern shore before them. "That used to be the Victoria and Albert docks before the war, the heart of the Empire's merchant fleet. They were something to behold in their day. Now, look at it."

The fog had burnt off in the morning sun, leaving an inland ocean. Rooftops poked their heads above the surface, but most remained submerged, a modern-day Atlantis, sinking below the waves.

Nathaniel surveyed the scene. "Where are we headed?" he called back to Isaac.

"I know folks around St Mark's who can help Simmons."

"That's good enough for me," he replied. "How is Rosie doing?"

"I'm fine," she said, poking her head out of the canvas tent. She emerged, wrapped in one of the large grey blankets Isaac had rustled up for her earlier and proceeded along the deck towards Nathaniel.

Her bare feet fell silently on the wooden boards. The blanket reached only to mid-calf, and Nathaniel averted his gaze, but the image remained etched in his mind. She seemed like some strange mixture of a Scottish Highlander, with her shock of dark red curls, and a pirate captain, walking the decks inspecting her crew for shirkers.

Nathaniel tried his best smile, not confident enough to look her in the eyes.

"I'm glad to hear it, how's your chest—your breathing?" he corrected himself. *What is it about talking to women?* He always became flustered, stuttering or saying things that came out all wrong. Why couldn't they be more like men? He could speak with them without faltering or feeling a fool.

Rosie just smiled. "I'm fine, Nathaniel. No signs of wheezing, coughing, bleeding, or red weed erupting through my flesh." She continued up the boat to stand beside him, joining his gaze northward across the submerged city.

"Are your clothes dry yet?" Nathaniel said, cursing to himself as soon as the words left his mouth. *Of course they weren't. Otherwise, she'd be wearing them, fool.*

"Not quite," she replied. "Isaac said it wouldn't be long though. Apparently, the engine runs hot, and with them packed around the pipes, they are steaming along nicely, much like us."

He bit back his urge to mention it was a diesel engine, which reminded him of Simmons.

"How is Simmons?" he asked instead.

"He was struggling for a while when he came to an hour ago, but another shot of the morphine seemed to help. We need to get him to St Mark's. I'm concerned about his eye and any other internal injuries."

"The sooner, the better," Nathaniel agreed. "I did what I could, but I'm no surgeon."

She took his hand. "Nathaniel, you did a marvellous job with the resources you had available. You can't blame yourself. Without your intervention he'd be dead, I have no doubt about it. You saved his life. You should be proud of that. I'm sure Simmons will thank you himself once he's able." She smiled up at him. "And I haven't forgotten your involvement in saving me—"

"Oh, it was nothing," he interjected.

"You're wrong," she replied, her voice low. "If it weren't for you slowing me, I'd have plunged into the water and been beyond the reach of that damned stick you jabbed me with. As you're the reason I'm still alive, you don't get to leave without me, agreed?"

He raised his head from staring into the river meandering past them. "Agreed," he said.

"That's more like it," Rosie said. She adopted her gruffest imitation of Simmons. "Now get on with it, you blithering idiot, we haven't got time for melancholy, we've work to do."

She coughed, her throat still sore from her attempt at drinking the Thames, but it had the desired effect rising a smile and a chuckle from Nathaniel.

"He says that sort of thing a lot, doesn't he?"

"Yes, he is the epitome of a miserable old git, but that, I suppose, is part of his charm." She laughed. "Isaac, let's get to St Mark's and don't spare the... horses?" She looked to Nathaniel for confirmation. He nodded in approval as the engine roared into action, propelling them inland.

∾

St Mark's church rose from an island ahead of them. Its Gothic spire shone as the sun caught it, and Isaac steered them past a huge building where a large sign announced 'The India-Rubber, Gutta-Percha and Telegraph Works Company, Limited'.

Within the confines of an old dock to the east stretched the corpse of a massive steamship, collapsed on its side and devoured by rust. Its back was broken, and two vast sections lay half-submerged. Three circular funnels reminded him of large rusty tunnels cutting through the water's surface, wide enough for Isaac to steer the vessel through if he so desired.

A few scrapes accompanied their final approach to St Mark's as the water level lowered. As usual, Isaac drifted and moored the boat next to a wall. "There you go, ladies and gentlemen," he said. "Please disembark in an orderly manner, women and children first. No pushing or shoving if you don't mind."

The large double doors, set in the centre of the church, creaked inwards and a figure emerged from the darkness. Nathaniel thought he saw a rifle in the man's hand before it disappeared behind the leftmost door.

"Isaac?" the man called down the three stone steps leading from the doorway. "A long time since we've seen you here at St Mark's, what can we do for you this day?"

"Reverend," Isaac responded, tipping his cap. "I've got some folks in need of serious medical help."

"And they're not in a position to get into the city, I take it?"

"That's right, so I brought 'em here, hoped you could lend a hand."

The man moved towards the boat. "Let me look at them, and we'll see what I can do."

Isaac made his way forward, grasping the man's forearm and pulling him up onto the deck. "This is Reverend Brown," he said as he introduced each of them.

"I'm called Jack," Brown said with a warm smile. "Only call me Reverend when you have something to confess." His handshake was firm, speaking of strength of body as well as spirit. Jack stood an inch or two shorter than Nathaniel, but his frame was stocky, a similar build to Maddox. Though the man was a lot older, he must have been formidable in his youth. "So where are the injured parties?"

"This way," Nathaniel said, leading him toward the stern. "His name is Simmons, and he's lost an eye. I tended to it as best as I could, but I'm not trained in medicine. He may have other internal injuries, and has had two doses of morphine for the pain."

"Thank you, Nathaniel," Jack said. "It's a good starting point for me from which to work. In here?" he motioned towards the canvas tent. At Nathaniel's nod, he pulled back the flap at the entrance. "Give me a few minutes to look him over, then I'll check at that nasty bruising around your throat."

"Don't worry about me, I'm fine."

"If it's all the same to you, I'll still have a look after I've checked on your friend," Jack said before dropping the canvas behind him.

Isaac caught Nathaniel's eye. "He's a good man. An ex-military surgeon who tired of all the needless bloodshed and took a calling to the church. Simmons is in safe hands."

They moved towards the prow to meet with Rosie and Maddox who were deep in conversation.

"If Isaac says he's all right, then I trust him," Rosie said.

Maddox shook his head. "I don't know him and until I do..."

The sentence trailed off as Nathaniel and Isaac approached.

"I don't need you to like him, or even trust him," Isaac said. "All we need is for him to help Simmons, get him back on his feet."

"I still don't like it," Maddox said to Rosie. "There are too many people getting involved in our business. All our eggs in one basket. Come on, Rosic, you know better than that."

Rosie sighed. "We'll wait and see what he can do for Simmons, and then I'll make my decision."

"And that's it, we all bow to your superior intellect?" There was a snarl in the way Maddox spoke the words, but Rosie wasn't backing down.

"Look, John, it's simple. Either stay or go, it makes no difference to me. But I'm staying to help Nathaniel and Simmons do whatever has Josiah so riled up. This has got to be the right choice. It's taken me too long to realise how twisted he has become, or maybe he always was, I just didn't see it before."

Nathaniel stepped forward. "Mr Maddox, Rosie is correct—"

"Back up there, Bazalgette." Maddox pushed Nathaniel, almost sending him sprawling. "Who asked your opinion? This is between her and me. I have nothing against you or your friend at the moment, so let's not get into something you can't handle. Remember your place and who you're dealing with."

Nathaniel stepped back, catching his balance as Rosie's face grew dark. Maddox loomed over him, having matched his step. A flurry of motion and the harsh echo of a slap rang out, followed by the thump of Maddox hitting the deck in a crumpled heap. Rosie stood there, between him and Nathaniel, hands on her hips, defiant. "And you, John Maddox. You remember *your* place in this. Don't make me kick your arse up and down this damned boat."

Maddox snapped his head around to face her. Nathaniel felt his stomach clench. Maddox reached up and rubbed his jaw, a thin trickle of blood ran from the corner of his mouth and smeared under his meaty hand. He laughed. "Well, at least one thing I taught you stuck in that messed-up head of yours, kid."

The anger seemed to drain from her, and she was a petite young woman again, albeit dressed in a shabby grey blanket held together with a few hairpins. She reached down to offer the big man a hand up, which he accepted. With a quick tug of her arm, she pulled Maddox to his feet. It was all wrong, the angles and moments of leverage and force didn't work. Nathaniel was silent, recreating the event in his mind. No, it just didn't make sense. She couldn't be that strong.

"John," she said, "in fact, Nathaniel, Isaac this involves you too. We need to stick together. We can't afford to quarrel and fight amongst ourselves, especially now. I'm not afraid of anything, John will attest to that." Maddox nodded his assent. "The only thing that worries me is Josiah. There's something about him that's just wrong, broken. He doesn't care about anyone else. He'll take everyone down with him if they get in his way."

"So, you're saying we should all kiss and make up?" Isaac asked, his face creasing as he puckered his lips.

Rosie stared at him for a moment, then sighed. "Has anybody ever told you that you're just a dirty old man?"

"All the time, love," he croaked, nudging Nathaniel with his elbow and winking. "All the time."

~

Brown complimented Nathaniel on the job he'd done treating Simmons' injuries as they moved him to the makeshift surgery set up in the church's back room. "I need to clean the socket. If we leave the remains of the sclera and flesh untrimmed, it will lead to infection."

"How risky is the procedure?"

"All surgery carries a risk, but at least we don't need to open him up."

"Could I assist?"

The reverend thought for a moment before replying. "I don't see why not. It would be useful to have someone to help, and you seem to be a talented amateur already. Yes, let's talk a little about the requirements."

It took just over an hour. Nathaniel watched and provided instruments while Jack cut away the excess tissue while describing what he was doing. He finished by allowing Nathaniel to sew the eyelid shut.

There was nothing further to do for the fractured lower orbit around the eye. It would have to heal naturally but didn't appear to be too extensive, and the prognosis was good for a natural recovery over the next couple of months.

Nathaniel joined the others in the rectory and explained everything had gone well. "Jack expects Simmons might be mobile in a day or so. He's provided extra morphine and two bottles of laudanum for the pain."

"That's great news," said Rosie. "I suppose we shall have to see how he handles the loss of his eye, and when we can move on from here."

"Yes, he's sleeping now, but I will stay at his bedside, so he has a friendly face when he wakes. Before that, we should discuss our plans."

"Where are we headed next?" Rosie asked.

"Strange as it may sound," Nathaniel said to the others. "We are searching for the crash site of Angel-One."

"Well, from what I hear," Isaac said, "we're in the right area. It crashed east of the city near Canning town if I recall."

"That's useful, Isaac," Nathaniel said. "Does anyone else know anything more?" He looked to Maddox and Rosie, but they were silent.

"Oh," Rosie said. "Isaac, didn't you say Jack has been here for some time, even before the invasion?"

"That's right. I suppose we could ask him."

"Ask me what," Jack said as he descended the stairs into the living room.

"We were talking about the end of the resistance during the war when Angel-One came down in flames. You was here then, weren't you?" Isaac asked.

"Yes, it was a tragedy. Crashed north of Canning Town right on top of the Holy Trinity Church. Thousands had been seeking refuge from the Martian Fighting Machines, none I know of survived. Of all the places, it had to come to earth there."

"You're sure?" Nathaniel asked.

"I saw it for myself from the bell tower. Terrible, and so unfortunate."

"Why do you say that?" Rosie said.

"Well, if it had crashed earlier, it's all fields and farmland, once you clear the gasworks. And if it had stayed in the air a little longer, it would have plunged into the Plaistow Marsh. But no, it fell dead into the centre of the housed area between the two. Some would say the Devil was at work that day."

Isaac stood. "Holy Trinity is just off the tramway on Barking Road. I've dropped there, before the war when I was driving cabs. It's about three miles from here."

"Can you take us there?" Nathaniel asked.

"It's not possible," Isaac replied. "The river runs dry north of here, can't get old Betsy through, I'm afraid. I could draw you a map though, not sure how useful it will be now, but it might help get you close."

"Can't you come with us?"

"As much as I'd love to go haring about in the middle of the desolation Fogside, I need to look out for Betsy. I'll hang around here for a while, catch up on old times with the Reverend. But no, I'm not leaving her on her own, she's too precious. Besides, who'd look after Simmons?"

Nathaniel was silent for a second. "No problem, Isaac. The map will do fine. I'm sure that between us we'll find the church, won't we?"

Maddox turned to Rosie, who was already smiling. He hung his head and blew out a long breath. "All right then. Overland trip it is. I best get packing my gear."

Nathaniel gave Rosie a slight nod of thanks. "We can set off tomorrow morning. That will give us time to have the Reverend check us over, and I want to speak with Simmons before we leave. Make sure he's coping."

~

Simmons woke with a blinding headache in darkness. His mouth was dry and tasted of something vile and bitter. Sweat dripped from him, soaking the bedsheets. He reached up to massage his sore head, his fingers caught on gauze covering the right side of his face. *What was going—*

"Bazalgette," he shouted, the crumpled form lying on the observatory floor came flooding back into his mind.

"Simmons, it's me. It's all right, you were injured, but you're fine now."

Bazalgette's voice was a more welcome sound than he could ever have imagined. If he was talking, then he was safe.

"Josiah? Are you all right?" Simmons asked. "Why is it so dark?"

A blue spark of electricity leapt into being and ignited a candle wick, shedding a small glow. Within a few seconds, the room came into focus, or half of it did.

"Whoa, let's slow down a little," Bazalgette said. "First things first, we escaped from Greenwich and Josiah. Second, I'm fine, fully recovered. And third," Bazalgette seemed to pause as if thinking through his next statement before speaking, "you received a serious injury. I did my best to patch you up, but you've lost your right eye."

"What?" Simmons said. "What happened?"

"I presume you must have fought with Josiah after I passed out, do you remember? Josiah turned on us. All he wanted was the microfilm."

"The schematics," Simmons said, his fingers reaching to probe at his bandaged face.

"Try not to touch it," Bazalgette said. "It's been cleaned up by a surgeon, but it will be sore as hell. He only finished," Bazalgette checked his pocket watch. "About twelve hours ago. You need to let it heal. Also, you have fractured the orbit, so don't go prodding at it."

"The orbit?"

"The bone around your eye got broken in several places. Jack, the surgeon I spoke of, did his best to position it all so they would heal, but it will be a while. We can't do anything to hold them in place. Your body needs to do the work."

"Oh," was all Simmons heard himself reply. "Well, it explains the damned headache."

"You can take this for the pain," Bazalgette said, handing him a glass of water. Simmons had to orient his head to see it from his left eye. He took the offered drink and lifted it towards his dry lips and paused, running his tongue over them, feeling cracks and rough flakes of skin.

"What is it?" he asked, fixing Bazalgette with his good eye.

"Laudanum. Twenty drops every three to four hours. It should dull the pain."

"Right, down the hatch then." He drained the glass in one, the water had a bitter aftertaste, but he felt much better for the liquid. "My throat is parched. Is that normal?"

"We gave you morphine. It's a common side effect. The dry mouth will pass as you hydrate. Drink plenty of water."

"I should have given him the film," Simmons said. "I thought you were dead. The bastard near choked the life from you while I watched, I could have saved you from it all."

"I'm fine now. It's not your fault. Josiah is the one we need to stop. We're heading out tomorrow morning to search for the original pocket watch."

"I'm not sure I'm up to it just yet, a few aches and pains, you know?"

Bazalgette swallowed. "Sorry, I didn't mean us. You should stay here and recuperate."

"Then, who?"

"Rosie, myself and… John Maddox."

"Maddox? Maddox is here? What the—"

Bazalgette pushed him back into the soft bed. "Whoa. It's not what you think. They rescued us from Josiah. Rosie brought Maddox to help."

Simmons tried to struggle, but his body was too weak. Bazalgette restrained him as simply as if he were a toddler.

"And you trust Maddox?"

"Rosie says it was all part of the Black Guard's plans. They set up the job and laid the false trail of terror Maddox had perpetrated. It was all a ploy to get rid of someone they couldn't find themselves. So they hired the best."

"The best bloody idiot. So they suckered me into finding Rosie for them and now it turns out I'm stupid enough to have been used to locate Maddox as well?"

Bazalgette released his hold on Simmons. "It's what they do. They have a vast network of operatives, and they do whatever they need to get their way."

"Is that supposed to make me feel better? Because I can tell you it's not working. I'm a useless, gullible fool, who's too long in the tooth to finish the job anymore. And with one eye to boot. Bah. Just leave me be, go find your damned pocket watch with your new friends. You'll be better off without me."

"Simmons—"

"Just get out."

Bazalgette rose and reached over towards the candle.

"Leave it," Simmons barked. "I might need it to burn out the other eye."

Bazalgette stepped back, seemed as if he was about to say

something, then thought better of it. The door closed with a soft click as he left the room.

Damn Bazalgette and his righteous ways. Damn Josiah and his scheming. He was too old for this, far too old.

Surita, why did you leave me like this? Why couldn't you let me go with you?

31

Simmons hadn't risen by the time Nathaniel led Rosie and Maddox northward, picking their way through outcrops of collapsed stone between the flood surrounding them. Rubble shifted underfoot, and rocks splashed into the water, dislodged by their passing.

As promised, Isaac had produced a detailed map to their destination, though Nathaniel wasn't sure how much help it would be in the changed landscape since the war.

The clouds hung heavy in the sky, full of potential to release their vast quantities of rain. Nathaniel moved the group onward, and after a few hours, they entered a narrow gulley between two part-collapsed structures. The water had dwindled to mere puddles, ankle deep or less, and their progress quickened.

As Nathaniel suspected, the landscape had changed, but the map still proved useful in pinpointing key landmarks, even through all the chaos. They moved in formation with Nathaniel taking the lead, followed by Rosie and then Maddox bringing up the rear.

A large junction appeared before them, and they turned to head north-east along Barking Road. The rusted iron tracks of the old tramway led off into the distance.

As they drew closer to the remains of Holy Trinity Church,

Nathaniel noted the decline in stable structures as the area changed to an ever-increasing scene of destruction. Rubble lined the streets. The buildings all around were ruins of charred brick which grew more ravaged the further they travelled north.

They stopped to rest, Maddox took a long swig from a canteen and passed it to Rosie who followed suit. Nathaniel drew out the frequency detector and attached the power leads to the battery at his waist.

"What's that?" she asked him, wiping her mouth on the back of her sleeve.

"This is a resonant frequency receiver; it's how we'll locate the original watch if it survived."

She stoppered, then handed him the canteen. "You made it?"

"Yes, just a little something I pulled together in my workshop."

He looked down to the device and tapped the glass cover on the gauge to check it was working. There was no trace of anything on the receivers frequency range, and he took the offered water.

Maddox turned to face a street to their left. "What was that?"

Their conversations halted as they all listened.

"What did you hear?" Rosie asked.

Maddox pointed his pistol in the direction. "It sounded like rubble shifting."

They waited a long, tense sixty seconds. "Whatever it was, nothing is happening there now," Rosie said. "Let's keep moving."

Maddox nodded but kept the gun aimed over there as they continued along the ruined street. As they reached the epicentre of the destruction, tangled tramlines bent out of the ground snapped and melted into slag by an incredible heat. All that remained of St Mark's was a corner of the building that, despite the surrounding carnage, had stood the test of time.

The asymmetrical twisted remains of the spire hung

there as if suspended from the heavens, refusing to bow to the will of gravity. It was apt for a religious structure, he thought.

"Wow," Rosie said, peering down into massive gouges through the edge of the consecrated ground and street beyond. They reached down over six feet, having strewn brick and earth over the entire area heading east.

Nathaniel lifted a misshapen cobblestone, its surface cracked, bubbled and shiny.

Most of the stonework looked discoloured and burnt. The inferno that had swept through had reduced the rock to a molten state which had run and then solidified again as it cooled, forming elongated drips of stone.

Nathaniel surveyed the crash site in a widening spiral as he monitored his receiver for any sign of the watch's frequency. After fifteen minutes of careful checking, he'd had enough. "There's nothing around here, not a trace."

"Should we follow the destruction eastwards?" Rosie asked from her makeshift seat, on an untouched stretch of wall.

"Where's Maddox?"

Rosie pushed herself upright. "He said he wanted to check the surrounding area. I saw no harm in it."

"No, sounds like a good idea. We might be here some time."

Nathaniel kept a close eye on the receiver as they followed the line of devastation to the east. The rubble mixed with huge sections of steel, the backbone of the great airship which plummeted from the skies in its final valiant attempt to resist the Martian onslaught.

Maddox caught up with them after an hour. "It seems quiet out there," he told them. "No signs of life. Not surprising though, everything around here's flattened."

Even after four hours, there was no sign of what they were hunting. Nathaniel rechecked the machine, but it appeared to be working well within parameters, just nothing in range for it to detect.

He sighed, returning the device to the belt clip he'd fashioned. Through the mass of shattered rubble, they arrived in an area where long sections of steel grew from the ground like massive ribs, broken and torn from some metallic beast.

There was a low click. "Shh," Nathaniel said, holding a hand out for quiet. It repeated a few seconds later from the device at his belt.

He reached down, unclipping the detector to inspect it in more detail. He waited. The needle flickered up on the gauge, accompanied by a soft tick from the speaker.

"It's close," he said. "We just need to track it down."

Rosie rushed up and hugged him. "You've found it, Nathaniel."

"Let's not get too excited quite yet," he said as Rosie almost spun him off his feet in excitement. "It could be trapped under tons of rubble or girders. We need a more precise location. But it's here somewhere. Somewhere close."

It took another few minutes to locate the strongest signal, and as Nathaniel had feared, it seemed to emanate from below ground level. The area was on the far side of where they had first seen the metal struts which looked like the remains of the great airship's ribs.

The steel was thick but had circular holes cut through it. Sufficient to allow the running of cables and supports, but small enough not to damage the internal strength of the structure. Most of it was still in reasonable condition, though there were severe bends and creases through some smaller sections.

A few pieces had sheared from larger struts and lay embedded in the earth, surrounded by the boulder-sized remains of housing and molten cobbles.

"It's under here somewhere, within ten or twelve feet by my guess. How the hell are we going to move all this rubble?"

Rosie looked to Maddox, whose shoulders slumped. "Really?" he said. "I'm the pack mule and the navvy? Bloody typical."

"We'll help you," Rosie said, her honeyed words seeming to raise Maddox from his aversion to the role.

"Fine," he said, dropping his backpack to the ground, rifling through it, producing an assortment of tools. They looked well-suited to breaking and prying through the rubble.

The light was fading by the time they had their first breakthrough. They'd all been working solidly for the last couple of hours, either lifting, rolling or otherwise shifting some heavier stones and metal fragments. They used hammers to break up anything too heavy to move, crowbars to lever their way under the larger items, and resorted to brute strength when all else failed.

Maddox's non-stop approach impressed Nathaniel. He was a machine, powering through when Nathaniel and Rosie paused for breath and refreshment. But it was Rosie who continued to confound his understanding of physics. She moved pieces that were beyond even Maddox. How was she able to force her slight frame to perform at that level of effort? It was astonishing.

As both Maddox and Rosie pushed down on one of the metal ribs, a troublesome boulder finally broke free with a resounding crack. They both fell, cursing, as the great steel section clanged off the mound of debris around them.

Nathaniel checked they were all right, but they'd only received minor cuts and abrasions. A rumble of shifting rubble opened into a small passageway. It could have been part of a cellar or something similar.

With the main obstruction and the mass of stone removed, the detector increased its volume and clicked at his side. "It must be in there," Nathaniel said. "The rock would interfere with the signal, less than ten feet I'd say."

Rosie inspected the opening. "I might be able to squeeze through."

"As eager as I am, it's too dangerous. We need to move the smaller rocks now to open the entrance, and then we should try to shore up the sides before venturing in. There is still a lot of mass here that could crush us if it shifts."

"So," Rosie replied. "What you are telling me is, better safe than sorry?"

"Yes, I suppose—"

Maddox leapt to his feet. "What was that?"

"Are you hearing rats again, John? I didn't hear—"

A distant howl reached them through the descending darkness.

"That's no rat," Maddox said.

"I've heard that before," Nathaniel said. "It's bleeders. Or worse."

"What do we do?" Rosie asked Nathaniel.

"There's next to no cover here," Maddox said. "We could make a run for the less damaged properties, but it's half a mile, and we've no idea how many of those damned things are out there."

"No," Nathaniel said. "We clear enough rubble for us all to fit through and get into the cellar."

"Really?" asked Maddox.

"If we are quiet, they might not notice us," Nathaniel replied. "Come on. We're running out of time as it is."

They set to work, forming a chain, and moved the rocks and debris hand-to-hand. Rosie stood at the front picking out and passing the items to Maddox. Then between Nathaniel and Maddox, they placed them away from the opening entryway.

As they worked, more of the foul creatures wailed in the distance. Every sound from placing a rock or section of scrap caused Nathaniel to stop and listen for changes in the noises that would signify the bleeders had sensed them.

The distant mournful wail of the fog warnings carried through the night air. It had grown cold, but they had made significant progress. Rosie had descended into the space and was handing rocks through from below. Nathaniel had passed the arc-lamp down to her, spreading a dim glow within, sufficient to see by, but not spill light from the opening.

Nathaniel gauged he could squeeze through the entrance, but more was required before Maddox could fit his broad shoulders through.

"Hey, Bazalgette," Maddox said, passing him another large stone. "You should go down there. There's a big enough gap for you now."

"I'll wait until we can both get through."

"Look," whispered Rosie from below. "Will you both just shut up and shift these rocks? Who knows how much time we have before one of those things stumbles onto us."

"Yes, ma'am," Maddox replied, rolling his eyes so only Nathaniel could see.

Nathaniel smiled, suppressing a chuckle which soon faded. "Maddox, do you hear that?" he whispered.

"I don't hear anything."

"Exactly. It's been quiet for a few minutes, a little too—"

A moan rang out from a behind them as rocks and debris crunched under something approaching.

"Shit," Maddox shouted, jumping to his feet and flinging the rock toward the foul stench of the dark shadow a mere arms-length away. A sickening wet crunch, then more shuffling footsteps approached as several new voices cried out their mournful songs.

"Get in the bloody hole," Maddox said, pushing Nathaniel, who lost his footing and bounced down the rough entry to the cellar. Rosie stepped to the side, avoiding being swept off her feet as Nathaniel landed on his backside with a thump.

Pain flared in his shin and lower-back as the air escaped his lungs. He saw a flash of bright light then his vision dimmed a little before recovering.

There was a scuffle outside—several moans and heavy wet thuds that changed to sharp cracking sounds of something solid crushing bone.

"Maddox," Rosie shouted.

"Rosie," Nathaniel called, "the arc-lamp. Crank it up to full. They are sensitive to brightness."

She froze for a second, taking in what he had just said, then grabbed the lamp, wrenching the dial clockwise.

A white beam exploded through the cramped space, then faded as she thrust it out of the hole. "John, take it and get down here. Nathaniel says they don't like it."

The moans grew louder outside, and the light dimmed further, as the scrabbling Maddox squeezed himself into the passageway feet first, lamp held between him and the bleeders beyond.

Dust fell around Maddox as he inched into the cellar. If it shifted now, the debris would crush him, but there was no other option. Rosie grabbed Maddox and pulled. They both landed in a heap on the stony ground.

"We can't fight them all. There are loads of the buggers," Maddox said, brandishing the arc-lamp in one hand, a stained and dripping crowbar in the other.

A snarling figure thrust through the opening scratching, clawing at Maddox, who brought the bar down onto the thing's skull with a crack. Its mangled head squelched, spewed dark viscous ichor, and fell silent.

Maddox hardly had time to blow out a breath between his teeth before another two burst into the space. They thrashed their way past each other to get to him.

"I can't do this forever," Maddox yelled.

Nathaniel looked up through the slithering shadows swarming across the rocky ceiling, cast by the lamp rolling on the ground.

"Bring it down," Nathaniel cried. "The rock, hit the one above you."

"What?"

"Hit the bloody thing as hard as you can."

Maddox blocked the swipe of the nearest bleeder, pushing it back, then looking up, he swung at the packed stone above the entryway. A resounding clang rang out, and an ominous creak accompanied the fall of dust.

"Again," yelled Nathaniel.

Maddox took the bar in both hands, and with a mighty upward strike, the rock cracked. This time it fell, it's neighbours following in a cascade. Rocks clacked and broke as they crunched their way through flesh and bone of the two creatures caught in the entrance. Maddox slipped as he backpedalled from the mountain of debris crashing into the small space. Thick dust swamped the room, and Nathaniel hacked and coughed as he tried to cover his mouth and nose.

Nathaniel watched as rocks tumbled, rolling across the floor, while motes swam through the chamber. As they started to settle, what had been the opening was sealed by tons of rubble. Rosie and Maddox climbed to their feet, coughing and laughing.

"Bloody hell," Maddox said. "I thought we were done for."

"Is everyone all right?" Nathaniel asked.

They both nodded while Nathaniel bent to retrieve his lamp, clipping it back onto his belt.

"Well, we won't be getting out that way," Rosie said nodding at the rubble-filled opening. "What now?"

Nathaniel finished attaching the connections to the scanner. It burst into life, giving off a load click every couple of seconds. He lifted the device and rotated it until he was facing deeper into the space they had uncovered. The clicking increased in both frequency and intensity. "This way."

∼

The receiver pointed at a pile of rubble, the ticking almost constant now. "It's got to be under here," Nathaniel said while panning it left and right.

As he panned it away, the tick slowed, returning to full tempo as it passed back across the collapsed masonry.

"What are you waiting for?" Rosie asked, "this is what you came here for, isn't it?"

"Yes," Nathaniel said. "I'm a little apprehensive of what

state it might be in. There's no guarantee it will even be in one piece, let alone working."

Maddox took a step towards the assorted, brick and stone. "There's only one way to find out." He bent and started the back-breaking job of moving the sizeable chunks from the pile.

Nathaniel placed the arc-lamp to illuminate the area, and the resonant frequency detector to point at the rubble then joined Maddox in moving fragments of broken wood beams.

They threw the smaller pieces from the old stack to the side, while all three of them hauled the larger sections with small shuffling steps and aching backs. The detector clattered as they raised another large segment of brickwork.

As Nathaniel rushed to inspect the new gap, a metallic glint caught his eye. He reached down and scooped up a circular shape covered in grime and powdered mortar, but the gleaming silver sparkled in the bright arc light. A matching chain skittered through the fob, torn links leaping into the deep recesses within the rubble.

"Is that it?" Rosie asked him.

"Yes, I believe so. It looks just like the one Simmons had, but maybe..." His voice faltered. "Oh my God,"

Rosie stepped towards him. "What is it, Nathaniel, are you all right?"

He stood there, immobile. His view transfixed on a dark recess near where he'd found the watch. There, poking out of the darkness, was a tubular section of dust covered brass, that ended in the unmistakable shape of a large finger.

"I think we've discovered an ArcAngel."

Nathaniel was on hands and knees, clawing through the remaining debris to clear away the obstructions to his view of what lay beneath.

Rosie and Maddox, who had both come to inspect the find, now aided him in uncovering the battered remains of silver and brass. They excavated the humanoid form, inch-by-inch, as they cleared the rubble. Scorch marks covered large sections of the armour, its surface a non-reflective black and brown in stark contrast to smaller plates that told of its original polished finish.

Gouges and dents showed where the material had suffered massive impact damage. Multiple twisted sheets of grey metal lay beneath, propping it at an odd angle, the edges rent and torn like a curtain caught by a threshing machine.

Nathaniel felt tears welling in the corner of his eyes. The construction was masterful, the joins between the armoured plates were almost invisible. He imagined the joy Tesla and Dent must have felt bringing such a marvel into being. A shining symbol of the power and technology they had created for Queen and Empire.

But it was dead. Whatever energy source it had utilised was long depleted after lying in its dark tomb of brick and stone for four years.

From the tales Dent had told, this had been the last of the ArcAngels, fighting in vain against a vastly superior foe. Gabriel sacrificed herself so the final survivors might flee the alien menace.

This was history, here before Nathaniel and he stopped, feeling he owed a form of offering, a prayer for the deceased. *Should we even open this*, he thought, *or leave it sealed like an old war grave, maintaining some level of dignity?*

What to do? They settled the question when Maddox removed another large piece of stone revealing the cracked helm.

Nathaniel wasn't sure what he'd expected: bone, withered flesh, a stench of rot perhaps? What he hadn't expected was the pale skin hidden beneath the splintered faceplate, with no signs of deterioration or decay.

"What on earth?" Nathaniel said, the surprise evident in his voice.

"Can you open it, get a better look?" asked Rosie.

"I can't see any obvious mechanism. It seems fused into the

helm." He reached for his toolkit and probed around the seams. "Well, I'll be damned."

"What is it?" Rosie asked.

"I thought it was dead, but I just had a small jolt, there must be a live circuit somewhere." Nathaniel's eyes widened as he inhaled. "It's still got power, a tiny amount, but it's there."

Rosie looked concerned. "What are you thinking?"

"If I can isolate a charging point, I might boost the suit's battery. It looks like it's almost empty. I'm astonished it has *any*thing left after all this time."

Rosie cast her eyes toward Maddox and then back to Nathaniel, shrugged her shoulders and gestured for him to continue. "If you think it's safe, then go ahead."

Nathaniel located a power inlet behind a warped panel which he had to force due to the distortion. He found himself alone with the ArcAngel. Maddox and Rosie were looking around the other side of the room.

The port was unusual in its design, but it conformed to Nathaniel's understanding of Tesla's Arc technology, and his jury-rigged wiring was passing current into the suit.

He stared in astonishment as he heard the power draining from his battery pack. It was already half depleted in a few seconds. He unclipped the wires, and felt a more substantial jolt, even through his insulated gloves. Short pulses of light flashed over the armour, most of its activity around the chest and helm. A rasping sound issued from the faceplate as it tried to flex. A grinding of gears heralded more intense flexing, and then a pop of metal as whatever was blocking the mechanism broke away.

It rolled up showing the pale complexion of a woman in her late twenties, surrounded by a halo of dirty, matted curls. Her angular features sat on a strong-jawed face, covered with years of settled dust.

The Victorian standard of beauty was for whiter than white skin. Nathaniel didn't understand the lengths to which some women went, painting their faces with all manner of oils, and other obscure concoctions, some of them toxic.

Her eyelids snapped open, and her throat shrieked as she sucked in a lungful of the dusty air. Nathaniel fell backwards, his backside bouncing off several broken pieces of masonry as he landed in a heap.

Rosie and Maddox turned at the sound and rushed across the intervening distance, Maddox arriving with a large pistol drawn.

"Stop, stop," Nathaniel cried, raising his hands.

"What the hell?" said Maddox.

Rosie's face asked the same question, her eyes wide.

"Gabriel's awake," Nathaniel said. "Don't ask me how, but she's alive."

To emphasise the point, Gabriel burst into a wracking fit of coughing. It was like she couldn't catch her breath.

Nathaniel pushed himself to his feet, rubbing his throbbing buttock. "Help me lift her to a sitting position."

The armour weighed a ton. It took all of them to force it into a near right-angle, and the cough diminished. The suit seemed to lock in place, allowing them all to step away, backs and shoulders burning from the effort.

He stepped back in front of Gabriel, greeted by blue eyes flicking from side-to-side, taking in her surroundings and then focussing on him.

"Where am—" she croaked, her voice cracking. She took another breath. "Where am I?"

"You're in London. It appears you became buried under rubble after the airship came down," Nathaniel said. "Would you like some water?" He turned to Maddox, who rummaged in his pack and passed him a canteen.

Gabriel concentrated for a moment, frowning. "I can't move my arms."

Both hung limp at her side. The left one marked with scorch marks and heavy dents.

"I can help you," Nathaniel said, taking a slow step towards her, canteen held as a peace offering.

She seemed like she would say no, but she looked him straight in the eyes and gave a single curt nod. Nathaniel placed the water next to her cracked lips and tipped it until a trickle bubbled out. She swallowed and nodded to him again, so he repeated the process.

"More?" he asked.

"No, that's fine." Her voice was much clearer, a deep contralto. "Are you refugees?"

"Refugees?"

"Yes, are you trying to escape the city, heading to the south coast? I'm not in good shape, but I'll do what I can to get you to safety."

Before Nathaniel could say anything, she was reeling off a series of names and numbers. "Priority One signal. Reference three five six nine two two. ArcNet, this is Angel-One, do you copy?"

"Wait," he said. Gabriel either ignored or didn't hear him, repeating the same message.

"You don't understand," Nathaniel said, catching her eyes. "They're all gone. It's been almost four years since you crashed here."

That got her attention. She remained silent for a while. "Four years?"

"Yes, it's May 14th, 1899. You've lain buried under a collapsed building all this time."

The confusion spread across her face. "That can't be right. I was piloting Angel-One just yesterday, heading to intercept more of the alien fighting machines swarming up the Thames."

"Okay," Nathaniel said, "let's do it this way. What do you remember from then?"

Wrinkles formed on her forehead as she scowled at him. "I engaged the enemy, but two more joined from the ruins of Westminster. I destroyed one, but the others caused severe damage to my suit, and I returned to Angel-One.

"From there, the weapons platform took a lucky hit, and vented gas, there was fire everywhere. I gave the order to abandon ship but had to keep her steady enough for the rest of the crew to get out. By the time everyone else who could leave had gone, it was too late. I tried to reach the Plaistow Marsh, but she was falling apart around me."

She twisted to look over her shoulder at the remains of the metallic feathers protruding from the rear of her armour. "My wings were useless, so I rode her down, crashing into the houses in a ball of flame. I remember the screaming of tortured metal as we hit the ground and the spare gas tanks exploded, searing flames, being flung through the air, and then waking up here."

"It may feel like it was just a day ago, but your suit has kept you alive for the last four years, somehow sustaining your body as the battery drained."

Gabriel looked up at him. "But what of the Martians? What's happened?"

"They're gone," Nathaniel said. "They only lasted a few months after they took total control."

"So we won?"

"In a manner of speaking," Nathaniel replied. "The fall of Angel-One was the end for the resistance. But we didn't defeat them. They were susceptible to the earth's bacteria. They had no immunity, and it killed them all in a matter of weeks."

Gabriel fell silent for a few seconds. "They're gone."

"Ah, but they have left us with some nasty surprises," Nathaniel continued. "The Martian weed has taken a stranglehold, and the wilderness is overrun. It's also responsible for the red fog, the pollen from the weed mixes with the fog, and it's deadly if you get caught out in it. Breathe enough, and it leads to all kinds of disease and death."

"And what of the Empire? Who rules?"

Nathaniel released a heavy sigh. "Well, that's a whole other story. Victoria's granddaughter returned as the oldest remaining in line to the throne, and she is now Empress."

"Then I must go to her. It's my sworn duty to protect the ruler of the Empire."

Nathaniel held up his hands to stop Gabriel. "We need to talk before you do anything, there's a lot you still don't know. We believe there is a conspiracy within the Black Guard, which means they may already have replaced the young Empress with an imposter as their puppet."

Gabriel's face hardened. The pale blue of her eyes was like ice, he could feel the anger emanating from her, and it chilled him to the core.

She looked at each of the assembled group and back to Nathaniel. "Tell me *everything*."

32

Another shot rang out, and Simmons cursed again. "I'm damned useless."

"It's not *that* bad," Isaac said from the chair behind the church.

Simmons snorted. "You'd be better off replacing those bottles with two barn doors. I might hit something then, but I wouldn't bet on it."

"It's bound to take time to adjust. You've spent your entire life sighting with your right eye, and now you're trying to shoot bottles on a wall with your left? You're expecting too much, Mr Simmons."

"If I am to be of any use, I need to adapt. My aim is God-awful. I'll be more of a menace to our side than the enemy."

Isaac walked over to stand beside him. "What you need is a break, you've been going at it non-stop for hours. How about a cuppa?"

Simmons sighed. "That might be wise."

"I'll go see what I can organise with the reverend." Isaac turned and headed back to the rectory, leaving him to his thoughts.

He'd tried an hour shooting with his right hand and hit nothing. His hold was steady, and the grip was solid. He controlled the trigger as he always had, yet his aim was woeful.

He hadn't realised how much his body naturally aligned arm and eye until now.

With the sight gone, it forced him to gauge the shot from the left, and it wasn't the same. After trying his usual stance to no avail, he attempted altering it to more chest on. When that failed, he swivelled his head to align his weaker eye closer to the line of the barrel, but that didn't work for him either.

After becoming fed up with continued failure, he tried shooting with his other hand for a while. His aim felt better, but his control of the pistol was poor. His grip was weak, and his command of the trigger was appalling. Instead of a measured squeeze, all he could manage was a reckless pull, all strength and no finesse. It was like learning all over again.

No, the left was even more disheartening than his right hand. His head ached—perhaps Isaac's suggestion wasn't a bad one. A nice cup of tea then back to it. *Maybe try the rifle*, he thought. *It can't be any worse than the pistol.* All he needed were a few consecutive hits on the target, something to give him an ounce of confidence.

He'd been a miserable sod with Bazalgette last night, and now he felt like a petulant child. Kicking and screaming at the world when it refused to bow to his will. As he unpacked the elephant gun, the tinkle of cups on saucers reached his ears.

Isaac returned carrying a tray with a pair of teacups. A steaming black teapot, wedged between them, caused the rattling, as it pushed the china to the edge, tilting everything just enough to be touching the pot's bulbous sides.

A small silver sugar bowl and blue porcelain jug of milk sat precariously, tempting gravity to give them a tiny pull.

"Tea?" Isaac said, "with milk and sugar if I remember right?"

"Yes, thank you."

They sat and drank. Isaac watched the waterway and the idle rise and fall of his vessel. "I miss her, you know," he said without warning. "Betsy, that is. That's why I couldn't leave her here to go gallivanting about with the others. It's like being wed again, I think. She needs me to spend time with her to make sure she's happy. I take care of her, and she looks after me in return. I'm getting on, and I've found I dislike change more than ever before." He turned to Simmons. "Don't suppose that makes much sense to you? Ignore the ramblings of an old man."

Simmons looked up from his tea. "No, I understand what you mean. I've resisted it, and perhaps it's part of the problem I'm having with adapting my aim."

He found himself believing what he'd said. Rather than wallowing in what had been, if he embraced the change, would that work?

"Right," he said standing. "Let's get back to shooting the air around these damned targets."

"Right you are, Mr S."

Simmons reached down to pat the beautiful wooden stock of the Holland & Holland rifle and strapped it back into its case. *No, I'm not giving up on the pistol. I will master this or exhaust myself trying.*

Instead of aiming, he let his body and muscle memory take over. With the Mauser hanging at his side, he brought it up to position and fired in one flowing motion.

He missed—but it had been much closer. The chip he'd made in the wall was about an inch from the target. He reset and repeated the process. Shattered glass tumbled to the ground as the bottle exploded.

Isaac leapt to his feet, whooping in delight. "You only went and bleeding done it."

"Let's keep things in perspective, that could have been pure luck. With the number of rounds I've shot today, I was bound to hit something sooner or later."

Turning to the other bottle, Simmons raised and fired again. It stared back defiantly from the wall, but he was sure he hadn't been far off. "Perhaps I'm being too harsh on myself. How about we round up something a little more man-sized?"

They spent half an hour locating various items and laying them out, creating a set of four crate-legged, barrel-chested, bucket heads. Isaac secured the parts together so he wouldn't always be walking over to reset them. Kind of him to express that much confidence in his ability to hit them, let alone dislodge any. All that was missing was the black paint for their uniforms, but he had a good imagination.

"Now these evil fellows are in for an unpleasant surprise," he said as he reloaded his pistol.

The Mauser barked four rapid shots, each followed by a clang as the round punched through each of the metal buckets. They were less than perfect, the third shot had clipped the edge, but the others were solid hits around the centre of their heads. Three dead and one writhing on the floor, screaming. It was a more than satisfactory result this early in his retraining.

A smile brightened his dour expression, and Isaac grasped him with a hearty handshake. "Well that showed them now didn't it?"

It had indeed, and more importantly, it had shown Simmons he was capable, he could do this and get over his injury.

He spent the rest of the afternoon making new holes in his makeshift enemies. They had proven quite the opposition against the pistol, but as he switched to the rifle, they disintegrated leaving heaps of splintered wood and mangled metal.

He packed his weapons away as dusk descended, and took a sip from his engraved hip-flask before offering it to Isaac. "I feel this calls for a celebration."

33

Nathaniel brought Gabriel up to speed on everything that had happened in the four years she had lost. He finished the tale with the recent events leading them to the pocket watch and finding her in the cramped cellar.

She sat in silence, absorbing the news and what it meant for the Empire. "We need to find your other friends and make plans. Maybe ArcNet has been in shutdown for the last four years, much as I have."

"What does that mean?" Nathaniel asked. "What is ArcNet?"

"It's the network that linked all the ArcAngels. It was a secretive project, few people even knew of its existence, let alone where to find us. If anyone else survived the war, that's where they would go."

"What about Robertson and the Black Guard? Would they know where it was?"

"No, the Empress didn't trust them. Things were changing during the last couple of years before the invasion. The military split when they formed, a lot of bad blood between the different commanders. Robertson was a junior officer then, but from what you have told me, it seems he has risen through the ranks. He seemed to be the kind of man to exploit the smallest opportunity to advance his agendas. There was talk of several of the more experienced officers being forced out by a scandal. However, everything changed with the chaos that ensued when the Martians arrived ."

"So, where is this ArcNet?" Rosie asked.

Gabriel glanced at her for a second. "I'm not sure I can tell you," she replied. "It's not that I don't trust you, I need to get my bearings, to work out where it is relative to our current location. I know it sounds vague, but you'll have to bear with me on this."

"That's fine," Nathaniel said, "but before any of that, we must get you on your feet. I doubt we can carry you, even with myself and Maddox, unless..." he paused as his brain clicked into calculation mode.

"Unless what?" Gabriel asked.

"Unless we removed the armour and left it here. We could come back for it. I'm sure with the rest of our group, we could do it in a few trips."

The smile fell from Gabriel's face. "That's not possible," she said, her voice monotone. Her eyes settled on the rubble strewn across the surrounding ground. "It's more than just armour."

Nathaniel felt the frown as his eyebrows bunched together. "What do you mean?"

"Most of it is no longer removable. It maintains what is left of me." She let out a long breath, returning her eyes to meet Nathaniel's. "Almost half of my body is useless or destroyed. The ArcAngel program was the last resort, the final chance at living a fulfilling life. They told us there were no guarantees, but our lives were over otherwise, so what the hell? Die there, no use to anybody, or take the risk to be reborn as protectors of the Empire? It was an easy choice."

Nathaniel's eyes widened. "Hence, the name. They created you from ruined flesh into bio-mechanical perfection. This was Tesla and Dent's true work, producing a hybrid man-machine?"

"Yes," she said, blinking back tears. "I wasn't the first. There were four before me. I was the only one to survive the process."

"This is remarkable," Nathaniel said. Rosie and Maddox stood in silence, but their faces spoke volumes.

"What's the matter?" he asked Rosie.

"Don't you see?" she replied.

"See what? It's an incredible leap forward, imagine what they could do with this technology. The medical implications alone are staggering. Someone who had lost limbs or—" Nathaniel's eye's widened as the realisation struck him. "Dear God, it's what *he* was after all along, isn't it?"

Rosie nodded. "It's not your fault, Nathaniel."

He clutched his head in his hands. "Not my fault? It's all my fault. It was the schematics for the armour he was after. Josiah means to rebuild himself as an ArcAngel. What have I done?"

≈

Gabriel pulled her lower body from the remaining rubble with ease but mentioned her batteries were at almost minimum power.

Nathaniel shrugged. "I could give you a little more from my arc-lamp, but I've already half-drained the battery to get you up and running."

"Don't do that," she replied. "I'll reroute some less critical systems and focus on mobility so we can get out of here."

"We should wait until daybreak," Maddox said. "There's no point trying to dig ourselves out of this hole just to be set upon by those beasts out there."

Nathaniel nodded. "I suppose that makes sense. I am feeling rather tired, let's rest until the morning, then we'll find a way back to the others."

≈

Sleep was slow in coming, and transient when it finally arrived. Nathaniel woke several times during the night, aching and uncomfortable no matter how much he tried to cushion the floor with his coat.

He gave up at six, clicking his pocket watch closed and began analysing the fallen debris, for a way to escape to the surface. Two hours passed in a flash as he assessed their options. Gabriel opened her eyes on the chime of eight and stood. The movement caused a scuffing sound, and soon, both Rosie and Maddox were stirring.

"I think the rubble where we found Gabriel looks most promising," he said. "If we can dislodge a few key stones, we might squeeze through a gap to the surface."

The others agreed, and they started the excavation.

It turned out to be a far simpler task than he had expected. Gabriel could lift larger and heavier pieces than the rest of them and had much superior grip when trying to remove stubborn sections of the debris.

With her faceplate closed, she shrugged off any falling masonry, which bounced harmlessly from her armour.

A ray of sunlight broke through as a tumble of smaller stones parted revealing a route out. Nathaniel felt as he imagined Orpheus must have when escaping the underworld, but hoped for a much better outcome.

They scrambled up the steep incline of rock, emerging in the ruins of a large building with only one remaining section of wall. From the size of the place, Nathaniel imagined it once to have been a public house or something similar. He surveyed the surrounding area for any signs of movement. Apart from the trickle of shifting rubble, all was silent.

"It looks clear," he called to the others as they emerged. Like moles surfacing, they each squinted, shielding their eyes from the intense sunlight.

"I'll take a scout around," Maddox said, drawing his pistol and disappearing behind the wall. He was quiet for a man his size.

Gabriel insisted she go last, being the one most able to withstand any further collapse if it occurred. She emerged, surveying the scene of desolation. "Is it all like this now?" she asked, eyes boring into Nathaniel.

"No, this is some of the worst around the area. Angel-One exploded when it crashed here."

"And the rest of the city?"

"We'll show you once we make a little distance south," he replied, waving for both Gabriel and Rosie to follow as he picked his way through the remains.

After ten minutes, Maddox rejoined them. "All looks clear if we're headed back the same route we got here."

"Good," Nathaniel said, then pointed to the southwest. "There's the city."

Gabriel stood, staring at the vast black walls in the distance. "It's a monstrosity."

"But it is necessary to keep the fog at bay," Nathaniel replied.

"Do you really believe that? What of those who live outside the wall?"

"Well, they survive as best they can. They have fog-curtains fitted around doors and windows. That stops most of the ingress, but it's not foolproof."

"So they succumb to the disease carried by the alien spores, and become these bleeders you mentioned? How uncivilised have we become?"

Nathaniel turned to face her. "Well, essentially that's what happens, though the taint passes through two preliminary stages first, wheezers, then bleeders. But, yes that's the essence."

"And the politicians do nothing to improve the situation?"

"No," Rosie said. "All decisions come from the High Council now. They're a group of over-privileged toffs and military, led by the Lord Commander of the Black Guard, Sir George bloody Frazer-Robertson."

"And there," Gabriel said, "lie all the problems. Do any of you have detailed maps of the city, from before the invasion?"

"No, but I bet Isaac does," Rosie said. "He's a magpie for anything like that."

"He does," Nathaniel added. "I've seen a couple on his boat

when we were fixing the engine, but I'm not sure how old they are."

"Let's get back to this Isaac then," Gabriel said. "With an adequate map, I should be able to triangulate where ArcNet is."

～

Isaac rummaged through the tarps at the stern of his vessel, searching for any more extra cans for target practice. Shots continued from behind the church where he'd left Simmons practising again this morning. The reverend had rustled up eggs and bacon for their breakfast, but he wasn't sure it was any kind of bacon he'd tried before. More likely, it came from something more urban than pigs. However, food was food, and the taste had been better than a lot of what he'd sampled in the past.

The sky was grey this morning, but at least it was dry. The rear of the boat was a mess. He hadn't had the opportunity for a clear out, what with the rush to get away from Greenwich in the night. It was time he started on repair work.

With that thought now nagging in the back of his mind, Isaac stood and moved forward to inspect the damage Betsy had received during their escape. How could he have neglected her for so long?

The front quarter, on the port side, had taken the most severe beating. The broken rail and scorched deck cried out for attention, and he felt a physical clenching in his gut as he inspected the blackened and blistered wood. A smell of burnt timber assaulted his senses as he peered over the edge, following the charred planks down to the waterline.

"I'm sorry, my dear," he said out loud. "I'll get Simmons organised with extra targets, then be right back. We'll get you looking good as new in a few days."

He returned to the stern, and after a few minutes, walked ashore with an armful of emptied cans ready for Simmons to kill.

Simmons turned as Isaac entered the area at the rear of St Mark's. The buckets were ruins of torn metal, sharp edges jutting out as they lay discarded on the ground behind the splintered remains of the barrels.

"Reinforcements?" Simmons said, pointing to the armful that Isaac carried.

"Right you are, Mr S," he replied, depositing the liberated cans beside the mangled targets. "It looks like that rifle isn't conducive to the health of your enemies."

Simmons chuckled. "Yes, it has that effect, whether they be metal or the more fleshy variety."

"And the aim?"

"It's not good, but better than I feared. As long as I keep aiming for the centre of mass, I'll manage. The sight requires adjustment, but it won't compensate that much, so I have to lean my neck across to position my left somewhere near where it needs to be."

"What about Nathaniel? I bet he could devise something."

"Yes, I thought about the same thing. An offset scope—it's right up his street." Simmons paused. "How is he? Have you heard anything from him? I fear I was a dreadful arse when we last spoke."

"He's fine. Said you were still in significant pain, and the morphine wasn't helping your state of mind."

"That man is much too nice for his own good. I near as dammit had a tantrum with him, shouting and screaming like a spoilt brat. I don't know how he puts up with me."

"He's a good man," Isaac replied. "The kind of chap you want around to watch your back, and by God, what he didn't know about Betsy's engine? And all book learnt from what he said."

"It's true, but he can put his mind to almost anything to do with technology."

Isaac nodded. "Yeah. So, more practice?"

"Yes, I'll try shooting a few more Black Guard without wasting too much ammunition. You?"

"Betsy demands tending to, and I've neglected her too long as it is. I need to repair the deck and side rail. I have the wood for that, but the hull around the waterline might prove difficult. It needs curved sections. That's normally done under pressure and steamed to maintain the shape. It's a job for a dockyard to get that fixed proper, so I'll have to patch it the best I can for now."

"Well, good luck with that then," Simmons said.

"And you with your shooting," said Isaac. He held up his palm in farewell and headed back to Betsy.

The unmistakable roar of Simmons' rifle echoed through the intervening rubble as Nathaniel led his small group back towards St Mark's.

"That's Simmons," Nathaniel said. "What the hell is going on?"

The church was only a few hundred yards distant, but the debris obstructed their view.

"The quickest route is down by the waterside," Maddox said as he checked his pistol. "But there's not much cover."

"Can you take a closer look from somewhere? Get an idea of what's happening?" said Rosie.

He looked from Rosie to Nathaniel then nodded, ducking out of sight around the edge of the ruined wall they leaned against.

"We'll wait and see what he comes back with," Nathaniel said.

What else could they do with Gabriel requiring the help of both Maddox and Rosie to support her? The stumbling steps she made slowed their progress across the uneven terrain to little more than a crawl. It looked like a storm was approaching, and the sky had darkened, clouds amassing in thick grey clumps overhead. The wind had picked up and was shifting restlessly as if waiting for an opportunity to gust and blow into full force.

Another shot rang out, and a crunch of stone heralded Maddox's arrival. "I can't see anything unusual. No sign of anyone around and no return fire. Isaac is on his boat, looks like he's doing repairs."

"What do we do?" Rosie asked her eyes flitting from Nathaniel to Gabriel.

Nathaniel had worked most of his life in isolation. He wasn't used to giving orders or having to decide for others. He preferred working to his own schedule. "We continue as before, but let's keep an eye out for anything unusual. We'll find out what's happening when we get to St Mark's."

They all resumed their positions, except Gabriel. "You should leave me here and check that it's safe. If it is, you can retrieve me then. I'm not going anywhere."

"No," Nathaniel said. "Nobody gets left behind. Come on, let's move."

Without another word, Rosie and Maddox thrust their shoulders under Gabriel's arms hoisting her to her feet as they continued their slow progress, Nathaniel leading the way. *When did I become the leader of this group?*

As they approached along the water's edge, they made use of what little cover there was. Another two shots exploded from behind the building in rapid succession. They stopped, checking for any movement, but there was nothing to indicate any problem.

"Look," Nathaniel said, pointing ahead then holding his arm up acknowledging the figure on the boat waving to them.

"Nathaniel," Isaac shouted through cupped hands. "Good to see you're well."

"Yes, fine. What's going on with the gunshots?" he replied.

"Oh, that's just Simmons shooting the Black Guard," he called back, his tone calm.

"What?" Nathaniel asked, his stomach lurching.

"We made some targets. He's practising."

Nathaniel felt a wave of relief pass over him, and he

nodded for the others to follow him toward the boat. Isaac jumped to the shore as they reached him, he looked at Nathaniel, then froze as his gaze passed to the trio that followed behind. "Is that—" Isaac's voice faltered. "Is that an ArcAngel?" he said, clasping his right hand over his heart.

"Isaac, this is Gabriel," Nathaniel said. "Gabriel, Isaac."

"Pleased to meet you, Isaac," Gabriel said. "I've heard a lot about you."

"Oh my God," Isaac said, dropping to his knees, his eyes locked on hers.

"Isaac," she said with a shocked tone. "Please get up. I'm no different from you."

"But you're..."

"I'm a woman in ArcAngel power armour. Not a holy relic of worship, regardless of our proximity to a house of God." She ended with a short laugh.

Isaac still seemed a little stunned, Nathaniel walked over and offered his hand, helping the older man back to his feet. "It's true, she's just like us. We need to talk with Simmons and Jack. Oh, do you have a map of London, something detailed, from before the war?"

Isaac flicked his eyes towards Gabriel, still unsure, then refocused on Nathaniel. "Yeah, course I do. I'll go ferret it out."

The arc-lamp sparked and hummed in the dim living room, shedding a bright glow over the table and all those seated around it.

Gabriel tapped a metallic finger down on the old map between them. "That's ArcNet, there at the centre of the three access nodes."

"You're certain no-one else knows its location?" Simmons asked.

"I assure you, Mister Simmons, only those working on the ArcNet project knew of it. The ArcAngels, a handful of technicians, all of whom I would trust with my life, and the creators, Tesla and Dent."

"And you're sure that none of them would have turned over the information, even under severe duress?" Simmons continued.

"I have been out of commission for four years. There's no way I can be certain of what happened in that time, but if you want to find a place any survivors would return, then this is it. It's locked down and requires ArcAngel technology to gain access."

Nathaniel looked up from the map. "So, if the Black Guard somehow found their way in, they could stop us?"

"If there is anyone inside, they could refuse entry to anyone else, other than me. I have the sole override," said Gabriel.

"Okay, so we have a way in," Nathaniel said. "But where is it? Where's the entrance, that's the middle of Ravenscourt Park?"

"It's on a section of the Piccadilly underground line."

"What?" said Nathaniel. "Piccadilly doesn't run that far. It stops here at Hammersmith." He emphasised the point, tapping on the map.

"No, Mister Bazalgette," Gabriel said. "They extended and then blocked the tunnel, stating it was too unstable. But they used it for the ArcNet project as the central hub of operations. There are feeder lines to the other three sections I needed to triangulate its location."

Simmons scowled. "And what of the other locations, what if someone compromised them? Wouldn't that give access to the core through these lines?"

Gabriel smiled. "There are plenty of security measures, any of which would make it difficult for anyone trying to force their way in. Presuming they even knew where to look. The final option is to flood the tunnels from the sewage network."

"Really?" Nathaniel asked. "But how—"

"Bazalgette," Simmons said with a laugh, "can you just for once get your mind out of the sewers?"

A wave of laughter rolled around the assembled group, and

Nathaniel held his hands up in mock surrender. "Fine, fine. Perhaps we could talk in more detail later?"

Gabriel nodded and returned her gaze to the crumpled paper, edges ripped and covered with spots of oil and grease. "So, we have a target and three access points. I have the means to override any lockouts if we encounter them, but I need more power. We won't manage this with you having to carry me around everywhere. Have you been able to come up with anything to help us with that?"

Nathaniel grinned. "As luck has it, I picked up two extra energy cells when I took the Arc-Rifle. I recharged them at my workshop so they might give you enough charge to keep you running until we reach ArcNet."

Gabriel nodded. "That sounds good, but the sooner we get to ArcNet, the better."

34

They planned their travel, with Isaac able to take them most of the way before they would have to hike through rougher and drier terrain. As the entrance Gabriel had shown them was outside the city walls, Nathaniel didn't feel the need for travelling under cover of darkness.

It took all the power cells to charge Gabriel's armour enough to get her moving, and then they boarded as bright rays of morning light crested the church roof.

Jack wished them well as they left, offering them the hospitality of his humble abode if they ever required it. Nathaniel watched the old man wave them off as Isaac increased the power and the roar of the boat's engine thrust them west back towards the city. He noticed Simmons fire the reverend a sharp salute before returning to his preferred location at the prow. Jack had tidied Simmons' bandages, and he now sported a leather eyepatch. It looked much better, but angry bruising covered a large area of his friend's face. Black around the bottom of the patch and running through purple and into a green and yellow mass that reached down to his jawline.

Simmons didn't seem to notice Nathaniel's stare and looked like he was almost back to his old miserable self. *Well, better than that,* Nathaniel thought. There appeared to be a new purpose in him, an enthusiasm for life again. Nathaniel smiled, perhaps Simmons had finally come to terms with not being able to do everything himself.

"How long, Isaac?" he called to the stern.

Isaac popped his head above the canvas awning. "We're going against the tide, so I'd expect somewhere around two hours."

Nathaniel nodded his thanks and found a place among the others near the prow as they progressed towards ArcNet.

Nathaniel checked his watch, Isaac was spot on. They sailed into sight of Hammersmith with ten minutes to spare.

They splashed through the muddy water, picking their way between outcrops of rubble and the rusted remains of exposed rebar. The smell of salt from the brackish pool, caught in his nose. It must have been standing for some time.

Gabriel led them into a tunnel. Two beams of light cut through the darkness from her armour, and he and the others followed. The rays bounced around the walls as she got her bearings and headed toward a blank wall with a sturdy steel door. It looked like it belonged on one of the great ironclads of the Royal Navy. Six feet tall with rounded corners and a circular wheel mechanism in the centre. It stood there, imposing its will on those who would attempt to breach it and the secrets it protected.

Nathaniel searched the room, his arc-lamp casting shifting shadows. The interior was sparse, and with no sign of any recent habitation, he felt a little more reassured. They might be the first people to enter the complex in some time.

"There's no power," Gabriel said, looking back at the assembled group. "I will have to force it open."

"Is that going to damage it?" Simmons asked.

"No, it has a manual override, but it may take a while, even for me." The wheel screeched as Gabriel wrenched it, rusted metal falling to the ground in thick flakes.

Simmons approached Nathaniel, stopping before him. "I've been a cantankerous old goat, and I wanted to apologise."

"For what?" Nathaniel said.

"Damn it, man. You're the reason I'm still alive. If it wasn't for your help..." the sentence trailed off into silence as Simmons looked at him then grabbed his hand in a firm shake. "Well, at least let me thank you. It feels like I've been wallowing at the bottom of some dark pit for eternity. Now there seems to be a spark of light even if I can only see it from one eye." He smiled at Nathaniel, their arms locked. "You are the only person I trust, the only one I can truly call a friend."

"It's mutual, and I'm glad you are feeling better about the world and your place in it," Nathaniel said, the corners of his mouth rising. "The eyepatch suits you. Makes you somehow more dashing and dangerous at the same time."

Simmons laughed. "Well, it's better than being told it makes me look like I should learn to duck quicker."

"It's good to have you back."

Simmons smiled, turning towards Gabriel as a resounding clang rang through the confined space. "Looks like our new friend has cracked the seal, shall we?"

Nathaniel fell into line behind the older man, and they headed to the door. The metal squealed in protest as Gabriel heaved it open, onto a narrow set of steps descending into darkness.

Isaac stayed when the rest of them started down the stairwell. His obsession with the boat wouldn't allow him to leave it. He told them they could find him later at one of his usual haunts along the river. He needed to return to business and hope that his involvement at the incident at Greenwich hadn't come to Josiah's attention.

The stairs descended for some considerable time, and much to Simmons' relief, Bazalgette suggested they call a short halt. His injured muscle burned and spasmed from the constant descent step after step. He stood flexing his leg, trying to hide his discomfort.

Bazalgette looked at him and tilted his head with a questioning look on his face. Simmons smiled back at his friend, and that seemed enough for Bazalgette who returned to his conversation with Gabriel.

They had each broken into smaller groups. Bazalgette and Gabriel spoke about some technical matters and whether the power coupling would be adequate for something or other. Rosie and Maddox whispered off to one side, leaning on the metal rail where the steps continued their steep descent. It left Simmons on his own to work on his aching thigh.

With a sigh, finally giving up on the pretence, he rubbed his leg. It helped. He turned to catch glances from Rosie and Maddox and stifled a silent curse. "So are you ready to move on, or are we going to stand around here all day?"

They continued for what seemed ages, snaking back on themselves as they disappeared into the depths. "Shouldn't be far now," Bazalgette called out. After the next switchback, the stairs opened into an underground station, abandoned for years.

They stepped down to a single platform with rails running on either side. The curved arches of the tunnel dripped with moisture and were home to a green moss that lived in thick, damp strands along its length. It reminded Simmons of seaweed and was visible wherever light fell on the walls and ceiling. Rust caked the tracks and disappeared into the darkness. Orange puddles formed on the ground and the sound of steady dripping echoed through the area.

"So this is part of the Piccadilly line?" Bazalgette asked, looking at Gabriel.

She nodded. "Yes, they kept it quiet, which was a blessing when we set up ArcNet. It doesn't seem like there's any power running here at the moment, we might have to improvise."

Simmons saw the smile grow on Bazalgette's face. He was in his element down here. In the dark, underground, and with problems to solve involving electricity? This is what he lived for.

They split up. Gabriel and Bazalgette went in search of a depot she thought lay beyond the station's eastern end. Simmons and the others stayed to keep watch in the other direction.

"So, Mr Simmons," Rosie said, breaking the silence. "How are you managing?"

"Fine."

"Really?" Maddox said with something that almost resembled a smile.

"Yes, really."

"Looked like you needed that rest back there," Maddox added.

"Oh, I'm sorry," Simmons said. "I thought we were waiting for you to catch your breath, seeing as how you needed the rail to lean against."

"What?" Maddox replied, a hint of menace in his voice.

"And the girl. Did you need her to hold your hand? Were you frightened?"

Maddox drew himself up to his full height. "I don't have to take this shit from you."

"No, I suppose not. Go back to taking your orders from your mistress like a good dog."

"Fuck you, Simmons." The big man took a step towards him.

"John, not now," Rosie said, her voice clear and calm.

He stopped, mid-stride and spat on the floor at Simmons' feet.

"That's right, do as she says. You might get a biscuit."

"Oh, that is it," Maddox said, rolling his sleeves up his meaty arms.

"John. Stop." Rosie said. Her tone sharp, just how Simmons would expect someone to address a misbehaving dog.

Simmons let the chuckle that had been growing out into the open space between them. Maddox, red-faced, stepped back beside Rosie, who caught Simmons' eye.

"Mr Simmons, I'd appreciate it if you would remember we are all on the same side here and that antagonising each other will not help our cause."

"Really," he replied, "and here was I thinking we were finally getting somewhere with all the trust issues I have."

"This is neither productive nor conducive in our attempt to defy Josiah and find the Empress."

"Is that what we're all trying to do?"

Rosie paused for a second. "Of course it is."

"Oh, I thought we were insulting each other with insinuations of weakness and frailty. I do beg pardon, milady."

Rosie sighed. "Must you do this?"

"Look, just keep it on a leash and out of my way. If I want to talk to it, I'll whistle. All right?"

Rosie's eyes narrowed, jaw clenching. "This isn't productive, Simmons. John has been nothing but helpful since he carried your body from the observatory. I don't know what it is you think he's done to deserve your contempt, but you could at least show some civility. You of all people should see that. This behaviour is not becoming of a knight of the realm." She whipped around, leading Maddox away along the platform.

"Ex-Knight," Simmons spat through gritted teeth.

35

Bazalgette and Gabriel returned with a railway handcar. Simmons stared warily at the contraption. It looked like an upturned table on wheels with two rows of stained leather chairs facing each other.

Between them stood a large, centrally mounted lever that resembled a child's seesaw. Simmons walked to the edge of the platform to get a better view. "I hope you're not suggesting we need to pump that contraption to move it?"

"No," Bazalgette replied with a laugh. "That's the manual override. It's used to recharge it."

"It's powered?"

"Yes, and it seems to be in a reasonable condition to say it has sat abandoned for all these years. It's flat, but it is charging as we speak."

Bazalgette motioned to a section at the rear behind the seat where a cable ran to a spare battery. "If we give it a few minutes, it should have enough to get us underway, and it will continue to charge as we progress to our destination."

"The core," Gabriel added. "Once there, we can access some real power."

"How far is it?" Simmons asked.

"I'm not sure of the precise distance, but it should only take about fifteen minutes. Nathaniel cleaned up most of the rust that was caking the wheels and brakes and it rolls smoothly on the tracks again."

Bazalgette looked up the platform past Simmons. "Where are Rosie and Maddox?"

"How should I know?"

"Because you were here with them when Gabriel and I went in search of something to get us to the core? You three were on lookout to ensure we had no uninvited guests."

"They wandered off that way," Simmons said, pointing to the far end of the platform.

Bazalgette frowned. "Have you upset Rosie?"

"What makes you think it was my fault?"

"Experience?"

"I don't trust him."

"Maddox? What's he done now?"

"He hasn't *done* anything. It's just a feeling in my gut, and in my time, I've grown to respect that feeling. It's kept me alive on a good few occasions."

Bazalgette let out a deep sigh. "I'll go talk to them."

"Don't you dare apologise on my behalf."

"Fine, fine," Bazalgette said, hands before him in a placating stance. "I'll try to smooth it all over so we can get underway."

Simmons turned to Gabriel. "So shall we board this contraption then?" waving for her to climb up first. She obliged, and he followed, sitting beside her, facing in the direction he presumed they would travel. The bulk of her armour meant the seat would only fit the two of them. Well, that was fine by him. If Bazalgette wanted to side with Rosie and Maddox, then he could sit with them.

The light from the bobbing arc-lamp indicated the three of them returning to the carriage. Was that a hint of disappointment in Bazalgette's expression? Maybe Gabriel and Simmons had taken the best seats.

The others climbed aboard facing them while Bazalgette checked his pocket watch. "We should be good to go."

Gabriel reached down to her right and pushed a lever.

With a clunk, the carriage lurched forward a foot amidst a grinding of gears. She pushed it again, and the noise ceased. She turned the handle on a brass wheel clockwise, gripping it in her armoured fist. A growing hum of power, then the vehicle leapt into motion, and they forged ahead into the darkness.

The clickety-clack of the wheels crossing the tracks reached a slow but steady rhythm as they got up to speed. It wasn't the breakneck pace of a hansom cab skidding across the slick London cobbles, but it was much faster than walking. Simmons relaxed into the worn leather upholstery and revelled in the relief of taking the weight off his feet. He felt the tension melt away, and he became accustomed to the vibration of the carriage, subtle shifts in direction dampened by some form of suspension.

Bazalgette's arc-lamp split the darkness, and it now provided a shorter but broader beam before them. Dark side tunnels swallowed the light as they passed, the central section looked more finished here, fewer tools and much less rubble lay against the walls. "We're getting close to the core," Gabriel said, rotating the wheel and slowing the vehicle to just above walking speed.

Ahead, beyond the reach of the lamp, two dim red lights appeared in the darkness.

"Well, it seems there is power down here," Simmons said.

Gabriel nodded. "Yes, it looks like someone is at home."

"Let's hope they are accepting visitors."

Gabriel stopped the carriage ten feet from a solid wall of metal blocking any further progress. The tracks disappeared under it, and she climbed down to the track. "There is an access point over here. I'll see if I can get the gate open."

She popped a panel out of nowhere on the blank surface, then jammed her hand into it, rotating it until a loud click sounded from within.

The lights flashed from red to amber for a few seconds, then to green. The massive bulk split in the centre then moved sideways, receding into the wall on either side. The track continued, recessed into the floor, matte black and in pristine condition. The doors glided effortlessly across the surface and disappeared into their snug housing.

As Gabriel got them moving again, they passed between the heavy gates, each at least a foot in depth. It was like a bank vault.

Arc-lights blinked on as they entered the area ahead shedding a pale light onto a platform that rose from the ground on their right-hand side. It was a station, large enough to hold a full underground train with around four carriages. The transport came to a halt, and Gabriel leaned out, re-engaging the brake.

"Is it all like this?" Bazalgette asked, his eyes flitting from one amazing piece of technology to another.

"The three stations are almost identical," Gabriel replied. "They're arranged at the edge as spokes on a wheel. We will head inward from here, to the core."

The gates behind them rolled back out of their respective walls, closing the exit with a dull thud. Gabriel stepped out of the vehicle and then turned to offer her hand to assist them all up. Their carriage sat a lot lower than a traditional train, and they had to step up almost a foot to reach platform height.

Simmons was still getting his bearings when they heard the slap of metal falling as square recessed holes appeared in the wall ahead of them. Half a dozen rifle barrels popped into sight, followed by a distorted voice through a speaker. "Drop your weapons, step back with your hands raised, and nobody needs to die today."

～

Simmons turned to Gabriel. "Nice reception."

"I suggest we do as they say for now," she replied.

The group raised their hands as requested and waited. The voice from the speaker returned. "How did you get those entry codes?"

"They are my codes. Are there any members of the original crew with you?"

"We are asking the questions here."

Gabriel tilted her head as if recalling a distant memory.

Simmons scanned their surroundings. This wasn't a good position. With solid cover, numerical advantage and knowledge of the battlefield, their opponents held the better hand. Overall, this was not the time or place to force a conflict.

The speaker crackled again. "What is your business here?"

"Callam?" Gabriel asked. "Is that you?"

"Gabriel?" came the stunned response a few seconds later.

Simmons waited, observing the interchange, lowering but not dropping his pistol as instructed.

Gabriel moved forward into clear view. "Yes, Callam, it's me. It took a little longer than I had hoped, but I'm back now thanks to these fine people." She nodded at Simmons and the rest of the assembled group.

"Damn," replied the voice through the intercom. "Open the doors."

Rifle barrels remained trained on them as a large section clanked open between the firing positions. A muscular figure thrust the door outward and walked towards them.

He was bigger than Maddox, almost six and a half feet was Simmons' guess, and broad with it too. Spots of oil discoloured his grey coveralls, and he carried a rifle in a professional, but relaxed stance. His eyes were wide and fixed on Gabriel as he approached, a smile breaking across his face.

"Damn, Gabriel, but it's good to see you. All this time, we thought you were dead." In contrast to the size of the man, Callam had a soft tone with a lilting Welsh accent.

"It takes a lot to kill an ArcAngel," she replied, grabbing him in a tight embrace.

He clapped her on the back. "I know that, but you'd be surprised at what's gone on since... hell, what happened to you? Where have you been hiding all this time?"

Gabriel held up a hand, halting the barrage of questions. "Later. We can catch up later. First, let me introduce some new friends." She turned, motioning to the group. "This is Sir Pelham Simmons—"

"Just Simmons will do."

Callam's massive palm dwarfed his hand as he shook it with enthusiasm. "Happy to meet you, Simmons."

"And this is Nathaniel Bazalgette, John Maddox and Rosie." Gabriel looked towards Rosie, a puzzled look on her face. "I'm sorry, dear. I didn't catch your surname?"

Rosie fashioned a grin aimed at Simmons. "Just Rosie is fine, thank you."

Simmons wondered if she was making some jibe at him, but let it pass. Better to play happy families for now. *Best not to wake the beast.*

Callam grasped each of them, including Rosie, in a firm handshake as he introduced himself.

"Don't worry about Callam," Gabriel called over to Rosie. "He's a top-class mechanic, but he knows little about etiquette. In fact," she turned her attention to the big Welshman. "Speak with Nathaniel. He's the one who got my systems back up and running."

Callam nodded at Bazalgette in recognition. "But first," Gabriel continued, "let's get to the operations centre, and you can tell me about the setup here."

"Fine," Callam said, heading back to the doorway. "We noticed your approach about half a mile out, we have motion trackers out in the tunnel but didn't know who to expect. It wasn't a worry though, ArcNet is locked down tight. So imagine my shock when the place opened with your override code. I thought someone must have stolen it, and I mobilised the whole damn lot of us."

"Which is?" Gabriel asked.

"Not as many as I'd wish."

Simmons positioned himself so he could still hear Gabriel and Callam as he moved to walk alongside Bazalgette. As they stepped through the large metal doorway, he saw the massive bars that secured the thick slab of steel. This would be a formidable structure to defend if the need arose, and a complete nightmare to breach.

"What do you think?" he asked Bazalgette who was examining the mechanism with particular interest.

Bazalgette pushed his index finger up the bridge of his nose, shifting his spectacles. "Very impressive," his friend replied. "If it is as Gabriel said, and they can flood the approach tunnels at will, they have a sturdy defensible position."

"And the technology?"

"From what I've seen so far, it looks every bit as advanced as the ArcAngel suit. Did you notice the power conduits?"

"Surprisingly, no. I hadn't noticed."

Bazalgette raised an eyebrow and Simmons wasn't sure if his friend was intentionally failing to understand the sarcasm in his tone, or if he really didn't get it.

Whatever was going on in that brain, Bazalgette continued unfazed. "So, here," he said, pointing at a recessed panel above head height, "that's the main junction box, but the amount of power it's carrying is astounding."

"How on earth can you tell by just looking at the damn thing?"

As Bazalgette opened his mouth, Simmons jumped back in. "No, don't explain it. It's a waste of your time and mine. I wouldn't understand, would I?"

"It is a rather tricky concept."

They followed Gabriel and Callam into a corridor lined with bright arc-lighting set into the ceiling. Ahead of them stood a group in dark grey uniforms. They carried weapons similar to ArcRifles, but there were subtle differences in the size and shape, which made them look a little more streamlined.

They all received suspicious glances from the uniformed group of three men and two women. One of the women watched Simmons as he passed, her intense green eyes holding his gaze as she and the others waited. The grey-clad militia closed ranks behind and herded them forward. There was no menace or physical interaction, but they knew their trade. Ex-military, Simmons thought. By their bearing, and how they reacted without instruction, these were seasoned troops. Green-eyes was most likely their leader.

Bazalgette continued talking about power regulation, voltage and capacitance. It might as well have been Chinese for all the sense it made to Simmons. He nodded and smiled when he felt it was appropriate. He didn't want to upset the poor chap when he was in full flow.

"So," he started as Bazalgette concluded. "What you're saying is that this is all powered by the same technology as your arc-lamp and Gabriel's armour?"

Bazalgette stopped mid-stride and stared at him. "Yes, I suppose I am. I didn't think you were paying attention."

"I got the gist. You have a knack for describing things in such a way I get enough to understand and not feel like a complete buffoon."

"Sorry, I didn't mean—"

"No. It's a good thing. I need it simplifying. Heaven knows I'm no engineer, especially with all this high energy malarkey from that Tesla chap."

They crossed an intersection where Bazalgette pointed out markings on the walls which he thought might be recessed bulkheads. Half a dozen doors lined the side corridors on either wall to their left and right.

They continued along the grey steel corridor until it ended abruptly. The only feature that marred the polished metal was a communications array. A grilled speaker hung there, and Callam made his way over and pressed a series of buttons before speaking. "Open up. I've got a surprise for you."

Silence.

"Come on, Raph. It's me."

A low, sullen voice responded. "I don't like surprises. You know that. What have you found?" The crackling reply had a suspicious tone, and it hung in the air before them. Simmons looked to Bazalgette, but he only shrugged.

"Open the door, and you'll see."

While Callam waited, tapping his foot, the intercom remained silent. "Raph?"

"I'm thinking," came the reply.

"Raph, are you going to open up or not?"

"No."

"What?" Callam said.

Another short pause. "No, I'm not opening the door. There's something odd about your behaviour. I don't think I can trust you."

"Look everything is fine, I thought you would like this surprise, just open the door. Please?"

"No. I'm flooding the compartment."

"What? No," Callam shouted.

The corridor plunged into darkness as the arc-lights dimmed, then glowed red. A blaring klaxon accompanied the change of lighting, deafening in the tight confines.

Green-eyes shouted, "Shit. Pull back, now." Boots shuffled then ran towards the intersection but halted with a resounding metallic clang. Simmons glanced over his shoulder to a bulk-head now trapping them in a twenty-foot coffin of steel.

"He's sealed us in," she called back. "Callam, do something."

While Callam continued shouting at the speaker, trying to get some response from the person beyond, Gabriel moved to stand before the intercom, a picture of calm.

"Raphael," she said, her voice barely audible above the klaxon. "This is Gabriel. Let us in."

Silence.

She repeated her request.

"Gabriel? No, it's a trick, some ruse to gain access to the core," came the sharp reply.

"Raphael, this is a direct order. This is ArcAngel-One, cease the alarm and open the door. Do you understand?"

"No, no, it can't be. She's dead." There seemed more than a hint of panic in the voice. "She's dead."

Dark water burst into the room, spraying from vents in the ceiling. The familiar smell of the Thames flooded the room as torrents of the brown muck splashed from the floor rising quickly around the beleaguered group.

"It's her," Callum yelled over the wailing alarm. "Raph, it's Gabriel, she's back."

"No, she abandoned us. Left us all to die. She would never have done that if she was still alive."

Gabriel shook her head, and her shoulders slumped. "Priority override one six two. Code gamma delta alpha omega." She shouted the syllables out thick and fast, fighting against the deafening siren. "Cancel alert. Access the core."

The klaxon cut off in an instant and left most of the occupants with their hands still over their ears. A grating sound of metal came from above, and the deluge ceased. With a gurgle the waist-high water started to recede, several small vortices appearing as it drained from the compartment. A bright arc flickered behind the rising bulkhead before them. As the thick steel wall approached its zenith, Simmons saw what lay beyond and gasped. He wasn't the only one.

Patterns of light strobed within the dark circular chamber ahead of them. Cables cascaded down the walls and snaked across the floor to a central dais. Upon it sat the shredded remains of an ArcAngel torso, built into a fused mess of metal, wires and tubes. The blue energy pulsed along the cables and glowed as it climbed the body, past the stump of a ruined metallic arm to a half crumpled faceplate.

The thing creaked as it shifted, appearing as though it was tilting the remnants of its head to inspect the trespassers. Amid streams of warped and melted metal, a single ocular lens whirred as it turned to focus on Gabriel.

"But you're dead," it said. The crackling was a feature of its voice, not the intercom. "You left me all alone. So alone."

"No, Raphael, I'm alive, and I'm here," she reached up, wiping a tear as it slid from her watery eyes. "Dear God, what did they do to you?"

∽

Callam conducted a brief tour of the facility on the following morning. It seemed designed for a crew of at least four times their current number of twenty-three. Bazalgette stopped at a workshop where a group of technicians greeted him. They all wandered off discussing the equipment and issues they had problems with. Word had spread of his repair of Gabriel's armour, and now he was being treated like royalty.

The rest of them moved on to the security area where green-eyes and four military types sat in discussion. Callam introduced her as Major Lynch, and it seemed she ran a tight ship.

Simmons continued the tour keeping as much distance as possible between himself, Maddox and Rosie. If Callam noticed the tension between the three, he said nothing to show it.

"So what was all that nonsense about yesterday?" Maddox asked.

"I'm not sure, to be honest," said Callam. "Raph has become increasingly paranoid over the last couple of months, but we've never encountered an incident like that before. Gabriel is spending some time with him, to work things out."

Maddox pushed on. "But there must be something that triggered that behaviour? Doesn't it worry you he flooded that compartment with us all in it?"

"Could he do it elsewhere?" Rosie added looking towards Callam.

"Yes, he could. He's wired into ArcNet."

"Wired in?" Maddox asked.

"Yes," Callam replied. "they designed ArcNet to have a direct interface with one of the ArcAngels at all times. It's part of what made them so effective."

Maddox raised an eyebrow. "So he's got full control of the place?"

Simmons had heard enough. "As interesting as all this must be to you, I'm sure Callam here has much better things to do than answer all your questions about how this facility operates."

Callam sighed. "I do have a considerable number of tasks I need to get on with, so if you will excuse me?"

"Of course," Simmons said with a nod.

Maddox stared at him, his eyes dead like a shark. "What was that all about?"

"I don't know what you mean?" Simmons replied, keeping his face and voice relaxed.

"I was trying to find out if this Raphael might be a problem."

"Yes," Simmons said. "You seemed a little too interested for my liking."

"What's that supposed to mean?" Maddox shot back.

"Oh nothing, just commending you on sniffing out trouble."

"Simmons," Rosie said. "I thought we'd been over this at the station?"

He flashed his most innocent smile. "I'm complimenting Maddox. He's the one that seems to be taking offence. Anyhow, I'm parched, and I'm sure I noticed a tea urn when we passed by the mess hall." He turned on his heel, leaving Maddox and Rosie as he strode back towards the central hub and their quarters. His leg hurt like hell, but he was damned if he would limp in front of them.

They all met that evening for supper. The food was simple but tasty. Bazalgette was full of the ideas he and the technicians had been working on. "The facilities here are astounding, and the power grid? That's something else."

"So, you've enjoyed yourself today, I take it?" Simmons asked between bites.

"Oh, yes. They are a knowledgeable group, all excellent scientists, well versed in Tesla's theories and principles. I would even say I've learned a few new things."

"No, surely not?"

Bazalgette smiled. "I don't know everything, Simmons."

The two friends chuckled until they heard the ringing of a spoon on china. Looking to the head of the table, Gabriel stood holding her teacup before her. "Apologies for my absence today, but I needed to spend time with Raphael. He has endured a lot these past four years, as most of you well know. Thanks to the efforts of our newfound friends, and to Nathaniel for his work restoring my systems." Applause rang out led by the technicians.

"Thanks to their help, they have brought news about our Empress and details of the peril she faces. Now, some of this we already knew, but there is more interesting information regarding the Black Guard. Nathaniel?"

Gabriel motioned to Bazalgette as she took her seat.

"Yes, today my colleagues and I discussed the disturbing new technology that has come to our attention. Mainly, we spoke of the Watchmen and the timepieces created for them by Dent."

Simmons leaned back and listened as Bazalgette told the tale of the murder at The Britannia Inn through to the present. It included the use of the watch, Josiah's involvement and the retrieval of the schematics. Bazalgette's story held nothing back. His memory was astounding, but Simmons wondered if this was the right place or time to be revealing all the information in full. Gabriel must have spoken with Bazalgette about this and convinced him it was a good idea, so who was he to argue with the will of an ArcAngel?

As Bazalgette completed his story and took his seat amongst the murmur of conversation, Gabriel stood again. "Now we know the full extent of what the Black Guard have been plotting, the exchange of the Empress for an imposter and her imprisonment somewhere in the Inner-City. We must plan a means to retrieve Victoria and restore her to her rightful position."

Gabriel glanced around the silent table. "To achieve this goal, we have several areas that require attention. Raphael has informed me of increased activity among the Black Guard, centred on Kensington Palace. We believe this is where Victoria is held captive and where we can locate the imposter. Both of whom we need to retrieve."

A murmur of assent flowed around the room until Gabriel once again called for quiet. "Besides retrieving the Empress, we also have to deal with the High Council, including General Robertson and his Black Guard. We don't know how many of the members have become involved in this conspiracy or if they're just afraid to oppose Robertson. It may be fear of reprisal against themselves or their families that are keeping them in line. Regardless we need to look for allies and any information that could be of benefit to us. Our final issue is that of Josiah Dent," Gabriel cast her eye to Rosie. "Is there anything you would like to add about him and his organisations?"

Rosie stood. "The first thing is you shouldn't underestimate him. Josiah is a brilliant man, regardless of his quirks, and a Horologist to boot as Nathaniel will attest to."

Eyes turned towards Bazalgette, who nodded his assent.

Rosie continued. "I worked with him for a time, and his influence reaches far across London and beyond into the wastes. He has already united three of the four main gangs, only the Elephant and Castle oppose him, and that's because they have leadership issues and hate the Red Hands. He also created a lot of support from the working class by using political agitators to cause unrest and turn them against the government, but they remain fiercely loyal to their Empress. When Josiah found Nathaniel and Simmons, his approach changed somewhat, leaving them to locate and retrieve the schematics."

She paused for a while, her eyes lowering. "I feel now that he used everyone around him, including myself, to further his agenda. I don't expect sympathy from any of you. I have done *questionable* things while working for Josiah."

Her eyes caught Bazalgette's for a moment, then dropped to the table before she continued. "Regardless of all that, He's been planning this for some time. Now, with the schematics to the original Dent designs, he's set to become the greatest threat to the city, and to the cause we follow to rescue the Empress."

Bazalgette raised his hand. "I suppose the question in everyone's mind is 'could he fabricate the watches and the armour?' Well, with the watch stolen from Simmons and myself, I would have to say, 'Yes'. From my brief introduction to the man, he has the skills and access to all the industry required to manufacture. The only saving grace is getting the components to power the devices is difficult. Tesla obviously didn't leave a stockpile of energy-cells, and they now need items of Martian technology, and as far as I am aware, the government jealously hoards these."

"I wouldn't be too sure of that, Nathaniel," Rosie replied. "He is a resourceful man, and his gang contacts give him easy access to the black market that trade in those sorts of artefacts recovered by independent scavengers. So Josiah may already have them. Even if he doesn't have them yet, be assured he will organise raids on storage facilities. His ambition knows no limits, and he's not afraid to waste a few lives to achieve his ends."

Gabriel returned to her feet. "Thank you, Rosie. So, we have several issues, and the clock is ticking. I suggest we think about this overnight and reconvene in the morning. We have people we are trying to contact that may provide help for our cause. Once we know their situations, we can divide into working groups to investigate each specific area that requires our attention. Are there any questions that need addressing now?"

The room was silent as the gravity of the situation sank in.

"Good, let's meet here again at seven am. Dismissed."

36

Simmons woke early, the sky only just starting to brighten. He kept irregular hours, but with the dull aching pain from his leg, he wouldn't get back to sleep again.

He rose and dressed, relishing the cold running water from the basin in his room. Drying his face on the soft white towel, he patted the area around his right eye, conscious of the bruising below it.

He lifted the black leather patch from the bedside cabinet, raising it to his socket and positioned it by touch. His fingers probed the edges, making subtle adjustments until it felt comfortable on his face. It would have to do. He thought he was becoming more adept at fitting it, but it was still early days.

Back to the table, he plucked a dark-coloured bottle from the top drawer and took a few sips of the mixture. He'd added a decent whisky which improved the taste of the laudanum no end. None of the bitter tang remained from his initial exposure to it mixed in water.

He placed it into his inside coat pocket and left in search of the messroom. The corridors stretched ahead, lit by the dimmest of glows from the overhead lighting. Simmons moved through the quiet halls with just the sound of his boot heels clicking on the polished concrete floor.

To his surprise, the place wasn't empty as he'd expected.

The large frame of the engineer lay slumped at a table, head resting on folded arms. As Simmons entered the big man inhaled sharply, his eyes cracking open at the approach. Callam brought his hand to his mouth, stifling the long yawn that forced itself from him.

"Didn't mean to wake you. To be honest, I wasn't expecting anyone else to be up and about at this hour."

"Don't worry about it," replied the Welshman. "I only meant to have forty winks." He picked his half-drunk cup from the table and took a sip, screwing his face up at the taste.

"Cold, eh?" Simmons asked. "Perhaps you needed a little more than a nap?"

"Right you are, it's been hectic lately. What with your arrival, Raphael's mood and Nathaniel's suggestions, there's a hell of a lot that needs to happen and soon. Sorry, where are my manners? Do you want tea?"

"That sounds splendid," said Simmons taking a seat opposite Callam. "So what's Bazalgette got you doing?"

Callam stood and walked over to a large metal urn. "He's offered a few profound ideas that have us thinking along different lines." Steam hissed and rose as he filled a teapot with boiling water. He placed two tin mugs onto a wooden tray, adding a milk jug and a bowl of sugar cubes. "It's quite the intellect he has, isn't it?"

"Yes," Simmons agreed. "He continues to amaze me, not that I'm any great thinker."

"Now then, we're not all men of science, are we? I've heard about your exploits in and out of the city."

"Really?" Simmons squinted at Callam. The huge man looked like he was carrying a child's tea set in his oversized hands. But to give him his due, he had a delicate touch as he laid out the items from the tray - his placement of each piece measured and precise.

"Oh yes," Callam continued. "Your name is all over the bloody place. The Black Guard are having a fit."

"You have access to Black Guard communications?"

"Ah. Has no-one mentioned that?" Callam's face was

quizzical for a moment as he mulled thoughts over. "Well, what the hell. You are causing them some right royal mischief. The enemy of my enemy and all that?"

Simmons nodded and Callam continued. "It's part of what we have been doing for the last few years. We have gathered a lot of intelligence, intercepted messages and, Raph's cracked most of their cyphers and encryption."

Simmons raised an eyebrow. "I see."

"Well, we've had a little help here and there. A few people in positions of influence have given us an edge. That's what I've been discussing with Gabriel, bringing her up to speed. She'll cover it at the briefing this morning. We know where they are holding the Empress, we just need to find a way into the Inner-City."

"You have spies placed in the Black Guard?"

"Oh yes, and a few people within the government too. Nothing like council members, so don't get too excited, but they hold positions that give them access to useful information."

"You realise what will happen to them if they're caught?"

"We are all aware of the disappearances and what they mean. These are all royalists, brave men and women who have done more than sit by and watch this country collapse from the corruption that festers within the halls of government."

"But are they willing to die for those convictions?"

"Every last one. Many have already given their lives to get information out so we would be ready to strike back when the opportunity arose. And it seems there will never be a better time than right now."

"I agree," Simmons said.

"It gets my goat. I can't believe how the Empire is teetering, how anyone could become involved in something like this. It's treason, that's what it is." He slammed his hand onto the table, the silverware leaping and clattering against the china. "Apologies, but I'll be happy to see the back of all those traitorous bastards. How could Robertson do this? He was the bloody regent, there to look after Victoria, help her rule not bloody usurp her power. If he's laid a finger on her, he'll have me to deal with. Well, I suppose whatever's left of him after Gabriel's finished with him."

"I don't think I'd like to get on her bad side," Simmons said. "She seems incredibly... focused."

"Too bloody right, and that's not the half of it. I was here during the invasion when she, and the others, took the fight to the Martians. It was incredible, seeing them at the height of their power, resisting those alien bastards." He stopped, a long sigh escaping his lips. "But all in vain, wasn't it? They're all gone now. Michael and Uriel. Only Gabriel and Raph survived, and he struggles day by day."

"What happened to him?"

"I've not heard the specifics, and he doesn't talk about it." Callam's voice dropped to a whisper. "The Martians captured and tortured him, but he never broke. They ripped him apart and then reconstructed what they needed to keep him functioning. I've seen the weld marks, and I've done as much as I can to fix the metal, but it's his mind that's failing. He was mistrustful after we recovered him, but now he's downright paranoid about everything. Well, you saw yesterday, he almost drowned the lot of us."

"Yes, that was more than a little worrying."

"A bloody good job that Gabriel was here, isn't it?"

"Very fortunate." Simmons realised he hadn't touched a drop of the tea and reached for his mug.

"Apologies, Simmons," Callam said, noting the movement. "Too busy gabbing about all that's wrong with the world. Here, let me get that." He lifted the large teapot and poured the dark, steaming liquid into the two mugs. "Here you want a quiet cuppa, and I'm giving you my bloody life story of doom and despair."

"It's fine," Simmons replied. "Useful to understand what you and everyone down here has been up to."

"Well, that's kind of you to say. I feel better having had this little chat. Got a few things off my chest that maybe I needed to air."

"Anytime."

"Right you are," Callam said, upending his tin cup and downing the contents in one long gulp. He stood and reached out his hand. "Nice talking with you."

"Likewise," Simmons replied, shaking the Welshman's meaty paw.

Callam turned and left. Simmons found himself alone in the mess hall as he'd initially expected. He looked down at the tray and dropped two cubes into his mug. He gave it a quick stir then topped up with milk.

Now where was I? he thought, taking a slow sip. He cast his mind back to leaving his quarters. *Oh yes, what to do about Maddox.*

≈

Bazalgette screeched to a halt, avoiding bowling Simmons over as he rushed around a corner. "Sorry, Simmons. Didn't see you there."

"No harm done," he replied, stepping back to check his friend over. "Are you all right?"

Bazalgette's face had an almost deathlike pallor. "Nothing that a few hours sleep wouldn't fix."

"I ran into Callam earlier. He looked a little worse for wear too."

Bazalgette nodded. "Where is he now?"

"I think he was heading to the lab to meet with you?"

"Good, I need to get going, lots to discuss."

"Could you spare a few minutes before you go?"

Bazalgette's hand shifted towards his waistcoat pocket, where a silver chain disappeared under the fold of grey cloth, but halted. "What can I help you with, old chap?"

"I wanted to catch up about what you said last night. You know, before today's meeting gets going."

"Anything in particular?"

"I was wondering if we should have kept the bag a little tighter closed?"

Bazalgette frowned, his pupils darting to the lower right as he considered. "I don't understand. What bag are we talking about?"

"The metaphorical one, as in letting the cat out of it too early?"

"Oh," Bazalgette replied as comprehension dawned on his face. "You think I should have held certain details back?"

"Well, I wouldn't have put it like that, but yes."

"Why? Aren't these our friends? Surely they need the information so we can coordinate our efforts?"

Simmons stifled a sigh. "Are they?"

"What do you mean?"

"Are they our friends? We know almost nothing about the ones down here."

"I think you're a little over suspicious. These are people hand-picked by the ArcAngels, all ex-military and loyal to the Empress. Don't you trust Gabriel's judgement on that?"

"Gabriel isn't the one who bothers me."

"Hang on," Bazalgette said. "This is still about Maddox, isn't it?"

"Yes, damn it. There's something not right about him."

"Everything I've seen him do has been to help us, to help you. If he and Rosie hadn't been there at the observatory, I'm not sure we would have escaped. He carried you on his back while we were being shot at."

"Yes, I know all that," Simmons said. "But it still doesn't mean I'm wrong. Look at the way he tries to pick fault at every opportunity."

"From what I've heard, you haven't made it easy for him either."

"What are you talking about?"

"Rosie spoke to me, said you were fanning the flames somewhat, rather than dousing them."

"Whose side are you on?"

"I'm not taking sides, or at least I'm trying hard not to. We need to stand united. There are few enough of us as it is. Can you put it to one side?"

339

"What, you want me to ignore it? Let him get away with whatever he's up to?"

"No, I don't want you to ignore it. Just set it aside while we organise things. If you think there's a problem, then keep an eye on him, but surely it would be better doing that when he isn't aware. If he *is* up to anything, then he's unlikely to let anything slip while you call him out on everything he does."

Simmons knew his friend was talking sense. He just didn't want to accept it. There was something wrong with the way Maddox acted, and he would expose it. "Maybe you're right. It takes a thief to catch a thief, eh?"

A smile crept across Bazalgette's weary-looking face. "Thank you for being reasonable."

"Perhaps the injury and the pressure we've been under was getting to me."

Bazalgette broke eye contact, his view dropping to the ground. "How are you doing, Simmons? With all that's been going on, I get distracted and sometimes forget it's still only been a week since..."

"Don't worry about me. I knew this was an occupational hazard, right from the off as a young officer. Few men of my previous and current occupation live to retirement without picking up a few war-wounds." Simmons groaned inwardly at how that sounded but kept his face straight and hoped Bazalgette wouldn't see through the charade.

"That's good, and the pain? You're managing all right?"

"Yes, I take a slug of the laudanum if it gets too much, helps me sleep too."

It was true. Well, most of it. Simmons wasn't ready to tell his friend it was more than just a night-time dose, and in truth, didn't help his sleeping at all. If anything, it was worse than before his injury, but that was his cross to bear, he'd sort it out. *Once the pain recedes enough, I'll cut out the laudanum.*

"That's... good," replied Bazalgette. "Oh, and it reminds me. I've been working on something for you. I'll bring them to the meeting."

Simmons tilted his head to the side. "Them?"

"Yes, it's a surprise. You'll like it," Bazalgette said beaming. "But I need to dash. I don't want Callam thinking I've abandoned him in the middle of things now it's getting difficult."

He turned and left at a pace that spoke of his excitement at what he and Callam were working on. Simmons pulled the chain, flipping his watch into his hand and opening it in a smooth, practised motion.

It was still an hour before they were all due to meet, time enough to make final preparations and do his packing. They would head back to London soon. It was no secret that he was to accompany Lynch's squad in their attempt to retrieve the Empress.

∼

The meeting passed much quicker than Simmons had expected. As they outlined the plans, Lynch caught his gaze on two occasions, most notably when Gabriel announced that Simmons would lead the rescue along with Lynch and her team. If she was unhappy about it, she didn't show it in front of her troops. That was good, but he knew the moment was fast approaching for an interesting discussion in private. He hoped that she was the type of officer who could move past any first impressions and could follow orders. If she was like the spoiled brats who had bought their way into their commissions through wealthy parents and privilege, that would be more challenging. Time would tell.

Rosie and Maddox would scout the outer areas of London to see what they could find about Josiah's plans, while Bazalgette was staying to help Callam and his team. They would work with Raphael to repair ArcNet and Gabriel's damaged watch. If they could get that up and running, it would provide a considerable advantage for them all.

The meeting concluded with the information they had a contact within Kensington Palace for Simmons and team to meet. The password was 'God save the Queen'. He smiled, it was unexpected, but welcome news. He'd been thinking about the time it might take to find the Empress, let alone rescue her unnoticed.

Bazalgette cut his way through the crowd of people, his face alight with wonder and mischief. "I've got something for you, in fact, two somethings."

Before Simmons could say anything, he felt a polished wooden box thrust into his hands. "These should help you," Bazalgette said, his voice filled with anticipation. "Go on. Open it."

The matching brass clasps clicked open at Simmons' touch, and he pulled the lid which lifted with a slight pop of air. The mechanism rolled back on smooth hinges, revealing a lined velvet interior. It looked like an exquisitely carved gun case to Simmons, but a little on the small side.

Within lay a pair of beautiful brass and leather goggles. The lenses appeared to have a subtle shade of red to them, and Simmons threw Bazalgette a quizzical glance.

"Goggles?"

"Yes," Bazalgette replied, "try them on."

"Wouldn't a single lens have made more sense?"

"Just try them."

Simmons realised it would be easier to go along with it. He reached towards his eyepatch.

"No, you needn't remove it," Bazalgette said. "Over the top is fine."

"What are you up to?"

"Come on, old chap. Put them on."

"Very well. If I must."

He manoeuvred the goggles into place, surprised to see the room was bright, not tinted as he'd expected.

"Here let me look at that," said Bazalgette taking the straps from Simmons and adjusting them until they were snug. "There you go. How do they feel?"

They were, Simmons found, extremely comfortable. "Yes, they fit well."

Bazalgette walked around in front of him so he could inspect the device. "Now, how's your sight, everything clear?"

"Yes. Clear as normal."

"There are two switches on the outer edge of each lens. The left one toggles them on and off."

Simmons looked Bazalgette in the eye, still humouring him, and reached for the switch. A quiet whir sounded as an internal mechanism released the lenses which lifted out of his line of sight.

Bazalgette studied the movement and made small adjustments with a jewellers screwdriver. Once satisfied, he backed away. "Try it again."

Simmons did so, and they returned to their original position with a soft hissing sound. "So, they open and close without having to remove them. That's... interesting."

Bazalgette was smiling. "Press the other one."

Simmons flicked the right-hand switch. His vision slewed, and he experienced a wave of nausea for a moment. "What just—"

"Have a look around. They might take a while to get used to."

Simmons scanned the area, there was something unusual, but he couldn't place it.

"Maybe you should try aiming your pistol?" Bazalgette suggested.

The room had almost emptied, so Simmons unclipped the Mauser and brought it to a firing position, and aimed at the far wall. He targeted at one of the junction boxes and froze. "My God," he said. "I'm sighting it clearly."

"You're getting the sight from the right optic. I wasn't sure how well it would work, but you should be able to aim and see as if it were from that eye. It was for the rifle. Isaac told me you had an unnatural stance when trying to use it, so I thought of this."

Simmons laughed. A few people stopped in the doorway looking at him, but he didn't care. "I've said it before Bazalgette, and I'll say it again, you are a damned genius."

"The transition should become easier with practice, you'll

feel a bit woozy at first, but that should fade as you get used to it."

He flicked the switch back, and felt the strange shift in his visual field again, this time a little worse than before. He reached out to support himself on a chair.

"Is everything all right?" Bazalgette asked.

"It's fine. The disorientation was a touch stronger. I just need more practice, and now I know what to expect, I'll manage better."

"Don't overdo it." Bazalgette shrugged. "As if that's likely."

"I will try," Simmons replied with a grin, "but with a gift like this, I want to be back to my old self as soon as I can."

"Who am I kidding?" Bazalgette asked. "I give you a new toy and then tell you not to play with it."

"There is that," Simmons said. "Why are the lenses red?"

"Are they affecting your vision?"

"No, I just noticed it before I put them on."

Bazalgette gave him a knowing nod. "That's something else I'm working on, but I haven't had a chance to complete it with the tight timescales. When I have a little more time, I'll finish them."

Simmons clapped Bazalgette on the shoulder. "Thank you. This will make a world of difference. I'll catch up with you on my return."

He turned to leave, but Bazalgette caught his arm. "You'll need this before you go," he said, handing Simmons a ring box.

"What's this?"

"I re-engineered the device we used to locate Gabriel's watch, and from what Dent told us, I've created something that should interfere with the Watchmen's devices. It's on a chain, and I'd suggest you wear it next to your skin. It reacts when any of the watches are active or in your general vicinity."

"How does that help if they are in use?"

"It will deactivate the time field if they come within ten feet. You'll feel a tingle if there's one close by."

"How close?"

"Within thirty feet or so."

"All right. Good to know."

"All the best out there Simmons," Bazalgette said clasping and shaking his friend's hand.

"Look after yourself while I'm gone."

"You too. God save the Queen."

"God save the Queen," Simmons replied, turning to leave the room, not knowing if that would be the last time he ever saw his friend.

37

The contact was due at six, and it was already a quarter past. Simmons stalked back towards the Lamb and Flag. The public house was on a narrow alley which somehow had managed the far grander title of Rose Street. Perhaps it had come about from its proximity to the Covent Garden Market just around the corner. Or, maybe the name had been a joke. The odour was more akin to offal and manure, with a strong dose of human sweat from the packed bodies along its length.

The smell of tobacco smoke caught in his nostrils as he returned to the raucous din. Lynch had told him the locals called it 'The Bucket O Blood' for the bare-knuckle boxing bouts held each night. It seemed to Simmons a much more honest name for the establishment.

The patrons spilt onto the narrow cobbled street, milling outside the building. Sloshing tankards of ale and loud conversation filling the tight brick-lined space. A match was due to start in the next few minutes, and the alley was rowdy with arguments and betting before the fighters began their craft.

Simmons passed two revellers slumped on the cobbles having already overindulged in the cheap beer. There was no point in trying to get into the place, it was full of jostling bodies either seeking to make a wager or fighting to reach the bar for a refill. Instead, he found himself a section of wall to lean against and lit his pipe. Streams of blue smoke coiled into the air, mingling with the existing clouds.

Shouts from inside, announcing the fight was about to begin, filtered into the alleyway. Another shoving match started as patrons pushed closer to the door and windows to see.

"Spare a light, sir?"

Simmons hadn't noticed the man at his elbow approach. With all the commotion around, he'd blindsided him, coming from his right. He needed to get used to that. The fellow dressed in working clothes with a flat cap, the brim concealing his eyes in the poorly lit alley. "For a pipe, is it?"

"No, it's a little early in the evening for a pipe."

That was the passphrase Simmons was waiting for. "Never too early in my book," he responded as instructed.

The man pulled a cigar from his inside pocket and moved back from the crowd, now baying for blood, as the fight began. "Where are the others?"

The ArcLighter produced a brilliant cross of electricity which set the dried tobacco smouldering. "They're waiting a few streets away. Why are you late? Is there a problem?"

"No, there was an inspection that ran later than expected. Everything is fine. Let's take a walk, and then we can get you on your way. Follow me, then lead on once we reach the main street."

He turned, walking back along the alley. As they approached the end, the man knelt to tie his lace and Simmons passed him, heading to the waiting squad near the marketplace in a pair of hackney cabs.

He pulled the door open to the first black cab and climbed in to find a pistol aimed at him from the seat opposite. Lynch sat there, face a mask of calm and said nothing. The barrel didn't waver in the slightest. Her eyes asked a question to which he nodded a silent yes. The Mauser lowered but remained in her hand.

Their contact entered, sitting beside Simmons. "My name isn't important. You can call me Smith if you must. Before I say any more, I don't want to know anything about you or the rest of your team. I've been paid to get you into the rail yard and onto a carriage. After that, I'm done. Everything else is up to you. No names, no information, no questions. Is that clear?"

"Crystal," replied Simmons.

"Good, now let's go." Smith tapped on the cab roof, and they lurched into motion with the crack of a whip.

Lynch sat with the Mauser on her lap, looking as relaxed as if they were on a simple trip to the theatre. She showed no sign of concern about their plan to break into the Inner-City and invade the Queen's residence in Hyde Park. Simmons had found her to be a woman of few words, and that was fine by him. Nothing worse than idle chatter on route to important business. He realised he hadn't thought about quiet in some time, having become accustomed to Bazalgette's tendency to blurt something out when it went silent. If it wasn't the latest tweaks he'd performed on the arc-lamp, it was some other techno-wizardry he'd come up with.

Simmons tried to convince himself it was better this way. But damn, he missed the sound of Bazalgette's excited tones describing his latest discoveries. A smile crossed his face thinking about it, and Lynch raised a quizzical eyebrow. He shook his head at her, and they continued in silence.

Smith directed them onto a labourer's omnibus a few streets from Hampstead Road, and they travelled with the rest of the late shift to the engine yard at Euston.

With the clothes provided, they blended in with the other workers and the checks at the gate went without a hitch. The overhead rails from all the Inner-City areas converged here. Silent carriages hung in the darkness, awaiting repair.

Lynch and team found an empty work-shed where they could change out of sight. They unpacked the tool-bags they each carried, which held their equipment rather than the expected engineering tools. They had packed the top layer with spare coveralls and an assortment of spanners in case of inspection.

Now the squad constructed the devices they knew and loved. Pistols and holsters along with a variety of hand-to-hand weapons and even a few rifles and a shotgun were being rebuilt. Simmons busied himself with his rifle. The speed at which Lynch's crew organised themselves was nothing short of amazing. There was a little chat between them, jokes poked at each other, but all in good humour. As they prepared for action, he could see this was an elite force of veterans, as disciplined as any he had served with.

The rifle he'd spotted was approaching completion, and it was unlike anything he'd seen before. It reminded him in part of the arc-rifles used by the Black Guard, but a much slimmer, streamlined design. The other woman in the team, Fletcher, had pieced the remarkable weapon together in a few minutes. She spent a few seconds checking the mechanism. It appeared conventional enough, a breach loaded round, though the bullet itself looked unusual.

She noticed him watching and smiled with a chuckle. "Simmons, isn't it?" Her accent was sharp and clipped Scottish dialect.

Simmons hadn't realised he had been staring. "Ah, yes. Yes, it is. You are Sergeant Fletcher if I'm not mistaken?"

"You're no mistaken," she replied, "but it's no me you're interested in now, is it? It's this wee beauty." She tapped the stock of her weapon and looked back over to him. "It's no quite the brute you have there," she gestured at his rifle. ".303 Holland if *I'm* no mistaken?"

Simmons stood and crossed the distance to take a seat beside her. "You've a damned fine eye for weapons. Yes, I've had this old girl for a good few years, been through thick and thin with her out to India and back."

"Really?" Fletcher said. "Was it all hunting, or has she seen any real action?"

"A little of both to be honest. More so since returning to Blighty. It was just before the invasion, you see."

"Which regiment did you fight with?"

"Ah, long story," he replied. "Let's say I was freelance and worked with the resistance."

Fletcher smiled with a knowing nod. "Enough said."

"So," Simmons continued, "what the heck is this contraption you've got yourself hooked up with? I've not seen one before. It looks like the bastard child of an arc-rifle and something much more elegant."

Several groans issued from the team. "For the love of Christ, don't ask her that. She'll tell you *the story*," the big man, Blake said.

"Shut your yaps," Fletcher said. "Just cos you lot cannae hit a barn door at arm's length."

A few more friendly jeers followed before she continued. "Dinnae listen to them bampots, they wouldnae know a good tale if it danced in front of them and kicked them in the balls."

"Two minutes," said Lynch. Silence filled the shed in an instant as all the humour ceased.

"I'll tell you later, Simmons," Fletcher said. "It's worth the wait."

Nathaniel watched the readings from Raphael with a sense of despair. It wasn't a feeling he was used to. Callam crossed the room. "It's no use. I can't boost the signal any further. The relays won't take it."

"Why is it degrading so quickly? The power outputs haven't changed. It's almost as if there's a new resistor or capacitor in the loop somehow."

Callam turned to face the mangled remains of the ArcAngel amongst a mass of wires and tubes. "Raph, can you detect any changes to the network since the last diagnostic?"

Power lines pulsed around Raphael, and a rising hum filled the room. "I'm sorry, Callam, the system appears to be identical to our previous baseline."

"Shit," Callam said, thumping the workbench with his fist.

Nathaniel looked pensive for a moment. "So, if what we are seeing is accurate, then there's nothing different with the systems. No change in the power input, so what does that leave?"

Callam's face lit up catching Nathaniel's inference. "If it's not external, it got to be internal. Raph has changed."

"When did you notice the fluctuations?"

Callam shook his head, the shock of realisation sweeping over his features. "It was after I plumbed him into the core. I can't believe I didn't see it myself. I suppose they were only minor to start with, and that could have been the system reconfiguring. Then it's been difficult trying to keep everything else going with such a skeleton crew."

"Raphael?" Nathaniel asked.

A screech of metal accompanied the ArcAngel turning his head to focus across the room. "Yes, Nathaniel?"

"Can you run a self-diagnostic? See if there have been any changes in your processes since your integration with ArcNet."

"Sorry, Nathaniel, I can't do that. My internal diagnostics are offline. They are one of many non-functioning systems from the damage I sustained during my detention."

"So you don't know if something has changed in how you are processing the data and power inputs?"

"No, I can only tell you I feel no differences, and I have started no new protocols."

"Okay," Nathaniel said, turning back to Callam. "We need to work around it. What are the chances we could run additional feeds straight from the core?"

"You mean to bypass Raph? There will be no failsafe if we pull raw power. It is doable but dangerous."

"As long as it's possible, we can deal with the safety factors. I'm thinking of running through a series of capacitors to ramp down the output to a safe level, and then link it into the dormant systems. It's not as good as everything coming from a central point, and we won't be able to adjust the flow—"

"But it *will* get those systems operative," finished Callam, a huge grin spreading across his face.

The carriage clanked into motion. While the squad crouched between stacks of wooden crates, Simmons couldn't resist the urge to examine the contents of the one nearest him. It contained an assortment of fresh vegetables and salted meats. *How the other half lives.*

Their carriage joined three others, all of them rising into the air. Cogs clacked above them, and sparks rained down as they passed a set of points where different overhead tracks crossed. Carriages banged together, and a few crates shifted, but the straps in place prevented them from moving more than a few inches.

He caught Lynch's eye. "So this is how the nobility travel? They're braver than I thought."

"This is a goods carriage," she replied. "The ones for passengers are a lot more luxurious, and they have hydraulic suspension for an almost smooth ride."

Simmons nodded. "I'll have a word with Smith, see if he can upgrade us to first-class next time."

"With any luck, there won't be a next time."

A steady clicking sounded above them as they climbed at a steep angle. Some clever connection to the rail kept them horizontal.

"We're approaching the wall," Lynch said. "Lights out and keep your heads down. We don't need any eagle-eyed guard spotting anything in here and raising the alarm."

The carriage interior was pitch-dark, and Simmons didn't think anyone could see them, even if they peered in with their noses pressed against the glass. Clearing the wall was much easier than expected. They passed over ten feet from the walkways, and high above the soft glow of street lights below.

With a lateral sway, their carriage veered to the left, snaking along after the others southwest towards Hyde Park. They'd travelled around fifty yards when they lurched forward with a squeal from ahead, then swung back, leaving them rocking to-and-fro in the night sky.

Lynch shot out a burst of hand signals to one of the squad obscured from Simmons' view, fingers pointing to her eyes then back to the team member. She turned to him and whispered, "Simmons, keep yourself between those crates and the rear window and see if there's any unusual activity from the wall behind us."

Their connection to the overhead track creaked as they continued a subtle shift back and forth. The sound wasn't dissimilar to old sailing vessels riding a calm sea. Nodding his acknowledgement, he made his way to where the crates stood high enough that his head wouldn't rise above them as he peered through the rear window. He rose until his nose rested on the rubber seal holding the glass in place.

Through the darkness, he spotted floodlights on the walls behind them, all pointing down into the city. Uniformed figures moved along the wall, two-person patrols and groups that huddled at sentry posts every few hundred feet. It was many years ago, but he remembered his early days as a young officer being garrisoned and ordered to watch the perimeter through the night. Cold work if you stood still. He'd always preferred to keep walking, inspecting the positions where there would be a brew on, tea or coffee, it didn't matter as long as it was hot.

He ducked back to floor level and located Lynch. "Everything seems in order. No signs of any excitement, they're scanning the ground with the spotlights as usual."

"Good," she replied. "It looks like there's a passenger transport ahead. It will have priority if it needs to cross our path. Fletcher is keeping an eye on it, but we need to sit tight until it's out of our way."

A faint blue light flickered on the rails above them to the north as power streaked along before the approaching train. A shower of brilliant white sparks accompanied the clanking of the other vehicle crossing tracks ahead of them before carriages hurtled past. Simmons tried to follow one of the bright windows and glimpsed a scene of luxurious upholstery and several seated figures. In the brief glance, he could swear those were champagne flutes in their hands. Then the other black carriage was a receding blur suspended in the heavens as it sped across the night sky like a shooting star. *Now that's the way to travel.*

A moment later, a hum heralded the power increase before they bumped forward, resuming the journey towards Hyde Park and their target—Kensington Palace.

~

The train crested the wall surrounding the northwest corner of Hyde Park. They had been running parallel a hundred feet north for some time. Now they rounded a sharp bend to head due south, descending into the grounds of the royal residence.

Once across, the team jumped into action. They adopted positions to exit the carriage. If their information was correct, they were aboard a scheduled shipment which would end in one of the warehouses near the Palace. The crates should remain overnight, transferring to the stores in the morning. However, they'd received no intelligence, so they couldn't rule out a night shift with workers waiting to unpack anything that might spoil.

This was where they needed to play it by ear and react to the environment they faced. Lynch and team seemed relaxed and ready for business, no matter what the evening threw at them.

Lynch had made it clear to the squad that the ideal operation was to sneak in and out with the Empress without detection. If things became dangerous, their first encounters were to be silent. It would only get noisy if their plans all went to hell.

A dull glow rose towards them as the carriages descended into a group of large buildings and Simmons soon saw the warehouse loom into view. The train rattled on the overhead track and clanked as they crossed under the supporting pylons as it slowed, now only a few feet above ground level.

A series of Arclights hung from the beams of the deserted

area shedding a dim light. Everything was quiet except for the rattle and hum as the carriages came to a shuddering stop.

Piles of boxes and crates littered the platform, providing reasonable cover, at least from sight. The team surveyed the scene for a short time planning the safest route from the carriage and through the warehouse towards the Palace.

A crackle of electricity sparked overhead, and the interior lights brightened.

"Shit," said Lynch.

Simmons looked at her. "I take it we weren't expecting that?"

"No, we were hoping we'd have free rein until a morning unload."

Her face was grim but determined. "Fletcher, what have you got?"

"Nothing new," came the Scottish drawl.

A single bell rang from the interior, and the doors hissed open.

"Talk to me, Fletcher,"

"I'm telling you, there's nothing —" she replied. "Oh, just a minute we've got movement from ten o'clock. Five—no, eight figures."

Lynch wasted no more time. "Move out, take cover and let's keep this quiet."

"Wait," said Fletcher, holding a flat palm up at her side. "They're bloody automatons."

"Orders stand, move out."

The team slithered between the carriage doors staying low and pushed into positions between the crates. Simmons felt a tap on his shoulder, turning he saw Fletcher beckoning to him. "Follow me. I got a wee plan for us."

He crouched and followed the woman who ducked behind a set of boxes further along the platform. As he rounded a crate, expecting to see Fletcher holed up there, she shuffled between them and disappeared off the other side. He crawled across to investigate.

She'd dropped four feet into the areas designed for the

carriages and, he presumed, inspection by technicians. He caught up halfway to the next platform. "Where are we going?" he whispered.

"There's a gantry at the far end of the warehouse. Noticed it as we were coming in."

"Ah," he said, realisation flooding his features. "And you want a better vantage point?"

"That's my boy, Simmons. Aye, I like to see what's happening down there, a bird's-eye view helps a lot in my line of business."

"Right you are then. Come on, what are you dawdling for?" he said, pushing ahead.

They checked the progress of the automatons when they reached the base of the ladder. The things looked to have entered the warehouse and then stopped on the platform by the front carriage. They stood in four pairs and seemed to be waiting for something.

Simmons followed Fletcher up thirty feet onto the gantry that spanned the width of the building. Narrow railings ran on either side of the five-foot-wide metal beam, and Simmons had to admit it was a massive section of steel. Bazalgette would have loved it.

Fletcher took up a position where she had cover near the control unit, and he followed her lead. Simmons hadn't noticed her unsling her rifle which was now aimed it at the train they'd arrived on.

"What's happening?" Simmons asked.

"Have you no got any lenses on those goggles of yours?"

"Nothing that magnifies, no."

"Well, the team are still in cover. The doors are open to each of the carriages, and those metal monsters are just standing around."

"What are they waiting for?"

"Damned if I know. There are binoculars in my belt on the left, use them if you want a look-see. I need to call in."

Simmons wasn't sure what she meant but found the pouch. After unbuckling a strap, he reached in, withdrawing a fine-looking pair of binoculars constructed in black leather and brass.

There were a series of quiet clicks, soon followed by a few more.

Simmons looked to Fletcher. "Was that Morse code?"

"Oh, look who's mister technology now," she said.

"What was that? Two dots, that's an I, and dot-dash-dash-dot, is that a P?"

"Not so rusty after all eh, Simmons?"

"But what's IP?"

"Oh," she replied, still scanning the platform through her sights. "It's short for 'In Position', I cannae be arsed tapping everything out, life's too short for all that shit."

"I suppose," Simmons said, "but how have you got a Morse key working up here?"

"Oh, just another toy from Mister Tesla's collection, the transceiver, that's what *he* called it. It's a poncey way of saying transmitter and receiver. It's in my jacket button, transmits a radio wave that's picked up by the rest of the squad."

"So you were just 'calling in'. Ah, I understand now."

He adjusted the binoculars and brought them to bear on the unmoving automata. They leapt into focus, the magnification was impressive. All eight were identical in construction, brass, wood and gun-metal grey. They seemed almost skeletal, except for a solid wooden torso's peppered with valves and dials. Each was a little broader and shorter than the average man and looked like service or manual labour models. He said as much to Fletcher. "Aye," she replied. "Well as they're still deciding if they want to dance or no, I'll get the lads and lasses moving this way."

Another series of dots and dashes clicked by too fast for Simmons to follow this time and a few seconds later a single click in response. "Here they come," Fletcher said, pointing back towards the crates and boxes nearest the last carriage.

It was incredible to see from above. They rolled in two teams, moving to new cover, then waiting for the other team to slide past them taking an advanced position before the whole fluid motion repeated. As Simmons watched, he knew these weren't as good as the best troops he'd ever worked with. They were much better than that.

~

The squad crossed the warehouse while Simmons and Fletcher observed from their vantage point. There was still no sign of life from the automata.

"Movement, one o'clock," Fletcher whispered as she tapped on her button. Simmons oriented ahead and noticed what she had spotted. Someone was moving through the shadows outside towards the warehouse.

The team moved in response to her warning, taking cover focused in the same direction he was. *That transceiver is impressive.*

He watched the scene unfold as Lynch made a series of hand signals and two of them peeled off. They headed in opposite directions but seemed to be moving to intercept the approaching intruders.

A figure in a black uniform pushed the door a little too hard, and it clanged from the wall. An almost identical form followed and said something to him. By the second man's body language, Simmons could tell he was less than impressed by his colleague's inept entrance.

As 'Clumsy' turned to apologise, Lynch's men struck from either side, and the two Black Guard troopers slumped to the concrete.

A low laugh came from Fletcher. "Ooh, they'll have sore heads tomorrow. Blake and Turner are the best at that quick takedown shit, silent as a shadow then bang, like a steam-hammer."

Simmons had to agree. He'd lost sight of the men as they stalked their prey, moving between cover. They were chalk and cheese: Turner had an athletic build, short and lithe while Blake was his opposite, a great hulking fellow, made of muscle. It surprised Simmons how he moved with such grace for someone who looked more like a prize-fighter. Full of surprises, this team of Lynch's.

"Best get yourself down there, Lynch will want to know what you prefer to do with those lightweights," said Fletcher as she continued surveying the warehouse.

"Right," Simmons said, making his way back to the ladder.

By the time he reached Lynch, the two bodies lay gagged and bound in a pile. The squad had established a perimeter with a clear line-of-sight to the remaining entrances and the still immobile brass and wood statues.

"Simmons, enjoyed your little jaunt with Fletcher, did you?" Lynch said.

"Yes, a remarkable performance. It was quite the show from up there."

Lynch smiled at that.

Well, there's a first time for everything.

"What do you want to do with the prisoners?" she asked.

Simmons thought for a few seconds. "Let's see what they can tell us, then we'll decide."

"Right you are." She turned to her team. "Look lively, lads. We need to have a chat with these two when they come around, and I don't want them making any noise when they do."

Blake and Turner watched the captives between them. Turner picked at his fingernails with a thin blade while casting his gaze about the room. Blake sat in silence, keeping both prisoners in his view.

A few minutes passed before 'Clumsy' showed signs of coming around. Blake tapped Lynch with his boot and nodded towards the groggy guard. Their prisoner's eyes snapped open, and he made a few mumbled sounds, lost in the fold of his gag.

"Whoa there," Blake said, pressing onto the knotted rag,

359

forcing it further into Clumsy's mouth. "No talking until the boss asks you something, or it will be the last thing you ever say. Understand?"

Clumsy nodded his comprehension, his eyes wide and shifting between the surrounding figures.

Simmons leaned forward into his sight. "I'm going to ask you a few questions, and you shall answer them quietly. If you make too much noise, my friend here," he motioned to Blake, "well, let's just say, he won't be pleased."

Another vigorous nod from the prisoner.

"How many Black Guard are there?"

Clumsy mumbled four syllables through the damp fabric.

Simmons turned to Blake. "We need to take that off him. I can't understand a word he said."

Blake looked past him. From his peripheral vision, Simmons detected an almost imperceptible nod from Lynch and Blake removed the gag, pulling a wadded ball of cloth from the man's mouth.

His eyes still wild, Clumsy whispered, "God save the Queen."

38

"Try it now," Callam called from beneath the central console. All Nathaniel could see of him were his legs. The rest of his body lay crammed into the guts of the unit under cables that spilt onto the ground like a mass of writhing snakes.

"Are you sure?" Nathaniel asked. "You are in the thick of it if anything goes wrong."

"Yeah, it's fine. What's the worst that could happen?"

Nathaniel didn't want to say the first thing that came into his mind and instead settled for, "Okay. Powering up in three, two, one."

A loud click of the heavy switch preceded the growing hum as power found its way into the new circuits. "See," Callam said, "what did I tell—"

A shower of sparks exploded amid the crackling of angry electrical current and an even louder series of curses from the Welshman ending with, "Turn it off. Turn the bloody thing off."

Nathaniel slammed his hand against the switch, killing the power. "Are you all right?" he shouted at the legs protruding beneath the cables. A few of the smaller ones smoked and the acrid smell of burning wires and hair hung thick in the air.

"Yes, I'm great. I love getting ten thousand volts up my backside. What do you bloody think?"

Nathaniel was ready to apologise, but Callam beat him to it. "Sorry, it's not your fault. I'm just frustrated at this whole mess. I thought we had it this time."

"It's fine," Nathaniel replied. "We've been at it for hours. Maybe we should take a break, look through the schematics again and see what we're missing?"

"No, we've gone through it, and your calculations are correct. We both agreed that on at least three occasions. There's something else we must have missed."

Nathaniel smiled. "All the more reason for a cup of tea and a rethink. If we recheck the circuits, with clear heads, we're bound to work out what we are overlooking. It will be something obvious."

With a heavy sigh, Callam agreed. "All right, you smooth-talking devil, pull me out of this nest of vipers. We must have been at it for bloody hours?"

"Three... and a half hours," Nathaniel replied glancing at his pocket watch. *It was three hours and twenty-seven minutes.* It felt odd not to say that, but he'd grown accustomed to having to limit his accuracy when referring to time. Most people seemed unable to appreciate the finer details.

He reached down, grabbing Callam by the boots and hauled him from the mess of smoky cables. Scorch marks ran across his clothing in a web of dark lines, and his thick black hair was a smouldering mop jutting out at all angles.

"Are you sure you're all right?" Nathaniel asked as he helped the big man to his feet.

"Yes, I've had worse." Callam thought for a few seconds. "Well, probably not. That hurt like hell, my body's still buzzing from it." He slapped Nathaniel on the back. "But nothing a good cuppa won't cure, eh?"

∼

"What?" Simmons said.

"God save the Queen," Clumsy repeated.

"You're the contact?"

"Yes, it was all last minute. I had no way to get free of my associate, that's why I stumbled into the door, hoped it might give you enough warning." He paused, rubbing his neck. "What the hell did you hit me with?"

"Sorry about that," said Blake.

"No, it will make it seem better when I'm found with Jackson later," he glanced at the other unconscious form.

"You're not what we were expecting," Simmons said.

"I'm sure that's true, but we haven't got time to talk about it now. The Empress is in a cell somewhere in the cellars, while the imposter will be in her rooms upstairs with two guards on the door. I think they are planning to take one or both of them out of here in the early morning, so you need to get moving."

"What about the other guards and the household staff?" Simmons asked.

"There is a garrison of twenty-four Black Guard troopers and two officers. They work twelve-hour shifts with a change at six o'clock."

"So," Simmons said, "with you and your colleague incapacitated and the two guarding the imposter, that leaves eight troops and one officer on duty until six?"

"Yes, but they might miss us after a few hours, so best get your job done quickly."

"And the staff?"

"They should be sleeping until they rise between four and five to provide food for the shift changeover. I don't expect they will cause you any trouble, but the Black Guard employs them, so they have no loyalty to the Empress, they are just paid to play a role. They arrested the original staff months ago. God knows what happened to them."

"What about access to the Palace and the cellars?"

"Right. I can reprogram the automatons to transfer the goods to the stores in the main house. There are tunnels between here and there and if you travel with them, it might offer you cover with the movement and noise."

"Ah," said Simmons, "so that's what they've been waiting for?"

"Yes, they follow basic pre-programmed tasks. They will continue their current task unless you get in their way. They can make simple decisions, such as stopping to wait until their path ahead is clear, or if they cannot complete their instructions, they go into a standby mode. That's all I know about them. The orders come on punched cards." He pulled a stack from inside his dark coat. They were seven inches by three, grey in colour, and full of tiny rectangular holes.

"That's what gives them their instructions?" Simmons asked.

"Yes, I need to load each unit with one of these and then tell them to process them."

"Thank you."

Clumsy smiled at him. "Let me get these automatons running, then make it look convincing with dumping Jackson and me someplace they won't find us for a good long while."

Lynch took over. "Turner, Blake, once those things are moving, bag our two friends and stash them somewhere safe. Everyone else prepare to move out in five."

She tapped her top button three times then turned to face the gantry. When she received a single click in response, her hand was a flurry of movement telling Fletcher what they were planning. It was too quick for Simmons to understand, but from the few signs he recognised, Lynch was relaying the same message she had given the rest of the team.

He followed Blake and Clumsy to the group of eight wood and metal statues on the far platform. He had a strange feeling of unease as he approached them. Their identical frames were humanoid in design, but their heads recessed into the torso as if they had no neck. Their eyes were lifeless, glassy baubles surrounded by copper sitting in the gunmetal egg that resembled a head.

Clumsy walked between the two rows of four, inserting a punched card into a slot into the middle of each of their wooden chests. They remained inert, dead to the world and might as well have been statues.

"Automata, attention," he said to the assembled group. A

series of clicks and whirs sounded as their glassy eyes lit with a dull blue glow.

"Process new orders."

A cacophony of scratches and clicking issued from the machines. The sounds like an army of angry old women knitting for their lives. It stopped after a few seconds.

Clumsy stood to one side. "Execute new orders."

Each machine burst into action, marching in unison, their metal arms down by their sides like a group of newly appointed butlers. They split into four groups of two, each moving to a carriage to unload the crates and boxes onto the platform.

"All done?" Simmons asked.

"Yes, best get me stashed with my colleague," he turned to shake Simmons' hand. "Good luck. God save the Queen."

"God save the Queen," he replied as Blake led the black-uniformed figure across the warehouse and out of sight.

Simmons watched the automata following their new orders. *I must tell Bazalgette about this.* They lifted the crates with ease as if designed to fit them, or vice versa.

After a few minutes, the cargo stood stacked on the platform. From there, the automata picked up a container and headed to where they'd entered, and Simmons followed.

He stopped at the exit from the warehouse that led to stairs descending into darkness. As Lynch approached, he made his best attempt at a courtly bow. "After you milady." She sneered as she passed with the first half of her squad, but he was sure he'd glimpsed the merest hint of a smile.

∾

Lynch's team activated torches in the pitch-black passage. Some attached to their weapons, others hand-held. They illuminated a brick-clad tunnel wide enough for two of the machines. Simmons guessed they were about twenty feet below ground level.

Lynch sidled over to him. "Best you stay close for now, my

girls and boys know how to play nicely in the dark. I'd hate for you to walk in front of one of them when they think they have a clear shot."

"Fair comment," he replied, matching Lynch's whisper. "Where on earth did you find all these people? You don't have an entirely conventional approach to..." He stumbled for how to finish, "well, to anything really."

"Long story, maybe I'll tell you sometime. If we get out of here with our cargo."

"I look forward to it."

They travelled slowly, carefully. Light from the surrounding team moved to check walls, floor and ceiling. The sound of metal scraping and wood creaking ahead of them, a constant reminder of the silent automata as they progressed through the cold brick tunnels. It hadn't looked that far between the warehouse and the Palace as they approached, but it had been dark, and they took care with their cautious progress.

Simmons felt a hand on his arm. "Hold up," Lynch whispered.

Looking ahead, he noticed the torches had stopped. Then soft clicks followed as they switched off. The automata continued moving forwards into an area which began to resolve with a dull glow of light.

Lynch moved forward, reaching out to squeeze two of her team on the shoulder. He wasn't sure exactly what happened, but there were quiet footfalls as the pair selected sneaked ahead hugging the walls of the tunnel. Silence hung heavy in the darkness for minutes, then out of nowhere a black shape appeared speaking in whispers to Lynch. It was Turner's voice. "Opens into a large storeroom packed with boxes, so there's light cover. It has electric lighting, but there doesn't appear to be anyone there other than the machines stacking the crates."

"How far have you seen?" Lynch asked.

"Without going into the room, only about thirty feet, but it looks like it continues for some distance. A heavy door opens into the area. It's open at the moment, but who knows once they finish lugging that food about."

"Blake?"

"Yeah, he's still at the entrance."

"Okay. Head back, and if everything is the same in two minutes return and we'll move in."

"Done," Turner replied, his footsteps receding to nothing in less than three steps.

∾

The storage space was large but poorly stocked. Discoloured wooden crates sat in a puddle which produced a sickly sweet odour from their rotting contents. *Damn*, Simmons thought, *this is the royal residence. What the hell is going on?*

The exit was unlocked and opened onto a dark passage. It ran in a slight curve towards the low glow of lighting from beyond the corner. The light from the storeroom crept in, illuminating arched brick ceilings which were much lower here, only a few feet above head height.

Blake and Turner sneaked away into the murk, becoming one with the shadows. If he hadn't seen them leave, Simmons would have sworn there was nobody in that dimly lit tunnel.

Fletcher took a position outside, aiming along the corridor with her rifle. The rest of them taking places either side of the door into the storeroom, ready to move in an instant. Lynch closed it and received a reassuring click of Morse.

Five tense minutes passed as Simmons waited with Curtis and Lynch. Eyes flicked between the three, but they remained in silence. Simmons knew the least about Curtis. He was a young-looking chap with a thin styled moustache which ran parallel to his top lip. It seemed to defy gravity, tapering to fine points at each end with a distinct peppery smell from the wax he used to tame it. The only thing Simmons could remember mentioned, other than his name, was engineering. That had stuck with him, because of Bazalgette's skills, but he envisaged a different style of problem-solving from this fellow.

Like most of the team, Curtis carried a Mauser pistol, but this one had an extended box magazine. It dropped below the base of the grip, and Simmons wondered how many rounds it held. He also wore a selection of waxed leather pouches around his belt and across his chest on a harness.

Simmons checked his watch. It was approaching six minutes when a double click sounded on Lynch's comm-link followed a few seconds later with two soft knocks on the door.

Lynch pulled it open, and Turner squeezed through, pushing it closed behind him.

"The approach to the cells is clear. There is a stairway leading up to the ground floor just around the corner. From there, this passage continues across into the cellar. Plenty of light cover then it opens out into a larger area with at least four guards."

"Four?" Simmons asked.

"Yes, they look like they're having a party. Lots of wine bottles on the table. If we leave them for another hour, they'll be unconscious."

Simmons glanced at Turner. "We don't have the luxury of time. We need to move now."

"Understood. Blake is keeping an eye on things down there."

"Good," said Lynch, running her hand through her hair. "Any sign of the cells or the package?"

Turner shook his head. "Not that we've seen so far, but with the guards there, it's a safe bet she's somewhere close by."

"Any signs of movement upstairs?" Simmons asked.

"No, it's all quiet. But we should leave someone to watch the stairs for anyone poking about."

"Fine," Lynch said. "Head back to Blake, and we'll follow. Is there enough room for Fletcher to tag a couple before you and Blake do your work?"

Turner considered for a moment, then nodded. "Yes, it's doable."

"Take her with you, then get into position. We'll meet you as soon as I'm happy the stairwell is secure."

They left Curtis guarding the stairs. He propped his shotgun against a wall before unpacking a few unusual looking discs from his pouches. They were the size of a saucer but maybe an inch thick and a rich black.

As they moved forward, Simmons turned to Lynch. "What's he up to?"

"Curtis?" Lynch asked. "He's just laying out a few toys, so we aren't surprised if anyone heads down before we're ready."

Lynch stopped, looking back at Simmons. "Best not be the first to climb those stairs. Make sure Curtis or one of us has cleared it."

"So these are dangerous little surprises then?"

"Yes, deadly."

They continued through the brick-lined passage, noting short corridors leading off either side, each stacked with barrels. As they approached the lit area, their progress slowed to a crawl.

Fletcher knelt in a firing position, leaning on the corner of a wine rack for cover. It ran from floor to ceiling and contained smaller square partitions filled with bottles. Each section had a black slate hanging from it with a chalk description. Among the signs proclaiming 'Musigny', 'Richebourg' and 'Beaune' with dates ranging back to the eighteen-thirties, were several recent additions chalked over the slates. These proclaimed such esteemed vintages as 'Rat Piss', 'Vinegar' and 'The Good Stuff'. It seemed the new residents had an affinity for the finer things in life.

Within the room, a low murmur of voices split the silence and glasses clinked. From his position beside Fletcher, half the table was visible, the edge of the doorway obscured the other side of the chamber. Two guardsmen lounged in plush green chairs, their tunics thrown over the chair backs while they nurtured crystal glasses of red wine. Empty bottles lay strewn around the floor.

Lynch leaned over to Fletcher. "Set?"

"I've got clean shots on this pair, but Blake and Turner will need to cover the distance to the others. Might get messy."

"I don't mind messy," Lynch replied. "As long as it's quiet."

"Aye. In that case, set."

Lynch nodded and turned to Simmons. "You stay here while I check with our scouts. Fletcher, be ready for my signal. Everyone else will go on your first kill."

She disappeared into the gloom ahead almost as quickly as he'd seen Blake and Turner do.

"Now you're in for a treat, Simmons," Fletcher whispered to him. "You get to see this wee beauty in action." She pulled the stock tighter into her shoulder and waited. It wasn't long before a single click came through her comm.

"Showtime," she whispered. That was all Simmons heard. The next second the nearest guard slumped from his chair, a spray of bloody mist bursting from the back of his head and speckling his neighbour's face.

The unmistakable silhouettes of Turner and Blake burst into the light from their position in the shadows. Neither of them worried about the extra distance required to go round the table. Blake went over while Turner slid under as both disappeared from view.

The only movement came from the second trooper in Simmons' line of sight. He was blinking and wiping at his face as he struggled to make sense of his friend's body collapsed on the ground in a spreading pool of blood.

A crash from the far side of the table and two heavy thuds were all the sounds that issued from that room. Before the final guard could shout for help, a low click beside Simmons announced Fletcher chambering another round. Getting to his feet, the guardsman tumbled backwards over his chair as the silent rifle took him in the forehead.

The three seconds of chaos ended. All that remained was the sound of a glass rolling on the floor and the steady glugging of wine splattering onto the stone floor.

"Clear." It was Blake's voice.

As Lynch stood and crossed into the light, Fletcher rose

and motioned to follow. "Come on, Simmons. You dinnae want to miss all the fun. We've got an Empress to rescue."

A little too dazed to utter any words, he followed her into the lit room. It had been so fast, three seconds, if that. In that time, Fletcher had dropped two guards with headshots, while Blake and Turner had covered the distance to engage in hand-to-hand. He shook his head in wonder.

"Everything all right?" Lynch asked him.

"Fine," was all he could manage as he absently rubbed his injured leg.

~

The cells were easy to locate, but try as he might, Turner couldn't find a key on any of the guards or in the surrounding area.

Simmons ventured, "Perhaps only the officers carry keys."

"It's a reasonable assumption," Lynch said, "but we don't have time to go hunting for them."

The main entrance to the cells was behind a sturdy grille of black steel. The bars were an inch thick with just enough space to get an arm through between them.

"What now?" Simmons asked.

"Turner, go relieve Curtis on the stairs, we need him up here," Lynch said.

Simmons looked at her through a frown. "You're not thinking of blowing the doors, are you? That will bring all the remaining guards running, won't it?"

"You don't know Curtis well, do you?" she asked with a twinkle in her eye. "He's got a bag of tricks that would make Houdini blush."

"Fair enough. I shall wait for the show."

It was only a minute before Curtis made his appearance. He headed over to Lynch. "Major, Turner said you needed me."

"Mister Curtis, we require your expertise." She motioned him to the metal doorway. "I want in as quietly as possible."

He examined the gate for a few moments, checking the locking mechanism and the solid bars. "Five minutes?"

"Proceed," Lynch said, smiling at Simmons.

Curtis rummaged through his leather pouches and produced a sticky substance. He picked pieces from it and packed them around the lock.

"What is he doing?" Simmons asked.

"Ask him."

Simmons turned his attention back to the engineer. "Excuse the interruption, but what is that?"

He looked up from his work. "Thermite." When that garnered no response, he continued. "A mixture of ferrous oxide and aluminium which burns fiercely once lit. Hot enough to melt the steel of this gate."

"So, not explosive then?"

"Not in the sense you're thinking. It's quick and quiet, just gives off intense heat and light."

"Isn't it awfully dangerous to be carrying around in your belt?" Simmons asked.

"No, it's stable and requires high temperatures to burn—about three thousand degrees. I use a magnesium fuse, burns hot, but much easier to ignite."

He produced a small strip of silvery metal from a different pouch and placed it into the sticky substance.

"Ready to go when you are, Major."

"Take cover," Lynch said leading Simmons ten feet away from the barred gate and around a corner.

"Could I watch?" Simmons asked.

"Yes, but don't look directly at it once it's lit. Curtis says it can damage your eyes."

"Ah, like staring at the sun?"

"That sort of idea."

Curtis gave a hand signal showing he was ready to go in five.

Simmons waited as the engineer produced an ArcLighter much like his own and applied it to the fuse. It burst into a brilliant light. The whole room lit up as Curtis retreated towards them.

The magnesium impressed Simmons, but the thermite was amazing. Hissing and spluttering, the entire lock glowed yellow then white. Sparks flew from it, flung five feet bouncing from the walls. Molten metal dripped from around the mechanism, then a resounding clunk as the whole section fell onto the ground.

Well, there's something to impress Bazalgette with, my newfound respect for thermite. What had Curtis said? Ferrous oxide and aluminium, I'll remember that.

Curtis pushed the door open after kicking the molten slag to one side, which had pooled on the brickwork floor along with the remains of the lock.

Blake was first through into the secure area beyond. It turned out to be another part of the cellar with six dark alcoves, not deep enough to be called passages in their own right. In the farthest of them lay a filthy mattress with a dishevelled figure sprawled atop it. The place stank of human waste and Simmons noticed a slops bucket near the makeshift bed. It lay on its side, contents spread across the floor, a stain crawling up the bottom edge of the mattress.

The young woman wore soiled and stained clothing, a mismatch of once beautiful garments, now fit only for an incinerator. Beneath a mass of matted hair and layers of caked dirt, she had an unmistakable look of her grandmother. Her chest rose and fell, but her breathing was shallow. A distinct chemical odour clung about her, both on her breath and from the clothing.

"Looks like we've found our Empress," Lynch said.

"Yes," Simmons replied, "but she's drugged up to the eyeballs."

"We haven't got time to mess about explaining the situation to her. We should keep her under and get the hell out of here."

Simmons blew out a sharp breath. "I don't like it, but agreed."

Lynch called across the room. "Blake, get ready to check upstairs for the imposter, I'll take the Empress."

"Whoa," Simmons said. "You can't do that. You are too—"

Lynch whirled on him. "Too what? Too weak? Just a woman?" Her eyes didn't hide the fury behind them, and Simmons stepped back. *Damn, I was trying to be gentlemanly*.

"I'll have you know I've carried that great sack of coal," she pointed to Blake, "for three miles. You think I can't handle this young lass?"

Simmons held out his hands. "I'm sorry, Lynch. I wasn't questioning your ability, just trying to say you're too valuable."

The fire behind her eyes still burned but seemed to dial down from incandescent to merely white-hot. Her face regained some of its usual composure as Turner appeared at a breakneck run.

Lynch turned her ire towards the new arrival. "What the hell are you doing here? I told you to watch those stairs."

"Sir, I've been outside, and we've got company. Another train just arrived, looks like a whole platoon of the Black Guard decided it was party time at the Palace. They're already fanning out through the grounds and advancing on the main entrance, armed and ready for contact."

Lynch drew in a breath and looked around the room. "Blake, wait. There's no time to hunt for the other one. Simmons, get that cannon of yours fit for action, we might need it."

"Which way, sir?" Turner asked.

She paused a second in contemplation.

"Back to the storeroom," Simmons said. "We'll head for the train. If we get stuck, they won't be able to surround us."

Lynch nodded. "Curtis, get some of your tricks ready. Something to slow them down. Let's move, people."

She hoisted the unconscious body and headed to the passageway. Turner and Blake raced ahead to check the route was clear, disappearing around a corner.

Fletcher caught Lynch's eye. "I'll go with them. See if I can find a location to support you."

"Go," Lynch said, waving her off. "Simmons, it's up to you and Curtis to watch our backs. I think the time for stealth is over, so make as much noise as you have to."

He looked at Curtis, who was checking through yet more pouches. He nodded to Simmons in acknowledgement.

"Clear, move on, move on," said Turner as they reached the stairs. He waved them through, and as if hearing a silent question from Curtis said, "Everything's armed on the stairs, and I added a little something—"

An explosion echoed above them as brick dust and mortar rained down.

"I guess they found it," Curtis said with a grin, it was the first time Simmons had seen him smile since meeting the man.

"That's the front door," Turner said. "Best get moving. Go, go, go."

Simmons turned, backing up behind the others as he kept his eyes on the stairs. Something bit him, a sharp pain in his chest and he cried out.

"Are you injured?" asked Lynch.

"No," he replied. He realised it wasn't a bite. It was the device Bazalgette had given him to identify the pocket watches. "Damn, there's a Watchman with them."

39

Nathaniel looked on, impressed by the work he and Callam had achieved. The power flow wasn't as stable as he would have liked, but it was good enough.

It was Callam who spotted the mistake which had gone unnoticed for their last three attempts. As Bazalgette had suspected, it was a simple oversight. A hastily written seven which looked more like a one which had compounded calculations based on it.

"How about that?" Callam said, moving to stand beside him. "It's a thing of beauty, isn't it?"

They'd taken power feeds from the core and routed them through a series of complex circuits, enabling them to supply the remaining systems that Raphael couldn't handle directly.

"Hmm," mused Nathaniel.

"Come on, it may not be the prettiest of wiring jobs ever, but it works like a bloody charm."

Nathaniel scrutinised the tangle of jury-rigged connections that ran the length of the control room. *Well, done is better than perfect*, he thought. There would be plenty of time to tweak and improve the weaker links once the systems were operational. He'd already collected a mental list of six items that required urgent attention.

"Yes," he said, "it is marvellous."

Callam turned towards the centre of the room, at the twisted figure sat amongst the high energy cables. "Raph, how are you doing?"

"Everything is working. There seem to be a few deviations from baselines, but they are within safe tolerances."

Nathaniel scowled. "So you still have variations even now we've reduced your raw power input?"

"Yes, though it's becoming easier to monitor and maintain reliable levels across all the systems I have control of."

"Job for another day, mate," was Callam's reply. "I don't know about you, but I'm shattered. A cuppa, a bite to eat, and a good night's rest are in order if you ask me."

Nathaniel nodded in agreement. "Sounds like a fine plan." He checked his pocket watch, twelve fifty-two. They'd been working flat out for over twelve hours. There had been only the one tea-break where they had resolved the problems with the calculations. It was the only time either of them had stopped.

As they turned to leave the room, Callam called back, "Goodnight, Raph, give me a shout if you notice anything untoward with those levels."

"I will, Callam."

"Goodnight, Raphael," Nathaniel added with a small wave of his hand.

"Good evening to you both," Raphael replied then returned to his silent contemplation of all the systems he managed.

"So tea then?" Callam asked.

"Thinking about it, I might get straight off to bed. Still a lot to do tomorrow."

"Right you are then. I'll see you bright and breezy in the morning." Callam headed off down a corridor towards the canteen, his heavy footfalls receding while Nathaniel turned the corner to head back to his room.

He spotted a technician in the communications centre and wondered if they had drawn lots for who got the night shift. His thoughts wandered to Lynch's team, and how they and Simmons were faring in their attempt to find and rescue the

Empress. They would be sneaking onto a train any minute now if they were running to schedule, then heading towards Hyde Park.

Another wave of fatigue crashed over him. He hadn't realised how tired he was, and with relief, he pushed the door open to his small room and collapsed onto the bed.

～

Nathaniel awoke with a start to the sound of klaxons blaring and flashing red emergency lighting. *What the hell?*

Still dressed, which in this case was a blessing, his hand fished around in his waistcoat pocket for the watch while he tried to force the sleep from him. He felt the cool curved metal under his fingertips and flipped it open. Five minutes past two, he must have been asleep as soon as his head hit the pillow.

He stood, his legs wobbling until he caught his balance with the help from a small bedside table. He reached over, dipped his hands into a bowl of lukewarm water and splashed it onto his face.

The shock did the trick. He grabbed his glasses and pulled the door open. The corridor pulsed from dark to a dim red light and the damned klaxon hammered into his head. He set off at a run to the operations centre. There were sounds of voices and scurrying feet all around, and he saw a group of technicians already equipped and speaking with their on-duty colleague.

"What's going on?" Nathaniel shouted over the commotion.

The man looked up. "Something has tripped the alarms in sector three," he said. "There's a lot of movement down there, and we've just lost our first sensor."

～

Lynch and Blake hustled into the storage area, and Simmons followed. He turned looking back down the brick-lined passage waiting for Curtis to catch up.

Simmons had left him laying more of his surprises for any pursuit, while he escorted Lynch and Blake. After the deafening explosion of the front door, it had been quiet as they covered the two hundred yards of the dark corridor. The advancing troops must have slowed their pace once they realised the place was booby-trapped.

Simmons turned to enter the storeroom and heard a distant pop and fizz, akin to a firework. A gurgling scream followed but cut off abruptly.

"Well, that's the stairs cleared," said Curtis as he caught up. "It sounds like the razor-wire took at least one of them though."

Those were the things Simmons had worried about when searching Silas Cooper's house. The tripwires on the stairs might have triggered something similar. Mini explosive devices that spun then disgorged strands of deadly wire designed to slice through both flesh and bone, eviscerating anyone caught in its path.

"Report," Lynch's voice called out ahead of them as Curtis closed the door and set to work with his latest surprise for the advancing Black Guardsmen.

Turner crossed from the far side of the room, and his face didn't look as if he had good news. "The tunnel to the station is sealed. All the automatons are lined up ready for inspection, but powered down."

"Can you get it open?" Lynch asked.

"I don't know how. There are no obvious controls, and it's a solid old beast. Maybe Curtis?"

Curtis continued his work, but shouted back, "Sorry, all out of explosives. Left it for our friends outside. I've got a little thermite, but not enough if you want me to secure this door."

"Damn," Lynch said. "How much time, Curtis?"

"Two minutes."

"Seal it. We need another option for getting out of here. I'm open to any ideas at this point."

"Can we brute force it?" Blake asked as they all moved past the line of identical unmoving labourers.

379

"I can't see that working. It's sturdy," Turner replied.

"Is there a lock to pick?" Lynch added.

"Nothing I can find," Turner replied.

"Forget about the door, how about going through the wall?" Blake said.

Turner looked up at his friend. "It's possible, but it will take one hell of a time. I'm thinking a few hours, and we still might not get through. Even with your puny muscles swinging the hammer. Oh, and a hammer would be useful too."

"It's probably opened remotely," Curtis called to them.

Lynch turned. "Fletcher, can you do anything with the transmitter? Switch frequency try to activate the door mechanism?"

Fletcher shook her head. "I cannae do it here, I've no got the equipment, and to be honest, it would be pure guesswork."

"Fine," Lynch replied. "I was grasping at straws with that one."

Simmons scratched his mutton chops. "What would Bazalgette do?"

"What's that?" Lynch asked.

He looked up, not realising he'd spoken out loud. "I was just thinking about how Bazalgette would approach the problem."

"And?"

"Well, he would review all the evidence we observed about access through the doors then reverse it and search for patterns."

Lynch thought about it for a second and nodded. "Okay people, what do we know?"

Fletcher spoke up. "We saw the automata arrive so they must have come through at each end to get onto the platform. So did someone else open them?"

"But there was nobody else around," added Blake, "other than our friendly Black Guard and his colleague."

A loud hissing noise erupted from behind him as Curtis joined them. The entrance had a thick steel bar welded across the frame. The golden glow of molten metal dripped like hot wax to the floor, pooling into red lumps as it cooled.

"It's sealed, but it won't last forever."

"Come on, what else do we know?" Lynch asked.

"Well, the door was open when we left," Turner said. "Now all the automatons are in here, and it's closed."

"So who shut it?" Blake asked.

"Just a minute," Simmons said. All faces turned towards him as he thought.

"Yes?" Lynch prompted.

"What if we're looking at this wrong? There wasn't anyone around to close them, no-one else knew. So what if it's the automata that trigger the controls?"

Curtis nodded. "It would be a slick solution. If they have a transponder coded to the door systems, they would have access whenever they needed it."

"Exactly," Simmons said. "If we can get them headed back to the platform, it may be possible to follow them again."

"I like it," Lynch said. "And it's the only option we have that might work. Simmons, you saw them being programmed?"

"Yes, me and Blake."

"Right, you two get these things moving and find us a way out of this mess."

Curtis moved to take the girl Blake was carrying and laid her down next to their sealed escape route. Blake crossed to where Simmons stood before the eight static machines. "After you, Simmons."

He cast his mind back. "Automata, attention," he said to the mechanical squad before him.

They clicked and whirred to life, their eyes filling with a blue glow. Blake nodded and gave him a thumbs up.

Simmons looked at Blake. "Should I tell them to do the same as before? Will they go to the station or just pack boxes here?"

Blake shrugged. "Your guess is as good as mine. Try it."

Simmons turned his attention back to the waiting group. "Process new orders."

As they had before, the automata issued a mass of clicks and scratches as they processed their instructions for a few seconds, then returned to their usual state of inactivity.

"Execute new orders," Simmons said, a slight hesitation in his voice. Nothing happened. He looked at Blake and shrugged. "That was the same as what he said, wasn't it?"

Blake nodded. "That sounded right."

A dull bark came from beyond the entrance, and the room vibrated, shifting more dust to hang in the air.

"They're getting closer," Curtis called. "One more charge and they'll be at the door."

Simmons looked at the static automata before him. The incredible, but stationary machines stared back at him. *What did I miss?*

He took a step towards Blake ready to discuss what else they could try, and with a whir, they stirred. "Of course," he said. "I'm in their damned way."

As he moved to the side, his new troops cranked into motion, changing their formation to fit through the passageway. As they reached the door, it recessed into the wall with a loud mechanical grinding of metal on stone.

"Squad two ready for duty," he called to Lynch.

She smiled. "Let's move out, people."

Simmons split his squad of automata into two halves by jumping between them and blocking their path. Lynch and team slid in between them as the first four continued towards the station.

Fletcher tapped him on the shoulder. "Do you think we could get ahead of these things, so they don't announce our presence to anyone on the platform?"

"I can't see why not," he replied. "If you push in front then move slowly until the doors open at the far end then I'll try to deactivate them."

Lynch had been listening. "Blake, Turner. Take point with Fletcher. Let's keep this quiet."

The warehouse door slid apart as they approached, and Simmons cancelled the automaton's orders. They each slumped into their static state, their eyes fading to black.

The advance squad moved to survey the scene while Simmons, Lynch, and Curtis squeezed between the four remaining machines ahead of them. By the time they reached the others, only Blake and Turner remained.

"Report," Lynch said almost as a reflex. "Whoa, where's Fletcher?"

"Ah," Turner replied with trepidation in his voice. "We have a squad of Black Guard armed with arc-rifles on the platform next to ours. They are alert and patrolling the area, but other than that it looks empty. The main body of the force must still be at the Palace."

"And Fletcher?"

Blake cut in. "I instructed Sergeant Fletcher to find high ground to cover our arrival."

"No, you bloody didn't," Lynch said. "Gone walkabout again, hasn't she? I'll skin the bitch when she's back."

"She'll have headed for the gantry again," Simmons replied. "It provides an excellent view of the entire warehouse from up there."

Lynch nodded. "You two better get your act together and sort out these Guards, and hope that Fletcher's all right. Otherwise, I'll kick your arses up and down the barracks so hard you won't sit down for a week. Understood?"

Blake and Turner looked to one another and then back to Lynch. "Yes, Major." They disappeared into cover and out of sight, glad to get as far from her as possible.

"A little harsh?" Simmons whispered.

Lynch turned. "They're experienced soldiers and make informed decisions. I'm sure Fletcher will be a valuable asset in that position, but I'm not letting them know I approve of her disobeying orders."

Simmons chuckled, he liked Lynch's attitude. He could have done with more officers like her in India.

～

Blake and Turner made quick work of the six Black Guards, accompanied by Fletcher from her vantage point. Within five minutes, the platform was theirs, and they transported the unconscious Empress into the carriage on which they'd arrived. It became clear the troops pursuing them must be having difficulty accessing the storeroom as there was still no sign of anyone from the passageway to the warehouse.

Simmons and Lynch agreed something was required to stop the Black Guard following them in the other train that sat at the adjoining platform. They only needed ten minutes to get to the edge of the wall around the north-west corner of Hyde Park. From there, they could climb down the outside and escape Fogside into the darkness.

Their other main problem was getting their carriage mobile and heading in the right direction. Once they could attach to the exit rail, the system of cogs would haul them up to the electrified tracks. From there, they would progress on a standard circular route between each of the Inner-City areas.

Curtis knew they could get onto the riser, and the carriage had an emergency brake which he planned to engage when they reached the point they wished to disembark. Lynch's concern was if anyone contacted the controllers who oversaw the rail system, they could halt the train. Or worse, redirect it to arrive in a location full of armed guards waiting for them.

Curtis was out of explosives, so Simmons suggested the gantry could detach the other carriages from the track, making it impossible for them to follow without considerable time and effort.

As it had been his idea, he headed up to tell Fletcher the good news, and to help her position the crane above the other train. He crossed between the platforms as he had done earlier and was soon climbing the steel ladder. As he peered over the top rung, he saw the rifle muzzle pointed his direction from ten feet away.

"Ah, Simmons," came Fletcher's dulcet tones. "Thought it must be you with all the bloody noise. Have you no heard of stealth?"

"Didn't want to scare you when I popped up unannounced," he replied.

"You didnae, I've seen you all the way across the yard."

"We need to move the gantry, see if we can unhook that other train, or disable it so it can't follow when we leave."

Fletcher moved her rifle back to survey the rest of the warehouse. "Why doesn't Curtis weld the bugger to the tracks?"

Simmons shrugged. "He says he's all out of toys, used the last of the thermite sealing the storeroom door."

"Aye, sounds about right. He enjoys playing with it too much, never saves enough for a rainy day."

"Do you know how this thing works?" Simmons asked nodding at the vast metal beast they stood on.

"It's no my speciality." Fletcher looked along the massive walkway. "The controls are over there. I'm sure a man of your calibre will figure them out."

"And I suppose you'll just wait here while I do all the hard work?"

"Aye. I dinnae like moving once I've found a comfy position, no unless we get to shooting. And this spot is proper cosy."

Well, my idea, my task to determine how to move the beast.

The central section housed a control unit similar to a locomotive cab, and he stepped into the box-shaped structure looking at the vast array of dials and buttons. Though he didn't understand what most of them were for, he identified the large red switch labelled 'power'.

A huge earthy roar issued from somewhere below and the booth shuddered then thrummed to life. He could just make out Fletcher's voice over the noise. "Seems you're on the right track, Simmons. Good on you."

With his inability to understand the dials, Simmons went

for the most obvious choice, a large four-way control lever that looked like what they used to change railway points. He thrust it from its central position across to the left. It jarred amidst a squeal of protest from gears. He released it to return to the centre, then tried again, this time engaging the clutch plate and shoving it over harder. Another grinding of metal, and then it popped into gear. The whole cab shuddered and rumbled along the gantry arm towards the train awaiting detachment. Lights flashed, and sirens blared. *Not the stealthiest of approaches,* he thought. He cast his eyes over the console, but nothing was flashing or labelled to allow him to cancel the wailing noise. He ignored them and concentrated on positioning the crane over the carriages.

The first he knew they were under fire was the spang of rounds on the exterior of the cab. He turned towards Fletcher as she fired back. From her expression, he presumed there was one less enemy. She loaded another round into the chamber with a smooth push on the bolt handle and was scanning for a new target.

A few more shots sounded from below and the unmistakable hum and whoosh of an arc-rifle discharging. Simmons risked poking his head out to see what was happening. A team of Black Guard had established a position at one end of the platform and were exchanging fire with Lynch's squad. As he watched, another burst of sizzling electricity arced through the intervening space, splintering and scorching the corner of a large wooden crate.

He pulled his head back in, focusing on a small glass plate sat in the floor, the opening about a foot square. Below he could see the huge set of clamps used to attach and lift carriages or large crates. *How the hell does this work? I'll have to sort it out when everything else is in place.*

He saw the overhead line come into view and reached to pull the lever back to the central position, remembering to engage the clutch this time. The cab shuddered to a stop in line with the track and carriages below.

"Simmons," Fletcher shouted. He turned to see her

kneeling beside the cab. "We need to get out of here quick. There's more of them coming. The team will get swamped if we don't move soon."

"I'm trying to grasp how this damn thing works so I can grab the carriage."

She scanned the console. "What about that big red button there?"

"I've no idea what that's for," he replied.

She smiled at him as she hit it. "Let's find out."

A loud bang sounded below them, and the gantry shook. As he looked down, the clamp below them dropped, crashing into the overhead line with a sound of splintering concrete and screeching metal. As it slid to one side, the right-hand jaw wedged itself into the carriage amidst shrieks of protesting steel.

"Okay," Simmons said. "That will do it. Tell the team to get the train moving. We'll meet them over there." He pointed to the end of the walkway.

"You're barmy," she managed, clicked her button five times in rapid succession and took off along the metal limb.

He followed her lead, his leg was much improved, but he couldn't match her speed. The firefight below was intensifying and looked like Lynch was trying to lay enough suppressing fire down so they could get into the carriage. It wasn't looking good.

He pulled the Holland & Holland from his shoulder and aimed at one of the arc-rifle holders as he lined up a shot. He clicked the button on the goggles Bazalgette had given him, and his vision swam for a second before resolving. The beast roared, and a hole the size of a man's fist ripped through the makeshift cover. It flung the Black Guard backwards to lay sprawled against a wall painted in crimson. Lynch took the opportunity, and her team bundled into the carriage.

As a whir of electricity sparked along the line above the carriages, another of the Black Guard popped up to take a shot, but Simmons was waiting for him. The Holland roared again, dropping the trooper, a thick spray of blood splattering the splintered wooden crates behind him. Simmons reloaded as he walked.

The train lurched forward and stopped as cars clanged into each other, screeching in protest. Blue arcs of electricity leapt along the line again, the intensity of their hum increasing, and the carriage surged again. This time it caught the first of the cogs that would pull it up the steep incline.

"Simmons, get your lazy arse over here, they're leaving."

He turned and fired another two rounds at the figures huddled behind their inadequate cover, smiling as he picked out a grunt amidst the splintering wood. He ran to join Fletcher, noticing for the first time the distance to the track below them. It was at least ten feet to the train roof. Their landing zone on top of the carriage was only a few feet wide if they didn't want to fry on the central electrified arm.

There's a chance we might not die. He turned to Fletcher. "We can do this."

"Really?"

"Yes," he replied, hoping his features weren't betraying his thoughts.

"I think we'll break our bloody legs and either be electrocuted or fall to our deaths screaming in agony."

"I'm not sure you would get on with Bazalgette," Simmons said half to himself. "He's more of an optimist."

"What are you blabbering about?"

"Nothing important."

Shots resumed from the Black Guard troops, arcs of electricity struck the rearmost carriages and flew around the gantry. Simmons and Fletcher climbed down the side of the gargantuan structure to hang down, trying to minimise the drop. As the first carriage clanked under them, sparks flying from the rail, Simmons released his grip.

His right leg hit the roof and gave way. Simmons flung an arm out grasping for anything to stop his slide off the edge. His gloved left hand caught on something sharp, but he gripped, ignoring the pain that shot into his wrist. His legs dangled out into open space, and as his foot clattered into the carriage window, he saw Fletcher falling towards him. *This is going to hurt.*

Her knee dug into his bicep, and he grunted through gritted teeth. His hand felt as though he'd thrust it into a furnace, and his brain screamed for him to let go. His grip weakened as darkness welled around the edge of his vision, but then his arm wrenched upward, gripped by Fletcher from above. The pain fled for an instant. As his sight returned, Simmons noticed movement at the rear of the train as a dark uniformed figure pulled itself onto the last section's roof.

Grating metal sounded below as the door opened and hands grasped and supported his feet. The carriage clanked over the cogs drawing them up the incline and sparks flew as they crossed each section of the overhead rail. They bounced off his jacket, leaving tiny black scorch marks, as he pushed against whoever had hold of his boots. The grip on his arm strengthened, and he slowly shifted upwards.

As they left the protective cover of the warehouse roof, the gale struck them, sending the whole carriage lurching. "Watchman," he shouted, at the telltale sting of Bazalgette's device, but the gusting wind stole his words. Fletcher struggled to hoist his weight, ignorant of the black shape approaching leaping between the carriages.

Simmons felt the drip of something hit his face and saw a smear of red liquid on his lens. His wrist was damp, and as he twisted to get a better grip, a few more droplets fell, torn away by a violent gust into the dark void around him.

The officer made his way onto the adjacent carriage and sauntered towards Fletcher, who was still unaware of the threat. Simmons shrugged the rifle from his shoulder, catching it awkwardly, then flipped it to get his finger inside the trigger guard. He grimaced as they jolted across another cog and peered up at the approaching figure. The officer spotted him fumbling to keep hold and pulled a short sword from his belt.

A deft flick of the wrist and it expanded to twice the length with a click, audible even through the growing gale.

Fletcher's head spun as she heard the sound, but it was too late. The pocket watch glinted in his other hand, and in an instant, he vanished.

∽

As the officer appeared with his blade ready to plunge into Fletcher's neck, his sneer transformed at his premature return to the time stream. A gasp escaped his wide-eyed stare as the barrel of Simmons' rifle rose over Fletcher's shoulder and into the man's face.

By instinct he tried to pull back from the weapon, but not before Simmons squeezed both triggers. *Surprise*, he thought.

The hammers fell, driving their force into the firing pins of the heavy calibre rounds. Click, click. Disbelief, then realisation flooded him. He hadn't had time to reload before they leapt from the gantry.

The officer regained his composure and steadied himself to strike. Simmons slipped as Fletcher released his wrist. Another sharp stab of pain tore through his hand. Then he was falling again.

As he fell back off the carriage roof, Fletcher whipped her foot out from under her, striking the man in his knee which crumpled with an audible crack. He staggered to his right with an angry roar. As his blade crossed the centre line, electricity arced from above, engulfing his body in a burst of sparks and flame.

Simmons smiled at the almost poetic justice as he fell away from the scene into the void that would soon become solid ground.

∽

Pain lanced through his knees as he swung upside-down below the train. Strong hands gripped his ankles and then calves as Blake heaved him upwards. Somehow he'd kept hold of his rifle strap, the Holland bouncing wildly beneath him.

Simmons felt his heart thundering in his chest as he was hauled into the safety of the carriage. He lay there on his back, trying to get his breathing under control.

"Feared we'd lost you there, Simmons," Lynch said. It was the first time she'd sounded concerned throughout the evening.

Blake blew out a huge breath. "Let's not do that again. Next time I might not be able to keep hold of you." He sat leant against the wall beside the still open door, his breathing heavy.

"Thank you," Simmons replied. It seemed inadequate, but he had nothing else at that moment.

"Is he all right?" Fletcher's voice called from above, her head and shoulders poking through a hatch in the roof.

"I'll live," Simmons said, giving her a tired wave.

"Thank fuck for that. I thought I'd killed you."

"No, still here." His left hand throbbed, and now the adrenaline was dipping, the pain returned. Blood seeped from his glove down his sleeve.

Lynch noticed the damage and rummaging through her pack. "Let me look at that."

"Right, if nobody is dying down there, make a space," Fletcher said. "The stink up here is worse than Blake's arse."

The clanking continued overhead as they maintained their steady rise. Fletcher lowered herself and dropped to the carriage floor. The squad watched as Lynch patched up the tear in Simmons' hand. It was a nasty ragged cut, but after being able to move his fingers, Lynch seemed happy there was no permanent damage.

"You should've seen that bastard's face," Fletcher said. "When I kicked his knee out, it was a proper picture. And you?" she said, orienting on Simmons. "Balls of steel. Bluffing him with the rifle like that when you knew it was empty. He nearly shat himself."

Simmons smiled, not wanting to spoil her enthusiasm for his inspired plan. The squad broke into laughter with Fletcher until they left the riser onto the electrified rails. Then it was all back to business.

Curtis motioned from the controls for Lynch to join him. While they discussed where they would disembark, the team prepared for their exit over the outer walls. Rope and climbing gear appeared from packs.

40

Simmons led the way towards the water's edge where Isaac was waiting as planned. The whole operation of getting the team onto the wall and then rappelling down with an unconscious body had gone like clockwork.

They were off and moving through the rubble-strewn cobbles before any of the guards realised what had happened. Sirens sounded shortly after and spotlights scoured the streets, but by then there were rows of derelict buildings between them and the wall.

Lynch equipped the young girl with a fog mask and dosed her with something to keep her unconscious. It made sense. Trying to explain what was going on just wasn't worth the effort, better to carry the sleeping *package*, even if she *was* the Empress.

They progressed west along the river, and then the engine cut out. For a moment, Simmons thought there was a problem until he felt the boat turn, coasting towards the bank, silent except for the gentle lapping of the Thames around them.

With his usual aplomb, Isaac brought them to a stop where they could disembark. It was only a short walk to where they had entered the abandoned underground station before, and the squad disembarked with their precious cargo.

Simmons offered Isaac a hand securing the boat. They

jogged to catch up with Lynch and team who crept between outcrops of rubble and the remains of buildings. They stopped, each member dropping to a crouch. Simmons slowed and kept low as he covered the last few yards to join them. "What's happening?" he whispered.

Lynch looked up. "Turner says there's been organised troop movement around here."

"Black Guard?"

"That's what he thinks."

"How many?" Simmons asked.

"Difficult to say, but enough to cause us a problem."

"Damn. So what now?"

"Blake, Turner, Fletcher. See what you can find near the station entrance, then report back."

The three of them disappeared into the darkness in silence, leaving Lynch and Curtis with the Empress. Simmons took up a position where he could keep watch in case any of the troops were still about.

Ten minutes later, Turner appeared out of the night. "We watched a couple of Black Guard sentries at the entrance and were just about to take them down when a pair of officers joined them from within. The usual saluting and fawning you'd expect, but they didn't seem interested. Headed off to the east with a heavily built civilian."

"Maddox," Simmons said.

"Yes, I'd say so."

"I knew he was up to no good. Damn him."

"We've more pressing issues at hand," Lynch said. "We need to take the Empress to ArcNet, to safety."

Simmons nodded. "Agreed, but if he's brought the Black Guard here, it's treason."

"We're walking a fragile line regarding moral high ground," Lynch replied. "Turner, get back and clear access to the station. I want to walk straight in and down to that platform. You, Blake and Fletcher need to make a path. Go."

Turner didn't even reply, he disappeared around the corner and was gone.

Lynch picked up the young girl, swinging her over a shoulder, pulling a Mauser pistol from her belt.

"I have to leave," said Isaac.

Simmons turned to shake his hand, and the older man smiled. "I'll be back, just got a favour to do for a friend."

"Right," Simmons said. "We'll catch up on your return."

Isaac waved as he headed towards the river. A few seconds later, the engine purred to life, and the boat pulled into the main flow.

Simmons checked his rifle and then hustled to walk alongside Lynch. It only took them a few minutes to reach the station, and as they approached, Simmons heard the distinct click of the communication buttons they used.

"It's clear," Lynch said. She crossed the area of open ground before the deserted entrance. Blake appeared from behind the doorway and motioned them in.

"Report," said Lynch.

"Sentries neutralised. Turner is scouting the stairwell, and Fletcher is keeping an eye out for any more targets."

"Right," Lynch said. "I'll call her in. You head forward to support Turner. Simmons will—"

"Simmons will stay here and put down that treacherous mad dog," he said.

"We need you to—"

"No. I can't allow him to get away with this," Simmons said. "Your team is more than capable of getting the Empress to safety. My being with you won't make any difference to that. In fact, I'm more of a liability to your operation as it stands. Let me do what I do best, hunt down crazed animals that are too dangerous to leave running free."

She wasn't happy, but he could see that Lynch realised he wouldn't change his mind about this. "If this is really what you want?"

"It is."

"Look after yourself, Simmons. Don't go getting heroic, shoot the bastard from a distance."

"That's the plan," he replied, accepting her handshake.

"You take care of the Empress."

"That's the plan." Lynch smiled, tapped her communication button three times, then turned heading for the stairwell.

Fletcher almost bumped into him at the entrance as she bustled in. "Simmons, you're going the wrong way. Stairs are over there," she said, pointing past him.

"I'm headed after Maddox."

"Aye, of course you are," she said. "Didnae take much to spot the bad blood between you. If it wasnae for that Rosie lass, I think we'd already have been tearing your hands from each other's throats."

"Did you see where he went?"

"Aye, out to the north-east, some buildings look in half-decent nick over there. That's where I lost sight of him."

"Thank you, Fletcher."

"It's no bother. Just a word of advice."

Simmons cocked his head, waiting for her to continue.

"Dinnae let him dictate the game. I get the feeling he's canny one, you shouldnae to go toe-to-toe with a thug like that. No disrespect, but you are getting on a wee bit. You're no the prime stag anymore, so don't try to be. Be the hunter that takes him down from five hundred yards."

She slapped him on the shoulder. "All the best, Simmons. I hope we see you again. I've still got to finish that story."

He smiled as he walked out into the early morning air. It was cold and damp. The terrain was crisp underfoot, and the sky was showing the faintest hint of light. Perfect hunting conditions.

They assembled a team of technicians and equipped them with weapons. As they left to search the tunnels, Raphael called out. "More sensors are down, and I'm getting reports of multiple intruders."

"Do you have any details on numbers?" Nathaniel asked

"I can't be certain, but between fifty and a hundred."

"Shit," Callam said. "What about the other sectors, Raph?"

"No signs of activity in one or two, though signals were intermittent over the past week."

"So what are you telling us?" Nathaniel replied.

Raphael's joints whirred as he oriented his ruined features to face him. "Just that we cannot rely on any signal coming from there."

Callam shook his head. "Great. Another problem we don't have time to fix."

Nathaniel surveyed their makeshift wiring from the previous day. In the red emergency lighting, it looked ugly. "We need to prioritise. So let's work with what we have and ignore what we can't repair now. Is it possible to get word to Lynch and Simmons?"

"There's no way to communicate with her squad while they are outside ArcNet," Callam said. "We can speak with Peterson's team in the tunnels, but that's as far as it goes."

"I have a list," Nathaniel said. "Six items from yesterday need urgent attention. If we don't resolve those, we might end up with system failures from any significant power fluctuations."

"Right," Callam said. "Let's get cracking on those until we hear from Peterson. Raph, keep us informed if we lose any more sensors or if any alerts trigger in the other sectors."

"I am already monitoring for..." Raphael sagged in the wires that supported his system, his voice slurring to a stop.

"Raph! Raph, are you all right?" Callam shouted, rushing over to him.

Nathaniel followed, all thoughts of the systems in need of attention gone in a flash. If Raphael failed, they would lose power to the core, plunging them into darkness.

Callam checked the primary feeds into the ArcAngel's body. "Raph?"

"...any unusual activity from all three sectors," Raphael continued, his voice returning to normal speed like a newly wound gramophone.

Callam held up a hand. "What just happened to you,

Raph?"

"What do you mean?"

"You cut out for a few seconds there."

A few more whirs sounded as the ArcAngel turned to look down at where Callam was inspecting his power feeds. "I'm not aware of any period offline."

"Perhaps you should perform a diagnostic. Cross-reference your internal clock with ArcNet."

"Very well."

The ArcAngel's eyes dimmed while he sat motionless for ten seconds. "I have completed the primary analysis and can find no prob—"

This time it was an instant cut-off. Raphael's head sagged, and the blue lights showing energy transfer to his metallic frame died.

"What the hell?" Callam said.

Nathaniel checked the nearest console of dials and gauges. Needles flickered as power levels failed. "We're losing the core, and all the systems Raphael was controlling are failing. We need him back online in the next few minutes or the new circuits will overload, which could lead to a full cascade failure of ArcNet."

Simmons approached, keeping to cover as the sky brightened to a dull grey. As Fletcher had mentioned, the buildings seemed in reasonable condition and had once been a factory with warehouses around it.

The tracks left by Maddox had been difficult to follow; the man knew something of sticking to the rockier ground, but Simmons was a seasoned hunter, and the two Black Guard were easier to spot. He picked up the telltale traces that showed their recent passage.

He'd travelled about a mile from the underground station entry, but had taken his time, staying alert for any signs, but so far nothing. As he circled the buildings, he found no further tracks heading away. So they were still here. *What are you up to, Maddox?*

Wary of traps or an unexpected welcoming committee, he stalked between the warehouses towards the factory at their centre. Quarter of a boot heel left its imprint on a patch of softer earth. It looked like Maddox had headed straight to the central building.

In the near-dark, Simmons saw a tiny glow of light from the upper floor and moved away from the main entrance. No way of knowing what nasty surprises might protect that door.

After five minutes of scouting, he located a window at ground level that gave as he pushed at it. The frame was rotten but held together as it opened. Checking inside, rows of machinery ran in parallel lines along the length of the huge room within. Though it was dark, his eye had adjusted enough to see an open space where he could step down to the floor without fear of disturbing anything.

He stalked between the silent looms, long beyond their useful lifespan. Rust clung to their sharp angles, while any sign of wool had rotted away into a dried sludge beneath them. He made slow and quiet progress towards the far side of the room where stairs led up to the next floor.

Simmons kept his weight on his rear foot as he tested the first stair. As he placed his boot on the outer edge of the step, he applied more pressure onto it, hoping for a sturdier construction and not a loose or squeaky floorboard. It accepted him without protest, and when he had transferred all his weight forward, he moved his back leg to take the next step, repeating the slow and painstaking process.

He poked his head around the top of the stairwell, finding a long corridor leading towards a series of doors, probably offices or storage areas. A pale yellow light seeped beneath the third one, and faint sounds of murmured conversation came from behind it. He approached with great care and measured steps, choosing every footfall until he was beside the doorway. He hadn't made a sound.

From within, there were two voices. It was difficult to make out what was being said, but they sounded like they were to the right of the door which, luckily for Simmons, opened inwards.

A third voice, deeper and louder issued from inside. "I don't care how you do it. You need more men." Maddox.

He was somewhere to the left of the room. *Damn, it would be tricky to get the drop on him.* Simmons decided the best option was to be direct. Burst in, take out the two to the right with the Holland, then use the Mauser to deal with Maddox. He reached down and unclipped the holster providing easy access to the pistol, already cocked and ready to fire. He'd made sure of that on his way across the rough terrain from the station. It wasn't something he wanted to do within earshot of his prey.

He aimed the rifle towards the right side of the room and prepared to kick the door from its hinges. He counted down, mentally. *Three, Two, One.*

The wood splintered around the lock and flew open. Two Black Guard officers sat at a rickety table. They lurched to their feet, knocking a wine bottle which smashed against the wall. The Holland rifle roared, blowing a great hole in the nearest one's chest and sending him flying backwards into the other. There was a sickening crunch as the back of his head smashed into the others face, and they both fell in a bloody mess onto the floor.

Oh, Lucky Days, Simmons thought. He'd expected to have to use both shots and now had one barrel left which he whirled to bear on Maddox.

"I wouldn't try that if I were you," he said as his enemy reached towards a pistol on the table beside him.

"It seems you have me at a disadvantage, Simmons." Maddox's fingers twitched, desperate to grasp the weapon. He opened his hand, drawing it back into his lap.

"So it would seem," Simmons replied. "You'll pay for what you've done, traitor."

"I'm no traitor. I just know when to support the winning side."

Simmons smiled. "So this is all about money then? I will put you down like the mad dog you are."

"That might be harder than you think." He nodded past Simmons where the door creaked on ruptured hinges.

"You don't expect me to fall for that, do you?"

"Your funeral," Maddox replied, shielding his eyes.

A fizzing noise burst from the frame behind him, and Simmons ducked to his right. Light exploded, leaving just a blur of bright white etched in his vision. Then Maddox hit him at a charge, lifting him off his feet as they crashed through the splintered remains of the flimsy entrance.

∼

Callam fought to re-establish a link to Raphael. "I don't understand it. The power coupling is fine, and there's plenty of juice, he's just not functioning. Maybe you should try?"

Nathaniel shook his head. "You have far more experience. I wouldn't know where to start."

"Other than having seen the schematics?"

"Well, yes," Nathaniel said. "But that's no substitute for the practical skills you've gained over the last four years. I only skimmed through them, so I have an incomplete technical schema and nothing on which to relate. I'll try to stabilise the power flows before anything fails. The others can limit any further damage."

"Right you are," Callam replied as Nathaniel left to face the assembled technicians with Gabriel at their head. He explained the vital functions they needed to repair and sent teams scampering off along the corridors to begin their tasks. With luck, that might be enough to save ArcNet.

Nathaniel returned to the central console with Gabriel, and after a minor change to a power dial and a few flicks of switches, the Klaxon lapsed into silence.

"Thank God for that," Callam said. "I felt like my bloody head would explode."

"Sorry it took so long, I should have thought of it earlier."

Gabriel turned to Callam. "How are things going?"

"I think I'm making progress here. It looks as if Raph started the shutdown himself."

"Why would he do that?" she replied.

"I'm not sure. Whatever the reason, he's gone into some form of lockdown. It must have been an intentional decision, but it's strange how he cut-off mid-sentence."

"Can you bypass the lockdown?" Nathaniel asked.

"Well, I think I can," Callam said. "I'm just not sure if I should."

"Why's that?"

"If he locked his systems down intentionally, we've no idea why and what we might do in unlocking them."

Gabriel sighed. "It's a fair call, but if we don't get him back up and running, we'll lose all the work you did to bypass the core. The teams are out there doing their best to protect the essentials such as air circulation and power distribution, but without Raphael controlling them, the whole place will shut down."

"Damn it," Nathaniel said.

Callam was silent for a few moments. "There's no other choice, is there?"

"No," Nathaniel replied. "I can't see any way past this."

The big man blew out a long breath. "Right, let's get Raph unlocked then."

Callam removed a metal plate on Raphael's torso, revealing a tangled mess of wires. He placed it onto the floor at his side and pried at sections around the data feeds that plumbed Raphael into the workings of ArcNet.

Nathaniel returned his attention to the power. Two of the six dials he was most worried about had slowed in their increasing energy consumption. At last, something going right. He almost jumped when a loud buzzing sounded next to him, breaking the near silence. Gabriel reached down, flicking a switch to open the intercom connection with the communications room.

"Peterson?" she asked.

"Yes, ma'am. I thought you should know I've heard from the team investigating section three."

"Good news, I hope?"

"Not sure yet. They've taken a railcar to investigate and should be at the halfway point shortly, where I expect another update."

"Keep me informed."

"There's something else," Peterson said.

"Go on."

"Well, it might be nothing, but I just received a new set of movement signals from section one."

Nathaniel's brow creased. "Raphael mentioned that the sensors there were unstable. Haven't there been problems over the last week?"

Peterson paused. "There have, but these are different. There seems to be something approaching rapidly from the north. From the readings, I'd say it was a railcar."

"How long till it arrives?" Gabriel asked.

"If it continues at its current speed, and the sensors are correct, then no more than ten minutes."

"Thank you, Peterson," Gabriel said, stifling a groan. "Nathaniel, get a team ready to check the northern tunnel."

Nathaniel stood, wondering where he would find a group of technicians not already engaged in emergency repair work. Callam caught the end of the discussion and turned towards them. "Everything all right?"

"It looks like we have a railcar heading down the tracks in section one," said Gabriel.

Callam frowned. "Could it be Lynch and Simmons."

"I hope so, Callam," Gabriel said. "I really do hope so."

~

The air exploded from Simmons as he and Maddox hit the wall outside the room. He felt his knee connect with Maddox's stomach as the larger man fell on top of him with a loud grunt of pain.

Simmons tried to blink his vision clear from the white afterimage which blocked his sight, damn, it was almost as bad as staring into Bazalgette's arc-lamp. He struggled to his feet, sucking in a great lungful of air. His chest burned, and he looked about, unsure where the rifle had landed when they had burst through the rotten door.

He backed up the corridor, trying to buy himself some time but heard Maddox getting up.

"Simmons, you stupid old bastard. Why couldn't you leave things be?"

"If you think I'd let a treacherous dog like you get away with treason—"

"Oh, who are you kidding? You had me in your sights, and now here you are. No rifle and blinded in a confined space."

Maddox's voice was below head height. *He's crouching, ready for another charge* Simmons thought, reaching for his pistol and slipping it from the holster on his belt. Before he could aim, he heard Maddox racing across the distance between them. He managed to fire once before Maddox struck him again.

A second shot rang out as he fell backwards and there was a yell of pain, Maddox's body rolling off him. He fought to bring the pistol round towards the blurry shape, but something hit his wrist like a hammer, sending the Mauser tumbling from his numb fingers.

"You'll bloody pay for that," Maddox spat between gritted teeth.

Simmons kicked out, pushing himself further away from the hulking figure. "I hope it's nothing minor," he said, pulling himself up on the railing by the stairs.

"I'll live," Maddox said.

"More's the pity," Simmons replied, glancing about the poorly lit passageway. His vision was a little better, but not good enough to pick up where the pistol was in the darkness. Maddox stood before him, gripping his left side with a meaty paw. He was leaning that way too, with luck the shot might have clipped his liver or broken a rib.

Maddox crept forward, using the knowledge of Simmons' injury to blindside him, but with the goggles, he noticed the approach. However, in the dim light, he misjudged Maddox's strike. He raised his arm to block the backhand flying towards his face, twisting his body away from the blow, so it glanced off his forearm. He didn't notice the secondary punch that landed hard into his right leg, struck just where Bazalgette had removed the shrapnel.

White-hot knives stabbed into his brain as his knee gave way. He yelled in agony as he collapsed, grabbing at the stair rail for support. His numb fingers couldn't arrest his momentum before he crashed through into the open space below him on the stairwell.

He bounced down the stairs, amidst splintered wood, to lie crumpled at the bottom among the shattered remains of half of the wooden spindles, head still ringing. Pain coursed through his entire body, nausea threatening to overwhelm him.

The salty iron taste of blood filled his mouth, and he spat a mouthful onto the floor. He must have bitten into his tongue on his descent too. His ribs screamed as he tried to stand, but he knew he had to move, and fast.

Gritting his teeth, he dragged himself towards the nearest aisle of rusted machinery. Through the rushing of blood in his head and his laboured breathing, he heard movement at the top of the staircase. *Move it, old man. Got to get out of sight.*

He clawed himself between the first two rows of looms, and gripping the rusty undersides of the machines, pulled himself under them.

Solid footsteps reached the factory floor. Simmons couldn't see a thing in the darkness. He just lay there, trying to keep his breathing quiet and winced with pain with each ragged breath. He'd cracked at least one rib in his fall.

A few scuffs broke the silence as Maddox crunched through the splintered debris at the foot of the stairs.

"Oh, that must have hurt," Maddox called out. "I heard a few nasty cracks on the way down, I was expecting to find your broken bones at the bottom, but this is much more fun. Now I get to break the others, one by one."

Light filtered into the structure as dawn approached, the grey gloom becoming lighter by the minute. Luckily for Simmons, it was brightest at the other side of the room, but it wouldn't take long for it to seep over the entire factory floor.

"The amount of shit I've had to endure from you so that Rosie could keep up appearances with your group. I've killed men for much less than that. You should think yourself lucky. But now it's just you and me Simmons, you old goat." Maddox continued his slow approach. He was almost at the end of the aisle. "I have the entire force of the Red Hands at my beck and call, and what do you have? Nothing."

Simmons held his breath as Maddox stalked towards his hiding place, but the pressure in his side was unbearable. He coughed, a dribble of blood speckled his lips, and he groaned in pain.

"There you are, you slippery old bastard. Now come out from under there and let's finish this."

Maddox knelt and reached under the broken machinery, his fingers mere inches from Simmons' boots.

A door crashed open, flooding the northern side of the factory with pale grey light.

"Leave him alone. Why don't you pick on someone your own size?"

A thin figure stood silhouetted in the doorway. The thick London accent was unmistakable - Isaac.

"What the hell?" Maddox said, standing to face the visitor. "Is this some old git's convention that nobody told me about? Go home, Isaac, you're even more decrepit than this old bastard."

A female voice replied. "I think you'll find he means me."

A tall figure pushed past Isaac. Starlight sparkled from ringed fingers catching the first glints of the morning sun, as Diamond Annie strode into the room. "Isaac told me there was a mad dog needed putting down. So here I am."

41

"Callam, I need these doors open. Lynch has the Empress outside."

Nathaniel waited on the northern platform. He knew Callam was doing his best, but that didn't curb the anxiety he felt.

"That should do it," Callam said. "I'm bringing Raph back online now."

"No!" Raphael shouted, his crackling voice piercing through the intercom.

"What's happening?" Nathaniel asked.

"He's fighting it, trying to shut down again."

"Can you stop him?"

"Gabriel bypassed the cut-out he used last time."

"Get him to open the security gate. We need Lynch inside."

A loud electrical hum rose, and the solid steel section clanked into movement, recessing into the thick protective walls that blocked the rail access.

"Nathaniel, he's complying, but he's not at all happy. There's something seriously wrong with him."

"Tell Gabriel. She can talk to him."

"She's already doing her best. Callam out."

The opening gate spat a widening cone of light into the dark tunnel illuminating the packed railcar. Lynch sat in the

407

driving position and disengaged the brake as soon as it was wide enough for them to pass between. The rest of her team clung to the sides of the makeshift vehicle. Nathaniel scanned, but found no sign of Simmons.

He pressed the close button as they passed through the massive black gates. Nothing happened. He pushed it again, clicking in response to his touch, but still, the steel slabs continued into the walls leaving a twenty-foot-wide hole into ArcNet.

Nathaniel punched the intercom. "Callam, we've got a problem with—"

He realised he wasn't transmitting, the light beside the speaker flickered then cut-out. He turned to one of the three armed technicians he'd poached on the way here.

"Head back to the core. Tell Callam and Gabriel what's happened here, that systems are failing and we have a damned huge hole in our defences. You two," he said, pointing to the remaining techs. "Take up a position here and lock down as much as you can. Get it done quickly, it needn't be pretty. Weld the doors, stack heavy equipment behind them, whatever works."

The other men nodded their understanding, discussing ideas while Nathaniel moved onto the platform to meet Lynch. By the time he'd covered the distance to the railcar, Lynch's team were lifting an unconscious young woman from the vehicle.

"Curtis, Blake," Lynch called. "Take the Empress to secure accommodation and tell Gabriel."

"She's in the operations centre," Nathaniel said, extending his hand. She took it in a firm handshake. "Major Lynch, your mission looks like it was successful."

"Yes, Nathaniel, but what's going on here? We encountered Black Guard forces in the east entrance and had to make our way onto a loop to get to this line."

"Sensors identified a large group of intruders, Peterson led a force to investigate."

"We'll be lucky to see them alive again. These are seasoned

assault troops, he won't stand a chance." She looked over her shoulder towards the gate. "Why is that still open?"

"We are having systems problems with Raphael. He shut down, and Callam is fighting to bring him back online. That's why we had the delay in getting you inside. Now the mechanism seems inoperative, along with the intercom here."

"We have to get it secured."

"I've got two technicians doing the best they can."

"Curtis, belay that last order," she shouted as he was about to pull the young girl onto his shoulder. "Give her to Blake. I need you to coordinate efforts here. Secure the area. Take whatever you require and seal that gate."

The man snapped a sharp nod and handed the girl to his colleague.

Lynch looked back to Nathaniel. "You said Gabriel was in ops?"

"She's with Raphael, trying to find out what's wrong. It looks like he intentionally shut himself down earlier and is now struggling with being reactivated."

"Shit. It was bad enough when he was just paranoid. It's risking the whole bloody network."

"Where's Simmons?" Nathaniel asked, his voice catching.

"He's fine. We left him topside. He insisted we got the Empress to safety while he went to track Maddox."

"Maddox?"

"Yes, it appears he led the Black Guard here. Simmons was insistent that he didn't get away with it."

"Oh," was all Nathaniel managed. Maddox was the reason Simmons had become involved in the whole affair. He'd never let that drop until one of them was dead.

⁓

"Don't go anywhere," Maddox said sneering at Simmons' broken form as he stood to face Annie. He was a beast of a man. Heavyset, muscular and though there was a growing bloodstain on his clothing above his left hip, it didn't seem to slow him in the slightest.

Annie was an athlete, lithe and fast. Simmons had seen it in the way she moved at their first meeting. He still couldn't get over how tall she was, standing two inches above Maddox.

"What are you doing here, Annie? Got a soft spot for old farts like Simmons, eh? I don't think he's in any state to keep you entertained, love."

"No, me and him made a deal. I'm here to collect my pound of flesh on Gracie's behalf."

"Gracie?" he feigned ignorance tapping his finger against his temple. "Sure I've heard that name before somewhere."

"Stop fucking about. Let's get to breaking bones."

"Oh, that's it," he said, face lighting up with mock surprise. "The bitch whose neck I snapped after she gave me this," he pointed at a scar on his left cheek, "with that sparkly shit she called a diamond."

Annie stared at him, eye's smouldering, her lip lifted at the corner as she exhaled. "Enough."

"No, there's more. You should know how she squealed and begged before I offed her. Promised me anything I wanted, the filthy whore. I beat the crap out of her first though. She was screaming and weeping, tears, blood and snot everywhere. Her face was a right mess, not so pretty any more. But I didn't realise she was your favourite plaything. If I'd known, I would have been more creative, gone to town on her with my knife."

He was goading her and Simmons could sense the anger in her building, a volcano ready to erupt. *Keep your head, girl*, but it was too late. She exploded at Maddox like a wild beast, covering the last ten feet in a flash. Maddox turned his body to absorb the punches and kicks on his bicep and thigh. He weathered the flurry of blows waiting for an opportunity that inevitably presented itself. His upper torso rotated from the hips pulling his right arm back as he unleashed a powerful left.

The crack as his knuckles struck her chin echoed across the room, and Annie spun from the blow, collapsing to the dirty ground like a rag doll. Maddox let out a hoarse laugh.

"Fucking women. Think they can fight. This isn't a scratching competition, love."

He turned towards the doorway. "Isaac, just get the fuck away from here, or do I need to give you a slap too?"

The old man leant on the doorframe, chuckled and crossed his arms.

"Didn't you hear me? What are you waiting for, my boot up your bleeding arse?"

"No," said Isaac, his voice calm. "I'm staying for the next round." He nodded behind Maddox to where Annie was pushing herself to her feet. She spat out a mouthful of bloody saliva. A blood-beaded string hung from the corner of her mouth. "Not a bad shot, Maddox," she said, rubbing her jaw, "for a girl."

He whirled on her, eyes wide. "You should have stayed down."

"What, you think this is over? I'm just getting warmed up. I've had worse than that while romping around the bed with Gracie. If you want to feel a real punch, come and bring your ugly mug over here."

Pain flared as Simmons turned for a better view of the two fighters. Blood smeared Annie's face from her swollen split lip, and her jaw was already darkening. This time she let Maddox throw the first shot and slipped it effortlessly. As it glided from her left forearm, her body swayed like a cobra, her right fist leaping to catch him a solid blow. His head snapped back, and he grunted.

He stepped away, and Annie grinned. "Look, you have a matching scar on that side now."

Maddox reached up to touch his face. His hand returned dripping with blood from three gashes which tore across his cheek.

Annie caught his eye and winked. "You know what they say, 'that which doesn't kill you only makes you uglier'. And fuck me if you haven't been near-death on way too many occasions."

"You fucking bitch!"

Maddox came on like a raging bull, his fists flying at her. She ducked and weaved, dodging or blocking the storm of blows, but gave ground, allowing him to unleash his anger and frustration on the space between them.

Simmons shuffled and found an angle to see them as they approached the end of the aisle. The barrage was unrelenting. It seemed only a matter of time before Annie missed a block. She couldn't withstand this constant assault forever, could she?

She stumbled as she moved backwards, her guard dropping on her right side, exposing her head as she backed into the wall. Maddox took the opening, firing a powerful straight left into her eye. A gut-wrenching crack of splintering bone, followed by a roar of pain burst from the large man.

Annie was a seasoned street-fighter, she'd played him with a move so beautifully orchestrated that he'd ploughed on thinking he could finish the fight in one blow. But she hadn't stumbled. She'd exploited his instincts to go for an obvious opening, then swayed out of the way allowing the full force of his punch to strike the brickwork behind her.

He stood, cradling his ruined left hand, his face contorted with agony. The strange sound from him was somewhere between a whimper and the feral growl of an injured predator.

"Oh, that was close," Annie said shuffling in a boxer's stance. "You nearly got me that time, lucky I slipped, eh?"

He roared in defiance and charged her, ignoring the pain that must be raging through his shattered knuckles. They collided with a flurry of blows from Annie, glancing from his solid guard. He propelled her into a wall with a sickening crunch. They both cried out, but Maddox had her by the upper arms, limiting her strikes into his torso with no room to build any power.

He pulled his forehead back, ready to drive it into her. "No," yelled Isaac. The rippling muscled neck snapped his head forward into Annie's unprotected face. The crack of bone and cartilage made Simmons' stomach lurch, and he watched in shocked silence as Maddox stood then stumbled, his features a bloody mess. Annie lashed out with a knee into the bloodstained area above his hip, and as he buckled, finished with a vicious left hook. A spray of blood-flecked spittle flew from him, and he slumped to the ground in a boneless heap.

Annie reached up, rubbing her head, hair matted in a dark mass of sweat and stained crimson. "Fuck, but he's got a bony nose."

She bent to retrieve a chain from around Maddox's throat, a red stream dripping from the rings on her left hand. Holding the silver links before her, a single ring sparkled in the sunlight. "This was for you, Gracie," she said, stamping down on the thick bull neck with a resounding crack.

Isaac was running from the door towards her. "Annie, I thought you was a goner," he said between gasps for breath.

"Nah. It's a prize-fighters trick, pull your chin down when someone tries to butt you, let their soft squishy bits hit your bony ones. My dad taught me that when I was a nipper."

Isaac hugged her.

"Calm down, fella. Is that any way to be treating the new leader of the Elephant and Castle gang?"

"No, I suppose not," he said, releasing her and stepping away. "But you'll forgive an old man for hugging his favourite daughter now, won't you?"

$\sim$

The place was in an uproar as Nathaniel and Lynch arrived. Technicians surrounded Gabriel and were all shouting at once, and nobody could hear a thing.

"Shut up!" roared Lynch. Nathaniel jumped from the unexpected noise from the usually soft-spoken woman. The room fell into silence. "Let Gabriel speak," she continued.

"Thank you," Gabriel said. "As I was trying to say. Neither myself nor Callam fully understands what has happened to Raphael, but all three security gates to the tunnels are locked open, and we can't close them. The most pressing is the south-east gate where we've identified intruders on the tunnel sensors. We need people there to defend that area while we

413

continue to work on getting the systems back online to seal the entrances. With Major Lynch's return, I shall hand over defensive operations to her and her team. You will follow her instructions as if they came from me, understood?"

Gabriel waited as the group mumbled their agreement. She motioned for Lynch and Nathaniel to approach, and they retreated to an office for privacy. "Please give me some good news, major."

"We rescued the Empress though she has been heavily sedated. She needs cleaning up and a medical check-up."

"Great news. I'll get onto that straight away. In return, as I mentioned to the crew, you need to take over defensive preparations and get the south-east tunnel defended. We received a garbled message from Peterson that shows he encountered trained military troops."

"Yes, It's a Black Guard assault unit. We saw them when we first arrived and had to move around them. As far as I am aware, they didn't spot us."

"Good to know who we are fighting against," Gabriel said. "Nathaniel, help Callam. He's struggling with Raphael. I've tried to talk to him, but Raph is babbling nonsense about being a danger and needing to be shut down. I need to understand what's happening here and get it sorted out. If he goes offline, we lose main power, and all the other systems fail. I can't allow that to happen."

"I'll get right on it," Nathaniel said, standing to leave.

"Before either of you go. Thank you for all your efforts. I may not have another chance to say this and I wanted you to know how much it means that we've rescued the Empress from the Black Guard. Let's hope we can all make it out of here in one piece."

With that, they each left to carry out their appointed tasks. Nathaniel could hear Lynch barking orders to both her team and the assembled technicians as he ran up the corridor to see how Callam was getting on with Raphael.

Callam spun as he crashed through the operations centre

door. "Nathaniel, thank God you're here. I need your help with Raph. I've tried everything I can think of."

Nathaniel stared at the dejected figure plugged into a mass of cables in the middle of the room. "What's wrong with him?"

"I have no idea. It's like he's given up on life."

Raphael lifted his head as he heard Nathaniel's voice. "Kill me, shut me down. It doesn't matter how, just do it now."

The dented and ruined half-metallic face twisted and scowled at him, but beneath it all, Nathaniel could see the torment in him.

"We can't," he said. "Why would you want us to?"

"There's something wrong with me. If you don't stop me, I'll destroy this whole place."

"You'll be fine. We'll sort this out."

Raphael didn't answer. Instead, he tucked his chin into his neck and closed his eyes.

Nathaniel and Callam moved to the side of the room to discuss their findings. The systems Raphael oversaw were fluctuating but stable, much better than when he had shut down.

An alarm sounded, and they both jumped. The communications channel was flashing, Callam reached it first pressing the button to open a line. Lynch's voice crackled over the airwaves. "We have contact with the Black Guard. Taking heavy fire." The sound of weapons discharging was clear in the background. "We need all the manpower you can spare down here, or they *will* overrun us."

Nathaniel turned to Callam. "Do we have a lens down there?"

"Yes, I'll patch it through."

He pushed a few buttons, and the screen nearest them blinked into life. Dim at first with a green haze, then resolving into a view of the platform where they had all met. The viewpoint was somewhere high looking down towards the open gates into the tunnel. Lynch's team were in cover near the entrance, exchanging fire. Flashes of light and arcs of electricity flashed back and forth in a silent exchange.

The image fuzzed and wobbled, a strange glow around the outer edges on the screen.

"What's that?" Nathaniel asked. "It looks like magnetic distortion."

Callam thought for a second. "Perhaps it's Fletcher's rifle. It uses a magnetic field to propel the projectiles. Maybe she's situated somewhere up near the lens?"

As the combat continued, the image distorted again, and an attacker dropped while trying to change cover.

"Good guess," Nathaniel said.

The communicator crackled into life. Lynch's voice rang out amongst the raging battle. "Taking too many casualties, we're pulling back to ArcNet."

A huge explosion burst from the speakers, and their eyes shot to the screen. Dust filled the shaft beyond the gate, rolling into the platform area obscuring the camera's view.

"Did it collapse?" Callam asked.

Streaks of light cut into the cloud from above, and a towering shadowed figure rose from a crouch in the swirling eddies of fine particles. Shots pinged off it from the troopers further down the tunnel as a familiar form resolved within the light and thinning dust.

Callam squinted at the screen. "Is that another ArcAngel?"

The bulky armoured shape stood, rising to stand ten feet in height and whirled to face the Black Guard troops. Twin rotary cannons spun up to speed then disgorged a raging torrent of electrical firepower into the darkness. The sound from the communicator cut in and out, the noise of the automatic fire deafening.

"My God," Nathaniel said as the figure turned towards the platform. It raised its half-ruined face, perfectly framed on the screen, tendrils of smoke rising from the slowing Gatling guns attached to both arms. "It's Josiah."

≈

"Callam, you need to tell Gabriel about this," Nathaniel shouted.

"What about Raph?"

"I'll deal with Raphael. Gabriel is the only one who has a chance of standing against him."

Callam jumped to his feet, heading for the exit. "Best of luck, Nathaniel," he called over his shoulder as he left.

"You too, my friend," he replied. "Now, what next?"

"Destroy me." Raphael's voice made him jump, and he turned seeing the ruined ArcAngel's eyes following his every movement.

"I can't."

"Callam was incapable of doing it. You are strong enough to do what's required. Can you not see the ruin I have already caused? It will only continue to worsen."

"What is the problem?"

"I'm not sure, but I am corrupted. It has been eating away at me like the taint."

"You aren't affected by it," Nathaniel said. "You're mostly machine."

"I didn't say I had contracted the ailment. There is something hidden in my systems. Now I spread it as a disease, infecting all I touch, and I am connected to almost everything here. I have links to over ninety percent of ArcNet. That is why you must shut me down. It may already be too late for this facility, but you might still save the crew."

"Even if we followed your idea, how would that help? We have the Black Guard and now Josiah on our doorstep."

"If I manage to wrestle control back for the security gates, I can close them and flood the tunnels. There is an escape route through the core for the staff. Everyone will need to retreat inside ArcNet, to safety, or they'll get locked out once I deactivate."

A flicker of movement caught Nathaniel's eye, and he examined the view screen. From the high vantage point, the lens captured groups of rough-looking men and women descending on ropes from the hole Josiah had crashed through in his dramatic entrance. They wore bright colours proudly announcing their gang affiliations. Red Hands, Black Canary and Silver Hatchets stood shoulder-to-shoulder, a brotherhood of street thugs.

The defenders had withdrawn to safety behind their steel shutters. A lone figure walked from them towards the assembled crowd who jeered at Gabriel's approach. The microphones near the lens were working better now. *Perhaps Fletcher had moved, and her rifle was no longer interfering with the electronics.*

"Josiah, isn't it?" Gabriel asked as she approached. Her armour made her an imposing figure, but she looked like a child next to Josiah's monstrous machine, she barely reached his chest.

"Yes," he replied. "You must be Gabriel. What an amazing facility you have hidden away down here. No doubt filled with all manner of exciting toys."

"Why are you here?"

"For all this," he said, turning with arms outstretched. "I want it all, Gabriel. All of your heavenly technology, and this fine establishment too."

"It's not mine to give."

"Come now. You are lord and ruler here. Let's not delude ourselves about that."

Gabriel shook her head. "No Josiah, I follow a higher power."

Josiah's laugh echoed from the walls, and the crowd followed his lead. "I fear you have been in storage too long. You are the creation of man, not some God."

"You misunderstand me," she replied. "I serve the Empress and take my orders from her alone. Only she could allow me to hand over property of the crown."

"Victoria is dead, you fool. Destroyed by the Martians years ago."

"No, she lives on through her granddaughter, who is alive and well. She does not wish to relinquish her estates to you or anyone else, including the Black Guard."

"And how have you come to this deluded ideal?"

"Because I spoke with her just five minutes before I came out to meet you."

Murmurs spread among the assembled gang members until Josiah reasserted his position. "If you are unwilling to give up the prize, then I'll take it from you, as the strong have always taken from the weak."

"I will die before relinquishing my duty," Gabriel said, planting her feet.

"Make your peace with your God then. You're about to fall from Heaven once again."

Josiah's guns spun into motion belching gouts of electricity spraying over the heads of the crowd. Panicked screams filled the area as gang members dived for cover from his indiscriminate attack. Scorched remains marked the spot of those too slow off the mark. As the line of fire reached its intended target, it found only empty space.

The roar of Gabriel's power-assisted leap resounded throughout the station. She hovered in the air as a mighty pair of silver wings sprung from her armour. Electricity rippled over her suit, and she flung one hand out towards Josiah. A flight of six sword-like feathers arced into him, striking with a thunderclap and a shriek of tearing metal. The gun on Josiah's right arm shredded, shrapnel exploding in all directions. Fragments ricocheted off his armoured torso cutting down swathes of the fleeing gangs as he stumbled back, bracing himself.

Callam's team had achieved great things with the ArcAngel armour. Nathaniel had focused on fitting the new wing unit while working on the amazing technology.

Josiah roared in anger, shaking the molten remains of metal fragments from the arm as he tried to sweep the other weapon into Gabriel's path. The firepower he brought to bear was immense. Rounds pounded into the station with dents and holes the size of a man's head, but Gabriel was a seasoned veteran. Her armour was part of her, a second skin, and she'd lived and trained in it for years. It showed in her agility and with her precision.

Dodging the hail of fire from the other cannon, she unleashed another volley of the charged feathers. They curved through the air to find their target. This time, the Gatling gun didn't explode, but fell to the ground split into several pieces.

Josiah kicked the useless remains which careened off the platform edge striking gang members who were hiding there. All that remained were smears of crimson gore across the platform's surface.

Amid the carnage and chaos of people escaping into the tunnel, Nathaniel noticed a skulking figure. Dark clothing wrapped around its form as it maintained a stealthy profile at the edge of the gates. Nathaniel's heart almost stopped as a curl of bright red hair slipped from beneath the hood.

Isaac leaned on the tiller and watched London burn. Thick black clouds rose from behind the walls, who knew what the hell was going on? It seemed the city had abandoned any semblance of law or order when the gangs entered. Their plan was nothing more than chaos and destruction on a grand scale.

Gunshots echoed within, and Isaac counted himself lucky to be floating along the Thames. Betsy's engine was smooth, and they left a small wake as she cut through the gentle waves of the outgoing tide pushing against them. "How's he looking?"

Annie poked her head out of the canvas and crossed to the tiller with two steaming metal mugs. "Sleeping. Perhaps that's for the best, looks like a few broken ribs and lots of bruising coming through. He's taken a right kicking, but he'll survive."

"Good."

"Is that it?"

"What else do you want me to say?"

"So you're still a man of few words?"

Isaac smiled. "Yeah."

Annie passed him the tea. Dark with the merest hint of milk and plenty of sugar, just the way he liked it. Isaac worried where the milk came from though. It was some time since he'd seen cows. With the black market, it was better not to ask, but thoughts always lingered on the edge of his subconscious. Images of giant-rat farms. Could you even milk a rat? He shook his head, chuckling. Or what if it was human? No, that was plain disgusting. He screwed his face up at the thought.

"Everything all right?" Annie asked. "Not having a seizure, are you?"

"That's the problem with the youth of today, isn't it?"

"What's that?"

"No bloody respect."

"That's not true," Annie said. "I respect many things—strength, cunning, intellect and beauty."

"What about tradition or your elders?"

"Well, I respect you, don't I?"

"Do you?"

"Course I do. But not only cos you're my old man. I value what you taught me when I was little. How to fight and shoot, how to look after myself."

"Life's more than just fighting, girl."

"But you were one of the best."

Isaac shook his head. "That was a *long* time ago. As you get older, it changes. Things what didn't seem of any use when you was young become more important. Others you thought you wanted more than anything else in the world lose their charm."

Annie looked at him, a quizzical expression on her face. "What do you mean?"

"Oh, I don't know. Shit just changes, and you got to be ready to change with it. If you can't adapt, then you either get left behind or one day find you aren't no use no more. I wish your mother could have seen you like this."

"Like what?"

"All grown up. Look at you, Queen of the Forty Thieves and leader of the Elephant and Castle at twenty-four. She'd have been proper proud, she would."

"I'm twenty-five."

"What?"

"You heard."

"When did you get another year older?"

"Well, it happens *every* year," Annie said with a grin. "You must be going senile."

A sigh escaped Isaac's lips. "There you go again, no bloody respect."

〜

The battle raged between the two behemoths into the tunnel system just outside the station. Gabriel's aerial advantage ended with a sputtering from her power circuits as the wing unit failed. Nathaniel cursed the lack of time they had in completing and testing the refit.

Now they fought on the ground, trading punches and kicks. The pinnacle of technological warfare reduced to a common street brawl.

Gabriel was still quicker, her reaction speed was incredible, but all it would take was one direct hit from Josiah, and that might finish the battle in an instant.

As Nathaniel watched everything playing out on the viewscreen, Raphael's voice crackled back into activity.

"You must help her."

"Rosie?" Nathaniel said, looking up. "I mean, who?"

"My analysis shows Gabriel cannot win this fight alone."

"What makes you so sure?"

"Look at her power levels," Raphael said, pointing to another screen. It depicted a schematic of the ArcAngel suit and a battery draining rapidly.

"How is it so low already?" Nathaniel asked.

"She can't afford a direct hit from his attacks, so she's over-clocking her systems, to stay ahead of him."

"How long does she have?"

"At the current rate of consumption, a matter of minutes."

"But what could we do? We've not got anything that will stand against that monstrosity?"

"I fear *we* can do nothing. But Gabriel could."

"How? You said yourself she's running out of... *time*."

Raphael's neck plates squealing as he rotated his head to face him. "Precisely. She needs more time."

Nathaniel's eyes widened. "Her watch?"

"Give her that, and everything changes. She could freeze Josiah in place and disable or destroy him."

"But, we've been over this. The power unit is dead, and we have none of the alien technology. It's hopeless."

"There's always hope, Nathaniel." A click from Raphael's torso exposed the edge of a panel in his upper chest. His right arm reached across and flicked it open, revealing a recessed mechanical heart. A mass of cables sprouted from it and connected into the armour, while a red glow pulsed from behind the device in the grim parody of a heartbeat.

"Is that?"

Raphael nodded. "A Martian fusion cell. The same one you will use to power Gabriel's watch."

"But won't you die?"

"Yes, but that has been my intention for some time." He held Nathaniel's gaze with newfound resolution. "This is my fault. I've carried this disease since I returned here after escaping from the Martians. But I realise now they planned it all, and my escape was but a catalyst for their ultimate ambition: to destroy ArcNet when it suited them."

"But that means—"

"Yes, there may still be remnants of the alien intelligence in league with powers within the city. We have little time. The longer we discuss this, the weaker Gabriel is becoming. Her power *will* run out unless we do this now."

Nathaniel hung his head realising Raphael was right. Gabriel was taking more glancing blows in her fight against Josiah. She was slowing, and it wouldn't be long before they became solid strikes, disabling or even destroying her.

He turned back, nodding. "What do I need to do?"

∾

Raphael explained the process as he set up the commands to route power to capacitors in the emergency door controls. As soon as he went offline, the overrides he maintained would drop. The doors would revert to their normal state—closed, powered by the reserves in the capacitor. The flood system was on an isolated circuit which they could link to once they had sealed the security gates. But it would require manual intervention at the gate control.

Nathaniel opened a panel on the main console and triggered the emergency evacuation. Red lighting flickered then pulsed to match the wail of a klaxon. A wax message drum rotated dragging a stylus across the grooves in its shiny surface. Speakers throughout the complex burst into life repeating the monotone warning. "Emergency evacuation. Proceed at once to the central core. This is not a drill."

"Are you ready?" Raphael asked.

Nathaniel shook his head, eyes wide as he paced. "I can't do this. There has to be another way?"

"There isn't, not with the time we have left. You must get the watch to Gabriel."

Nathaniel swallowed past the knot in his throat and nodded.

Raphael smiled at him. "It's the only option to save you all. I cannot do this myself. You need to give me the authorisation."

Raphael gripped the heart-like mechanism that pulsed within him and Nathaniel clasped his hand over it as he issued the command sequence he'd been given. "Alpha-Omega-Sigma-Epsilon-Epsilon." He felt Raphael's fingers constrict under his palm. "Goodbye, Raph."

"Goodbye, Nathaniel, and thank you."

Raphael's arm yanked away from his chest with a series of pops as cables and power lines ripped free. Sparks flew, and his eyes glowed an intense blue for an instant, then faded to eternal black.

The heart pulsed, the last living remnant of what had been an ArcAngel. The metal fingers slackened, leaving the red pulsing device in Nathaniel's grip. He reached up, wiping the stream of tears from his cheeks.

"I'm sorry, Raphael," Nathaniel said, his voice catching. "I should have been able to find another way, a better way."

He took a deep breath and turned to his next task—powering the watch.

42

Nathaniel rushed through the dim metallic corridors. The pulsing red lighting reminded him of the alien artefact, which now powered Gabriel's timepiece. He heard footsteps running towards the core and wondered for a second why he was headed the opposite way.

The clang of boots on the metal plates ahead snapped him from his thoughts. He stopped in his tracks, realising he had no weapon. What if this was one of Josiah's men, or worse, the Black Guard? He reached for his trusty arc-lamp as Fletcher came barrelling around the corner. She yelled in surprise, almost crashing into him. "Shit, Bazalgette. What you doing? The core's that way." She pointed back where he'd come from.

"I'm going to the platform."

"Are you fucking barmy? We need to evacuate."

"No, I have to get the watch to Gabriel before the gate seals." He pushed past while she mumbled something behind him.

"Fuck it. Wait up. I'm no letting you do this on your lonesome."

They stepped out onto the dark platform, the grinding of gears was deafening as the security gates edged closer together. The gap between the two colossal steel structures was shrinking at a rapid rate, and Nathaniel lit the arc-lamp as he dashed to cover the distance. Beyond the gate, the battle of the titans raged. Resounding clangs and the shriek of metal straining and tearing pierced the void ahead.

A gunshot rang out from down the tunnel sparking off the rightmost wall. A figure moved in the darkness, hunkering into a recess against the wall. Nathaniel instantly recognised Rosie and stopped, staring at her in disbelief.

"Get down, you bampot."

Another shot whistled past, and he collapsed as Fletcher tackled him, the breath bursting from his lungs as he hit the ground.

"Nathaniel," cried Rosie.

He tried to reply, but only managed a gurgling noise. His chest felt like a horse had sat on him.

"He's all right, lass," Fletcher called back, "just a bit winded."

Fletcher dropped into a prone position, rifle extended ahead of her, waiting. "There you are, you wee bastard," she said.

Nathaniel heard the almost inaudible hum and then a sound as if she'd spat on the floor. "That'll teach you."

He pushed himself to his feet and noticed the clanking of the gates. They were almost closed. "Rosie, get in here now."

She wouldn't make it. The gates were closing too fast. He reached into his waistcoat for the watch, his decision made, but it wasn't there. Frantic, he checked the other pocket - nothing. He glanced about and there, where he'd fallen, a curved glint of silver caught the light from his arc-lamp. Nathaniel dived for it ignoring the pain as his elbow and knees found the concrete and steel where the tracks entered the station. His fingers pressed down on the latch release, the case flipping open in his hand. He continued the pressure pushing the crown into the body as detailed on the schematic.

He turned, taking in the strange scene. Fletcher still lay on the floor having discharged her rifle. A two-foot-long wake of dust hung suspended in the air where the passage of the bullet had disturbed it. The arc-lamp highlighted swirling motes all

427

around, reminding him of walking through thick fog. It was beautiful but strangely haunting. A moment frozen in time captured solely for him.

He shook his head, focusing on his immediate task. As he arrived at the gate, his heart sank. He'd been too slow. Less than six inches remained between the vice-like slabs of black steel. He could barely thrust his arm through, let alone pull Rosie back to safety.

He pushed the arc-lamp between the jaws of the metal beast separating them. The tunnel lit up. She stood in the alcove, dust clinging to her dark clothing, while her hood hung loosely about her shoulders, a bright red spray of hair cascading around her pale features. She must have been turning back towards the gates as the watch activated. The tail of her leather trench coat brushed the ground, sending eddies of particles swirling out from it to hang like raging sandstorms. She was beautiful, only ten feet away, but entirely out of reach.

"Rosie?"

His words echoed in the silent, frozen photograph. Nathaniel pulled his arm back. It felt wrong leaving her in the darkness with just the shafts of light from the hole in the ceiling for company.

He rushed to the wall panel beside the gate and tore it free. It still had power, the capacitors were doing their job, but they looked close to empty.

Can I reverse the closure, use the last precious joules to open the gates enough to drag Rosie through? How much time do I have?

The second hand swept backwards from eight minutes past midnight, so it was a reasonable estimate to say it gave him ten minutes from activation. *What can I do in eight minutes?*

∾

Nathaniel sat with his head in his hands. It was useless. He'd tried everything he could think of.

This was the sixth reset, and he was no closer to a way of solving the problem. Towards the end of his first ten minutes, he realised he couldn't allow the gates to seal, that would make it impossible. So, instead, he'd waited for the last few seconds before reactivating the watch. It had worked, resetting to ten past twelve and the second hand began its crawl back toward midnight. He seemed to have all the time in the world, but it made no difference.

An attempt to reverse the door closure led to nothing, other than draining the capacitors faster. Reset.

He routed additional power to the mechanism which resulted in sparks and blown fuses from other overburdened systems. Reset.

He'd scavenged energy packs and linked them in series to top up the primary capacitor. But they'd fused and melted as they overloaded. Now he had an odd sculpture of warped angular metal sticking out of the control panel at strange angles. Reset.

Crowbars and any other form of leverage had been a complete waste of effort, but by that point he was desperate. Reset. Reset. Reset.

He had no idea how many more chances to restart the watch he had. Now he was out of ideas. He'd failed, and it was torture listening to the tick, tick, tick of the second hand wasting what little time remained.

"I'm so sorry, Rosie," he said, reaching between the gates, unable even to take her hand in his.

He must have missed something. There had to be a way, but how? Maybe he should admit defeat, but he couldn't bring himself to do it. He pushed the crown into the case again to reset another ten minutes. Tick, tick, tick. The countdown continued. Five seconds, four. He pressed again. Three, two, one.

The frozen scene burst back into motion, dust swirled, clangs echoed from further up the tunnel, and Rosie dashed across the intervening distance to grab his outstretched hand.

"I can't open the gate, I've tried everything."

"It's not your fault," she said. "But why did it stop here?" She looked through the narrow gap between the steel jaws.

"The power failed," he replied, unwilling to go over the hour of desperation he'd spent seeking a solution.

The noises from up the tunnel sounded more like a forge with huge metallic clangs. Those weren't glancing blows anymore.

Nathaniel gripped her delicate hand. "You need to get out of here. Gabriel can't last much longer, she's running out of power. It's only a matter of time."

"I can do something," Rosie said, her eyes lighting up. "I'll persuade Josiah."

Nathaniel shook his head. "I don't think he's willing to listen to anyone now. He has his sights set on ArcNet, and he won't give it up. Our only hope was to..."

Rosie's eyes leapt to meet his. "To flood the tunnels?" she asked.

Nathaniel's eyes widened. "How did you know?"

"It was just there in your mind, like an unfinished sentence."

"It's too late. I've drained all the power from the control panel."

She looked up at him again. "But... there's an override in the tunnel? And you weren't going to tell me?"

She pulled her hand from his, stepping away.

"Rosie, no. You wouldn't survive, and I couldn't bear it."

Her face softened, and she stepped back. "I've done so much that I'm not proud of, Nathaniel. Horrible things, you can't imagine."

"I don't care."

"But I do". She lifted his hand to her cheek. "You see something in me that I can't. But I have this chance to do something right. To save Gabriel and defy Josiah, and if that doesn't work, I'll flood the damned place and wash away all the filth with it."

She gripped his palm tight in her own, her nails digging in, but he couldn't feel it for the ache that flooded through his chest.

"Rosie, please—"

"I wish this could have been the start of something. Something that might have lasted." She turned, heading into the dark void.

Nathaniel rammed his shoulder into the narrow gap, trying to maintain a few seconds of extra contact. Pain screamed along his arm, but he didn't care. "Rosie, no!" he yelled, his other fist hammering on the insurmountable mountain of steel between him and the woman he loved.

~

Rosie couldn't bear it, but she had to stop Josiah. It hurt leaving Nathaniel in such torment, a physical pain burned in her chest. She pushed it aside and steeled herself. As she hurried through the darkness, she focused her mind on the task ahead.

The sound of fighting up the tunnel had stopped. As she rounded a corner, a metal behemoth towered triumphantly over Gabriel, who had slumped to her knees before it.

Josiah laughed. "So, all out of power. No more bouncing about avoiding the fight now, is there?"

Rosie found the alcove from the mental picture she had somehow gained from Nathaniel and slid into it, peering her head around to view the scene. She focused as she breathed in and pushed her thoughts out towards Josiah—a subtle tendril of doubt.

He paused, looking down at the battered ArcAngel below him. Gabriel looked up, and surprise showed in her face at the unexpected reprieve. "I never wanted to fight you, but you must understand I cannot break my vow to my Empress. I am sworn to protect her as the ruler of this once glorious Empire."

He considered for a moment. "I can accept that. Loyalty is a fine attribute for one's subjects, but I mean to take this Empire and mould it to my ideals."

"Let Victoria rule," Gabriel said. "Make yourself an invaluable ally. You can find great meaning and reward from your skills. Look at what you have accomplished with that new ArcAngel armour, it's astonishing. You are truly a master Horologist."

Rosie pushed. *Yes, Accomplished. Horologist. Ally.*

"You think so?" Josiah said, contemplating his next words. "But why should I not just take what I want? I have the power and opportunity now."

"There's a better way Josiah, leave this petty feuding and join with us in making this city what it once was. The Empire will be great again. You don't have to burn it all down."

Rosie pushed for all she was worth, reinforcing Gabriel's words.

"Yes," he said. "I can see that."

It was working, though Rosie's head throbbed as if it were about to explode.

"An interesting idea," Josiah said, "but no."

His hand shot down, and metal shrieked from Gabriel's chest as he hefted the heart in his palm as if measuring the weight. "I will rule my own Empire, and all shall bow down before me."

Tears flooded Rosie's cheeks as she collapsed to her knees. "No."

~

Josiah jerked his head up to scan the area, catching sight of Rosie. "What do we have here?"

"No," she said again, trying to stifle the sob.

Gabriel's body toppled, crashing onto the dusty tunnel floor, a small cloud leaping into the air. Her head came to rest facing towards Rosie, but all the life had left the eyes, now just dark, glassy orbs.

Rosie whirled as she felt someone behind her. Her pistol was in her hand from a smooth motion that would have impressed even Simmons. But she was alone.

"What are we going to do with you, my dear?" Josiah asked, taking a step towards her. "Always popping up at the most inopportune moments. We must put a stop to that."

Puzzled and with her body on edge, she returned her attention to Josiah. There it was again, a cold, slimy movement coiled up her back and snaked over her shoulder in a sinuous embrace.

Her breath caught in her throat as she struggled to release herself from the sensation, but there was nothing there, nothing she could see. No, it was happening again. She'd experienced this before when they strapped her to that infernal machine. It had come back for her.

An ear-shattering scream shook the surrounding darkness. Only when she felt the hoarseness of her throat did she realise that she was making the throat-cracking sound. Her vision swam with tears as a curtain of red mist engulfed her. A cluster of oily black orbs emerged through the fog, locking their gaze onto hers, dragging her down into an endless dark abyss.

43

Rosie awoke to the sound of crying. She felt lightheaded and couldn't think where she was. Darkness surrounded her, wrapped her in its folds of black cloth. There was the sobbing again.

Her eyes opened to a scene of destruction. Thick clouds of brick dust billowed in the air, but she found no problem breathing. She was in a tunnel, the walls cracked and missing half their bricks. The arched ceiling sagged towards a pile of rubble in the middle of the floor while warped metal rails jutted up from the ground, embedded into the remaining brickwork. She heard the muffled sound again. It was coming from the mound.

It shifted as something moved, breaking through from below. A humanoid head and torso emerged, bricks rained down to crack on the floor as the thing pushed itself up out of the filth.

The memory came flooding back to her—Josiah. The metal monstrosity pivoted its mangled face towards her. Its left side was a ruin of exposed flesh and bone packed with dirt. One eye glowed with blue light from its dented metallic skull.

"You fucking hybrid whore! Look what your twisted mind has done."

He stumbled as he put his weight down on the ruined

remains of his right leg. It had sheared off above the ankle, trailing electrical wires that sparked as they brushed against the metal frame.

Gunfire rang out from the tunnel along with the cries of the injured and dying. Great arcs of electricity and gouts of flame lit the darkness, silencing the last screams of agony. In the distance, the sound of boots falling in unison approached.

As she peered towards the sounds, it brightened enough for her to see dark shapes in long trenchcoats—the Black Guard. In their midst was an officer, surrounded by a squad of heavily armed escorts. They marched through the carnage unfolding around them as the other troops finished the last survivors of Josiah's gangs.

"I'm going to rip your fucking arms and legs off and feast on your remains," Josiah screamed, his disfigured metal hands clawing himself through the surrounding rubble.

The honour guard moved into position on either side of the tracks, an aisle opening between them as the officer strode forward to survey the scene of destruction. "You did all this?" he said to her, motioning at the carnage wrought on the tunnel and Josiah. She didn't answer.

"Impressive," he continued. "Perhaps you are ready to come back where you belong." He brushed the shoulder of his uniform where dust had settled. The silver insignia must mean something she thought. There were a lot of daggers and crowns. "Do you even know who I am?" he asked. His voice was cold, reassured, commanding.

"I know you, Robertson, you arrogant whoreson," Josiah said, spitting the words as if they were venom.

"Ah, Josiah, isn't it? It seems you have finally shed that foetid skin of leather you called flesh and chosen something even worse." Robertson sneered at the ruined fusion of flesh and metal. "I am unaccustomed to being insulted. You will refrain from doing so."

"Or what? Do you think you can intimidate me like the rest of your spineless council?"

"I only give one warning," Robertson said his voice calm and unbothered by the outburst. "Dispose of it."

Four of the dark uniformed escorts stepped forward, levelling their weapons at Josiah. Three arcs of electricity leapt from rifles and a hum of power built from the fourth trooper. He flicked an ignition switch, and the tip of his weapon burst into life with a blue pilot flame.

Josiah writhed on the ground screaming from the constant arc-rifle discharge. Sparks arced around the mangled frame as ozone filled the air along with the smell of burning hair.

That was pleasant compared to when the flames rolled over him. Rosie turned her face from the intense heat across the tunnel, as the remains of Josiah's flesh melted and charred to ash. The screaming rose to a vile crescendo then broke off. All that remained was the greasy odour of smoke and burnt meat.

"Enough," Robertson ordered, and the troops ceased their fire and returned to their positions. He turned his gaze back to Rosie. "Before that rude interruption, I asked if you knew who I was."

"I do now," she replied, trying to look calm, though her stomach was roiling, and she struggled to keep it from heaving its contents onto the ground. Cold beads of sweat formed on her brow. "You're the Commander of the Black Guard."

"Is that all?" he asked.

"What? You want me to recite all your fucking titles?"

"There's no need for incivility, girl. I merely asked if that was all you know of me."

"You are the leading member of the High Council and a traitor who has usurped power from the rightful Empress? Was that more what you were after?"

Robertson held her with a stern gaze. Then with a sad smile, he shook his head. "This is disappointing, Rosemary, and I don't enjoy being disappointed, especially by you."

What Blakelocke had pleaded for her to listen to, it was all true. The realisation slammed into her like a black train. All the pain and anguish she'd suffered, the men she had tracked down and murdered in revenge for the ordeals they forced upon her. It all paled into insignificance. They weren't the ones she should have butchered, he was. General Sir George Frazer Robertson—her real father.

~

A single tear rolled down Rosie's cheek. "Don't call me that. Never call me that."

Robertson laughed. "Ah, so you do remember, girl."

"I'm not *your girl.*"

"Of course you are. Now let's end this nonsense and head home. There's still lots of work to do, and after taking time out of my schedule to track you down in person, I'm behind on other important business."

Rosie's eyes hardened as she glared at him. "I am not going anywhere with you. I'd rather die." She glanced at the smouldering remains of what had been Josiah and swallowed.

"Rosemary, no," Robertson said, his calm demeanour gone in an instant, he was all command and control now.

Something echoed in the back of her mind. "What did you say?"

"I said, No. You will not speak to me like a spoilt child."

'Rosie, no' she thought, where had she heard that? The idea scratched at her subconscious, unwilling to leave, then it flooded in, *Nathaniel!* She remembered what she came here to do.

"Apologies, father, you're right. I shall act like the adult I am and not the child I was."

"Excellent," he replied, his demeanour back to that of a loving parent.

"I have just one thing I need to say. Go to hell."

She reached back and pulled the emergency release switch.

"What?" Robertson bellowed, his face a mask of utter disbelief.

A rumble sounded from somewhere above, growling as it rushed to greet them. The Black Guard looked around, trying

437

to identify the unseen threat. Then it was upon them, a deluge of water roared towards them, filling the tunnel. They panicked, dropping weapons, turning in a futile attempt to outrun it.

"Sorry, Nathaniel," Rosie whispered, willing the words to reach him. She turned, her arms outstretched to embrace the thundering tsunami as it engulfed her.

44

Fletcher slammed the metal door closed behind them and stood there in the dark corridor leading into the heart of ArcNet. Nathaniel slid down the wall and slumped into the freezing water gushing through the grills from the platform.

"Get up," she yelled at him. "We havnae much time before we drown in this shit."

He sat there. All the life drained from him. "She's gone."

"Aye, she's fucking gone. And so will we if you dinnae get your arse in gear."

Nathaniel stared at the two inches of water as it continued to rise.

"Oh, for the love of Christ. Do you think I want to drown in this filth? Get moving, or you'll no just be killing yourself, you'll be killing me too cos I'm no leaving you."

"Just go."

"Look, I've lost plenty of friends. It's an occupational hazard in my line of work. It looks like you havnae, and I won't lie to you, it's fucking hard. But think about what she would have wanted for you. She did this so you could live. Imagine if the roles were reversed. If you'd been out there with the choice, would you want *her* to give up and drown?"

Nathaniel continued staring at the rising water. "No, I would have died to save her."

"I know you would, pal. Now you have to survive to make her sacrifice worthwhile. Otherwise, it was all for nothing."

Fletcher offered him her arm, and he grasped it, letting her help him to his feet.

"Good man, come on."

They ploughed their way through the frigid water as it rose steadily. A thick foam bubbled on the surface up to their chests as they approached the central core.

They both held their prized possession above their heads as they waded through the submerged corridors; Fletcher had her rifle, Nathaniel, his arc-lamp. He'd disconnected it from the battery just in case it shorted and electrocuted him, which would be somewhat ironic after finally deciding he wanted to live.

The repeating warning slowed, warbling to a halt. Water must have reached the console. The lighting still flashed red but was flickering. It wouldn't be long before the failing power thrust them into blackness.

"Where now?" Nathaniel asked as they entered the central core. In all the chaos, he realised he didn't know the escape route.

"Far side of the galley, there's a room that looks like a secure lockup, double bulkhead doors."

"I thought it was a cell."

"No, there's a ladder that leads up to the surface."

They pushed on through the rising water, the smell was the usual mixture of sewage and decay, but at least there were no signs of red weed.

Fletcher coughed and spat out a mouthful of the stagnant water. "I swear if we get out of this, I'm gonna kick your arse for fucking about back there."

"I'm sorry."

"Dinnae be fucking sorry, just be fucking quicker."

The bulkhead doors hung open. It would have been near impossible to pull them against the weight of the water.

Nathaniel gestured towards the ladder. "Ladies before gentlemen."

"No fucking way, pal. You might decide you want another wee sit down. Get your arse up there. I'll be right behind."

He smiled and reached for the first rung. Above them, a circle of blue lit the shaft, and as they began their ascent, faces appeared silhouetted against the sky.

"Fuck me, Fletcher. You smell like you shat yourself," Blake said, pulling her up the last few rungs.

They embraced. "You're not exactly roses yourself, big man."

"Glad you made it, lass. We were all worried."

"All of you? Oh, that's nice. Where are the rest of the uglies?"

"They're escorting the Empress to a safe house. Well, as safe as anything is now."

Fletcher turned to Nathaniel. "How you doing? Up for one last push? Then we can all put our feet up and have a wee drink."

"I wouldn't say no to tea," Nathaniel replied.

"Right you are. Blake, let's be moving. I need to get out of these wet clothes."

"No time like the present," he replied.

"In your dreams, pal. Here I am trying to be all fairy princess in front of Bazalgette, and you're ruining it."

Nathaniel managed a weak smile. Fletcher grinned, and Blake took point finding a trail for them to follow. Other than the black clouds of smoke rising from the fires within the city, there wasn't a cloud in the sky.

45

Simmons woke to a blinding hangover. He closed his eye, trying to blot out the bright light streaming in through the curtained windows, but could still see a red glow through his eyelid.

Piecing together the fragments of last night, he tried to fathom how he came to be in a luxurious bedroom. His stomach roiled and grumbled as he pushed himself upright on the bed and waited until he felt able to stand. He stumbled across to the window and flung aside the curtains, not wanting to prolong the agony. It was like taking a dressing off, best to get it done quickly.

He was high up, overlooking a flooded section of the Thames. Below was the rubble remains of an old church. *Ah, Morton's Tower, Diamond Annie's abode.*

Now he remembered Isaac and Annie plying him with spirits until... Well, he didn't recall them stopping, to be honest. His entire body ached from his encounter with Maddox, but his ribs were particularly sore on the left. He gently probed the bandaged area and regretted it, wincing.

A soft knock at the door interrupted his agony. "Come in."

Isaac poked his head into the room. "Thought I heard you shuffling about. How you feeling?"

"Like I went ten rounds with a mad dog," he laughed and grunted again, pain lancing through his left side.

"Yeah, maybe keep off the funnies until them ribs heal. Annie strapped you up, reckons you cracked three of 'em pretty bad."

"You must thank her for me."

"You can do it yourself. She's downstairs."

"Very well, lead on."

Isaac hesitated. "Perhaps put some trousers on first, eh?"

Simmons looked down at his stained undergarments. "Good call."

"I'll wait, give you a hand down the stairs. You know how tricky it gets when you're getting on in years." He winked then closed the door.

$\approx$

"So are you ready to move on?" Annie asked.

"Yes, and thank you again for your timely intervention the other day." Simmons raised his glass. "Cheers."

"Well, we had a mutual friend we both had business with. It were the least I could do."

"The least would have been to leave me there while you sat here drinking this fine whisky."

"I couldn't do that. My old man likes you, and what is it with this Bazalgette geezer? He won't stop going on about him. Keeps telling me to put him on the payroll, that he can fix anything."

Simmons smiled. "Yes, he has that effect on people. But I don't feel he'd fit in here. He has trouble turning a blind eye if you catch my drift."

"Straight-laced, is he?"

"You could say that. So what now for Diamond Annie?"

She tilted her head, eyes considering the rainbow-speckled ceiling. "I'm not sure yet. I think it's time for the Elephants to hang around for the looting and fighting to get out of control.

443

Perhaps then, we can move in on the City and see if we can't sort things out."

"So, wait long enough for everyone to lose hope, then swoop in and become saviours to the poor folk of London?"

"Something like that, yeah."

"What about the other gangs?"

"Nothing much happening. A lot of them are dead or scattered after Josiah led them on his fool's crusade. Their leadership is shattered and unpopular. Might be time for a new recruitment campaign. With the Black Guard in disarray, there may never be a better chance to stake a claim to part of the Inner-City, rather than living here in the fog."

"I never thought I'd be saying this to someone like you, Annie," Simmons said, taking another puff on his pipe. "But best of luck to you."

"Thank you. I've no idea what the future holds, but you're welcome back anytime you're in London. Come look me up, I hear Kensington Palace needs new tenants. It's a bit poky here, don't you think?"

Simmons tried to stifle a chuckle but instead grimaced with discomfort. "I never told you. I was sorry that Gracie didn't make it."

"That's kind of you to say, but she was in a bad way after Maddox. He got what he deserved. It don't bring her back, but I feel better about it, and it's what she would have wanted. Take care, Simmons. I hope you find what you're looking for in this life."

"You too."

"The old fella said he'd give you a ride to wherever you want. He's waiting outside on that bloody boat."

∾

"Good day, Mister S," Isaac called from his usual mooring by the ruined church.

"How do you do, you old dog? You kept things quiet about that daughter of yours."

"Well, it don't do to go gossiping about family matters when you don't know people proper."

"That's fair enough," Simmons said. "Permission to come aboard?"

"Always. Let me get that bag for you." Isaac reached out hooking the satchel from Simmons and helping him on deck. "So, I hear you might need a lift. Anywhere particular in mind?"

"Well, you wouldn't know where Bazalgette is, would you?"

Isaac smiled. "It just so happens that I do. Take a seat, I'll go put the kettle on."

46

The house was large enough that they weren't living in each other's pockets, but not so big they got lost in it. Fifteen had survived the escape from ArcNet. Callam had become the Empress' go-between after taking over from Gabriel when she went to face Josiah.

Simmons' return had been joyful. It mortified Bazalgette when he thought he'd injured his friend's cracked ribs after an overenthusiastic hug on seeing him. They caught up on the events over the past few days and exchanged their personal stories.

Simmons spun a tale about his encounter with Maddox and his rescue by Diamond Annie. He left out the part about her being Isaac's daughter, waiting for Isaac himself to chime in, but he remained silent about the matter.

Fletcher told of the escape through ArcNet as the floodwaters rose, but try as she might to involve Bazalgette in the tale, he made his excuses and found work that required his attention. She backtracked covering what they'd seen of Rosie, but it was a low point in the otherwise joyful reunion.

Lynch gave her update in the precise manner they all expected from her, then returned to organising her squad which had taken their role as the Empress' new bodyguard. Reports from Blake and Turner told of running battles in the city streets and fights over access to commodities and natural resources. Life in London sounded ruthless and bloody.

All that remained was for Simmons to meet the Empress. He wasn't sure why, but he'd dreaded this moment. It was early evening when Callam entered the kitchen. "She'll see you now."

He took the steps slowly. They'd established a few upstairs rooms as her living quarters, comfortable, but not lavish as one would have expected. He stopped outside the door and took a deep breath before knocking.

"Please come in."

The room was golden with the late sun, shadows starting to grow from the trees beyond the large window which overlooked an area of green woodland.

Empress Victoriana II sat at a writing desk scribing a letter while a small mountain of paper lay beside her. Simmons inclined his head. "Your Imperial Majesty."

She glanced up. "Please take a seat, Mr Simmons." She pointed with her left hand to a chair by the desk, "I shall only be a moment."

As she continued with her reply, he crossed the room and sat. Victoria was a long way removed from how he'd last seen her. Gone was the young ragamuffin, caked in her own filth. In her place was a lady of impeccable grooming and posture. Her sapphire gown enhanced the colour of her eyes, intent as they were on the letter she was completing. With a swirl and flourish, she signed and laid the fountain pen to rest, turning to face him.

"Thank you for indulging me, Mr Simmons, or do you prefer Sir Pelham?"

"God's no," he said. "Simmons is fine, your Majesty."

She smiled, and in that moment he was no longer stood by a late teenager, recently scrubbed of filth, but before the Empress of the British Empire. Something about her manner and poise put him at ease. And that smile, he felt the corner of his own lips rising in response.

"Mr Simmons it is then. I have heard much about you from

the others here, and it seems I am in your debt. You led the squad that rescued me from that squalid cellar in Kensington Palace, and for that, you have my eternal thanks."

"Oh no, ma'am. I was merely one of the group sent to locate and retrieve you. Major Lynch should take the credit for her team's performance in that endeavour."

"Hmm," she said. "I have heard Sara's account of things, and they tell a somewhat different tale."

"Sara?"

"Major Lynch."

Simmons nodded. "Apologies, I wasn't aware she was named Sara."

"Well, now that's cleared up, perhaps we can get onto more pressing matters?"

"I'm sorry your Majesty," he said, dropping his view to the floor. "I didn't mean to interrupt."

She laughed. "Please, Mr Simmons, do not apologise to me. If it weren't for your involvement, I would still be laying in a darkened cellar awaiting the next round of questions from my captors. Look at me."

He raised his eyes to meet hers, intense blue. "You and the others royalists within this house saved me from God knows what fate those monsters had in store for me. I am indebted to you, all of you, and I intend to make sure that everyone learns that once I return to power."

He sighed. "That might be a difficult journey ma'am."

She nodded. "I know that it will not be easy. I am young, inexperienced, and unfortunate enough to find myself placed into a situation where the regent was a man of considerable personal ambition."

"General Robertson has a lot to answer for."

"Yes, but it seems he has answered for it with his life, and that now we must think about how we move forward while the council is off-guard. I need to re-establish my position, but I fear that is not possible here. I have spoken with the others at length and made my desires known, but wanted to confer with you before making a final decision."

"What do my thoughts have to do with anything? You are Empress. What you decide, we obey."

"No," she replied with a shake of her head. "One thing I learned very early with my tutors was it is easier to lead than to push. It is better to have advisors, who know much more than I about their areas of specialism than to try to learn everything myself. With the right people around me, I can make informed decisions based on sound advice."

"And your dilemma at the moment is how to regain your power?"

"It is. And I would have your thoughts on it, Mr Simmons."

Simmons took a few moments. "Well, you have no obvious friends here in London with any force to support and protect you. The city is a mess. The remnants of the Black Guard hide within their sanctums while running street battles rage as people fight to take what they can and carve out kingdoms of their own."

"I agree with everything you have said. That is why I plan to leave London and head to Glasgow to meet with my grandmother's staunchest ally, John Brown."

"Is he still alive?"

"I am led to believe so, and that he rules the second city of the Empire in all but name."

Simmons nodded. "On the surface, it seems sound. There are a few minor inconveniences in our way, such as a means of transport, and travel through the wilderness is dangerous, even for those experienced in the wilds."

Victoria looked at him. "I hear, Mr Simmons, that you are well versed in trips beyond the protective confines of the city walls. And I am pleased that you say that these are difficulties in *our* way. I take it then you are on board with my idea?"

He hadn't realised he'd already accepted the task, but yes, he liked this young woman and her down-to-earth attitude. She was intelligent, charming and seemed mature beyond her years. She had a talent for making people feel comfortable in her presence and a refreshing ability to talk on their level. It boded well for her future as leader of the British Empire.

"Yes," he said. "I suppose I am."

The following day, Victoria formed a new council of three, with Callam and Lynch as the other appointed members. The Empress held only one vote but had the power to veto any decision she strongly objected to. It hadn't been her idea, the other two had demanded it. Victoria relented but insisted she would never need to use it. Hers was a route of diplomacy, and she had already shown excellent judgement when asking for advice from those around her.

Days passed as Lynch worked on the escape plan, and regular forays into the walled city netted a surplus of supplies for their coming journey. It would be difficult travelling through the vast tracts of wilderness, but there were options to make it somewhat easier. There was still a track that ran from London to Glasgow. The trains that travelled it were armoured beasts hauled by powerful diesel-electric locomotives. The Black Guard used them for transporting trade goods and important dignitaries when required. This had piqued Bazalgette's interest, and he was busy familiarising himself with as much as he could find about the vehicles. The train yard at Euston was their best bet, and Lynch was already planning the operation.

Along with the trips into the city came worrying tales of violence as factions fought to fill the vacuum left by the Black Guard. They'd retreated within their steel walls, licking their wounds while they planned their next move. The news of Robertson's death must have shaken them, and all kinds of rumours abounded as to what this meant for the council.

Isaac caught Simmons and Bazalgette's attention over breakfast. "I wanted to say farewell before I left."

"But I thought you'd come with us," Bazalgette said, fork halting halfway towards his mouth.

Simmons shook his head. "No, it's that girl of his."

Isaac stared back, wrinkles creasing his forehead.

Bazalgette laughed. "Oh, yes. How could you leave your blessed boat?"

Simmons threw him a quick wink and Isaac seemed to relax. "Yeah. You know how it is? London is my home, and the poor old girl still needs waterline repairs. I can't see myself leaving either of them, not for long anyhow."

He smiled at them. "It seems you lot have a long journey ahead of you, so I'll keep it short and let you finish your food in peace. It's been a pleasure working with both you gentlemen. If you ever need a waterman in these parts again, you know where to find me."

Isaac stood, his chair scraping the stone tiles, and reached his hand across the table. Both Simmons and Bazalgette rose, and Simmons clasped the older man's arm. "The pleasure has been all ours, Isaac. Never fear, we'll look you up on our return. Good luck, and I hope you and your family do well in the weeks to come. Things are changing."

Isaac nodded and turned to Bazalgette. "I was sorry to hear about Rosie, and I know how it feels to lose someone close like that. I understand there's nothing I can do to help while it's still this raw, but believe me when I say it does get better, Nathaniel."

Bazalgette sniffed, trying to keep his eyes on Isaac's. "Thank you," he said, his voice quiet. "I'll be fine, just keeping myself busy for now. Plenty needs doing here before we're ready to leave, and you best look after that engine. I don't want to return here to find it coughing and spluttering again."

The tension broke, and they all laughed as Isaac shook Bazalgette's hand. "No need to worry about that. She'll be good as new next time you see her." He slapped the younger man on the shoulder, then turned and left, arm raised in farewell.

Bazalgette fussed between his work and looking after Simmons, but sadness filled his eyes whenever he stopped,

451

and so he kept himself busy. Losing Rosie had struck him hard, and Simmons wasn't good at talking about his feelings. How he had failed to manage with Surita's death was no use in passing on. What advice could he offer? He tried to think of how to approach the subject with his friend, but there was always something else that required either his or Bazalgette's attention. Maybe tomorrow he'd find a way.

∾

Bazalgette slammed a battered copy of the London Standard onto the table. "Have you seen this? They've painted us as the bloody villains."

"Did you expect something different?" Simmons asked. "History is written by the victors, or at least by the power that survives."

"Well, no. I suppose not."

Simmons winced at the sharp pain that lanced through him as he lifted the paper. His ribs were still sore after four days, granted he hadn't rested as Lynch had told him, but damn it, couldn't they just heal already?

He read the headlines.

EMPRESS SURVIVES ASSASSINATION ATTEMPT

In a cowardly attack, a group of traitors to the Empire murdered over fifty of the Black Guard who valiantly fought to defend their beloved Empress from the vile assault.

WANTED: Pelham Simmons - disgraced former colonial governor, known dissident and murderer.

WANTED: Nathaniel Bazalgette - Bomb-maker and mastermind behind the terror campaign throughout London.

£1,000 reward for information leading to the capture of these wicked killers.

"A thousand pounds?" Simmons said. "I might hand myself in for that kind of money."

"This isn't something we should joke about. They're calling me a bomb-maker."

"Come on, Bazalgette, it's just scare tactics. They're trying to make it as difficult as possible for us. If they get hold of Victoria, they'll be right back into the same game with somebody new pulling the strings."

"Well, I suppose so."

"We're getting out of here tonight. Lynch has her team prepped and ready. Your technicians are in place at Euston, by this time tomorrow we'll be on our way to Glasgow."

"Yes, you're right. It just annoys me. All this work to rescue the Empress and they make us out to be bloody kidnappers."

"I know, but you've got to let it go. They're doing what they can to fix things—damage limitation. We know we're in the right. No need to worry about what they say about us."

"Fair enough, but it gets my bloody goat."

"You've been spending too much time with Callam. How many goats do you think he has?"

Bazalgette looked at him for a second, then burst out laughing. "He does say it a lot, doesn't he?"

"He's mentioned it once or twice," Simmons said.

The carriage rocked gently in the darkness, but sleep still eluded Simmons. Lynch's plan had gone without a hitch, and they now sped north away from London. Almost everyone else was asleep, apart from Blake who watched over the Empress, and Bazalgette who was driving the engine.

Large plush chairs and couches lined the walls making the carriage look more like an opulent living room.

The Empress took one of the couches along with the off-duty guards, Lynch, Fletcher and Turner. He wasn't sure where Curtis was, perhaps with Bazalgette playing trains.

Simmons peered through the thick metal shutters, just able

to see darker flashes of countryside flying by in the pre-dawn light. He pushed his face tight to the glass, peering ahead to the engine and the occasional sparks skipping off the track as they took a slow curve.

Glasgow, he thought. *Let's hope this John Brown is all he is rumoured to be*. Victoria, the old Empress, had trusted him with her life and he'd saved her from at least two assassination attempts. Perhaps he was just the man to raise a rebellion and put her Granddaughter back on the throne.

They had a long way to go, and treacherous terrain to cover. The unexplored wilderness between the few pockets of civilisation would hold plenty of unpleasant surprises. The red weed and the taint being the two main threats they would need to contend with.

Whatever the future held for him and this ragtag group, they'd find a way. He'd keep his promise to Surita. For the first time in years, he felt he had a purpose, a reason to carry on. She would have been proud of him.

He smiled, thinking of all the good times they shared in India and wiped the moisture from the corner of his eye. Now if he could just get some damned rest. He took a swig of laudanum, perhaps that would help him sleep. Only a dribble of the oily liquid remained in the bottle that should have lasted him another week, and he hid it in his bag along with the other empty.

Relaxing back into the soft cushioned chair, his Holland & Holland gripped lovingly across his legs, he closed his eyes and dreamt of India.

EPILOGUE

Water dripped steadily as the hooded figure was escorted into the dim chamber. Red fog clung to the far side of the unnatural cavern like a curtain awaiting showtime. From within, a multitude of shadows writhed but were too indistinct to discern their true form.

The two scarlet-robed escorts cast the body to lay prostrate on the wet stone before bending at the waist with arms extended towards the wall of fog and backing out of the area.

A sibilant whisper echoed around the cavern. It reverberated from the unusual rock formations making it difficult to place its point of origin. The figure pulled itself up to its knees, head still bowed and waited. The whispers focused into words in the figure's mind. "You know why you are here?"

"No, my Lord."

"No? You must realise you have failed us."

"Yes, but that is why I don't understand why I kneel before you now."

"Death was adequate punishment for your failure, but your weak bodies should not be the limiting factor of your usefulness to our plans."

The figure waited for what seemed an eternity in the silence. *Was the inquisition over?* The thought shattered as the swirling mass of hisses returned to their mind.

"We offer you one final chance to prove your use. To fulfil our requirements, we shall provide you with a gift to overcome your physical frailties."

"Thank you, my Lord—"

"If you fail again, the mere suffering of death shall be nothing compared to our wrath."

"I understand."

"Now, accept our gift and leave."

Fog swirled and pushed out from the wall, forming three thick tendrils that drifted across the cavern, coiling and twisting around each other. With a lurch, the tendrils pierced the body and thrust it high into the air. A prolonged scream burst from the impaled figure. Its back arched, the tentacles writhing like frenzied eels in a barrel. The cry ended with vocal cords cracking, as the ragdoll corpse smashed into the stone floor with a wet crunch.

Crimson pooled around the ruined body. The blood pouring from the wounds slowed to a steady oozing, and a few moments later were no more than slow drips. Within a minute, the bleeding had stopped altogether.

The figure gasped a ragged breath, fighting to control their broken shell and failed, throwing their head back, howling at the white-hot fire coursing through their veins. It came out as nothing more than a tortured croak.

Shattered bones cracked, knitting together while ripples rushed towards the outer edge of the bloody pool. The tiny waves hit the side and rebounded as if receding after crashing onto the shore. Converging at the centre, blood leapt forming a stream of crimson which branched into veins. The fibrous strands swayed, searching, then plunged into the wounds with a splattering sound.

Within seconds, the figure was whole again, brimming with untold energy. They stood, bowed before the retreating fog, then turned, striding from the now dark cavern.

The final unspoken command from the alien presence echoed inside their mind.

"Find the child empress and destroy her."

DEAR READERS

Thank you for reading Fogbound - I hope you enjoyed it.

If you would take a few minutes to leave a review, I would be very grateful. Reviews help others decide whether to spend their quality time and money on a book—as an author, they also help me improve my work. I take reader reviews seriously, as they help me publish better and more enjoyable books.

How to Leave an Amazon Review

- Go to your order detail page
- In the US - Amazon.com/orders
- In the UK - Amazon.co.uk/orders
- Click the **Write a product review** button next to your book order.
- Rate the item and write your review.
- Click **Submit.**

How to leave a Goodreads review

- Go to goodreads - bit.ly/goodreads-fogbound
- Click on the star rating under the book cover
- Then you can choose to leave a review

ACKNOWLEDGMENTS

I have to once again thank Jayne, my lovely wife, who has supported me through the writing and editing process to get this book into your hands (or e-hands). There were many times during the 12 months of editing, where my resolve seemed to waver. Whenever that happened, Jayne was there to support me — reminding me why I was taking this much time to polish the story of Simmons and Bazalgette's adventures.

> **BTW:** Sorry if this comes as a surprise, but Bazalgette is pronounced Bazzal-Jet. If you went for a hard G as in get (the hell out of here), then that's just what I did when I was writing Fogbound. It was only after looking up some background material on YouTube, about Sir Joseph Bazalgette, that I realised my mistake. And it took a long time to get used to pronouncing his name with a soft G.

Special thanks to everyone I've ever roleplayed with during my time at high school at Aireborough Grammar, through university at Brighton and the great friends I made in the roleplaying society - BURPS. And to all the groups I played with since then - including the longstanding association with the Wednesday Night Crew over the last thirty years! It's been a blast and provided 30 years of writing experience ready for this novel.

To all the people who have given me their feedback on the story - whether it be Editing, Proofreading or general pointers on what was right and what needed some more work. And believe me, there was plenty that needed work!

Thanks to all of you, but especially to both Fiona McLaren and Ed McDonald for your excellent editing advice. Also to all the members of Write Club who trawled through the book for all those comma's (Gemma, Lucy, Nick, Owen, Sara and Sophie).

> *I know I've broken the first rule of Write Club - "You do not speak about Write Club," but hopefully you'll forgive me this once.*

If you found my take on a Steampunk London enjoyable, imagine all the fun I had researching it. Many of the names and places come from real life around the turn of the century.

The Red Hands, The Elephant and Castle, The Forty Thieves, The Silver Hatchets were all gangs from that period. Even Diamond Annie was a real person and leader of the all-woman Forty Thieves and was pretty much as described, tall, covered in diamonds and able to punch harder than a lot of men. She lived a little later in the early nineteen hundreds, but once I'd found a character like that, she had to make an appearance in my timeline.

Joseph Bazalgette, of course, was the famous engineer responsible for building the London sewer system after the Great Stink. The Thames was so full of "raw sewage" (that's a polite way of saying it was full of little brown Richards - check your cockney slang if you don't get the reference) that parliament finally insisted that something must be done. So along came the genius Bazalgette who designed a system that is still in use today and coping with the considerable increase in demand.

Dents of London are indeed watch and clockmakers by Royal Appointment - among many outstanding achievements, they build the clock for the houses of parliament, familiarly known as Big Ben. Though, as we all know, that's the name of the bell.

I've used street names from 1899 maps of London, and again found a wealth of exciting info about places like Pye Street and the Lamb and Flag public house - though I must admit nicknaming it "The Bucket O Blood" was a concession to seeing a pub called that while I was on honeymoon in Cornwall nine years ago. It stuck with me all this time till I could finally use it.

If you get the chance, and have the inclination, take a look at all the amazing history around the turn of the twentieth century. You may find enough interesting nuggets of pure gold to inspire your own Steampunk adventure, as I did.

Last, but definitely not least, this book is for my mother Pat who sadly passed away in Feb 2019. She was a special person and a great mum who always supported whatever crazy venture I decided to follow: whether it be music, roleplaying or writing.

It was sad seeing her as a frail old lady when she had always been so vibrant and full of life. She suffered from Vascular Dementia, which progressed quite rapidly towards the end - with myself and Jayne almost becoming strangers to her when we visited.

I'll remember her as an amazing, positive person - always out with her walking club friends and always willing to help anyone - a believer in social justice and a true Humanitarian.

Thanks for all the support, mum. I miss you.

ABOUT THE AUTHOR

Gareth lives in make-believe worlds somewhere in the dark spaces between fantasy and science fiction. There he converses with imaginary friends and survives on a diet of tea, the finest curries available to humanity, and the occasional slice of Battenberg.

With over thirty years of experience writing for Roleplaying games through almost every genre that interests him, Gareth finally bit the bullet and decided to finish a full novel starting in November 2017.

From all his favourite settings which include fantasy, sci-fi, pirates and samurai, he eventually settled on Steampunk - and thus Fogbound was born.

To keep up with Gareth's latest work checkout his web page and signup for the mailing list at **www.GarethClegg.com**

 facebook.com/Fogbound1899

twitter.com/Fogbound1899

46031791R00277

Printed in Poland
by Amazon Fulfillment
Poland Sp. z o.o., Wrocław